Fixer

A Novel

Sally Vedros

First U.S. edition
Printed in the United States of America.

ISBN: 978-1-7345849-0-5 (paperback)
ISBN: 978-1-7345849-1-2 (eBook - ePub)
ISBN: 978-1-7345849-2-9 (eBook – Mobi)

Library of Congress Control Number: 2020902174

Cover photo: Brandon Nelson
Cover design: Christine Horner

For my mother, who taught me to be a reader.

PART 1

CHAPTER 1

Meghan

On the day she met Diego, Meghan lost her job. One door opened, another closed, and everything had changed. Just like that. Spawned from a few chats on Match.com, their first date was nearly eclipsed by the sudden upheaval at work. That morning, Diego texted her a breezy reminder: "Can't wait @Megsy!" Moments later, Meghan received an all-staff email: "Announcing company-wide restructuring." Funny how the harmonic convergence of two messages can shatter a life into its elemental pieces, like the ones and zeros of machine code ready to be compiled into something new.

The question was, what would she build with that code? Already a few years since graduation, a few years into the new millennium, and Meghan Miller's life still remained a black screen waiting to boot up, a blank canvas of possibilities. She could do anything, be anything. She could achieve greatness! Meghan's future self was a famous artist, or a celebrity chef, or a best-selling novelist. Her soon-to-emerge self would surely be an all-around cool person who did creative things, hung out with interesting people, and had lots of brilliant lovers. At the very least.

More than a passing desire or a pleasant daydream, a great well of need had thrust Meghan out into the world to find that pitch-perfect calling that would manifest an authentic life. Out there alone, unformed and adrift in the thorny wilderness of adult life, she explored, dabbled, started, and eventually abandoned dozens of projects. Poetry lost its gleam after a few lackluster pieces. Pâtisserie classes had produced ten extra pounds around her hips. Her watercolors were as amorphous as her pottery or prose. A string of boyfriends had been a secondary hobby, but none were capable of nurturing a specific passion within Meghan, for love or purpose. Year after year, her "real" self was ever elusive, teasing her from the shadows.

Despite Meghan's many false starts, the only constant had been her work life, which offered a straightforward career path, should she choose to follow it. She could not quite bring herself to embrace the identity of "marketer"—that conventional, corporate, *boring* person—even temporarily. Still, she had to make a living, and this was better than anything else she could think of for now. Within the bland, workaday world, Meghan found opportunities to grow her natural professionalism and even be creative now and then, which dulled the ache, just enough, to get through the days while she searched for her true North Star.

This day, however, would be different. Meghan sat at her desk struggling to cope with the prospect of sudden, involuntary change. "Today is the first day of the rest of my life," she whispered to the past. Six years at this job, and she was back to square one.

~

The game company was a sinking giant, desperate for a new generation to keep it afloat. Like a siren, Meghan's role was to produce enticing copy for websites, disk jackets, sales sheets, presentations—any marketing song needed in the frenetic swim of business to promote games, gamers, and the power and triumph of *fun*. The classic brand, beloved by the game industry for its enduring legacy and good-old-days console titles, now struggled to keep up with the quicksilver startups that were redefining *fun* out from under them. Who had time to lounge on the living room couch and play a real game these days? And for those few minutes of dead air in your on-the-go day, you could download thousands of micro-moments of fun to your phone. For free.

Although Meghan had never considered herself a "gamer," she relished the full spectrum of game genres and mega-hit franchises that her company produced. And she made sure that she tried them all—even the most testosterone-pumping, bikini babe-infested, first-person shooters, games that targeted the opposite end of the demographic spectrum from herself. Her personal tastes gravitated toward puzzlers and arcade-style games, where she would be challenged by a string of problems or tasks to complete while racing against the clock. Somehow, they were the perfect metaphor for her work life as she barreled through her everyday circuit of minor hurdles and small victories. If she could break away for a few minutes and narrow her focus to a puzzle game's simple, clear demands, she could feel utterly in control, even if she had to replay the tougher levels over and over. She either failed or won; there was no in-between.

Above all, she found it thrilling to work with colleagues who passionately loved everything about games—the players, the industry, game history, and the sweet ache of nostalgia for favorites from their youth. These guys fiercely debated game design strategies and talked for months about new titles on the product roadmap, only to drop everything when getting their hands on a pre-release copy. On those happy days, a crowd would immediately converge in the office lounge, a small, windowless room that was tricked out with worn, overstuffed couches and a full lineup of every game console ever produced. They'd play noisily, rowdily, their enthusiasm thickening the stale office air like overripe tropical fruit. She loved working for a legendary brand that represented something cool and edgy, and made her feel a part of an exclusive club of diehard fanboys whose lifelong passion and level of dedication she aspired to herself, whenever she finally found the "thing" she could love as much.

Lately however, the entire office had been on edge, fueled by an undercurrent of prickly tension that infused meetings and emails and the collective mindshare. Ambient chatter had died down to an eerie calm. Even the most dedicated workaholics among them found themselves distracted and frazzled. Fueled by rumor and an occasional reconnaissance mission outside the HR office, the prospect of layoffs had seemed like a tornado building in the distance.

Meghan often wandered past the office kitchen in hopes of picking up reliable intel. More often than not, what she got was speculation spun from the thinnest of threads.

"Quarterly earnings tanked again. Fourth quarter in a row. You know what that means," said José, the web team's lead engineer, as Meghan lingered with a few jittery co-workers one afternoon. He drew a slice across his throat. Meghan winced.

"Yeah. I was in the elevator this morning and heard the security guy say that he has to attend a new training session," replied Jim, a QA test manager, as he yanked an invisible rope above his neck.

"Nick's been out a lot lately, and he never takes time off," said Nick's junior producer, as he cocked his finger pistol at Jim's bulging belly.

"First, they cancelled Pizza Fridays, then the free sodas disappear, and now, no more watering service! We're all gonna die with the plants," snorted Milo, a user experience designer. Meghan saw Milo put a few extra tea bags in his pocket before filling his cup with hot water.

Listening to her team's spiraling morale, Meghan hoped selfishly that when the storm of change hit ground zero, it would zigzag over her cube and strike someone else's instead, wrenching others from their job security into the free fall of unemployment during the worst recession in decades.

However, today had begun like any other. A cold April gust swept Meghan's long coppery hair across her still-sleepy face as she quickly climbed the stairs to Market Street from Montgomery BART station. Downtown San Francisco was awash in bustling commuters, everyone bundled up against the blustery roar of spring. Meghan was greeted by a 360-degree panorama of San Francisco history—elegant old buildings shoulder-to-shoulder with sturdy newcomers—that spanned an entire century of optimism and aspiration. Rising from the ashes of the Great Quake, it was a city undefeated by earthly impermanence and determined to preserve its reputation as a haven for cheerful good living. Meghan stopped at a cable car-themed coffee cart tucked into the sheltered corner of a pocket park in between high rises. As she sipped her double latte, she felt her shoulders unwind a notch. What would the day bring? It was only Tuesday, which meant anything could still happen before the week wound down into slow motion by Friday.

Arriving at the office, Meghan ran through her mental data check of things that signaled "all is well." Her key card still worked (thank God). The vast armies of character dolls from various game franchises still stood guard above her colleagues' cubicles. The usual office early birds were at their desks with Starbucks cups in hand and eyes glued to YouTube. She relaxed, settled down at her desk, and booted up her day.

"Wow, I've got back-to-back meetings all morning. What's up with that?" she mused to Karen, a fellow marketer who shared her cube space.

"Yeah, I don't know why we're moving forward with any of my projects. Seems like we should wait until we know what the hell's going on," Karen replied.

"I hate wasting time, and I hate wasting work even more," sighed Meghan.

"Heads-down, girl. Keep looking busy," advised Karen, who'd already survived two layoffs in her fledgling tech career. "We've got to look indispensable, even if we're just spinning our wheels."

"My wheels are getting squeakier by the day," said Meghan dryly. She bustled around their cube tidying up pens and papers and jumbles of stuff in order to soothe her revved up nerves.

"Whatever you do, Megs, no whining! Not even once! That's a sure way to get on the blacklist!" Karen said.

"It probably doesn't matter at this point. The list is what it is. Our fate is sealed."

"I don't want to leave, but I also don't want to stay and be alone in this place." Karen looked so despondent that Meghan felt an intense need to tease her out of it.

"Oh, you wouldn't be alone. You'd be sitting with the testers!" Meghan pointed toward a remote corner of the office suite. The boisterous Quality Control team spent their days playing the games that were still in development in order to report on bugs and other errors. Occasionally, spontaneous swag fights broke out, with branded projectiles targeting rival cubes and inevitably catching the odd passerby unawares.

"Ugh, it reeks of old socks and stale burritos over there," replied Karen. "And that heavy metal playlist on low volume—I'd never get it out of my head. I'd go insane!"

The two women laughed, relaxing into their familiar camaraderie for a brief moment before turning back to the blank screens of their day.

Later that morning, the announcement that they'd all been expecting finally arrived. The company was going to reorganize and "right-size," which would affect a whopping one third of their workforce. The tip of the funnel cloud hit Meghan in the form of an urgent email summoning her to a conference room called "The Bunker." Appropriately named, it was the largest in their office suite and the only one without windows. She stepped into the sterile room and discovered it was already filled to capacity with dozens of other dazed souls, including Karen sitting stiffly at the back. Meghan touched her friend's shoulder briefly and took the empty seat next to her.

The unfortunate news was delivered to everyone at once in a single, efficient strike, HR staff circling like drones to ensure the mission was accomplished successfully. Info packets were distributed, Kleenex discreetly available.

"We are really, truly, deeply heartbroken to inform you of this," intoned Ros Blackwell, VP of HR. Standing in front of the room's only whiteboard, she paused and frowned in a show of compassion, yet remained arrow-straight in her silk navy dress and patent leather heels. "Due to company restructuring in response to dramatic market shifts, some tough decisions needed to be made. Unfortunately, we're losing up to thirty-five percent of our workforce. Peter wanted me to send you his condolences and sincere appreciation for your contribution to the company."

"How nice of our fearless leader," cracked production manager Jacob Green, his lip curled into a twisted smile. "Is Pete going to sponsor my rent next month?" Tense chuckles rippled quietly through the packed room. Ros furrowed her heavy brow, an extra dose of sorrow glazing her dark eyes.

"Every effort to support you in your transition will be made, including a month's membership at an outplacement agency. Again, thank you for your contribution. You'll find everything you need to know in your information packets." Ros nodded to her assistants, Tim and Ruth, who began quickly handing out thick manila envelopes, careful to deliver the correct packet to each person. Immobilized, Meghan had to consciously will her right arm to reach out to receive the one with her name on it. It felt unusually heavy and she let it drop onto her lap with a thud. Karen sniffed quietly next to her, looking utterly lost.

"Before you leave, please sign up with Jen here for an exit interview timeslot," commanded Ros. Sitting by the door with her laptop, Jen smiled weakly and waved to indicate her readiness for the onslaught of signups, only be met with stillness and stony glances.

Meghan dutifully scheduled her interview and reviewed the thick stack of paperwork that officially terminated this chapter in her career. It stated her legal rights, and at the same time required her to sign away her rights to any legal recourse. "In case I feel inclined to aim my slingshot at the corporate goliath," she mused to Karen, who smiled wanly in reply. As the two walked back to their desks, Meghan noted some stern looking strangers standing around. "And here's... Security."

Stacks of flattened cardboard boxes had suddenly appeared throughout the office. They were neatly piled next to the cubicles of the unlucky, including Meghan and Karen. As her initial shock from the news deepened into a greater realization of its implications—of change, unemployment, loss, mostly the great unknown—Meghan braced herself against a swirling fear that threatened to engulf her.

Back at her desk, she discovered that her email had been turned off, so there was no opportunity to send "Thanks and Farewell!" messages to her team that would somehow mark her exit with a sense of dignity and closure. Oh well. Meghan had already friended her favorite co-workers on Facebook and everyone else on LinkedIn, so no need for long, sad group hugs. Still, she knew that she'd miss the real-life presence of her office community, some of whom she'd never see again.

"Megs, I'm soooo sorry!" said her neighbor Mike, one of the lucky survivors. Irritation rose in her throat as Meghan began assembling one of the boxes. She hated pity in any form.

"I can't believe this is happening!" Mike exclaimed. "What a crappy way to treat people. Too cold, man. This company is fucking doomed." His voice fell to a whisper. Meghan could imagine the impact of this layoff on Mike and the remaining members of their broken team. Demoralized, they faced more work with a reduced staff. Their tournament buddies and morning chats were gone forever. The compassionate ones like Mike probably felt some survivor's guilt, or at least concern for favorite co-workers cast out into the wilds of the industry diaspora. *This sucks for us all*, she reminded herself.

"I just got the summons," shouted Jim. "Time for Wave 2!" Glum eyes followed his shuffling steps as he ambled off toward The Bunker.

"They're kicking us out of here in two hours. Unbelievable," Dan, one of the senior producers, spat bitterly. "I'm gonna need a U-Haul, and I took BART today. It's a long way to Castro Valley."

Every inch of Dan's double-wide cubicle was filled with game-related merchandize and memorabilia—stuffed character dolls, action figures, key chains, inflatable weapons, rubber masks, and even a few bizarre items such as limited-edition bubble bath and a backscratcher shaped like an alien arm. Dangling from the cube posts were close to a hundred nametags from different game conventions he'd attended throughout his career. Meetings in Dan's cube always felt to Meghan as if the team were building yet another brick to add to his shrine, paying homage to the game characters on his walls as immortals in a long and noble lineage. Meghan cringed at the thought of this proud industry veteran faced with the horror of job hunting (which was like practically begging) so that someplace (maybe anyplace) would pay his mortgage and family expenses.

"Now I can't wait to get the hell out of here," Meghan responded, rolling her eyes angrily. "Good riddance."

Dan flipped both his middle fingers at the ceiling in solidarity.

"Ditto," added Karen as she plopped down heavily in her desk chair. "The Corporate Reaper finally got us this time." She frowned and swiveled her chair from side to side.

"Yeah, I guess we didn't look busy enough," Meghan replied, recalling their earlier conversation. "We're dispensable after all." She reached down to give Karen a hug.

Unlike Dan, Karen was among the majority on the spectrum of staff ages. In her mid-twenties, she had no significant financial responsibilities beyond paying her rent and student loan. "I'm taking my severance and going somewhere," she declared. "Mexico maybe, or Guatemala. Somewhere far away from technology. Somewhere real." Her friend seemed to perk up a bit at the grand idea.

"Sure…good luck with that," teased Meghan. "The whole world is wired now. That's what's real."

"Okay, then you can write me a real paper postcard when you want to visit!" Karen quipped, as she began unpinning photos from her cube wall.

It didn't take long for Meghan to gather her personal items and the gaming merchandise she'd collected over the past two years. She took the couple dozen videogames that were lying around her cube, many still in their original shrink-wrapped packaging. She could get a good price for them and some of the premium branded items on eBay. *For my retirement fund*, she thought sourly and hoisted the boxes roughly onto a mail trolley. She'd have to call a taxi to get home.

All that was left now was to make a final tour of the office to say her goodbyes. Apart from Karen and Jess in Public Relations, she didn't socialize with anyone outside the office, so she wouldn't see most people again for a while, if ever. She was truly fond of them, and the loss weighed heavily on her heart. No matter how temporary or artificially formed, these were people who cared about each other.

Waiting until the beefy security guy's back was turned, she snapped a photo of her empty cube to post on Facebook: *2 years of my life, up in smoke. Behold the ashes.*

The brief exit interview was a formality meant to soften the blow on a more personal level, but Meghan couldn't stand to witness Ros's "brave face" for longer than absolutely necessary. She wanted to simply drop off her badge, phone, and laptop, and then leave. Fingers crossed that the cute IT guy that she occasionally flirted with was still employed and would erase her personal files from the phone and laptop, hopefully without snooping.

"Thank you again, Meghan, for all your hard work," Ros said, her broad face pulled tight in an expression that seemed to both empathize with, and distance herself from, Meghan's unfortunate situation. "Best of luck to you, and if I can help at all, you just let me know!" Meghan could hear the well-trained tone of optimism in Ros's voice—just enough to placate without promising anything.

"Sure, thanks," Meghan replied dryly. "It's been real." She heard her voice strain from the desire to burn this bridge to the ground, and hoped it didn't show.

So, with a knot in her gut and a quick handshake, Meghan walked out of the office, the building, and her former life. She felt like a character in some kind of tacky meme being retweeted and reposted across the social globe: *The door actually hit me on the way out!*

~

That evening, Meghan met Diego at the Atlas Café in San Francisco's Mission District. It was a windy spring—way too cold to sit outside, as she would have preferred, especially when meeting someone new. She had envisioned the two of them as Italian lovers engaged in an intimate tête-à-tête, trattoria-style, bathed in the glow of the late afternoon sun, enjoying crisp white wine and bubbly conversation. Instead, she had to settle for meeting him inside the café, which always felt to her like a somber, lonely workspace. Fueled by caffeine, it seemed fraught with expectation and purpose as everyone sat heads-down and hunched over their demanding laptops.

With a nod to her romantic vision, Meghan chose a light-splashed table by the window and settled into a chair facing the door. She wasn't nervous exactly, but she had purposely arrived early in order to savor the first glimpse of her date from a relaxed viewpoint. At six p.m. on the dot, a likely Diego candidate strolled into the café and scanned the room. Not classically handsome, this guy had an appealing, boyish face with a grown-up set to the jaw and an expression of cheerful curiosity. His ragged Levi's, black T-shirt, and grey hoodie reflected the current uniform of urban hipsters, but underneath, his body seemed to carry itself with a distinctive, quiet confidence. The man and Meghan caught eyes, and both raised eyebrows in hopeful recognition. Meghan held her breath as he approached the table.

"Diego Garcia," he said, reaching out to shake Meghan's hand. "But everyone calls me Digs." He flashed a warm smile and she exhaled in relief. A normal guy. Maybe a nice guy.

"Megs," she said, smiling back. "Great to meet you!" She noted happily that he looked better than his profile pic.

Diego ordered drinks and pizza at the counter, returning with two glasses full to the brim with house white wine. *Well, we get a taste of bistro culture after all,* Megan thought. A good omen.

As they sipped their drinks, Meghan had plenty to talk about after her action-packed day at the office. The dramatic tale gave them both the luxury of being able to avoid the awkward, generic blind date script: Where do you work? What do you do for fun? Meghan launched into a blow-by-blow account of her day with the cheerful zeal of a master storyteller with some juicy dirt to dish.

"I couldn't believe how utterly ruthless the whole thing was. A hundred of us booted out in one day, just like that!" she exclaimed, still incredulous.

"Sounds like a surgical cut," Diego said thoughtfully. "Try not to take it personally, Megs."

"One minute you're in your cozy little daily groove and the next you're completely stripped of every connection to the thing that you'd given your heart and soul to for so long. The thing you'd sacrificed your personal time for, your well-being. When I think of all the overtime I gave to those assholes, all the stress I went through on a daily basis, it just makes me nauseous!"

Diego looked bemused as Meghan grew more and more animated, feeling her cheeks grow pink with the flush of righteous indignation. She took a gulp of wine and leaned forward.

"These days," she continued, "a job is like a virtual thing, like a web page that—*POOF!*—can just cease to exist and just disappear without a trace, with no past or future, no legacy. You turn around and even the people you used to work with are gone. Not to mention all the virtual stuff you worked on for years. It's as if your résumé is your word against—what, nothing?"

"Hey, it could have been worse," Diego said smiling. "They could have found a stupid reason to fire you and not give you a dime in severance or benefits. I've heard that happen more than once."

He reached across the table to take Meghan's hand in sympathy. In that moment, she felt the whisper of possibility and also his realness—the warmth of his stocky frame, the faint whiff of his meat-pie scent, the brush of hair on his arms, his solidity shoring her up and holding firm. Diego's dark eyes belied a multilayered intelligence and intensity of will. She willed that will to envelop her.

"Yeah, hopefully my game industry cred will land me another job fast, before I break out the credit card...credit cards, plural..." She sighed, squeezing his hand and meeting his gaze full on. *Pick me! Pick me!* She hoped to knock out any Match competition for this awesome guy.

Digs not only picked her, but he also hired her.

CHAPTER 2

Diego

It had taken Diego two weeks to work up the nerve to message Meghan on Match.com. He was more of a lurker than an active member of the popular dating site, dropping in on occasion to browse profiles of pretty women, his private gallery of dreams. He tended to shy away from the awkward moment of reaching out, of revealing his interest and intention—only to be met by a cold void. So many women ghosted him, it was depressing. Even when the occasional woman responded to his outreach, or even agreed to meet for a date or two, she'd quickly disappear, leaving him feeling haunted by the fickle specter of hope. For many of his friends, online dating was like a fishing game—sometimes you caught a marlin, other times an old boot. For him, online dating was dependent on the kind of randomness he disliked most. The kind that tried to apply a mathematical approach to matching two random souls, yet completely fell apart when a lack of "chemistry" mysteriously factored into the equation.

From her profile, "@Megsy" looked hot—curvy in the right places, pretty face, copper waves curling down to her shoulders, and emerald green eyes. Diego loved green eyes, which he found rare in his experience with women. After breaking up with his last girlfriend almost a year prior, he was itching to find someone new. Linda, like previous girlfriends, had been impulsive and temperamental, which was something that Diego found intriguing at first, even sexy at times. But when her unpredictability inevitably began to erode his own equilibrium, he had to not only break up, but also sever all ties in order to reset his emotional compass. Diego hoped to break the pattern with the next one. He saw no apparent red flags with @Megsy, so he took a leap of faith and reached out.

@Digs: *"what's ur happy place?"*
@Megsy: *"i heart sunsets @ ocean beach. u?"*
@Digs: *"chatting with u"*
@Megsy: "LOL☺ OK, fave music? pet peeve? open the kimono!"
@Digs: *"in good time querida ☺"*

Diego tapped out his desire, heart not quite yet on his sleeve.

After the third or fourth date, Meghan surfaced persistently in the daily churn of his thoughts. A colleague could be talking about some mundane work-related matter and Diego's gaze would drift to his phone—had she messaged, texted, emailed, called? Out drinking with friends, he began wishing she were sitting next to him, close enough for him to smell the rosemary scent of her red curls. Dropping off to sleep between chilly sheets, he would almost feel not alone, his fantasies more vivid than dreams. Diego tried gaining control over the "Meg brain" as he called it, to minimize any risk that she would slow him down or disrupt his focus. Yet despite his intentions, he was unwilling, or maybe unable, to course-correct.

Each time they met, Diego paid closer attention to Meghan, noticing more and more little things about her. She would get upset about things that to him seemed like mere distractions, yet he found it oddly endearing.

"The city should ban all cars! It should be bikes and pedestrians only!" she would exclaim with naked self-righteousness as they crossed a busy street. On other occasions, she'd refuse to go into a particular store. "Can you believe they still hand out plastic bags? Have they not heard of the giant garbage patch in the ocean?!"

At first, Diego would try to bring Meghan back into balance, but quickly understood that his efforts were not needed. He'd simply stand by and watch the emotion breeze across her face like a cumulus formation until all was sunshine again.

Sometimes, Meghan would be moved to perform random acts of kindness, such as buying an expensive sandwich for a homeless person or allowing a stranger to rant on and on about their bad day. She was especially kind to Diego, bringing him the brownies he loved, suggesting interesting books, fussing over his clothes, playing his favorite CDs. She even occasionally expressed interest in the well-being of his family, whom she'd never met. He tried to reciprocate, yet often struggled to think of creative ways to express affection beyond the physical. He usually defaulted to taking her to a new restaurant, as they shared a passion for culinary adventure.

On many weekends, the couple would spend a happy afternoon together in Golden Gate Park. Meghan would bring breadcrumbs and a sketchpad in hopes of "capturing the winged spirit," as she called it. "If the birds don't show up, then it's time for ice cream!"

Diego admired his new girlfriend's unflustered, come-what-may approach to shifting plans. It was either a profound inner flexibility or a lack of true commitment; he couldn't quite tell.

Regardless of the source, spending time with Meghan felt like a string of everyday, micro adventures, doing new things from an entirely different point of view. It was almost addictive. Slowly, Diego's "Meg brain" melted into the background of daily life and he relaxed into the awareness of being "with" her, of her potential to be an unwavering presence in his life, as a pillar and pillow.

As the months passed, Diego sensed that Meghan had begun languishing in her unemployment, slipping into the quicksand of inertia. Stopping by Meghan's apartment after work, she would more often than not greet Diego puffy-eyed and groggy from having slept all afternoon. His concern grew as she confided more little slips in daily discipline.

"Can you believe I've worn the same clothes all week?!" Meghan reported one evening, as Diego scanned her crumpled sweatshirt for stains.

"I should probably shower before we go out," she continued, "I've skipped a few showers this week already." Diego simply nodded.

"C'mon, let me take you out," Diego said, "How about Osha Thai? My treat."

"Ooh, thanks babe!" Meghan replied. "I've been eating a lot of Top Ramen these days. And nights…really, at all hours!" She chuckled.

At dinner, she chatted animatedly about soap opera plot twists and late-night horror fests, the few things that could draw her out of hibernation. It all made Meghan seem a bit wilder to Diego, almost feral, which could spark his imagination in interesting ways. But underneath it all, he was worried about her. Despite her best efforts in reaching out to recruiters and LinkedIn contacts, sending résumés into the black hole of job postings, the employment horizon seemed bleak, even for experienced professionals. After all, the country was in a deep recession.

One foggy Friday afternoon in late July, Diego invited Meghan to join him for beers with Ken Thornton and Dave Harper, his current employers. The two were co-founders of Del Oro Games, a small startup barely two years old, yet already gaining some decent industry buzz. Diego was officially Head of Engineering and unofficially lead recruiter, having an innate ability for spotting exactly the right kind of talent that the company needed at any particular time. Currently, the marketing department consisted of a couple of part-time freelancers who were loosely supervised by Kari, officially Head of Product, and Diego's long-time best friend.

"It's time to bring on a full-time marketer," Diego suggested to Ken and Dave over a pint of schwartzbier at a lively sausage and brew pub. Rosamunde was hopping at happy hour on any day of the week, where conversation vied with hard rock for audible attention. Although typical July afternoons brought a blanket of fog across much of the city, the Mission District was usually blessed with the comfort of sunshine. Still, the pub's outdoor heat lamps were fired up for the chill-sensitive locals.

"Time to take it to the next level," Diego said, groaning inwardly at this dreadful gamer speak cliché, while sensing that his point would hit home.

"Totally agree, Digs," Kari said, sipping the dregs of his hefeweizen thoughtfully. "We could grow our user base exponentially with a dedicated marketing resource." He thumped his empty glass on the bar for emphasis and focused a cool gaze on Ken and Dave.

Ignoring Kari, Ken turned to Meghan and asked, "How do you feel about going from corporate to startup? It's hugely different. More hours for less pay, no perks except free bagels and donuts."

"But they're from GoNuts, the best in the city!" declared Diego, thinking of his favorite orange cardamom cruller.

"And we take turns taking out the trash," added Dave, as he took a first eager bite of curry bratwurst.

Diego wondered if a job offer would actually materialize. Leading with the downside of Del Oro life was not a good recruiting strategy.

"Don't forget the stock options," interjected Kari, eyeing Ken warily. "It's a job and an investment both."

"Anyway, we're more fun than the corporate game factories," said Ken. "We work hard, but we play harder."

"Hard work and hard play—both are ingrained in my DNA," replied Meghan. "I'm ready for a new focus," she continued. "And I can hit the ground running." Diego's heart echoed a hard rock beat. *She's into it!*

Before the warm buzz of her India pale ale set in, Meghan became Head of Marketing and Del Oro employee number sixteen. A third of the startup's staffers were "heads" of something or other, the rest having just taken their first few steps beyond college graduation. Diego took her out that night to celebrate in style with seafood paella and Rioja at Gitane, a hot new gypsy-inspired restaurant downtown.

"Congrats, *querida*," Diego said, squeezing Meghan's soft, freckled hand. "Del Oro is lucky to have you." He raised his wine glass, swirled the blood red liquid thoughtfully, and plunged his nose deep into its heady perfume. "Almost as lucky as me," he smiled teasingly, and felt a delicious tug when Meghan beamed back.

A few days after the job offer, Diego gave Meghan the grand tour of Del Oro HQ. The company was situated in a partitioned suite on the top floor of an old brick warehouse in the city's SOMA district—South of Market Street, the city's main commerce corridor and cultural artery.

During the "dot-com boom" in the late '90s, when Silicon Valley gold first flooded into San Francisco, SOMA began its metamorphosis from light industry to light corporate. The area's shabby, downmarket buildings had a "vintage" flavor that appealed to boutique design firms, scrappy startups, and specialty businesses that wanted to highlight the edginess of their brand. Walking its treeless streets, one could easily miss SOMA's white-collar newcomers sprinkled in between the neighborhood's auto body shops, leather bars, building fixture outlets, and other assorted trades. By the mid 2000's however, such old-timer territory was encroached upon by modern offices, trendy restaurants, and huge loft complexes, also known as "live-work spaces" where the "work" half of the equation was primarily telecommuting. Walking SOMA's streets, one couldn't miss the familiar tech company logos adorning business windows and doorways, as well as the T-shirts of workers enjoying pricey organic lunches or artisan coffee drinks.

Del Oro's office was a large open space laid out in two concentric squares of folding tables. Rows of computer monitors stood at attention as designated workstations for any of the company's staff to use. Creatures of habit, workers tended to sit at the same workstation each day, yet didn't really personalize their space beyond the detritus of their workday. Four well-worn couches formed the square inner sanctum of the space, and currently four worn-out humans were curled into them, fast asleep.

"All-nighter," Diego whispered to Meghan. The team leads sat at dedicated office desks that capped the outer corners of the square. Along the back wall near the kitchenette were Ken and Dave's offices that had glass walls on three sides, fishbowl style.

Diego showed Meghan to the workstation closest to his desk. It was strewn with fluorescent colored Post-it notes, tangled Ethernet cables, and a tidy row of empty Coke cans left by the summer intern. She looked a bit dismayed by her new surroundings.

"At least you're near a window," Diego said cheerfully, trying to guide her attention toward the view of 3rd Street and its cluster of industrial buildings.

"And I'm next to you," she replied, "so don't distract me more than the view!" He hoped she would distract him, just a little.

Meghan pointed out that everyone sat in a different style of chair. "It gives the office a patchwork homey-ness," she said brightly. *Or possibly a shabbiness,* thought Diego, *depending on your mood.* He left her to settle in and wondered if she would miss her shiny corporate cubicle.

Diego had come on board at Del Oro the previous year, followed by Kari Lehtinen and Ravi Desai, two of his closest friends from college. All three were drawn by the company's groundbreaking online role-playing game *49 Rocks* that had soft-launched a few months prior. It had hit the market with zero fanfare, yet was fast becoming a worldwide phenomenon.

For Diego and Kari, the choice to join Del Oro was strategic. Although the two friends' post-college career paths had led them each in a different direction, a few years of "working for the man" had galvanized their shared dream of building their own business. Before landing at Del Oro, Diego and Kari had consciously targeted small startups that were poised for acquisition by corporate giants, with the goal of landing contacts and possibly a stock option windfall that could fund their own dream company together. The game industry was rife with such hopeful players, and it was one of the few industries still thriving despite the country's economic crisis. Besides, Diego was eager to discover and deconstruct the complex, powerful technology behind the most sophisticated games, so he could tinker with it himself. "I'm like Indiana Jones," he would say to Kari. "The contents of the Lost Ark will reveal our future."

Diego had started at Del Oro as a lead engineer working on the computing engine that powered *49 Rocks*. His highly productive work style, intense focus, and rock steady demeanor quickly earned the trust of Ken and Dave. He'd then easily convinced the founders to recruit his talented, and at the time unemployed, friend Kari to lead product management. On the other side of the conversation, it took some work to convince Kari to accept the role despite his friend's reservations about the business. "It's a great opportunity, dude," he had enthused to Kari. "It's a stepping stone, not a dead end." Kari had simply nodded his reluctant acceptance of this fork in their path.

As for Ravi, a passion for games and compulsive socializing had made him a natural choice for Del Oro's Head of Community. Ravi had been working as a customer service representative for a corporate accounting software company, and at that time, Diego knew that his friend was bored and restless. Therefore, Ravi didn't need convincing. "I'm in!" he said as soon as Diego mentioned the role. Diego had had no doubt that Ravi would dive right into the company's gamer community, energize its members, and nurture its heart and soul.

After barely a year at Del Oro, Kari had clearly lost confidence in the company's potential to take them closer to their goals.

"Ken and Dave are stalling," Kari said, frowning, as the three friends met one evening at Thirsty Bear surrounded by a flight of artisanal, house-made beers and a generous selection of tapas. Trying to ignore Kari's point of view, Diego eagerly nibbled a plump shrimp, lost in concentration on its garlicky, spicy sweetness.

Kari continued, "We've had some game industry players sniffing around, but our fearless founders seem to be holding out for the big guns: Yahoo or Facebook, or maybe even Google. They'd better watch it or they'll overplay their hand."

"Dude, *49 Rocks* is white hot," replied Ravi. "Even the Hollywood celebs are playing! That's got to be worth what, eight, nine digits?" He popped a Spanish meatball in his mouth and flashed his boyish grin. "Someone's going to snap us up any time now."

"Doesn't matter." Diego pushed his plate away and took charge. "Our company will change the world. Eyes on the prize, people." The other two laughed. Diego clenched his jaw and continued, "Come on, don't lose track of where we're going. Our shit is going to be priceless."

"Yeah, Digs, man, you're totally right. We've got to stay focused if we're gonna cash out on this," agreed Ravi, as he idly thumbed through email on his phone.

"Hmm," replied Kari.

Although Kari was itching to move on, and Ravi dreamed of getting rich through getting acquired, Diego was happy to maintain the status quo for a little while longer. For him, the potential for a cash windfall was secondary. Del Oro was an opportunity to both learn on the job and apply those learnings to building the future. He could comfortably oversee Del Oro's code development and engineering team during a reasonable day's work. This allowed him to devote the best of his mental energy to brainstorming, researching, and creating his own technological masterpiece that would become the basis of their brilliant startup.

~

From childhood, Diego Garcia had always dreamed big. He was the fifth and youngest "late love child" of Mexican parents living in Southern California, conceived when his parents were already past forty. From a very early age, Diego thought of himself as grown-up as everyone around him, with childhood limitations merely a problem to be solved. His quiet intensity and startling intelligence were a frequent source of entertainment to his four teenage sisters, each taking turns to push his thoughts farther and attempt to shake his uncanny composure.

"Little Big D," Lucita would say, "how big is the ocean?"

"As big as the sky," four-year-old Diego would reply. "Which is the ocean in Heaven."

"What about America, *mijo*?" Melinda would ask. "How many people live here?"

"Millions and millions," the boy would say resolutely. "Enough to create new Americas on all the other planets." Maria and Teresa would always giggle at the serious expression on his cherubic face and tickle him mercilessly.

The Garcia family lived in a four-bedroom bungalow in a working-class neighborhood of San Bernardino. The house sat behind a modest but tidy garden of yellowed lawn ringed by overgrown jade plants with stems as thick as wrists. A sturdy stand of rosemary bushes in the front kept curious eyes from peering directly into the Garcias' windows from the street. A waist-high, chain-link fence wrapped the perimeter, preventing dogs, cars, and neighborhood troublemakers from encroaching on their homestead. Still, more than once the family had to suddenly rush en masse to the bathroom—the most central room in the house—to hide from some young thug darting through their yard to escape police sirens. Diego would count the seconds before his family was comfortable leaving their hiding place and compare it to previous occasions. Was it getting safer or was the family getting bolder?

Diego's math skills were more concrete when it came to practical matters. By age three, he was counting his mother's jar of loose change in his head. When he turned five, he calculated how many cookies he could buy with his birthday money. As he got older, the family began leaving more and more of the household accounting tasks to Diego, until he was creating budgets for weekly groceries and Sunday outings, and later, even balancing the family bank account.

Once Lucita asked him, "Big D, how much would I need to save each week to have enough to open my own beauty salon?" Diego considered her supermarket cashier's salary, estimated the cost of rent, equipment, supplies, and utilities, and produced a forecast that years later helped his sister realize her dream.

By the time Diego started middle school, he had skipped two grades and won a regional spelling bee, yet the boy was reluctant to socialize with the other kids. He didn't go out of his way to avoid them. He simply preferred the company of his homework or his family, where he felt safe and in complete control. There were a couple of boys at school whom he considered "sort-of friends." The three would sit together at lunch, eat in silence, and feel protected from gossip and the dreaded stigma of "loner." Now and then, the other two boys would try to persuade Diego to join them at the after-school math club, but to no avail.

"*Mijo*, why don't you bring a friend home for dinner?" his mother Luz would occasionally ask while she bustled about in the kitchen, chopping or slicing or frying. "Tonight, I'm making my famous *pollo yucateca*—your favorite! I'm sure your friends would like it too?"

"*Gracias no, Mamá*," he always replied. "I'm too busy." And when the inevitable disappointment flashed in her eyes, he'd hug her and say, "Besides, I don't want to share." He'd take comfort in her predictable response—first a chuckle, then a long sigh.

As an adult, Diego recognized that like all mothers, Luz wanted the perfect life for her only son. This meant success in the three pillars of childhood: family, school, friends. Her boy was a devoted brother and son, and he had certainly triumphed at school. How could she have helped him with the third? His sisters were so much older, and there had been no cousins in the area, nor any neighbor boys his age. No one whom his mother could have easily pulled into the family circle to spark camaraderie with her solitary son.

Once, young Diego had heard Luz speaking to a friend on the phone: "I wonder if there are tutors out there that teach children how to make friends? Or maybe Diego is simply too stubborn or, *Dios mio*, too cold-hearted? *Ay!* Sometimes I feel like I will never really know him. My own son!" Diego had crept back to his room and curled up on the bed. He had devoted his short life to studying every quirk of his beloved *Mamá*; did she not do the same with him?

Like all sons, Diego wanted the perfect life for his mother. And although he didn't quite know what that meant, from an early age he sensed the many little holes that could easily be patched. He always felt closest to his mother when he helped Luz do something she found difficult, including the many practical tasks around the house. Luz worked at a bakery and could make magic out of sweet dough. But when it came to repairing or calculating or organizing something, she'd throw up her hands and turn on a *telenovela*. Diego, the family fixer, would then quietly work his own magic.

One problem that Diego was unable to solve was his father's love of cheap tequila, which often resulted in the elder Garcia's absence from their lives for several nights at a time, especially when Jorge was in-between landscaping gigs or restaurant gigs or janitorial gigs. It was preferable by all Garcias that he stay away during those episodes, as he was a sloppy and violent drunk. Luz had become expert at sensing the warning signs, like the aura of a migraine, and she would lock him out of the house for good measure. During these absences, little Diego would invent a new father for himself, one that was vaguely Santa Claus-like, but younger with dark hair and a full beard, and who always had a warm knee ready to sit on. This Santa eventually arrived—and stayed for good.

One evening when Diego was twelve, Luz made two simultaneous and life-altering announcements to her five children over one of her most special dinners: chicken with homemade mole sauce. The rich, complex meal underscored the profound meaning of her message. As the six Garcias sat around the round oak dining table inhaling aromas of chili and chocolate, Luz stated that she was divorcing their father and that she had fallen in love with Jorge's younger brother. Luz looked at her offspring over her untouched plate, with a mixture of hope and vulnerability that Diego had never seen in her before. "Óscar will be moving in with us," she added, eyes fixed on the donkey-shaped salt and pepper shakers that Óscar had picked up at a souvenir market in La Paz.

"You're swapping *Papá* with *Tío* Óscar?!" exclaimed Melinda, the oldest and soon to be married herself. "*Ay, Mamá*, are you sure you know what you're doing?" She stared at her mother as the worry spread across her face.

"How could you do that to *Papá*!" cried Teresa, the youngest girl and their father's unwavering defender. "He needs you! He needs *US*!" She burst into hot, angry tears prompting Melinda to sit down next to her and rub her small back.

"*Tío* Óscar always smells like fish," stated Lucinda firmly. Óscar Garcia worked as a fishmonger at the local Safeway. In addition, he'd take occasional trips to Cabo San Lucas where he was first mate on tourist fishing expeditions.

"Can *Papá* live next door?" asked Maria, always the most practical of the bunch. "Then he could still have dinner with us?"

Silently contemplating this new turn of events, Diego saw no real problem with the novel arrangement and easily swapped this new father figure into his family structure, appreciating the increased stability it would produce. If his mother was happy, then it was perfectly fine with him. If his father was unhappy, that was perfectly fine too.

However, unbeknownst to him at the time, Óscar would prove to be much more than simply a different face on the same father character, replacing tequila with fish. His *tío-padre* became the only family member to fully recognize the boy's massive intellectual gifts, and Óscar pushed Diego hard to apply them at school and at home. Óscar's wide circle of friends and networking talents landed him a well-worn PC that he hauled home one day and presented to Diego like a trophy. Diego picked it up, tore apart its hardware and software, and slipped blissfully into his destiny.

CHAPTER 3

Kari

At the height of the dot-com era, before boom turned to bubble and coding bootcamps offered a short-cut to a high-paying job, a career in computer science was still considered "niche" across mainstream college campuses. Despite nearly a decade of Internet growth, it was only the brightest and most adventurous of students who were attracted to the esoteric challenges and awesome potential of computing technologies. In an effort to incubate the digital future, Stanford University built its Gates Computer Science Building, a sunny citadel of technological aspiration that stood immune to the vagaries of the economy it served. It was L-shaped, which for some could signify "learning," for others perhaps "lucky" or "lucrative" or simply "labor." Regardless of a student's journey, the building's yellow brick archway welcomed all onto the golden path of its illustrious namesake.

Beneath the Gates Building lay an L-shaped map of ordinary institutional life. Utility closets, storage lockers, maintenance areas, and a few all-purpose meeting rooms provided everyday support for the great think tank above. At one end of the basement, a small room had been converted into a mini computer lab. Folding tables lined each wall and a dozen computer terminals were set up and available for student use at all hours. The faint whir of hard drives mixed with the soft sound of HVAC blowers added a peaceful ambience and sense of refuge from the intensity of the building's main lab on one of the upper floors.

One sleepless night in the middle of the Fall '99 semester, freshman Kari Lehtinen sat down at a terminal in the hideaway lab, hoping to make progress on a difficult class project. The room was empty except for an intense-looking student wearing long gray surfer shorts and a black hoodie. There was something enigmatic about the guy who was intently scrutinizing a screen full of code, and Kari was reluctant to disturb him. But it was one a.m. and Kari needed to get some work done.

"Hey, do you know if they changed the network password?" he asked tentatively.

"Yeah, man, some jerkoffs tried to hack it earlier," the stranger grumbled, eyes glued to his monitor. The staccato taps of his keyboard seemed to echo his sentiments across the small space. "Try *f8kITorm8kIT*."

"Cool. Thanks," Kari replied, as he quickly gained access to the building's network.

Turning suddenly to face Kari, the guy said, "Don't I know you?" He narrowed his eyes to better study Kari's face in the dimly lit room.

"I think we're both in Feinberg's Programming Abstractions class," said Kari as recognition dawned. "And are you also in his Principles of Computer Systems?" Although both men had learned those basic concepts years ago, the classes were freshman requirements for all Computer Science majors and couldn't be skipped. The lecture halls were so crowded, that it was easy to blur out an individual in the sea of faces, especially when you were heads-down working on homework for some other class.

"Bingo!" The guy grinned, nodding with satisfaction. "I'm Diego. Digs for short."

"Kari." He smiled back at his new connection. "Thanks, Digs." Unbeknownst to Kari, this simple moment had catalyzed a new path for both men, one that led toward shared challenges and awesome potential.

Kari and Diego had each migrated to Stanford University from polar opposite worlds. Diego had won a full, four-year scholarship after having consistently been the highest ranked student throughout middle and high school, a first for both Westfield High and San Bernardino County. Kari, on the other hand, had received numerous invitations to attend colleges as far flung as Oxford, the Sorbonne, and Yale, but chose Stanford simply due to its proximity to the ocean and its distance from his parents back in Finland. Despite their disparate backgrounds, the two naturally gravitated toward each other like the opposite poles of a magnet, their differences being the energetic glue that kept the friendship strong.

"This here, this whole thing, is my checklist," Diego stated emphatically one day, a few weeks after their first encounter in the basement lab. The two sat outside the Gates Building on a break between classes, and Diego thumbed through his battered copy of the School of Engineering course catalog.

"Oh yeah?" Kari replied. *Is this guy for real or what?*

"I'm going to power through as many of these classes as I can until graduation," Diego continued, "then audit the rest until I get a job." He radiated confidence and determination.

"I admire your ambition, Digs, my friend," Kari replied with a nod of approval. "Me, I want to start my own company as soon as I graduate." He felt the blood rush to his chest when he said those words out loud, the certainty of vision making his pulse race and jaw clench. It would be so! It *had* to be so.

As their friendship grew over that first semester, Kari came to see Diego's thirst for knowledge as more about strategy than a manic intellectual curiosity (although clearly, he had a passion for learning). To Kari, his friend seemed to be driven by an inner calling to create something big. Something mind-blowing and indispensable, with Diego's brilliant code, like his personal DNA, running through it—the lifeblood of a new organism.

"Someday, man, my code will crack the walls of Jericho," Diego continued, taking a sip of his triple latte. "Crack open our whole way of being. Our whole perspective on *life*!" He gazed intently into the distance, seemingly distracted by his vision of the future.

"Okay, Dr. Strangelove," Kari replied, with a skeptical glance. "Tell me when you're ready to unleash the power. I'll help you open the hatch."

Kari's natural pragmatism bristled at his friend's grandiose talk, and for the sake of the friendship he tried hard to rein in his tendency toward sarcasm. But the very same pragmatism also took note of something else. He sensed a thin undercurrent of possibility, of Diego's special combination of talent and focus that could produce a bright future for him as well. And Kari always picked the good bets. He was like a bloodhound that way.

~

As the only child of a Finnish investment banker and French ballet dancer, Kari had learned at an early age to negotiate his way toward solid ground in the turbulent seas of family life. His father and mother fought constantly, often using their young son as a weapon or shield to be drawn out of a shared arsenal at any moment. Afterward, they would declare a truce behind locked bedroom doors, leaving Kari alone to find ways to steady himself as best he could.

The family lived in a luxurious, eight-room penthouse in downtown Helsinki, with a sweeping view over the city's main harbor. From their living room window, the family could watch massive cruise ships from Stockholm pulling into the harbor during all weather conditions. Even when the chilly waters of the Finnish archipelago were frozen solid—enough to drive a jeep across the ice to nearby islands—the mighty icebreaker ships would carve out a path for the Nordic shipping industry to prevail over the harsh northern winter. For the Lehtinens, when it was coldest outside the apartment, it was often hottest on the inside.

Jussi and Mirelle could fight about anything, from major infidelities to minor insecurities, and it often felt to Kari that their mere presence together in the same room was a tinderbox waiting for the smallest spark.

"That face again," Jussi sneered during one encounter, as Mirelle caught his eye. "You save the sourest one just for me."

"Yes, my love, you are my big pickle. One taste and my tongue rebels." Delicate hands on slender hips, Mirelle squeezed her face tight to underscore her point.

"And where was your tongue last night, out until dawn?" Jussi replied, challenging and ready.

Mirelle shot back, "It was not with your latest mistress!" thus launching herself headlong into battle.

Sometimes young Kari would try to play peacemaker by throwing a tantrum of his own in an attempt to be louder and fiercer than his parent's current clash. But often that strategy ended in several hours of solitary confinement in his room, which invoked an even greater enemy than anger—loneliness.

During some parental battles, Kari would wander around the apartment, anxious fingers resting on his favorite objects—a pair of alabaster Sphinx bookends from Egypt, glass coasters embedded with butterflies from the Amazon, a marble sculpture of a famous race horse, a tiny brass pillbox—things that felt cool and solid in his small hands, things that made him feel real.

Before Kari was born, Mirelle had tapped the family resources to plan every detail of her perfect child's life. She wanted him to have the best clothes, go to the best schools, and have friends and activities that would lead to a stellar future. She designed the perfect small boy's room herself, complete in every detail from a rocket-shaped bed, with matching linens and drapes, to a galaxy-themed, luminescent ceiling mural, to a working Italian train set that circled the entire room. Over the years, she would occasionally get an obsessive urge to re-do some aspect of it, devoting her time and energy to shopping, rearranging, and reshaping what would later become her son's only refuge. Mirelle saw herself at the center of this childspace; her sleek, chestnut beauty was the sun around which everything happily orbited, including both her model child and his model railway.

Kari adored his celestial mother, usually taking her side of a parental argument, even if silent support was most prudent.

"Kari, *mon cher*," Mirelle would turn to her young son, dark eyes blazing like hot coals, "do you not agree with me? *Maman* is always correct, no?" Kari would nod imperceptibly, eyes wide, hoping only she could read his thoughts.

"Stop baiting him, Mirelle," Jussi would sneer. "Don't be so pathetic. You think an eight-year-old's opinion is your best shot?"

Although both parents had a temper that could terrify the young boy, Jussi was physically transformed by his anger. Kari could watch the escalation manifest in his father—face reddening, veins twitching, voice deepening—until he looked just like the bad guy characters in his favorite cartoons. Although actual violence never entered such scenarios, Jussi's tall, muscular, Nordic frame, electrified by rage, underscored the very real possibility. Kari became expert at understanding the full spectrum of conflict, assessing each instance to determine if his presence could be an intervention or an aggravation.

In between storms, there were periods of calm where the household maintained a cautious status quo. Jussi frequently travelled for business, sometimes staying away for a week or two at a time as he hopped between European capitals and Asian hubs. Mirelle needed regular immersions in her beloved Paris and occasionally followed her dancer friends to performances in Milan or Vienna or London. When both were away at the same time, Kari and his best friend, the family's housekeeper Jana, would float through the Helsinki apartment like ghosts.

"Jana, I'm bored!" Kari would often complain, listless during his parents' absences. "There's nothing to do!" After conducting his private ritual of touching favorite objects around the apartment in a special rotation, along with each of his toys for good measure, Kari would still feel thoroughly ungrounded.

"*Muru*, my little crumb, at least you won't be eaten today by those bears who call themselves parents," Jana snorted in disgust and hugged the young boy tight, pulling him sharply into focus.

When he was thirteen, Jana had finally had enough drama and moved north to her hometown of Oulu. Kari moved as well, to an exclusive boarding school for boys in Stockholm, where his young life took an entirely new shape and form. Founded in the late eighteenth century, the school continued to run in its original modest yellow brick building on a narrow street in Gamlestan, one of the oldest neighborhoods in the city. However, nowadays the boys lived in a modern residential complex in nearby Sodermalm, allowing the school to accommodate nearly five hundred students from ages five to eighteen. The boys' daily walk from their residence to the school building felt to Kari like another quarter-mile toward freedom.

During his five years at the school, the predictable regimen of school life became a framework that helped Kari not only find his feet but sprint toward his future. In a few short months after arrival, Kari blossomed into an excellent student, popular with boys and teachers alike. "Like a born leader," Jussi would say to his colleagues. "Like a virtuoso," Mirelle would say to her friends.

Trips home during the holidays initially had a destabilizing effect on Kari's emergent new self, requiring a brief period of cocooning upon return to school, much to the dismay of his friends. But as the years passed, this need diminished, and Kari spent several blissful years at boarding school collecting friends, relishing the occasional spotlight, and finally feeling like a real person in a real world.

As his confidence grew, so did his ability to influence his peers, and sometimes his teachers. A lifetime of navigating conflict had given him an aptitude for reading people and situations, and a talent for finding the advantage. During his final year, he set up a network of contraband distribution, mostly cigarettes, beer, and the occasional porn DVD, and he ran it like a pyramid scheme.

"You want in?" he'd whisper to an eager classmate on their way to class. "Then you buy my inventory. The whole lot."

"But there's no way I could sell all that before summer!" the recruit would exclaim, clearly worried. "I don't want to drain my savings dry in one go."

"Then get some kids to sell for you," Kari would toss back. "Or better yet, sell wholesale to them and tell them to find their own sellers." His poker face was unsympathetic and unnerving. "Piece of cake for the pros. If that's what you are."

Kari would sense that the other's ego and hopes were in danger of collapse, and more often than not, the boy would invariably join up, saying, "Okay, let's do it!" Kari would seal the deal with his trademark handshake and handsome smile. He always made sure that his investors felt like a vital part of an elite operation. Kari didn't need the money (Jussi gave him a generous allowance each month) but he got a thrill, almost an adrenaline rush, from seeing his investment skyrocket while he kept a tight grip on all the moving parts. It wasn't about success; it was about mastery.

By the time he was ready for college, Kari felt fully forged. At eighteen, he packed up his belongings and headed as far west as possible, to California, determined to never look back. Once her son had gone, Mirelle quickly did the same, returning to Paris to focus on the ballet circuit and her coterie of dancer friends. Jussi remained in Helsinki, focusing on his love of work and his hobby of taking on new mistresses, particularly when the stock market was bullish and the winter early.

~

Soon after arriving at Stanford, Kari met Kira, and the heart behind his poker face splintered into a thousand fragments, each glittering prism-like and beckoning. Kira Bellows was his image of perfection: a tall, slim, chiseled beauty, with alabaster skin and dagger-straight, platinum hair—like the Arctic queen of his dreams. Her regal demeanor, ready to take charge at a moment's notice, made her all the more irresistible.

On a sunny afternoon in late September, Kari was shopping for textbooks at the campus bookstore. He pulled a crumpled sheet out of his black Savotta rucksack to check the required reading material for his courses. He found his way to the psychology aisle and stopped next to a beautiful stranger who was checking a similar list of her own. As they reached for the same book, Kari asked her, "Are you taking Intro to Psych as well?"

Kira turned a cool gaze on Kari and replied, "Correct. I'm a psych major."

"I'm just fulfilling the freshman requirement," Kari said. "Though, it is an interest of mine."

"I'm glad that it's required. Everyone should take it," the woman declared. "It's the key to understanding people, which is the key to understanding the way the world works." Her bright blue eyes locked onto his, rock steady.

"Yeah, I guess it's sort of like the brain's code base," Kari replied in a halfhearted attempt to steer the conversation toward a familiar worldview. He felt an all-too-human flush creeping up to his spikey blond hair.

"I'm Kira, by the way."

Kari noted that she had a habit of pausing for an unblinking beat before speaking, which added an aura of intensity that drew his heart like a magnet.

"Kari." He nodded stiffly. "Nice to meet you."

"Shall we grab a coffee and compare notes, Kari?" Kira suggested breezily. Kari froze for a microsecond before nodding. A coffee date with this enigmatic woman? Fantastic!

The first cup of coffee led to another the following day, and then another the day after, until new reasons to meet emerged organically. In between classes, Kari would head, on autopilot, toward Kira's favorite study spot in a corner of the stately Green Library. Sitting across from her at a polished oak table, Kari would relish the nearness of her, the silence and shared diligence. Occasionally, Kira would glance up at him from a book or laptop, a fleeting moment that added an exclamation mark to the prosaic hours. Tuesday and Thursday mornings, the new friends sat side by side in a massive lecture hall full of freshman psychology students. As the spirited middle-aged professor strove to capture young attention spans, the two often passed the time by passing notes, taking micro-steps toward each other on little slips of paper.

The Prof is roaring today, noted Kira in elegant, precise script.

No cowardly lion, he! Kari hoped that his cramped lettering was legible.

Then where's his witch and wardrobe? quipped Kira, as they watched the lecturer struggle with a stubborn projector. He was almost vibrating with frustration.

Well, his twitch is present and accounted for! Kari punctuated his reply with a lightning bolt.

The wardrobe is empty, clearly, replied Kira, alluding to their previous banter about the professor's lack of clothing diversity. The man wore the same plaid shirt and jeans to every class. Kari chuckled inwardly. With every note passed, their word sports grew richer, more distinctive, like a secret language unfolding to reveal a nascent couple-ness.

As the weeks went by, shared class and study time blended into shared meals, and then off-campus excursions. One Saturday, nearly a month after they'd met, Kari surprised Kira with two tickets to the San Jose Ballet, complete with a rented BMW and reservations at The Grill, a high-end steakhouse that had received four stars in the San Jose Mercury newspaper. Kira loved dance performances, and Kari loved Kira's passion for dance. To him, Kira was as graceful as any dancer. As graceful as Mirelle, the dancer he adored more than anyone.

That night, the friends became lovers. It started sweetly with a kiss at intermission and holding hands on the drive home, then moved into raw territory with a passion that threatened to engulf Kari as they made love in Kira's dorm room. Afterward, he lay with her in an opiate-like haze, arms and legs encircled, body and being hooked.

As that first semester rolled on, the couple began a daily habit of spending as much of their free time as possible together. To Kari, this was immensely nourishing. He had a girlfriend! And not just any girlfriend—he had a woman who matched him perfectly. Kira was so like him, that at times, she was his mirror, and at other times, his ideal self. The relationship made Kari feel stronger, more integrated. With Kira by his side, he felt capable of becoming the man that destiny had intended. It gave him the bedrock on which he could build his kingdom.

For Kari, the anagram of their names—Kari, Kira—was yet more evidence that the hand of fate had blessed the couple as soul mates. Kari's roommate Ravi once called them "K2," and the name stuck.

"You guys are like some beautiful, remote mountain!" Ravi once exclaimed to Kari over a few beers in their dorm room. "It's like living next to a Himalayan peak, man."

"Are we that cold?!" replied Kari, miming a wounded look. "Don't we hug you enough? Is that it? You want more hugs," he teased, but with an extra little dose just for Ravi. He knew where to aim.

"Fuck you." Ravi shrugged it off. "I'm just saying you guys are hard to get close to. You don't give a shit about the rest of us mere mortals down here on Earth." He flashed a wry smile.

"Thanks for the radical honesty," Kari rolled his eyes. He smiled inwardly, knowing that others thought that he and Kira were that solid.

CHAPTER 4

Kira

To Kira, Diego was reticent and inscrutable. On the occasions when he would speak more than a sentence or two, she noticed that her mind tended to wander away from his arcane territory. Whatever point that Diego was making in those moments did not register in her own mind map, so she sometimes failed to notice that he had spoken at all. Kira had an inner compass that pointed to overt certainty and verbal prowess, and the soft-spoken wonderers like Diego often fell outside her radar.

"I don't like him hanging around so much." Kira tried to put her foot down early in her relationship with Kari. At Stanford, Diego seemed to simply appear out of thin air, whether in Kari's dorm room or at the couple's table in the dining hall or their favorite coffee house. He'd stay for an hour or two and immediately suck up the whole of Kari's attention. Afterward, she resented having to guide her boyfriend, like an airplane in dense fog, back to their shared home base.

Nowadays, she especially didn't like Diego in their San Francisco home, their inner sanctum. Somehow, she always felt breached by his presence, which seemed to quietly fill up the room and push her to the sidelines. It was suffocating.

"He's like some kind of ghost that just won't go away," she complained on one occasion when Diego had turned up unexpectedly at the couple's Pacific Heights apartment. *More like gum on my shoe*, she grumbled to herself. Kira hated feeling pouty. Even more, she despised those moments that threatened to reveal her own neediness to Kari.

"Sorry, baby, but Digs and I have to work together sometimes. You get that, don't you?" Kari nuzzled her neck like a puppy, a trick that always worked to soften Kira's hard lines.

Ten years prior, when Kira met Kari at the Stanford campus bookstore, she'd conducted her usual crown-to-toe assessment of this new acquaintance. Within minutes, she had analyzed the essential components of Kari's profile, as if she were running a full blood panel, from the caliber of his physique to the structure of his character. She liked his tall, Nordic good looks, and she liked the way he smelled—simple, pure, unencumbered by fragrance or sweat. Above all, she liked his point-blank ambition, a trait that she found rare in their college-age peers. In that moment, she decided to explore possibilities with him, locking her inner tracking beam to draw him in. It worked immediately, to her slight dismay. However, as time went by, it became clear that the fit for both was so good, that she allowed herself to dive into the sweet, intoxicating dream of a future together. And now, for better or worse, that dream included Diego.

"Yeah, I know, I know," Kira acquiesced reluctantly, running her fingers through Kari's hair. "Digs is a ghost with magic up his sleeve." She forced a bright smile. Back on track.

"Or under his sheet," murmured Kari, running his hand under Kira's T-shirt to caress her belly. His touch fluttered through her.

Kari was often apologizing for Diego's intrusion on their life together, and there was little that Kira could do about it. Few people were freely granted such access privileges. Kira tolerated Mirelle, Kari's possessive and theatrical mother, who was both entertaining and exhausting. She also tolerated Ravi, who was sweet and fun and her own trusted confidant at times. But visits from Diego were usually something to be endured, and when Diego's girlfriend Meghan accompanied him, it was worse. On those evenings, the couples would reshuffle into a different kind of double date. The two men would immediately gravitate toward their private world and leave the two women to fend for themselves. It was death by mediocrity.

At first, Kira would steer the conversation toward the more obvious scrap of common ground between them, hoping to mine some interesting nuggets that could be useful in her own work life. "What are you working on these days? Any new marketing campaigns?"

"Oh, just the usual," Meghan would reply as if she were referring to breakfast. "You know, banner ads, email. Facebook and YouTube. That kind of stuff." The woman's interest in sharing details, ideas, even excitement about her work seemed equally elusive.

Kira would then navigate toward broader, light-weight territory like pop culture, hoping to discover some shared spark that could make the time pass quickly.

"Seen any good films lately? We've been streaming anything Japanese on Netflix. We especially loved some of the old Kurosawa classics like *Rashomon* and *Seven Samurai.*"

"I don't watch TV. It atrophies the brain and stifles the imagination." Meghan's interest in sharing her hippy-trippy ideas on what it means to be creative seemed remarkably, excruciatingly, endless.

Kira suffered through these "Digs & Megs" evenings, and she did so willingly. Such was the price of compromise. Or dreams, for that matter.

~

From the moment Kira was born, Congressman Bellows expressed only one dream for his tiny, perfect daughter, and that was for her to follow in his own impressive footsteps. At the tender age of thirty-three, Dave was the youngest elected member of the Ohio state legislature, and chairman of several bipartisan committees dedicated to the biomedical, transportation, and manufacturing sectors. Bellows's natural charm and cheerful disposition had allowed him to make many influential connections within the upper echelons of the Republican Party, and he'd quickly risen through the ranks. The family lived in the exclusive Cincinnati suburb of Indian Hill. Their Colonial Revival home had been featured in *Architectural Digest* magazine for its classic décor and in the *Washington Post* for its lavish political dinners.

Many visitors to the Bellows' home remarked on the charisma of its newest member. Created in her father's image, Dave's baby girl had inherited his white-blond hair and sky-blue eyes, along with a cool, clear gaze that demanded others to engage. In one particularly intimate family interview, the congressman revealed that whenever he held Kira, he would become absorbed in those eyes and discover parts of himself reborn in his daughter.

"God willing, this girl will grow up to be a winner. Just like her daddy," Dave smiled, as the infant grasped his little finger. "She's got a grip of steel. Ohio steel," he chuckled, pretending to shake off the tiny fist.

"If she's anything like you, my darling," his wife Gretchen beamed, "then she will be unstoppable."

Turning toward her cherubic daughter, Gretchen's smile tightened imperceptibly. Little Kira was just as much like her mother. Both Bellows females knew instinctively how to inspire adoration and attention from their beloved, and perpetually preoccupied, congressman. God only knew if, or more likely when, the girl would surpass Gretchen in Dave's eyes as she grew into her potential.

Unstoppable baby Kira had already surpassed her older brother. When Theo was born two years prior, Bellows had expressed no dreams for his son. An enfant terrible from birth, the tiny boy was often red-faced and cranky, beset by colic or ill humor or deep-rooted malaise. His cries swept through the grand rooms of the family home, like vengeful wraiths bent on quelling any effort by the household to control the unhappy creature. Whenever Dave cradled his son, Theo thrashed and squirmed, determined to escape his father's embrace.

"He doesn't like me!" Dave would exclaim, struggling to contain the writhing child. "Why doesn't he like me? I don't get it." Dave had no patience for what he couldn't influence, be it people or politics.

"Just give him time darling," Gretchen would whisper. She and her nanny May did their best to instill a sense of equilibrium in the boy, diligently following parental advice from pediatric experts. Sometimes Theo responded to their efforts and offered his mother a classic happy baby moment straight from the pages of her new mother books. Other times, he was inconsolable, and both mother and nanny were forced to wait for the tantrum to pass wearing noise-cancelling headphones.

Most of the time, Gretchen did her best to shield the rest of the family from Theo's unpredictable discontent. When Kira was born, the irrepressible toddler needed so much attention that Dave and Gretchen hired a second nanny just for him. This arrangement added another pillar to the weary household and gave Nanny May a well-deserved break. It was also a blessing for baby Kira. She could shine her light fully under May's dedicated gaze, her very own cheerleader, mentor, and mirror.

With May as mother figure, Kira's relationship with Gretchen unfolded on its natural course, unencumbered by maternal bonds. The innate friction between them developed into a low-grade current of hostility that guided most of their time together.

"You and your mom are like two magnets," May remarked to her five-year-old ward, as she folded pink sheets and polka dot panties after yet another mother-daughter spat. With a hyper-charged sense of discipline, Gretchen had confiscated Kira's favorite teddy bear for an entire week after the girl had brought it to the dinner table that evening. "But too bad you are both North Poles." She pulled the dry-eyed girl close, intrigued as always by her uncanny composure.

"Mommy is just plain mean," Kira stated emphatically, face rigid and fists clenched. She then decided to hug May back, gradually warming and softening in her nanny's arms as the two sat on the girl's pink canopy bed.

Gretchen's own steely composure was as carefully crafted as her glamorous appearance. With jet black hair, creamy skin, and classic curves, people often compared her to Liz Taylor, which she gracefully accepted. She had once seen an article about the actress's home in Bel Air, and Gretchen had instructed her decorator to furnish one of her home's sitting rooms to match the article photos as closely as possible. She spent many afternoons alone in the "Liz Room" drinking tea and gathering strength for her next cameo in family or public life.

"Darling, you must never—*ever*—embarrass Daddy like that." Gretchen reprimanded seven-year-old Kira to stop her whining in front of her father's colleagues. She always kept young Kira's outbursts tightly in check, never allowing the child's emotions full rein. "You must make him *proud* of his family."

Whether driven by rivalry or maternal duty, Gretchen's greatest gift to her daughter was her own expertise in self-control. She would bait Kira with promises, such as a new toy, a friend's sleepover, a late movie night, an ice cream treat. But Gretchen would delay fulfillment of the promise to the point where Kira was so fraught with frustration and longing and helplessness that the desire for what she had wanted would pass, leaving only a simmering, acidic ache. Over the years, Kira learned that dignity always won out over food or love or pleasure. It certainly triumphed over need. Dignity equaled true strength for both Bellows women.

"Nothing is as important as first impressions," Gretchen told her daughter one evening after fifteen-year-old Kira had sulked throughout one of her mother's many charity events. The Bellows women stepped out of a hired town car and strode up the long brick path to their veranda. Night security had already opened the front door for them.

"People don't like grumps and frumps," she frowned sharply to emphasize her point. It was a rare effort at motherly advice.

"People don't like control freaks either," Kira shot back, hardened against any overt life lessons from her mother, especially in the form of advice.

"Don't say 'freak' darling. It doesn't suit you," scolded Gretchen.

"It doesn't suit you either, Mother," Kira commented sourly, weary of the same old nagging. She rushed past Gretchen, up the grand staircase, and straight into her brother's room. She needed some cheerful distraction.

Teenage Theo could easily make the Bellows women laugh with a silly story or joke, and he often made family dinners bearable for Kira when Dave was working late or travelling. However, Kira knew that behind the clownish façade, her brother was often tormented by panic attacks and depression when trying to navigating the complexities of adult life. This meant that Theo had to try much harder to please their father. When Dave was at the dinner table, Theo usually remained silent, letting his father enjoy the full spotlight of attention from his mother and sister. Later, Kira would watch Theo escape into the easy camaraderie of his friends.

Like their father, both Kira and Theo were naturally outgoing amongst their peers, making friends easily throughout their K-12 years at the exclusive Seven Hills School in Cincinnati. Both siblings also excelled at academics and extracurricular activities. Kira was on the yearbook committee from sixth through twelfth grade, serving as chairperson for the latter half of her participation. In junior and senior year, she was elected as both head cheerleader and president of the student council. Dave was thrilled and took every opportunity to tell her that she was on her way "up, up, up!"

"I'm strategic with my time," she once told her fellow cheerleader Gina. "I pick the right activities for the right reasons." Unbeknownst to Gina, she also picked the right friends for the right reasons. All offered maximum return on investment.

During his sophomore year, Theo joined the Young Republicans Club to impress his father, and discovered a potential for leadership along with a passion for whisky, and later, cocaine. This was no surprise to his sister. For years, Kira had been indulging her brother's elaborate, funny stories of drunken high jinx and truant escapades to the local mall.

"I got a bunch of us to sneak out of gym class today and go to the arcade," fourteen-year-old Theo confided to his sister. "Whoever won at *Space Invaders* or *Donkey Kong* got to take a swig of Jack Daniels. And guess who kept winning? Ha!"

"We skipped geometry to go see Slash signing copies of the new Guns N' Roses album," fifteen-year-old Theo grinned with pride. "I gave the security guard a bag of weed to let us sneak into their launch party. It was killer!"

"We ditched the YRC to hang out in Mitchell's basement," sixteen-year-old Theo mumbled, pulling marijuana smoke deep into his lungs. "Just needed to chill out, ya know?" Exhaling, the smoke caressed his baby-smooth cheeks.

During the summer of his junior year, Theo's struggle with various substances caused a very public meltdown at Republican Party headquarters. This cost him a coveted internship and any hope of earning his father's respect. Theo's failure of self-control in this situation only highlighted his lifelong failure to do his part to make Dave proud of the family. After graduating the following year, Theo moved to Los Angeles to become an actor or musician or surfer or artist—whichever fate would bring.

Kira chose to follow her hapless sibling to California and enrolled at Stanford. From there, she could keep an eye on him more easily.

~

As an adult, Kira was always running somewhere—to business meetings or the airport, to Pilates classes or beauty appointments—or simply up the hills of her Pacific Heights neighborhood at six a.m. every day to stay fit and on top of her game. Her role as corporate communications director for a large software company kept her constantly in motion. The fast paced, ever-shifting landscape of the technology industry fed her deep need for action and mobility. Anything was possible! And she could make it happen.

"Politics is just excruciatingly slow," she confided to Theo on one of her visits to his studio apartment in Venice Beach. "You're constantly bogged down by setbacks and compromises. It's like always fighting inside a straitjacket." She took a sip of the buttery, oaky Chardonnay that she'd brought, frowning slightly at the juice tumbler in her hand. Theo had recently broken his only wineglass.

"And you have to smile like a crazy person at all times," replied Theo, "no matter how bad you're losing." He laughed. "Glad I dodged that bullet!" He took a swig of a local microbrew and continued rolling joints on his vintage teak coffee table.

Theo's small living space featured a jumble of furnishings from the '60s and '70s, many of which were badly in need of a good coat of polish. He was currently working in a high-end men's boutique on Abbot Kinney Boulevard, and occasionally he would pick up an interesting find at one of the vintage furniture shops nearby.

"Dad still wants me to join him as a congressional aide. He thinks I could go back to the business world anytime I want." Kira kicked off her strappy sandals and curled up on the tweed sofa. Her feet were tired from an afternoon of shopping and strolling around Venice.

"You mean to be CEO of Microsoft or something?" Theo chuckled, throwing his head and shoulders back, miming self-importance.

"Damn right, big brother!" she laughed, raising her glass high. Her heart skipped a beat. Yeah, maybe. Why not.

Kira loved the feeling of forward movement, of being on a clear path heading toward her best self. At work, she took on any challenge that was worthy of her attention—as long as it was the right challenge for the right reasons. She'd give it her personal best and feel the delicious surge of energy that arose from yet another accomplishment, another step ahead, another adrenalin hit. In the corporate world in which she thrived, such challenges surrounded her, as intoxicating as ripe fruit. Some projects were essential, but there were plenty of others that were waiting for a team hero like Kira to voluntarily pick them, own them, and make the senior leadership proud.

Kira often overcommitted herself, working long nights and weekends that invariably led to a post-adrenaline hangover. Once, a coworker told her, "You're too greedy. You take on too much and then get stressed out. No one can do it all—or have it all—not even you!" At the time, Kira was completely taken aback by this, having never associated the concept of greed with herself, let alone with work. Over time, she came to recognize a particular quality in herself that was indeed insatiable: the feeling of never accomplishing enough, never achieving enough, never being enough. Childhood had taught her the art of delayed gratification, of keeping self-love just out of reach. Paradoxically, her skillful self-control drove the engine of "greed" that consumed her work life, which in turn consumed most of her waking life. She was either greedy or a workaholic. Or maybe both. So what? She was *getting shit done.* Few of her colleagues could wear this badge of honor.

On top of work, Kira simultaneously juggled numerous goals in her personal life. In any one week, she could be laser focused on such micro-achievements as firmer abs, faster run times, wardrobe or furniture upgrades, or the perfect art piece for the living room wall. When talking on the phone or watching a DVD, she always multitasked to keep her hands busy or her body activated. It was rare that she could allow herself to stop, let alone rest. Downtime was scheduled, and like everything else, tended to include an agenda. Luckily, Kari was usually on board.

On any given weekend, Kari would suggest some activity with a destination or potential for completion. "Let's hike that scenic trail that was featured in the *New York Times*," he would say. Or: "Let's try that new Japanese place, you know the one that was on the cover of *Lucky Peach*?" Things to check off their shared, ever-growing, must-do list.

"Sure, okay," Kira would agree, adding her own line item. "Since it's near Bloomingdales, I want to drop in quickly to look at an evening bag that I saw online." Check.

"Great," Kari would reply amicably. "While you're there, I'll shoot over to the Apple store to play around with the new iPad." Yet another check.

At home, Kira would purposely make herself sit down in order to flip through the glossy fashion magazines that had piled up on the coffee table. A habit left over from high school, she still subscribed to paper magazines despite the plethora of similar content online. She had always loved the silky feel of the paper, the rich images, vibrant color, and heft of it on her lap that created a special moment of pure, easy pleasure. *Vogue*, *Cosmopolitan*, *Elle*, *Glamour*—they all had a nostalgic place in her heart. These days however, she was usually too busy for such indulgences, and the magazines had become more of a housekeeping task. She may as well just scan through a few web pages. "I'm moving them forward in their life cycle," she would quip to Kari as she diligently turned every page. "Toward their ultimate demise in the recycling bin." A very satisfying double check.

Oddly, the times when she felt most relaxed were when Kari was deeply engaged in one of his current passions. One weekend, when Kari binge-watched an entire five-season HBO series, she napped like a kitten curled up next to him. One morning, when he dumped a perfectly good pot of freshly brewed coffee because it didn't "smell right," Kira teased, "You're such a perfectionist! Nothing is good enough for your golden nose!" As usual, Kari dismissed her comment with a staccato grunt. Kira knew that he hated to acknowledge any of his idiosyncrasies, especially perfectionism, which, he had once confided in her, ironically made him feel less than perfect. Still, when Kari was at his most obsessive, Kira felt sublimely relaxed. It was a strange feeling, almost weightless and timeless, and she could take an unscheduled break from the burden of her earthly self by riding the magic carpet of her lover's personal agenda.

CHAPTER 5

Ravi

On a cool October afternoon, during his first semester at Stanford, Ravi Desai lay on a narrow dorm bed, nose deep in a thick calculus textbook. He was forcing himself to stay on that bed, hold that book, and read (or re-read as the case may be), every page of Chapter Three. Instead of learning about derivatives, he could be sitting at his desktop computer immersed in a massively multiplayer online game, or on his phone flirting with Mike, his latest crush. But games and guys had to take a back seat to homework. Stanford was serious.

Some quantum ripple prompted him to look up the moment a stranger in blue-gray surfer shorts, flip-flops, and a plain black hoodie materialized in his doorway, unannounced. Ravi was both startled and intrigued in equal measures. *Who is this guy? And isn't he freezing in those shorts?*

"I'm looking for Kari. I think he lives here?" The guy gazed calmly at Ravi, as if he had all the time in the world to wait for an answer.

"You are correct, my friend," Ravi replied, smiling broadly at this handsome stranger. "But he's at the library right now. Feel free to hang out in his waiting room if you like." He gestured expansively across Kari's half of the small dorm room with its limited seating options.

"No thanks, I've gotta run. Tell him Digs came by," Kari's friend replied. "Short for Diego," he added, and flashed a not-quite smile before turning and leaving as abruptly as he came in.

"Sure," said Ravi, hoping this Digs-Diego would stop by again sometime.

Over the course of freshman year, Diego did indeed stop by Ravi's dorm on many occasions. Often, Ravi would come home to Diego and Kari sitting side by side on Kari's bed intently writing code. Their rapid keyboard taps seemed to Ravi like a lively telegraphic dialogue, and he would try not to interrupt their flow with his own penchant for the verbal kind of exchange.

Occasionally, Ravi randomly encountered Diego and Kari at various points along his daily route across campus—in hallways or on walkways, libraries or computer labs, dining or café tables, sunny benches or grassy knolls. If he had some free time, Ravi might spontaneously tag along, usually uninvited, just to orbit their enigmatic world for a bit. His two friends might be in the middle of a passionate discussion on the best database architecture, or the right way to set up a web server—conversation that made Ravi's brain telescope out, to focus on the body language that articulated the depth of their friendship. Now and then, Diego revealed a glimpse of his non-technical life, such as the latest woman he was into (usually feisty-sweet, all-American types) or an anecdote about his family (usually involving high drama and tears). Ravi would zero in on these moments, marveling at the ease with which Diego seemed to handle whatever came up in life without judgment or blame. He never heard Diego rant about a point of view, worry about an important issue, or even express frustration at the hassles of everyday campus life.

In this secondhand way, Ravi slowly got to know Diego until a firsthand friendship unfolded between them. One Sunday, Ravi joined Kari, Kira, and Diego in downtown Palo Alto to watch a hot new film called *The Matrix*. Afterward, the friends exited the theater, eagerly debating the film's core themes as they stepped out onto the sidewalk. Which was the better choice, the red pill or the blue pill? Was the Matrix friend or foe to mankind?

"There's a lot to be said for the blue pill," Ravi enthused. "Reality is too harsh, man. And it's getting worse every day. I'd rather live in a bliss bubble." He was thrilled to be deconstructing this awesome film. "Who needs to know about all the shit in the world anyway?"

"Ignorance is shit," Kari snapped. Ravi couldn't quite read his roommate's mood. Had he actually enjoyed the film, or was that shit too?

"Ignorance does not stand in the way of enjoying life..." Ravi countered breezily.

"...with the best of every creature comfort," Kira interjected. "We would be happy hedonists!" She flashed Ravi a rakish smile. He beamed back, glad to have someone else in the blue pill camp.

"Yeah, but you'd be slaves to mediocrity," Kari replied soberly, "and hand over all your power to your machine master." Ravi detected anxiety surfacing in Kari, like the orange-red glow of a mood ring.

"A master with golden handcuffs," joked Kira. "No—fur-lined cuffs, for the true pleasure seeker." She slipped her hand in Kari's and tugged playfully.

"At least with the red pill you'd be free," Kari said. "That's better than living like a human bot. Live free or die."

"Wow, that's so American," declared Ravi. "I can just see you on a giant chrome Harley, popping your little red pill, and roaring off into the sunset." He let this intriguing image sink in.

"What if one little pill could turn us into cowboys?" Kari lit up a little, finally.

"Yeah, we could all be American icons," Kira mused, "proud and free, riding through majestic, untamed lands."

"Making our mark in the wild, wild West." Kari turned to Kira and nuzzled her ear.

"Sorry to tell you guys, but we already live in the Matrix," Ravi replied. "And all the cowboys have computers for horses. There's a lot of bliss to be found online nowadays."

"And big bucks to be made," added Kari as the friends headed slowly down the block toward their favorite pizza place on the corner.

"What if there was a middle ground," Diego pondered, "where you have the best of both? Freedom when you want it, and ignorance when you want it."

"You mean, a purple pill?!" exclaimed Ravi. "Brilliant, man!" He skipped alongside, jostling Diego's shoulder.

Suddenly, a car sped past them and a rough, disembodied voice yelled, "Faggot!"

In that moment, Ravi's personal Matrix hit a glitch, hanging for seconds that felt like minutes. This single, violent burst seemed to ricochet across the cityscape and strike deep in Ravi's gut, as if the drive-by shot was aimed straight at him, and only him. Was his gayness that obvious? He looked over at his companions strolling peacefully beside him. Did no one else hear that voice? To his friends, Ravi's sexuality was a non-issue, just another common variable in human code. For a moment, he envied their ignorance of this particular kind of ugliness in the world, the kind that lay in wait for people like him, and he envied their freedom to ignore it.

Without skipping a beat, Diego calmly put his arm around Ravi's shoulders and held firm until the group arrived at the pizza place. The glitch patched, Ravi plopped onto the cool vinyl of the restaurant booth, immersed himself in the bliss of friendship, and began to slowly relax on a profound, almost primal level.

From that day forward, Ravi considered Diego a close friend and one of the few people he truly admired. This was a guy who seemed like he could handle any situation with finesse, like some kind of Life Ninja. And like most superheroes, Diego was a man of action rather than words, which was fine by Ravi—he could supply enough words for the both of them. Diego's bulletproof cool sometimes triggered Ravi's inner clown, something that his moody roommate Kari rarely inspired.

One evening, Ravi and Diego were playing pool in the dormitory lounge and Ravi was feeling particularly revved up, and at the same time, sentimental.

"You and K2 are my little dorm family!" Ravi declared, as he inadvertently sunk the cue ball for the third time in a row. He frowned momentarily and then flashed his trademark grin. "It's nice to come home to you guys after a long, hard day pumping up brain cells."

"Ditto," replied Diego, chalking the tip of his pool cue. "You guys are cool." His tone seemed somewhat neutral, so Ravi shifted his focus on the other two.

"Kari and Kira are like the archetypal couple. Beautiful, brainy, and..." he paused, trying to find the right word.

"Badass?" Diego hoisted one hip on the edge of the table as he eyeballed his next shot.

"Bingo!" Ravi exclaimed, cocking a finger at Diego. He paced around the table, awaiting his turn. Kari and Kira were Adam and Eve, Zeus and Hera, Vishnu and Lakshmi, Father Sky and Mother Earth. Someday, his hero's journey across the treacherous landscape of the heart would lead him to a soulmate of his own.

He continued, "As a couple, those two are so connected that they're like two halves of the same person. Soon, they'll be wearing matching track suits!" Ravi laughed, trying to imagine them wearing "his and her" garish polyester. He couldn't wait to tease Kira with that image—oh, the horror! He always loved their playful banter about fashion or anything pop culture.

"Yeah, they're a cute couple," concurred Diego, banking two striped balls with one long shot. The loud double-thud turned a couple of heads studying quietly on a couch at the back of the room. Diego had delivered this statement in such an off-hand way that Ravi couldn't quite read him. Was he thumbs up or thumbs down on the Kira half of K2?

To Ravi, the Kari half of K2 was more than just cute. He was movie-star handsome. Even at his worst—like the morning after an all-nighter studying or partying or fucking—puffy and haggard, shaving at the sink in his underwear, Kari still looked amazing. His tall, toned body moved with certainty and purpose, as if it knew exactly what it wanted at all times and didn't need a single brain cell to call the shots. Shimmering beneath the surface of Kari's polished, European reserve was an undercurrent of sexuality that felt like it could strike like lightning at any moment. Sometimes it left Ravi breathless.

"I wish they could adopt me, and maybe get my parents off my back," Ravi joked to Diego, who chuckled amiably. But seriously, he had to come up with a plan. Despite Ravi's youth and focus on school, his parents were pushing him to find a wife—and find one soon. At least get engaged now and then marry after graduation! They were relentless, even threatening to bring in an old-fashioned matchmaker. What a train wreck that would be.

~

Arjun and Sarita Desai had longed for a son for many years before Ravi arrived to bless their family with an heir, and a future. Their late-born, golden child grew easily into his role, becoming like a bright star that drew all members of the extended family into his glittering entourage. Little Ravi was living proof of the family's hopes and dreams, excelling both at school and in their social sphere. Amongst his peers, Ravi became legendary for hosting exuberant birthday parties, which usually lasted an entire weekend. Amongst parents, he was well-mannered, gracious, and a frequent topic of discussion. To unruly offspring, it was "why can't you behave like that lovely Desai boy," and to young daughters, it was "keep an eye on this one, my dear." To Ravi's parents, it was "so lucky-lucky!"

The family was indeed lucky enough to secure a spacious flat on the highest floor they could afford in one of Mumbai's most modern apartment buildings. Sarita wanted her home's furnishings to escort her family toward its bright future, so the flat was decorated in gleaming chrome and glass tables, luminous lacquer cabinetry, and butter-soft leather chairs. The flat's officiously modern shades of blacks, whites, and grays allowed slight leeway for tradition, and vivid pink and green silk pillows adorned seating areas, and brightly colored, cosmology-themed artwork hung in each room. Potted palms spread their fronds wide like arms of the fierce goddess Kali, warning the past to stay back, or else. In addition, the Desai children provided a living palette of color as they noisily romped and played throughout the posh, polished flat.

Twin sisters Nita and Layla were a full eight years older than Ravi, and from the moment he entered their world, they pounced on him like two miniature, doting aunties. Ravi in turn adored his sisters and blossomed in the glow of their affection. Although the family had a live-in cook and nanny, the girls insisted on taking turns dressing or grooming the young boy, or making him special meals, which allowed the cook and nanny plenty of time for leisurely chit-chats on the balcony. Young Ravi was the sisters' favorite playmate, much more interesting than any toy or book or schoolmate. They loved to prop him up on the white leather day bed in the family living room and beg him to sing or dance. "Please *baccha*! Sing the spider song! Dance the frog dance!" Ravi would wrap himself in one of his mother's shimmering dupattas and joyfully perform to a rapt audience, and all three would fall on the bed giggling and happy in their private bubble. As the girls grew into their teen years, the sibling bubble began to deflate. The sisters' time and attention turned toward boys their own age, and Ravi was forced to do the same.

"Ravi, *beta*, ask Suresh to stay for dinner," his mother always encouraged social ties with children from good families, and especially with those boys who brought her son such joy. "This weekend, how about a sleepover with Raj or Harjit or Yogesh? Or all three, *beta*, why not?!!" The prospect of sleepovers was always thrilling, especially in the stillness of midnight, when Ravi could gaze at Suresh for as long as he liked, his friend's feather-light breath falling gently as leaves onto his boy-sized sleeping bag.

Throughout childhood, Ravi often overheard Sarita complaining that she did not have enough precious time for her beloved son. As Superintendent of Schools for their district in Mumbai, his mother seemed just plain tired much of the time, as if she couldn't prevent the job from consuming her energy reserves with its endless barrage of demands. Sarita was normally not an all-or-nothing kind of person, so this imbalanced lifestyle left her vulnerable to occasional fits of tears or migraines, which took even more time away from her children. Like it or not, the full force of her conflict would be expressed in some part of her body or being, like a still-active volcano.

"*Ma*!" little Ravi would say softly, "I'm sorry you're sad! You can have my blanket?" Nita or Layla would inevitably whisk him out of the room to allow their mother to rest and recharge in peace, not realizing that Ravi was his mother's comfort blanket.

By contrast, Ravi's father was an all-or-nothing kind of person. Early in his life as a family man, Arjun had gone all-in on his career. His role as Director of Water Quality for the Mumbai metropolitan area kept him at the office until late on weeknights, so his children only saw him on the weekends, and sometimes only at mealtimes when he emerged glazed and distracted from his study. Arjun would dominate the dinner table conversation, worrying about water contamination, water shortages, acts of terrorism—disaster could happen any time! Ravi grew to understand that his father worried even more about the whims of elected officials who could make or break the steady progress of his career. Arjun aimed to rise as high as possible before retirement, and he seemed to be obsessively looking for the next rung of the golden ladder.

When he turned thirteen, Ravi went from being the family's bright star to being its North Star, as Sarita and Arjun turned their compass toward the boy's career path. They addressed the topic as if it were the key to the entire family's future, with Ravi as simply the agent who would carry it forward.

"I want to do something creative, like fashion design or film," Ravi announced one evening at dinner. He felt the barely concealed tremor in his voice, not daring to share more than those two words. His true dream of becoming a Bollywood star had to be restrained, incarcerated, in the darkest corners of his heart, which was already crowded with secrets.

"Ravi, *beta*, computers are your ticket to the best future!" Sarita responded firmly, reciting what had become her weekly counsel. "You learn computers, then get a very good job in a big company. Maybe you'll become CEO one day!" To punctuate her point, she took a large bite of chicken vindaloo. Ravi watched his mother in dismay; his secrets threatened a prison riot.

Following his wife's lead, Arjun added vaguely, "Look at this Bill Gates fellow. Look at all he has done. You are a smart boy, Ravi, you could learn from his example." While taking a second helping of dal, Ravi noticed his father's eyes land for a millisecond on his watch, and then on the hallway that led to his study.

"You must not let your education go to waste, *beta,*" said Sarita with even greater tenacity, clearly relieved that Arjun was being a father for a change. "It's your duty to use it properly!"

"Yes, it's your duty to go as far as you can in life," agreed Arjun, "otherwise, you will live in bitterness and regret at the lost opportunities." The thought made Ravi's stomach clench, and he reached for comfort from a triangle of naan.

"But I want to be happy!" Ravi whined.

"Happiness—ay ay—it will come later, boy." Arjun dismissed this trifle with a wave of his hand. "You build your house, then happiness will knock on the door in its own time."

But happiness knocked sooner than Ravi expected—at the house of his uncle Sanjiv, far away in California. Sarita's older brother had moved to Berkeley fifteen years prior after marrying an Indian-American girl that he'd met at MIT University. He had become a highly successful structural engineer and marathon champion, and regularly sent postcards and letters to the Desai family from his travels around the world. Sanjiv and his wife had not been blessed with children and it was now almost too late. Sarita had even shed tears for the unfortunate couple.

"Ay, ay, can you imagine such heartbreak!" Ravi heard his mother lament loudly one day as he was doing homework in the living room. Sarita was having tea on the balcony with her closest girlfriend, Meera. "Sanjiv and Shilpa have tried to have children for years. Doctors, clinics—you name it." Ravi quietly moved to the edge of the couch just inside the sliding door, but well out of view of the ladies.

"Lucky in everything except the most important thing. Such a tragedy!" Meera commiserated, before proceeding to cycle through her own family setbacks.

Sanjiv and Shilpa lived in a three-bedroom, Craftsman-style home in the Berkeley Hills with a sweeping view of the bay and plenty of space—really, too much space for only two people. So, they offered a bedroom to young Ravi along with the opportunity to experience life in a different country. They would take care of the boy, make sure he got good grades in school, help him stay focused during this critical period in his youth. And once Ravi graduated from university, Sanjiv promised, he'd make sure the boy got on the next plane back to Mumbai—for good.

"Sanjiv said he would enjoy having a young person around," Sarita confided to Meera. Ravi thought—hoped—he heard a note of enthusiasm in his mother's voice. He held his breath, afraid to disturb the possibilities that had just breezed through this open door.

"He wants a little taste of fatherhood!" her friend exclaimed, teacup and saucer clattering. "Like every man!" Meera peered at the plate of chocolate biscuits, unsure which to choose.

Sarita leaned over to her friend's ear and whispered: "The boy needs a father figure now more than ever." Ravi strained to hear the spoken and the unspoken. "He's getting into those tricky years, where a strong father about the house," she paused, "I mean to say," another pause, "an *available* father, can make all the difference to a boy on the edge of manhood." Ravi winced in embarrassment for both himself and his father.

Sarita continued, heading toward more dangerous territory. "And he seems too attached to his friends, especially Suresh. Much too attached..." His mother took a noisy gulp of tea. Ravi swallowed hard.

"A change of scenery would be a fresh start," said Meera, kindly.

"Yes," replied Sarita. "In the right direction." Her sigh ricocheted across the balcony, into the living room, and straight into Ravi's gut, igniting panic. Could his mother peer that deeply into his heart? Had she discovered his darkest secret? California now beckoned even more loudly. Maybe it was a place where he could finally explore himself, bring darkness into light.

Over the course of a several weekend family dinners, Sarita floated the proposition of Ravi living with Sanjiv. Like a master negotiator, she started lightly and broached the subject as if she were simply entertaining an amusing idea. Arjun ignored her at first, and after the third or fourth dinner, he appeared to listen. Following this cue, Sarita finally closed the deal by weighing in with her most convincing one-two punch.

"You know Arjun, this could help Ravi get into a top American university! Living there would make it easier. It's like a shortcut for foreign students." She smiled and poured her husband a second glass of Chablis.

"Maybe, but those schools take plenty of students who live in India," Arjun countered, digging up examples from the family's social circle. "Just look at the Banerjee boy, or the Ghosal's eldest. Or the daughter of your friend Anika." He took a sip of wine. "Two got into Yale, no problem, and the other just graduated from Georgetown." He gazed coolly at his wife, while Ravi held his breath. He wished that Nita and Layla were there to support him, but both twins were now living in Delhi, finishing their degrees and planning their newly grown-up lives.

Undaunted, Sarita replied, "But what if it becomes a problem in five or so years, by the time Ravi is ready for university? What if they favor American students then?"

Arjun shrugged hesitantly.

"What if, Arjun, Ravi doesn't get in," Sarita drilled straight to the core, "and we have to live with the bitterness and regret of lost opportunity?"

After silence for a minute that felt like an hour, Arjan said simply, "Okay, then."

Ravi enthusiastically agreed to try it out for a year. After saying painful goodbyes to his family and friends, especially Suresh, he promptly packed his bags, unpacked his dreams, and arrived at the San Francisco airport ready for a new adventure with Sanjiv and Shilpa, and American culture at large. Like the suitcase full of food that accompanied him, his parents' anguished goodbye words—"*Beta*, we can't wait for you to come *home!*"—reminded him that he was a son first, and adventurer second. Duty would come calling at some point.

One year turned into four, and Ravi flourished at Berkeley High School, graduating with top honors and a full scholarship to Stanford, which was the best possible milestone on the golden path to his future. Ravi, however, was happy to live in the present. He missed his family and felt a bit tearful at times, especially after their weekly phone calls. But at the same time, he had adapted so fully to his new world, it often felt like he'd never lived anywhere else. The Bay Area was perfect for him. He could finally, simply, blissfully, be himself.

~

By the end of his freshman year at Stanford, Ravi realized that he actually enjoyed computer science after all. It was not as dry as he expected—not just all logic and math—but it also involved both creativity and problem-solving, two of Ravi's favorite skills. He was more interested in what computers could do rather than the nuts and bolts of code, which were simply a necessary means to an end. And some of those "ends" were simply awesome.

In his cramped dorm room, Ravi would often unwind from a long school day by playing video games. He'd just bought a Sega Dreamcast console and was addicted at first to the *Sonic the Hedgehog* franchise, but then moved on to games like *Phantasy Star* that had an online component. The Dreamcast let you play against other people over the Internet, and Ravi thought that was the coolest thing ever. He could easily feel the presence of those other players in his dorm room, as he chatted with them and then beat the pants off those suckers in battle.

Sometimes he tried to engage Kari in one of his latest favorites.

"Kari, man, play some *Quake* with me!" Ravi asked his roommate as he set up the Dreamcast with two controllers. "C'mon, it'll be fun. I've got some beer too—Stellas!"

"Can't tonight." Kari was changing clothes. "Digs and I are studying." He stood squarely in front of Ravi, barely two feet away. Hands on hips. Calvin Klein briefs. Piercing gaze. "Maybe some other time."

Ravi held his breath for just a heartbeat. "Okay, sure. Have fun." *He knows*, Ravi thought. *He knows full well the effect he has on people—and he dials it up whenever he feels like it. For his own reasons, whatever they are. The beautiful fucker.*

Although he knew that nothing would ever happen, Ravi held on to the fantasy of it, of an intimate connection with Kari that would take him somewhere transcendent and pure. It was a movie he would play for himself now and then, when he wanted to feel the intensity of desire. When he wanted to believe that magic really did happen in life. When he wanted to feel less alone. Usually it was a catalyst that got him off his bed and into the local gay bars, where he could meet men that he could actually date, but no one had yet stepped up to co-star in his love story. Besides, Ravi was thoroughly enchanted by the K2 romance. Despite some occasional drama, theirs was destined to be a lifelong narrative, and Ravi wanted a supporting role.

But when Kari was with Diego, there was no room for anyone else. The two study partners were in lock-down whenever they were together—heads bent talking quietly (planning? plotting? what?)—and sometimes Ravi felt like a bird smacking against a windowpane. But if Kira happened to be there, the window was open and she would eagerly wave him in. She was a fellow bird.

"They're always together, and I don't like it," she confided in Ravi once over a salad bar lunch at the student cafeteria. "Kari gets moody and possessive around Digs. Almost like he doesn't want me to even *talk* to the guy!" She frowned and looked so genuinely sad that Ravi reached out to pat her forearm.

"I hear ya," Ravi commiserated. "I'm in a couple of the same classes as them, but do they ever invite me to study with them? Hell no!" He spooned some macaroni salad into his mouth to soften the outburst. He didn't want to complain, not really, but he just couldn't help feeling left out.

"Sometimes I think Kari likes Digs more than me," Kira moaned, and Ravi sensed his friend spiral down into a rare pool of doubt. Kira's thick eyelashes fluttered, keeping the predatory tears at bay. Her picture-perfect salad sat on the table between them, abandoned.

"Don't go there, girl," Ravi advised firmly, enjoying this unfamiliar big brother role. "You two are solid. Solid like the mountain you are together." He flashed her his best smile and nodded fleetingly toward her salad, eyebrows raised.

"Thanks, Ravi," she smiled back and gave his hand a quick squeeze. "You always say the right thing." She pushed her salad over to him, gathered up her book bag and hurried off to the next class.

"Rock on K2," Ravi replied softly, digging into a second lunch.

But the Kari-Digs equation continued to puzzle him. What could possibly be so compelling between the two? The sex factor was definitely out. And the "best buds" chemistry—he couldn't really see that either. They had nothing in common except their major. But to be so intensely *together* despite the lack of any perceptible reason? Ravi was intent on decrypting that code.

CHAPTER 6

Ravi

Ravi was getting married in a week and he was anxious as hell. Stressed out even, to the point of holing up in his apartment and spending most of his free time playing *World of Warcraft* or grooming his Facebook profile or lurking in gay chat rooms for late night distraction. Like most husbands-to-be, he worried about the blind commitment that marriage demanded. He could feel the straps of societal convention and the gauntlet of ritual strangling his identity—on paper that is. Unlike most husbands, he was eager to get it over with, so both bride and groom could forget about it as soon as possible. He was marrying a lesbian, his best friend Veela.

"It's surreal dude," Ravi mused to Nico Costa, his boyfriend and best man, both on paper and off. "I'm like the clueless groom in some holly-bolly rom-com. But can I really pull it off? Me? So much pressure!"

"Babe, you'll be just fine," replied Nico, stroking Ravi's shoulder as they lay cuddled on the black leather couch in Ravi's Valencia Street flat. Nico's furry, muscular arms held Ravi firmly, unwilling to let go. Ravi knew how hard he was trying to be a supportive partner. Since they'd met at a house party two years prior, Nico seemed determined to prove himself at each stage of the relationship cycle. Date-worthy, he was fun and sexy and liked many of the same things as Ravi. Boyfriend-worthy, he was easy to wake up to, spend weekends with, celebrate or commiserate with—whatever the day may bring. Partner-worthy, Nico was willing and able to be fully present, just a touch or a text away at all times, to share anything from a joke to a secret and keep it safe and precious within the container of "us." Now, Ravi needed him to be best man-worthy—it was a lot to ask an already-generous man.

Nico rallied with a joke: "Your film will be like *My Best Friend's Wedding* except with a twist—you're both actually best friends!"

"More like *Monsoon Wedding*," Ravi said glumly, "with the rainbow coming out after it's all over." *Thank heaven it's a made-in-America wedding*, Ravi thought. Only one twenty-four-hour ordeal here in San Francisco, plus a couple of dinners before and after.

"I wish you'd fly that rainbow flag right in their face," Nico griped into the back of Ravi's neck. They were both utterly weary of this tangent, but Nico, as always, was unable to hold back. "Just get it over with. Come out to your family already. Set yourself free!" Ravi felt Nico's arms tightening around him, possessing him. Was love the opposite of free?

"You know I can't do that, Nico," Ravi replied quietly. "They would disown me on the spot." He couldn't manage to dive into their usual banter about flag waving or in-your-face pride. Not about this.

"And why would that be so bad?" Nico shifted on the smooth couch, rebalancing his stocky torso under the weight of Ravi's slender frame. "You have me. You have lots of friends—and you'll make lots more. We're your urban family."

Ravi felt like he was free-falling, paralyzed. A wounded bird unable to flap his way to a ledge, where he could rest and think clearly. His family was his family; he was their only son. He had a duty to uphold! And he had already refused to move home after graduating from university.

"So many excellent jobs here, *Ma*," Ravi had argued. "Right on the doorstep of Silicon Valley. Why give up that opportunity now?" His parents, disappointed, reluctantly agreed.

"Five years," Sarita had said. "Make lots of money and come home in five years." Okay, they would have this discussion every five years. He could tolerate that. But first—take care of obligation number one: Get married.

"You don't understand, Nics," he whispered, feeling a visceral rush of panic course through his body. Nico's arms were just a shadow without shape and form, unable to catch him before he crashed.

"I don't think marriage is the answer, babe," Nico said in his gentlest voice, and kissed his lover's furrowed brow.

To Nico, this marriage of Ravi's was more than surreal, it was like theater of the absurd—they were all puppets manipulated by an unseen force in some existential play. He had confessed these feelings to Ravi shortly after the plan was set. "The real absurdity," Nico had said, "lies in the bare fact that I can't marry the man I love. And I have no control over that." Ravi profoundly agreed, but he couldn't face it. Not yet, anyway.

To Ravi, the marriage plan felt like he was taking control of a particularly messy part of his life. This would be a simple, self-arranged marriage and, unbeknownst to both sets of in-laws (and to the law at large), one of mutual convenience. Ravi and his bride, Veela, were both pride-filled, happily partnered, gay BFFs who needed to get married soon in order to continue living their authentic lives in peace. Both had been feeling the growing strain of their familial and legal circumstances, and the need for action had become urgent.

Their brainchild was born a few months prior, over strawberry margaritas at Cha Cha Cha in the Mission District.

"My parents are nagging me *con-stant-ly*," Ravi lamented. "They want to see me settled ASAP with a corporate job, corporate wife, and two corporate children, preferably a boy and a girl." He began nervously shredding a cocktail napkin. "And I'm not even thirty!"

"I thought they wanted you to move back to Mumbai after graduation?" asked Veela, as she slurped her frosty drink. "It's been a few years now, and here you are, still *here*!"

"There's more money to be made *here*," he snorted. "And anyway, it's a better story for their friends. Successful son in America! Proud parents! Family legacy on two continents!" He waved his arms expansively with each point.

"Yeah," Veela empathized, "and you don't want to break their heart with the truth." She re-adjusted her soft, ample bottom on the hard, wooden barstool.

"I suspect they know the truth," Ravi replied sadly. "My mother, anyway. Hence the pressure." He pawed ruefully at his mound of napkin confetti.

"Me, I've got two terrible truths breaking my heart." Veela downed the last of her drink and exhaled deeply. "My parents have already lined up a suitable suitor for me in Delhi. And they've sent me a plane ticket to come home and meet the guy!" She signaled to the bartender for a second round.

"Man," commiserated Ravi, shaking his head. "And what's the second truth?"

"My H-1B visa is expiring, and it was the final extension. Marv, our HR manager, can't figure out how to secure a green card for me fast enough. So, I may have to go home anyway. And once I'm there, it will be a nightmare to try and come back."

"So, if your family can't force you back to India, the INS will."

"An unholy alliance." Veela was on the verge of tears, and Ravi reached over to give her a bear hug.

They fell into silence, sipping their fresh margaritas, which shot an icy shudder into Ravi's forehead. After a few minutes, they both perked up, sitting up straight on the rickety barstools.

"We should get married!" they both exclaimed in unison, giggling at the shared brainwave.

"No really, Vee, I'm serious," Ravi said, glowing with tequila-fueled inspiration. "Getting married could make this headache go away. It would be so easy!" He grinned wide, eyes sparkling.

"I don't know if I'd call it 'easy.'" Veela replied, practical as always. "But maybe you're right. We just have to convince our families that we've been secretly in love."

"And now we're ready."

"Well, from their perspective, we are a great match—on paper—with a similar family and religious background," she mused thoughtfully.

"And we're both gorgeous," he replied in all seriousness.

"They'll love 'Us.'" Veela made air quotes to punctuate this ephemeral concept.

“Then here’s to ‘Us’.” Ravi raised his glass, clinking heartily with Veela’s.

“I do,” she smiled.

“I do too!” declared Ravi, and tossed his napkin confetti into the air.

~

Veela lived with her girlfriend Bets in a ragged Edwardian shotgun-style house in Potrero Hill. Their small garden featured two gnarled apricot trees on either side of a redwood chicken coop that housed four hens adopted from a battery farming rescue organization. An aging golden retriever spent his days snoozing on the couch in the sunny front bay window. Ravi was not fond of urban chickens, but loved Peach, who always jumped up, paws-on-chest, to greet him with a hearty lick whenever he came to visit. Veela herself stood an imposing five feet, eleven inches tall, with a voluptuous physique that enhanced her stature, a velvety curtain of long black hair, and inquisitive, chestnut eyes. Bets Guilford was a petite, five-foot, two-inch redhead with short fiery curls and a smoldering disposition. Ravi often mused that Bets had a perpetual look of barely suppressed irritation.

“What’s wrong?” Ravi had said when he’d first met Bets, slightly alarmed at this inscrutable person whom his best buddy seemed to openly adore.

“What do you mean what’s wrong?” Bets had shot back. She glanced around sharply as if the ‘wrong’ were standing behind her.

“Oh nothing, no worries,” Ravi had replied hastily. “I just thought maybe I said something…” he trailed off. Was it nature or nurture, he wondered? Some people were born with a certain expression forever imprinted on their face, regardless of their life circumstances.

"People are always telling me to 'smile!'" Bets had said. "It's passive-aggressive. Basically, it's a command. I hate that."

"Yeah, me too," he tried to be agreeable, for Veela's sake. "None of their fucking business." He softened a bit toward her then. It must be hard to go through life like a coiled spring.

At the time of the marriage, Veela and Bets had been together for three blissful years after having met one rainy Saturday afternoon at the Lexington, San Francisco's only full-time lesbian bar. A week after she'd met Bets, Veela declared to Ravi: "I met my soulmate!" Ravi was happy for her, and sad for himself, partly because that meant he'd rarely see her now. But it also stung because, on some level, he'd felt like *he* was her soulmate. He and Veela did love each other, and had been intimate with each other's emotional landscape for many years. Is there such a thing as platonic soulmates? Maybe he was just being needy. He tried to shake it off and congratulate his dear friend on her new love. But the shadow of loss stuck. He consoled himself by deciding that the acrid feeling was some kind of existential loneliness.

Ravi's gut proved its authority once again. In the blink of an eye, it seemed, Veela had become submerged in domestic bliss with her girl and their urban homestead, rarely attending social events or seeing friends. Occasionally the couple would be spotted at Fort Funston walking Peach, or at Whole Foods stocking up on organic ingredients for their latest cooking project. They also had a standing weekly date with another lesbian couple at the Presidio Golf Course to practice their game in hopes of someday playing in a tournament. Ravi saw Veela only occasionally, and even then, it was often hard to get alone time with her as Bets always seemed present, either in person or in a constant stream of incoming text messages to Veela's iPhone.

One exception to the couple's social pattern was during the month of June, when the gay community came out to celebrate Pride Month. Veela and Bets made a great effort to get out and about. The two spent evenings and weekends in the Castro neighborhood, seeing friends and films at the Frameline Festival, parading through the Mission District with the Dyke March, or just hanging out at Dolores Park or Café Flor to soak up the festive atmosphere and people-watch. Ravi was also heavily into Pride Month, and he and Nico were typically on the go, attending house parties and dance parties and charity cocktail events. Nico belonged to the Gay Men's Choir, and every June, he sang at numerous fundraisers and throughout the annual Pride Parade as he marched with the choir's contingent. Ravi marched alongside the choir, just happy to be part of the momentum and cheered by the half-million celebrants lining Market Street in downtown San Francisco.

One June, Ravi had a grand idea for Veela. "Vee—you should get yourself a motorcycle. I'd love to see you ride with the Dykes on Bikes!" Deep down, he would love to ride with her and be a part of this formidable contingent that kicked off every parade with hundreds of revving, rumbling biker women.

"It would have to be a pretty big bike," she replied, "so me and Bets could both ride together."

Ignoring that comment, Ravi continued, "Imagine you on a big white Harley, with knee-high black patent-leather boots and a red feather boa. Fabulous, darling!"

"And wearing a leather bikini?!" she laughed, striking a pose.

"You'd look like an Indian Amazon!" It was one of their favorite inside jokes.

Veela and Ravi's Pride celebrations usually crossed paths here and there during the month's activities, but they always managed to see the Frameline Film Festival's short-format film program together—*Fun in Girls Shorts* and *Fun in Boys Shorts*. The films were shown in the historic Castro movie theater, and every year, the theater was filled to its gilded rafters with a noisy, spirited crowd of men in the morning, and equally lively women in the afternoon. Ravi wondered if there were any films about gay men and lesbians getting married. Maybe they should make one.

~

Once they had decided to be "engaged," Ravi and Veela had to take the first terrifying, yet critical step of informing their families. Their first commitment as a couple was to help each other traverse this rocky terrain.

Veela's parents seemed to take the news in stride, satisfied with the Desai family profile and Ravi's Stanford pedigree. "We trust your choice, my girl," Veela's father had declared benevolently, adding, "We'll send you both tickets to come visit!" Veela was able to easily postpone this prenuptial gift, due to visa complexities and the necessary timing of the marriage. However, Veela's parents were relentlessly flexible. "We'll come visit you!" Despite her family support, it was yet another layer to carefully manage.

Ravi's parents, on the other hand, reacted with surprising alarm. After years of pressuring him to get married, he imagined that they would be thrilled to hear the news. They're getting what they wanted, so what's the problem?

"*Beta*. Why have we not met this girl?!" Sarita had immediately scolded when Ravi broke the news over the phone. His call had come through as she was dressing for her weekly ladies' club luncheon. Ravi could almost hear his mother's mind flipping through strategies around how to reveal this family development to her friends.

"What's this about a secret girlfriend?" added Arjun, listening in from the extension in his office. "Who is this girl's father? I'll look him up straightaway." Ravi's father had such an extensive network of professional contacts, he could uncover many salient details about a person in his social sphere with just a few calls and emails.

"What are you not telling us, *bibi*?" probed his mother. The obvious was laid bare right from the get-go.

"*Ma...*" Words stuck in Ravi's throat. "I wanted to see how things went with the relationship first." He hesitated. "I didn't want to get your hopes up."

"My hopes up?!" his mother shot back with a tinge of anger before changing tack, "What does Sanjiv think about her, *beta*?" Ravi grimaced. He hadn't considered how and when he would inform his uncle and aunt, he had fallen out of the habit of seeing them regularly. Like many San Franciscans, crossing the bridge to the East Bay felt to Ravi like crossing state lines. But clearly his mother would be dialing in her brother as soon as they hung up.

"Um, well, I haven't introduced them yet. We've all be so busy over here." Ravi added "Visit Uncle Sanjiv" to the wedding to-do list that he shared with Veela online. "But I'll bring her over to meet Sanjiv and Shilpa this weekend," he continued, adding a star next to this task. "They'll love her. *You'll* love her!" He tried to reassure his mother of Veela's worthiness by giving her the highlights of Veela's background, career, and beauty, promising to send photos as soon as possible.

"Well, *beta*, you seem to have it all sorted out," Sarita commented, sardonically. "Just send us some photos please." Ravi agreed and ended the call, deflated and relieved to have gotten through "the announcement." Veela met him at Cha Cha Cha to help him decompress over a margarita and quesadilla. "Bravo," she had said. "It's all downhill from here!" Meaning easy, he hoped, not disaster.

Once the date was set, the two couples met regularly at the women's home for a night of wedding planning and wine—usually more wine than planning—and after a few weeks, the convivial collaboration made the marriage idea feel almost 'normal' to them all. Almost.

Bets had fully embraced the idea from the beginning, because to her it meant one thing only—Veela could stay in the U.S. She could finally get her green card after so many years of waiting and lottery disappointment, and the couple could continue building their dream life together, blessed by a city of dreamers. "The end is way more important than the means." She was openly gallant and generous in her support for the wedding. "Other than that piece of paper, nothing will change whatsoever." Privately, Veela had confided to Ravi, Bets had suggested to her that after the wedding they take a road trip to cleanse themselves of the event, like waving burning sage in a haunted room.

Ravi suspected that Nico needed more than symbolic smoke to move beyond his bitter reservations about the wedding, still simmering away on the backburner of his heart. Now and then he let a caustic comment slip through, citing the "tragedy of national politics" or the "straitjacket of societal norms," and sometimes "this ridiculous farce." Regardless, Ravi was grateful that Nico tried his best to immerse himself in the full boil of party-planning.

"As Best Man, I'm going to make sure the groom gets all the debauchery he deserves before the wedding," Nico declared to the planning committee. "Go-go dancers, strippers, porn stars—you name it."

"You mean a regular night out for you guys?" Veela teased, taking a big sip of Merlot.

"Funny, funny," Ravi replied, wondering why he felt slightly embarrassed at such silliness. "No kegs of beer please!"

"Only pink Cosmos for you, babe," Nico reassured him, putting his arm around Ravi as they sunk deeper into the plum velveteen sofa.

A fire blazed in the cozy living room, drawing out the intensity of its lush colors. Veela and Bets had wanted to compliment the period detail in the room—embossed tin wainscoting, molded fireplace, ceiling medallion—with furnishings that had some reference to the old home's heyday. The end result was half-way between then and now, with some references to the golden age interspersed with classic Indian and modern American accents from their individual pasts. As a couple, their tastes ran rich with ruby red velour curtains, brocade pillows, and Beaux-Arts style furnishings made the room seem more boudoir than parlor.

"As Maid of Honor, I'm going to make sure the bride gets showered with all the finery she deserves," Bets said as she stepped behind Veela, seated in a high-backed leather armchair, to lightly drape a gossamer green Indian shawl over her partner's head and shoulders.

"My love, could you bring out some more snacks?" Veela deflected, as she rearranged the shawl around her faded Trikone T-shirt. "I have no intention of embracing any more wedding traditions than absolutely necessary." Veela was resolute. "American or Indian."

"As you wish, My Queen." Bets mock-bowed to the back of Veela's head.

"Why can't we just go to Vegas?" Ravi whined, half-joking. "We could get married by Elvis and earn some dowry cash at the blackjack tables." The committee ignored this wedding tradition altogether.

Bets dutifully walked over to the antique oak sideboard near the window and poured vegetable chips into a cut-glass bowl.

"Sometimes, Bets is the Best Maid," Veela cracked and they all laughed.

"And Nico is always my Man of Honor." Ravi snuggled deeper into his partner's shoulder. Peach shifted his position under the coffee table to lie directly on top of Ravi's feet.

"Peach can be the ring bearer!" Ravi declared. It was getting late.

"And the chickens can sing 'Wind Beneath My Wings,'" Bets replied with her usual two-beat chuckle.

"No seriously, why not?" said Ravi. "We can make a little velvet pouch for his collar. Make him look stylish. You want to dress up, don't you, Peach?" He bent down to scratch the dog's chin while Peach thumped his tail loudly.

"If we call him, he'll come down the aisle no problem." Bets arranged herself on the voluminous cushions of the emerald velveteen couch opposite the men.

"Like one of those classic St. Bernard dogs," Nico added. "Peach to the rescue." Peach thumped his tail again upon hearing his name, seemingly confident of his rescue abilities.

"It probably has to be my little niece Laksmi," Veela said. "I hate to be a downer, but what would our parents say?" A dog in a wedding ceremony! Unthinkable. "She's five years old and adorable."

"But she's coming from Delhi, so she won't have much time to rehearse," Ravi replied. He envisioned Peach approaching the altar with all his canine joy and ring-bearing finery, lightening up the awkward ceremony.

"It's not really our wedding," Veela reminded him.

~

Ravi woke up on the day of his wedding with a lump in his throat and a fist gripping his heart. Was this all a terrible mistake? The deception, the waste, the demoralizing truth that lay behind this foolish spectacle; it all pressed down on him like a righteous force stopping him cold. Was the wedding idea so far off-base that it would ultimately end in tragedy? He, Veela, their partners and families seemed to be hurtling blindly toward mass collision, where no one would be spared. Ravi had been lying to his parents for years about little things, forgettable things, like how he spent his free time. But *this*...this was a huge, enduring lie. Ravi tried again to stabilize his inner compass so that he could lock back onto course. He loved Veela, his dear friend, so it couldn't be so wrong, could it? A marriage of two loving friends. Nothing could shake that truth, he was certain.

He'd met with Kira at Starbucks the day before, mostly to validate the plan one last time with a neutral friend. But he also desperately needed her confidence. For any of life's crossroads, big or small, Kira always knew the right way to go, and she never seemed to get hijacked by doubt or opinions. She was his oracle.

"Ravi, don't worry so much," Kira reassured him. "Like I've said a hundred times now, your plan is sound, your reasons are good, so don't ruin it by stressing." She sipped an unsweetened soy green tea latte, her usual breakfast. "And besides, everyone can only get married to one person at a time, so why not you?"

"I should be marrying Nico," he lamented. "Well, I'm not sure if I'd even want to do that. It's such a big step."

"Darling, you can get divorced later! When human rights finally become civil rights, you and Nico can have a big old gay wedding. Veela and I will be your bridesmaids." Her bright blue eyes pierced through his whorl of anxiety.

"Ugh, the thought of marrying anyone makes me nauseous right now." He grimaced and took a sip of too-sweet chai.

"I know, I know," she empathized, gently patting his forearm. "It's natural for the groom to have cold feet right before the Big Day."

"Cold feet, warm heart?" quipped Ravi glumly.

"Just don't trip over the altar." Kira flashed him her best smile and Ravi felt its tractor beam draw him into the warmth of conviction.

The rehearsal dinner convened at Royal Bombay, a four-star Indian restaurant in Berkeley, where the lively party of twelve had taken over the entire back wing. All members of each immediate family were present except for Ravi's sister Layla who, heavily pregnant with her third child, was forbidden to fly in her third trimester. Nico and Bets sat together at one end of the table, ensconced in a world of their own.

Ravi was on hyperalert during the entire meal, tuning in to the nuances emanating from both families. In between the mulligatawny soup and vegetable samosas, he overheard his mother, flush with triumph, whisper to his uncle Sanjiv, "This is all because of you, my darling brother."

In between the chicken tikka and mango ice cream, Veela's mother Bhavana, flush with relief, whispered to her husband Vishnu, "This boy is far better than the other."

In between the Bengali sweets and Italian cappuccinos, the two fathers turned to each other and simply nodded, their final signature on the situation that thankfully no longer required anything more of them.

As he absorbed the mood of the wedding party, Ravi sat with his bride-to-be, quietly eating at the head of the table with a full plate and a full heart, happy that everyone seemed so happy. He leaned over to Veela and whispered, "Is this the beginning or the end?"

"Or the beginning of the end," she mumbled, her mouth stuffed with naan.

~

On the morning of the wedding, Veela texted Ravi, "Ready or not, here I come!"

Ravi was indeed ready. "Let's do this, girlfriend."

Ravi didn't find out until later that Veela had woken up that day in a cold sweat, momentarily preventing her from getting out of bed. She had her own reasons to dread this day and everything it demanded of her, of all of them, including her family. It had been a huge ordeal for her parents, grandparents, and her brother and his family to fly all the way from New Delhi.

By the time Veela and Ravi convened that morning, though, she had shaken her fears back into the shadows. She'd had a blur of things to do before the female contingent of the family arrived at nine o'clock to help her with the finishing touches. Veela's mother had brought a luscious red and gold silk sari from India, and helped her arrange it just so. Its deep ruby hue would look even more vibrant against Ravi's jet-black tuxedo. Veela's sisters helped with hair, makeup, and jewelry, transforming her into a glittering princess. She knew the part well, and could play it easily with finesse and grace. As a final touch, Bets gently slipped a blue garter onto her thigh, hidden beneath the finery, their shared secret. This trite, but time-honored tradition of a culture that wasn't hers, from a partner that was hers, had somehow made it easier to cope.

Ravi and Veela were both determined to give their families a dream wedding with two stipulations. One: it would be a modest, and (mostly) Western affair. The wedding would reflect the simple and relaxed culture in which they had made their home. And two: the pair would pay for everything themselves. Although both held good paying jobs and were willing to spend a few thousand dollars between them on this commitment, they wanted to maintain damage control on all fronts, especially the financial front. "Cheap n' chic," as Bets would say, which somehow always made Veela think of "fish n' chips." After many frustrating overseas phone calls, some ending in tears on both sides, both sets of parents reluctantly agreed to the final plan. It may be disappointing, but it was also fashionably modern, like their children.

As a compromise between simplicity and grandeur, the civil ceremony was held at San Francisco's City Hall, with Veela's district supervisor serving as officiant. To the parents, this seemed like an appropriately official and grand location. To the bride and bridegroom, the solution ticked a couple of important boxes. The whole affair had to be quick, in and out in one hour. And the spot was eminently photogenic, giving the parents an impressive wedding album to share back home.

At the moment of untruth, Ravi and Veela stood under the building's rotunda, in front of the sweeping staircase that seemed to invite an ensemble of holly-bolly dancers to animate the scene. Their partners, in blue dress, blue tux, stood stiffly beside them.

As Ravi and Veela stated their vows, Ravi felt as if the marble floor opened up beneath them, sending them plunging into roiling, icy bay waters. His eyes searched hers for the life ring of their friendship, its familiar easy comfort, to save them from drowning. The quick obligatory kiss grounded them and they both breathed a deep sigh of relief as applause blurred the past few moments into a watery wake. Photos snapped furiously, and the thing was done.

As a compromise between Eastern and Western traditions, the wedding reception was held at a restaurant on The Embarcadero called The Palomar. With a large patio overlooking the waterfront and the dramatic suspension towers of Bay Bridge, it was perfectly situated for an urban celebration. The restaurant had dressed outdoor tables in the simple elegance of cream damask and pink roses (Nico's secret nod), and set up a lavish Indian buffet at the back. An unusually warm May sun showed up as a most welcome guest.

"Good job, dude," Kari slapped Ravi on the back. "You look very GQ in that tux," he said, his Nordic looks even more striking than usual in a pale grey Armani suit.

"It was beautiful, Ravi," Kira kissed him on the cheek. "Well done." Her silvery elegance matched Kari's in a dove grey crepe cocktail dress and white, strappy sandals.

"Congrats, man," Diego nodded as he held up a glass of Pinot in tribute. Ravi saw that Diego had made a great effort for the occasion by wearing a wool blazer and a button-down Oxford shirt. His pretty new girlfriend Meghan, in a 1950s inspired flower print dress and pale green cardigan, looked like a summer meadow. She smiled warmly and gave Ravi a quick hug.

At one point, Ravi looked around for Nico and found him in the Palomar's back lounge with Bets. The two seemed to be attempting to recover from the ceremony with a bottle of Champagne and a plate of portobello sliders. Bets had kicked off the ballet flats she'd worn with her long blue dress and propped her feet up on a plush ottoman.

"I have no desire to talk to anyone," she declared, pouring two glasses. She gazed glumly at the currents of bubbles rising from stem to rim. Ravi pushed away a pang of guilt.

"This day may be a sham, Bets, but we still win in the end," Nico clinked her glass gently.

"A sham or a shame? Or both," she replied tartly.

"We get the 'happily ever after'—that's the real deal."

"Cheers to that, brother," she smiled wryly. "Brother-in-law."

Outside, family and friends crowded around the newlyweds like a football victory scrum, each adding their voice to the chattering chorus of familial approval. Both sets of parents expressed a profound sense of completeness at this essential milestone in their journey as fathers and mothers. They could relax now, the burden of duty released. Ravi and Veela had never seen their parents look so happy. His heart swelled, displacing for the moment, the usual bitter lump of obligation and guilt, identity and lies.

No need to course-correct, thought Ravi. It's about love. Twisted and fucked up maybe, but at the core, it's still about love.

CHAPTER 7

Meghan

Meghan came home from her first day at Del Oro Games both exhausted and elated. She had given the day one hundred percent of herself—vastly more than most days get from her—and she felt deliciously spent. What better place to be than working at a fun young company with a lot of potential, side by side with the most exciting guy she'd met in a long time?

As Meghan climbed the narrow interior staircase to her upper story flat, Bummers the Cat stared down at her through the chipped white bannister railing. For the past few years, she had been living in this three-bedroom Victorian on Pierce Street, in the Lower Haight neighborhood, just east of the famous Haight Ashbury. Meghan would have preferred living in the Upper Haight, amongst the colorful array of head shops and vintage boutiques and neo hippies who lounged on the sidewalks infusing the legendary street with a mellow vibe. In the Upper Haight, the Summer of Love felt endless, and the tie-dyed flame of idealism burned bright. The true spirit of San Francisco! She could see herself rolling out of bed after a late night of making art, donning round, Lennon-style sunglasses, and lighting a clove cigarette on her way to pick up a morning latte. By comparison, the Lower Haight was a pale and shabby shadow.

Regardless, Meghan grew to love her first—and so far, only—home in San Francisco. The classic, turn-of-the-century flat featured small rooms with high ceilings, and it still retained some of its period detail, including embossed tin paneling along the narrow central hallway, ornate moldings around the doors and ceilings, and a grand mantelpiece over a tiled fireplace that had sadly been bricked in. There was a closet-sized room just for the toilet, which was handy when having roommates. Meghan's favorite feature was the massive iron bathtub, its curving belly perched on silver painted lion's claws. It was the perfect remedy for everyday stress, and she regularly took long, luxurious soaks, her head dipped low in its deep, comforting well. The tub had the magical ability to stop the headlong rush of her life, but only for a short while, until its hourglass of warmth had emptied out. If luck were on her side, Meghan's everyday worries would have emptied out by then as well.

When she moved in, Meghan had been a fresh-faced college grad, ready to jumpstart an urban lifestyle and career path that was worth her precious time and effort. However, what that career would be, she hadn't a clue. Six years and two jobs later, she still had no clue. The freedom and responsibility of choice continued to overwhelm Meghan's inner compass. Sometimes, random images arose in her mind that articulated this feeling for her, mirror-like. She was Dustin Hoffman's character in the film *The Graduate,* floating aimlessly in his parents' swimming pool. She was both Vladimir and Estragon, locked in an absurd dialog while waiting for Godot. She was the rolling stone of Bob Dylan's song, directionless and alone. How does it feel? It feels like crap.

"Hi, Bummers." She stroked the orange tabby's broad head. "Did you have a good day, sweetie?" Bummers blinked his answer and sauntered off toward the living room. Meghan had discovered the cat as a skinny street waif living in a raccoon-infested, no-man's land near her college apartment in Santa Cruz. His name was inspired by the look of abject despair on his furry face at that time. Meghan couldn't help naming him, then feeding him, and then letting him sleep over sometimes. When her car was packed and ready to move to San Francisco, she grabbed Bummers and plopped him in a box on the front seat. Neither one looked back.

"Hey, Bree," Meghan said to her roommate as she passed through the flat's cozy kitchen. Meghan and Bree had lived together for almost two years, and Bree was always surprising her with something new. New dresses, new projects, new temp jobs, new boyfriends. The woman never stood still.

"What's up, buttercup?" Bree chirped without looking up from her craft project. She was bent over the kitchen's vintage Formica table, which was covered in neat piles of jewelry-making materials.

Bree was braiding pale blue silk cord and silver beads into long necklaces, her slender fingers flying through the knots with long-practiced ease. Her delicate ivory brow was knitted in concentration as she peered intently through pink-rimmed cat's eye glasses. A hank of her spikey, jet-black hair was pulled into a whale's tail on the top of her head, little girl-like. Bree was wearing one of Meghan's favorite outfits: a sleeveless cotton calico dress with full skirt, black fishnets, and Doc Martens boots with pale orange laces. Her eyes look puffy and Meghan wondered if she'd been at this project all day long.

"What's up, girl? You're a one-woman Maker's Faire!" Meghan exclaimed, fingering one of Bree's finished products. "I like the silver and blue combo. Very nice." Bree looked up for a heartbeat and smiled gratefully before resuming her brisk work pace.

Bree was Meghan's most energetic and industrious friend. Although born in the '90s, Bree would have fit right in to the homespun '70s, expressing herself through practical, homemaker crafts. She was always making something—jars of homemade preserves or frilly retro aprons or beaded bags—any project that struck her fancy from the extensive library of crafts magazines that filled a large bookcase in her bedroom. But she was more whimsical than methodical. Although she sold her wares on Etsy.com and at craft fairs around the Bay Area, she tended to produce inventory that was short-lived.

"You should stick with one product category," Meghan advised on occasion. "So, you can develop a strong brand and sell through boutiques, as well as online. Make some real money!" However, Meghan knew full well that real money was a pipe dream for crafters.

"I know, I know," Bree agreed. "But I'm still in the R&D phase. Still trying to figure out my best product."

"I think you love the R&D phase too much," Meghan teased, then feeling overly critical she quickly added, "But we all love being your guinea pigs!"

"I'd make a great pioneer wife," Bree said emphatically. "I could shoot a snake at fifty yards while churning butter and breastfeeding my tenth child—all at the same time." Meghan had no doubt about that.

During Bree's pickling and dehydration phases, she was obsessed with vegetables and combed the weekly farmer's markets looking for perfect specimens to can or brine or dry. During her macramé phase, she revisited the iconic plant hangers from the '70s. She created dozens of intricate jute pieces with large colorful wooden beads that cradled unruly Christmas Cacti or wispy Boston Ferns. Several stood guard along the back stairwell, and one behemoth Devil's Ivy hung in the front bay window of their living room, like a gigantic spider waiting patiently for its next meal.

"To your point about branding, I think I'd like to focus on upcycling," Bree continued. "I love the concept of reusing throw-away materials to make beautiful new things." Recently, she'd found herself inspired by a Brazilian women's collective and was teaching herself how to make a belt using the pull-tops of aluminum cans.

"Great. Upcycling is going upmarket these days," Meghan replied. She picked up a bottle of Pinot Noir on the kitchen counter and poured herself a glass. French and probably fancy. Perfect for now—thanks, Rence.

Her other roommate Rence worked as Head Sommelier at the upscale Tuileries restaurant in Hayes Valley. At one time, Rence and Bree had had a thing going, or have a thing going—past and present seemed to switch places often and Meghan couldn't keep track. It had become a habit of hers to notice which doors were cracked open or closed shut in the middle of the night. Luckily, she had the master bedroom at the back of the flat.

Rence was short for Lawrence. He'd dropped the "Law" part of his name when he dropped out of law school, as a symbolic way to underscore this life-changing decision. Larry, his uncle's name, was never an option.

"The name Lawrence feels way too structured, too institutional," he had explained when he'd answered their Craigslist ad for a new roommate. "It's too controlling, and I need more room to breathe." He threw back his arms dramatically to underscore this point and inhaled deeply into his soft, round belly.

Instead of law, Rence chose wine and studied how to control oxidation in order to bring forth its possibilities. During the day, he painted abstract landscapes in an 10x10 cubicle in a warehouse on Harrison Street that he shared with seventy other artists. Now and then he'd bring home a sample of his current work, or a half-bottle of leftover wine from the restaurant, and the three roommates would have a nightcap and chat. But most of the time, they didn't see him much.

Meghan headed toward her room at the back of the house and kicked off her shoes. Once again, she admired her roommates for following their hearts. They didn't just wander down the road less travelled—they sprinted toward their dreams. Since her teenage years, when she dabbled in an array of domestic arts, Meghan had yearned to live "the creative life," which she envisioned as an alternative universe that glittered teasingly just beyond her reach.

"True artists," she said to Diego one evening over dinner at the Formica table, "don't just dress the part like so many hipster wannabes in this town." She took a bite of spinach lasagna as her conviction gained speed. "They inhale and exhale creativity in every minute of their lives."

"Oh yeah?" replied Diego skeptically, stabbing his fork at a large broccoli floret. "Do they live like bubble boys and girls, sucking in rarified air?"

Ignoring him, Meghan continued, "They lead more exciting lives than the average person because they see the beauty and potential in every single object, every single experience." To illustrate her point, she picked up the saltshaker, turning it over in her hand as if it glowed with mystery, spilling a few grains on the table. Bad luck?

"Megs, there's also a world of ugliness out there, with no higher purpose. It only proves that we live in an imperfect world that we can't control." Diego licked his finger, dabbed at the spilled salt, and let it sting his tongue.

"Yeah, but an artist can turn even the ugliest thing into something worthy of attention, and even appreciation. That's some measure of control." Meghan felt a current of irritation shoot through her spine. He wasn't getting her point.

"You mean they make something out of nothing," replied Diego. "Like software engineers."

She stared at him for a moment, and then inclined her head to concede his point, although reluctantly.

If anything in one's environment could stimulate creative ideas, where could she find inspiration? What ordinary thing could she make extraordinary? Meghan scrutinized her apartment. She was sure that interesting things could be done with her bedroom closet door. Or the stairway bannister. Or the long vertical nook built into the entry hall where a door chime had once been. All opportunities for art! And because art bred more art, once she got started for real, she'd soon be riding an unbroken wave of artistic expression that would permeate her life from closet door to gallery show to who knew where.

~

"For real." These were the two most exciting—and scariest—words in Meghan's vocabulary. Her journey to "real" was proving to be much longer, and much more treacherous than she had ever imagined. So many hurdles slowed her down, so many forks confused her, so many voices hijacked her progress. The greatest roadblock on Meghan's journey toward her dreams was the ever-present specter called "risk." Or was it "security?" Maybe both were like a bad cop/good cop pair that conspired to stop her dead in her tracks. She could not just rush forward, fueled by blind faith, into the murky future of a life lived for art. Not only could she not bear to face the raw nakedness of the blank canvas, the blank page, the blank mind, every single day. But she just could not commit to a path that was clouded by probable failure, certain doubt, and most importantly, certain debt.

As a freshman at the University of California at Santa Cruz, Meghan had gravitated toward humanities courses before letting her creative voice take center stage. She enrolled in a variety of art classes, which felt more like auditions that she fervently hoped would reveal a hidden talent that could be cast into a lead role in her life. Drawing and painting were painful exercises, manifesting more self-doubt than imagery. With every stroke, she flayed herself for her lack of natural aptitude, and with every stroke she felt her dream slip a little farther away. She was much more comfortable with art forms that included a mechanical process, such as printmaking, photography, or ceramics. Going through prescribed steps in the physical world, like following a recipe, felt grounding and almost comforting in the face of her fickle creativity.

"Maybe I'll become a professional printer," she declared once, to the great dismay of her mother. "I could specialize in high-end art production."

"Just get a degree first, honey," Sandy had replied. Meghan could see a flicker of anxiety cross her mother's face, one that seemed all too common these days. Was she that off-track?

The summer of her junior year, Meghan took a part-time job in low-end art production at a small printing company. Using a manual silk-screen press, she printed tourist-friendly designs on T-shirts and sweatshirts at a per-piece rate. She worked alongside men with muscular arms that had been toughened from long days of pulling squeegees loaded with heavy paint across taut print screens. She was more careful than the men, but also much slower, which meant that she didn't make much money at all. But it was okay with her because just being around the smell of paints and solvents, the clacking of presses, made her feel authentic somehow.

Occasionally, Meghan would drive home to San Luis Obispo, where her mother lived alone in a modest, two-bedroom bungalow at the end of a quiet cul-de-sac. When Meghan was three years old, her father Jim had disappeared one day, leaving a brief note scribbled on a yellow pad next to a pile of his dirty laundry. The note said simply that he loved Sandy and little Meghan, but he had to pursue his dream of becoming a professional golfer, which required him to live in Tempe. Jim apologized for leaving them so abruptly, and for the dirty clothes, which he would not need anyway since it was always hot in Arizona. Sandy soon discovered that their next-door neighbor Mindy had left a similar note for her husband. After a few tearful weeks, Sandy would cry "Good riddance!" after every thought or mention of the runaway couple. "Right, Megs?" she would say to her toddler, who always nodded, wide-eyed. After a few bitter months, "Good riddance!"

turned into "Whatever!" As the years flew by, a cynical shrug was all that was left.

At the time, little Meghan wasn't fazed by her father's departure, nor in fact did she miss him as the years went by. He'd come to visit once a year, but for Meghan, it felt more like meeting up with an old teacher than spending time with a father. As she grew older, her parents' story took on the plaintive wail of a country western song—the cheating hearts and crying eyes added a layer of romanticism to a painfully ordinary experience. Meghan secretly admired Jim for truly living his dream, especially after learning years later that he had won a regional golf tournament in Albuquerque. Good for him.

On the family home front, Sandy Miller had worked hard to build a good life for Meghan and herself. She taught high school English to kids from farm families, utility worker families, and prison guard families, encouraging them, like a teen-savvy Mother Goose, to articulate the rhyme of their lives. During summers, she immersed herself in the adult world, working as a temporary administrative assistant at the local community college. Teenage Meghan had been determined not to go to that college at all costs. Like her father, her dreams lived far away.

"Mom, I want to go to college back East," she had declared at the start of her senior year in high school. Her thoughts drifted toward the kind of adventure that only distance could bring. "Maybe NYU or Georgetown, or one of the Massachusetts schools. I'm flexible!" She'd be on board with any school that was located along the Eastern seaboard.

"Honey, that would mean out-of-state tuition, and travel expenses, and who know what else," Sandy replied cautiously. She was concentrating on pulling a heavy pan of roast chicken out of the oven, careful not to spill any juices. Meghan tried to read her mother through the hunch of her back and set of her shoulders. Was she worried? Critical?

"Maybe I could get a scholarship?" Meghan suggested hopefully. She felt the familiar sting of fear that typically arose with any reference to finances.

"Maybe..." Sandy said gently. "I think you'd need much better grades though." She set the chicken on a carving board and began vigorously mashing potatoes.

"Okay, I'll look at California schools too." Meghan tried to hide her disappointment. There was no way in hell she could burden her mother with more debt than was absolutely necessary.

Mother and daughter sat down to their chicken dinner in silence. Meghan gazed thoughtfully at the petite blond woman across the table. With Sandy's neat, short haircut and sky-blue jogging suit, her mother seemed to Meghan like the quintessential soccer mom, or maybe super mom, revved up and ready for anything. She may not have an athletic daughter, Meghan thought, but she does have someone to rescue now and then. As her mother smiled back in between bites, Meghan noticed the fine lines around Sandy's eyes, which made them seem sparklier, happier. When her mother smiled, Meghan's heart beamed.

In the spring of her senior year in high school, a compromise was struck. Meghan accepted an offer to attend UC Santa Cruz, bolstered by modest financial assistance and a few student loans. Sandy seemed to accept the imminent departure of her only child, expressing relief that it was only a couple hundred miles north. For Meghan, Santa Cruz was far enough away for her to have her college adventure but close enough to go home anytime she wanted. The perfect balance of risk and security for her emerging grown-up self.

As Meghan's college life unfolded, adventures, experiments, and dreams all clamored for a role in shaping her. She went to parties with the art students, she danced to vintage '70s disco, drank shots of Jägermeister, and made fast friends and faster dates. The academic and coastal landscape of Santa Cruz offered a cornucopia of new ideas and experiences, from post-feminism to political activism to hippie culture. She took classes across a spectrum of humanities and arts and social sciences. As the years passed, Meghan felt the contours of her mature self slowly materialize through youthful edges that were tender and permeable.

Toward the end of her sophomore year, another compromise was struck after numerous tense debates between mother and daughter.

"Honey, you're at a university to study academics," Sandy said over a strained Sunday phone call. "You're paying a lot of money and you should get a substantial education for it."

"But Mom, art is substantial!" Meghan cried, trying to stifle a tremor in her voice. "It's important now more than ever with big corporations trying to buy our souls with all their cookie-cutter crap."

"Yes, but you won't be able to buy any crap without a good paycheck!" Sandy shot back.

"I don't need any crap. I want to live minimally."

"Meghan, getting a degree that people will respect is a starting point for a good job."

"But what if I got a job doing art?" Meghan whined, feeling the cruel fist of doubt grip her gut. What if she couldn't get hired, then what?

"Honey, I'm just saying, give yourself options," Sandy replied evenly. "Options are your best strategy in life. In careers, in love—anything."

Sandy's fear conspired with Meghan's doubt to turn her away from her intended path. She would not study something as ephemeral and unemployable as art, especially after her numerous art classes so far had only produced lukewarm results. So instead she chose art history—an academic subject that was more solid and somewhat less unemployable. If she couldn't focus full time on art, she'd study the creative process of the masters and hope to learn their secrets.

"Maybe I could work for an art gallery," Meghan told Sandy, feeling sure that it was an option that her mother could accept.

Sandy hesitated a split second, then replied, "Sure honey, you'd enjoy that." Meghan could hear the heavy sigh that echoed two hundred miles away.

As Meghan shifted from college to career, her third compromise arose on its own from the momentum of the first two. This time, she barely noticed. After graduation, she moved another hundred miles north and found that art gallery jobs were hard to find in San Francisco. Eager to jumpstart adulthood, and standing at the crossroads of her new professional life, Meghan chose security over risk—she wanted creativity with a good paycheck. Taking Sandy's advice, she considered her many options: graphic designer (required drawing skills), photographer (required expensive equipment), writer (required a point-of-view), chef (required more years of school). The roadblocks threatened to keep her at a standstill, hemorrhaging both her meager savings and her fragile confidence.

One day Meghan came across a job posting for a marketing assistant at a game company. Games were creative! She could be working around digital art and animation, which definitely counted as a creative environment. Besides, marketing is also creative! It's all about telling the company or product story. And games marketing meant fun visuals and fun copy talking about fun products. How cool was that! Meghan launched herself onto this chosen path with hope that it might connect her two disparate selves—the artist and the career woman—and bring her the wholeness she craved. She sought out opportunities in her marketing job that offered breadcrumbs of creativity and she consumed them, hungry to keep the flame alive.

PART 2

CHAPTER 8

Kari

Kari came home from his day at Del Oro Games so frustrated that he wanted to cry, which of course was impossible. Instead he walked over to his collection of glass birds from Finnish design house Iittala and picked up his favorite—midnight blue, palm-sized, dove-shaped. The bird felt cool and solid in his hand as he followed the stylized curve of its back with his fingertips. He owned ten of the classic pieces, which meant that he had been home to Helsinki ten times since moving to California. One bird per year. Ten birds and how far had he come? Not bloody far! His jaw clenched and he imagined that his current mental state could shatter the collection into dust, like some telepathic monster. But paradoxically, the glass birds always seemed to have the opposite effect, de-escalating his temper with their timeless beauty and unflappable demeanor.

At the end of the workday, Kari had approached his bosses Ken and Dave, yet again, to uncover some clue about the company growth plans, but the pair were tight-lipped as always. It was like that with startups—there was never transparency around anything beyond the mad rush to meet the next deliverable, ship the next feature, bank the next media sound bite. There was no corporate communications department to drip-feed optimism to the general staff. Kari's optimism had withered months ago.

"Like I said last week," Ken stated slowly, visibly irritated, "our big, hairy, audacious goal is to acquire five hundred thousand users before we move forward with any planned growth steps like hiring and raising more capital."

"That's what we should all be laser-focused on," Dave added firmly. "Nothing else right now." The two turned their backs on Kari and continued to huddle over something on Ken's laptop. Their ivory tower was impossible to breach.

"Hairy audacious ass," Kari had mumbled to himself as he walked away. *Why don't they lose the fucking clichés and just shoot straight for once?*

He'd suddenly felt like a cliché himself—ambitious young tech worker treading water in a struggling startup that had tons of potential but quite possibly no vision. There were thousands like him in the Bay Area. Why should he be any different? The only way to be different was to be bold and start your own startup.

The next morning, Kari awoke confident and determined not to let his own potential get left behind. He would bolster this resolve with a steaming cup of ZenSip Rainforest Dark, his current favorite coffee. When the smart kettle showed exactly 96 degrees Celsius, Kari gently poured hot water through a coffee filter, careful to evenly soak the grounds and unlock the beans' full flavor profile. In addition to his morning ZenSip meditation, he often met Kira for an after-work debrief and pre-evening boost at ZenSip's flagship store on Fillmore Street. It had replaced a decade's old neighborhood café that could no longer afford the rent. Gone were the threadbare, overstuffed couches, '80s band posters, back wall full of community notices, and shabby décor that was as worn and comfortable as an old shoe. Now the space featured high-gloss reclaimed wood surfaces, oiled steel shelving, industrial light fixtures, and letterpress hand-printed menus. It spoke of a commitment to precision and process, high standards and even higher ideals. Coffee by design—just Kari's style.

Kari used to prefer ZenSip's hand-crafted blends, but after carefully studying their portfolio of single-origins, he had shifted his preferences to pure terroir, where he could easily identify the source continent, if not the specific country.

"It's about learning how to tune your taste buds," he said to Kira once, "and dial into a varietal's finer nuances." He rolled a sip of Columbian estate-grown Typica around on his tongue thoughtfully. "Only then can you really *get* its true nature."

Kira smiled and nodded agreeably, yet remained staunchly faithful to her daily soy green tea latte.

When Kari found something he liked, which wasn't often, he felt an urgent need to experience every aspect of it until he could fully know it, possess it, in his mind and in his marrow. It was like accumulating wealth. Each experience was another small deposit, another puzzle piece that, when compiled, would eventually produce a valuable asset that somehow made his life richer. It was also a relentless search for perfection. The feeling of missing out, of not experiencing the thing that could be the best of its kind, was simply unbearable.

With coffee, it was the global varietals and local artisanal brands. With authors, it was every book, blog, and essay that the author had published. With travel, it was every major highlight of a particular area or country. Kari couldn't go to a place like Hawaii and not visit every island or Paris and not visit every museum—and if it took several trips to catalog them all, well then, so be it.

The recent proliferation of hand-crafted chocolates across the already opulent foodie landscape in the Bay Area presented a treasure hunt of sorts that evolved into an ongoing side project. Kari combed the high-end markets—Ferry Building, Bi-Rite, Rainbow, Whole Foods—to find and taste every fledgling brand, every flavor of distinctive, inspired confectionary, but it was a challenge to stay on top of it all. Despite the fact that the country had nose-dived into economic crisis only a couple of years prior, it seemed that tantalizing new food ventures popped onto the scene almost weekly, practically taunting Kari to sample their delights.

"It's like trying to keep up with consumer technology," he'd say to himself. "These days both chocolate brands and mobile apps are breeding like rabbits."

At times, when stress was at its peak, Kari would get obsessed over entire categories or genres and go on binges. He'd spend a weekend alone eating one particular gourmet product line, such as every flavor of PopD small-batch, artisanal popcorn, and watching a string of Japanese classics, or Jackie Chan flicks, or all of Hertzog and Fassbinder. During those times, even Kira couldn't pull him out of it.

"My love, maybe you can skip that one?" Kira said gently one evening at the couple's favorite ice cream boutique in the Mission District. They had specifically come to try the squid ink and chili jam swirl, only to discover that the guy in front of them had ordered the last scoop of this discontinued flavor. Kira's question mark hung in the air as Kari drew into himself, brooding all the way home over the missed opportunity.

Kari juggled dozens of ongoing bucket lists at any one time, each one surfacing when needed to create structure with the trivialities of life and offer a sense of accomplishment, however small. He also juggled ideas—strategies, plans, hypotheses—whether fragments or whole. He turned them over and over in his mind like a prospector sifting out fool's gold. One of these days a nugget would surface that would lead him to the mother lode, he was sure of it.

~

"It's time," said Diego. It was long overdue, Kari thought, but finally his friend had uttered these magic words and suddenly the universe shifted. Potential transformed into possibility.

"Awesome, Digs," Kari replied. "I am beyond ready to jump start this thing!" He could barely restrain himself from leaping up from the biergarten bench with joy, like a schoolboy on the brink of summer break.

"I've got a solid architecture mapped out and a proof of concept up and running that demos some of the system's core functionality." Diego casually sipped his tall, golden weissbier. "Now it's time to bring in a couple more developers and step up the pace." He daubed a stub of bratwurst in grainy German mustard and popped it whole into his mouth. The late afternoon sun filtered through the eucalyptus trees that ran along the undeveloped space next to the outdoor restaurant, making Diego squint and look even more serious.

"Let's do it." Kari nodded and lifted his glass of dark amber doppelbock in a solemn, heartfelt toast. The pair fell silent. Auspicious occasions like this deserved a moment of reflection and respect.

Kari had watched Diego quietly tinker away for years on an idea that at first had seemed like an amusing, wild-eyed, sci-fi daydream. But hey, so was space travel once upon a time. So why not this? Although Kari could only follow Diego's complex technical vision so far, he'd kept a quiet flame burning inside himself that his friend would eventually pull through with something solid and viable. Something that could produce a marketable asset, a business, a name. Something that could someday earn them a seat at the table among startup unicorns and tech luminaries. Maybe now was the time!

Over the years, Kari had toyed with the idea of starting his own tech company, and had long deliberated over what type of business could eventually become a cash cow—some kind of eCommerce business? A social networking app? Live-streaming porn? Nothing felt quite right. After graduating, Kari's first job offered a rare nod to his heart over his inner calculator. It was a media company that provided film reviews and rentals, and Kari worked on their recommendation engine, helping to refine it so that film lovers could more easily follow their highly-specific passions. The company eventually added books, music, television, and magazine content, which greatly expanded customer choice, as well as exponentially increased customer data.

"We know our customers' deepest desires," he murmured into Kira's ear one evening as they cuddled on the couch. "We know everything they consume, and we can even predict what they'll want next."

"You mean you spy on them," joked Kira, as she snuggled deeper into the hollow of his shoulder blade.

"We're their best friend," he replied. "We never let them down."

Despite his degree in computer science, Kari much preferred working with concepts over code and found himself a natural fit for a product management role. He was a shaper rather than a builder. He enjoyed influencing the end user's experience of a product, ensuring that it met their needs with elegance and sophistication. Kari's entrepreneurial nature gravitated toward the business side of technology—in this high-speed, high-performance industry, a product needed to be stellar in order to not only survive but succeed. To dominate, it had to go beyond simply being best-in-class—it had to radically change the daily lives of its users. Kari would accept nothing less. At work, he was a demanding, tenacious stakeholder that frequently clashed with his engineering teams, especially when their disparate realities collided.

"On time, on target!" Kari would attempt to motivate the development team when progress seemed sluggish. Inevitably, his enthusiasm would be met by a dozen stone-faced engineers silently staring back at him. When this tack failed, Kari would try a tougher approach. "We need to ship this next software release as planned. We've got to get it out in the market pronto. No delays!"

"Impossible," the engineering manager would respond. "Too many bugs, not enough testing resources, system integration issues." He'd shake his head slowly from side to side, in the manner of all engineering managers when uttering the dreaded i-word: impossible. "The team's continuous delivery tools help us to maintain the fastest possible pace, but we can't work miracles."

"Well, we absolutely can*not* slip the release date," Kari would counter, feeling the anger rise quickly from his toenails to his hair follicles. “We’ll miss our market window.” There were always plenty of business reasons to release on time: beat the competition, showcase at an upcoming trade show, influence quarterly earnings, or simply launch a roaring public debut at the right moment on the world’s noisiest stage.

“Impossible to say when the release will be fully tested and ready to deploy to production. Sorry.”

“Marketing, Sales, Senior Leadership—they’re all depending on this release going out on schedule.” Kari would pull out his biggest guns. “We’re talking major business investment in this already. If we don’t deliver, heads will roll.”

“Then cut some features,” the manager would state with an end-of-story tone.

Inevitably, a fierce debate would result with both sides reeling from the gloves-off encounter. Kari often got what he wanted in the end, which meant the engineering team had to work significant overtime.

Kari’s persistence extended to building a promising career path for himself, and he chose to pursue emerging technologies that had a growth-fueled future. Online media and entertainment were hot in the early years after his graduation; then, with the rise of mobile devices, investors flocked to game companies as visually rich, social mobile games exploded onto the market. Kari followed, first working for a large gaming device manufacturer, then trying his luck with a gaming startup, Del Oro, hoping to get a foot in early and rise quickly. Now Kari had arrived at ground zero of building a start-up with Diego and was faced with navigating the rocky road that comes along with such an unpredictable venture. High-risk would bring high-reward, and Kari was ready to gamble.

Later that week, Kari took his first baby step as startup founder and attended a software developer meetup with the intention of sourcing technical talent. The monthly gathering was held at a brewpub in downtown San Francisco, and about a hundred engineers mingled amongst pool tables in the spacious back room. Kari was looking for developers who had deep experience with big data, machine learning, or predictive analysis. Winding his way through the crowd, he was struck by their similarities more than their differences—all male, twenties to early thirties, faded baggy Levi's, clever T-shirt designs, scruffy sneakers. Each seemed to wear a similar expression, a fusion of wariness and belonging. Kari had dressed down for the occasion, wearing his oldest pair of jeans, a Mozilla-branded fleece pullover, and even going out on a limb with flipflops despite the chilly April evening. He'd swapped his Finnish design eyeglasses for contacts and passed on his usual hair products, hoping he looked as unremarkable and American as possible.

"I've worked on a lot of games," said Dale, a husky Java engineer with food stains speckling his retro Atari T-shirt. "Mostly a series of digital pet titles—ya know, the kind you have to feed, walk, and talk to every day or else they die." He chomped down on a large beef empanada and gazed at Kari, cheeks puffed, chewing slowly. "If you play long enough, your pet starts talking to *you*, and gets to know your habits."

"Cool," said Kari thoughtfully.

"We just launched a feature that activates the laptop or phone camera, so your pet can react to your environment." Dale suddenly lit up, eager to share. "Your pet notices that you've got a new bedspread that's different from your usual style. Or that your eyes are red from crying. Or you're logged in from a café instead of school and your pet calls you out for that huge-ass cookie you shouldn't be eating and threatens to email your parents because it knows that you're playing hooky from class!" He looked smugly at Kari, chest puffed, proud of this piece of technical wizardry.

"Creepy," said Kari, suddenly interested in this sloppy-looking guy.

"I've been working on a tutor bot for a language education company," said Chris, a skinny software developer with a baggy "code eater" T-shirt and an enormous "Oracle World" backpack. "Along with teaching you Spanish, it learns from all your mistakes and anticipates the things you'll stumble over so it can give you extra support where you need it." He shifted the seemingly heavy backpack with great care.

"Cool," said Kari, wondering if there was gold in that pack.

"If you enable the 'Get to Know Me' feature, your tutor will scan your emails and pick out words it thinks you might want to learn in Spanish. It then develops practice conversations around those topics." Chris took a swig of cream soda, looking a bit like a lost high-schooler on his first day of Spanish class. "Believe me, some conversations can get pretty wild!"

"Creepy," said Kari, handing the guy his business card.

By the end of the evening, Kari had connected with four engineers who had the unique combination of experience, creativity, and daring that could help bring Diego's quixotic vision to life. Better yet—each was interested in possibly working on their project. He couldn't wait to introduce them to his new business partner.

CHAPTER 9

Kira

Sweat trickled down Kira's back as she waited for the 6:37 p.m. Baby Bullet train to whisk her from sunny Mountain View back to foggy San Francisco. That morning, when she'd put on her slim-fitting, Marc Jacobs merino dress with matching jacket, she'd forgotten how warm it could be as soon as you went a few miles south, north, or east of the city during the summer months. It was a peculiar kind of amnesia common to San Franciscans who were held captive by the marine layer of fog that covered the city in summer gloom. Somehow, it was too easy to forget that real summer existed elsewhere around the Bay. Kira's heavily air-conditioned office complex also masked the true warmth of the day. Yet it wasn't always comfortable to dress in layers—so confining! At least her feet were happy in commuter sneakers, the office dress pumps packed away in her oversized Kate Spade carryall.

Kira watched the bicycles and passengers milling about on the long Caltrain platform. Some commuters seemed to cheerfully anticipate their train, perhaps due to evening plans waiting at the end of their ride. Others stood by looking worn and blank, the demands of their corporate day having wiped them clean like slates. Tech branded backpacks—LinkedIn, Yahoo!, Netgear, Cisco—were pervasive, creating some semblance of community amongst the disparate passengers. Although the "cool factor" of each brand was debatable, the logos not only broadcasted who you worked for, or had done business with, but they also served as a badge of belonging to an undeniably cool profession.

For this latest Bay Area in-crowd, meaning was everything, and "doing" felt vastly more meaningful than simply "being." Nearly everyone had a smart phone in hand, idly thumbing through apps or already-read texts and emails. Who knows, maybe a new message might pop up just then and kindle a brief sense of worthiness—of a person worth existing, of a life worth living—and a high as fleeting as a crack hit. It was no longer the "turn on, tune in, drop out" of the counterculture '60s, but the "always connected, always-on, fear of missing out" of the tech culture millennium. At the very least, anything incoming provided a momentary spark of relief from the dreaded monotony of waiting.

"I'm messaged, therefore I am," Kira once commented wryly to a fellow passenger, when she'd noticed that they were the only two people in the train car not glued to their phones. She had heard that there was a bar car during commute hours, and she imagined a convivial crowd of regulars enjoying beers and banter, like the old TV show, *Cheers*. It sounded nice—in theory. Kira later discovered this to be an urban legend, unless the rumor referred to the seasonal throng of black and orange-clad baseball fans en route to an evening Giant's game in the city.

"Too much beer and too much cheer," she had said to her colleague Darryl, the morning after a particularly rowdy ride home. "Better to get all that cheer in before the Giants lose again," Darryl had replied, flashing an impish grin. His handsome features evoked a fleeting, long lost sense of cheer deep within Kira, making her blush.

Like most Caltrain commuters, Kira preferred a quiet window seat where she could keep the work day going a little longer, get a few last emails in, maybe review tomorrow's presentation one more time.

When she first started taking Caltrain, Kira thought it would be as awkward as navigating the thirty miles of choked freeway to and from her company's massive campus in Silicon Valley. But she was pleasantly surprised. She usually telecommuted once or twice a week, and on the days that she went into the office, either Kari or a taxi shuttled her to and from the 22nd Street Caltrain station. Kira enjoyed her relaxed routine and quiet work time on the train. The soothing motion of the carriage, almost womb-like, carried her forward until she emerged onto the Mountain View platform, fresh and ready for a new day to unfold.

As she waited on the platform for the 6:37 p.m. train, the 6:15 rushed past at top speed, not scheduled to stop at Mountain View. Kira braced herself, unable to take her eyes off the flat grey engine front as it came hurtling toward her. For a split second, her chest clenched against the sheer power and velocity of the massive steel machine as it whooshed past, whipping her hair into her face. Even though this train passed by at the same time every day, and Kira could see it coming in the distance, the fright of it always took her by surprise, unbalancing her momentarily until she could re-settle herself, as well as fix her hair.

Lately, she found herself thinking: what would it be like to take a slight step right? She'd imagine gently tilting her body and toppling toward the tracks as the 6:15 transported her out of this world. Would she join those souls also commuting to the next world? What about those who never arrived in this one? She'd feel a sharp tug, and then the shadow sensation of falling down, down, before she could pull herself back up into the present. Grim thoughts! She'd scold herself, unsettled by their intrusiveness. Such a drama queen! Though she was certain that these thoughts also haunted other passengers standing on that platform, those who were lost or stuck or bled dry by demanding lives.

~

Kira had begun commuting via Caltrain a few weeks prior, after she'd checked her beloved BMW into an auto body shop for extensive repairs. After the cracks started to spider through her perfect life. After the "incident."

One morning Kira had woken up, felt a seismic shift in her abdomen, and dashed to the bathroom to vomit. Her volcanic stomach had settled down a couple hours later, but the tremor in her core remained and she knew something was up. Potential had transformed into reality. A blood test confirmed that she was five weeks pregnant. Five weeks since that brief lapse in birth control, when she had been so consumed by work that she'd forgotten to take her daily pill. She hadn't thought much about it at the time, assuming that the hormones were still flushing through her system during those few pill-less days. But now, the forces of nature had replaced artificial chemistry to govern her body, and by extension, her future. She could not stop thinking about it. How could she have been so stupid! For the first time in her life, Kira felt like a cliché—girl forgets pill, girl ruins promising future—following in the footsteps of countless women, yet walking the path completely alone.

"Theo, what do I do?" She called her brother in southern California, relieved that it was his sober, mature self who answered, and not one of his other selves.

"What do you mean, babe?" he replied. "You must be thrilled! You *are* thrilled? Or not...?" Blinded by distance, Kira struggled to gauge his expression over the phone. Why couldn't he learn how to use Skype or FaceTime, for God's sake.

"Kari is working two jobs now—he's still at Del Oro and now he's launching this new start-up company with Digs," she said, panic rising in her voice. "It's totally the wrong time for having a kid!"

"Yeah, but when is the right time? There's never a right time. It's one of those things in life that we just have to deal with when it comes." She knew that Theo was indexing all the words of wisdom he'd ever stored in his head, trying to pull out the right thing to say. And she appreciated every word.

"But..." Kira hesitated, afraid to speak her deepest fears. "But...I'm afraid he'll be angry about it. He'll be furious with me. I know him. He may appear to take the news in stride, but deep down he'll blame me. He'll hold me accountable for the situation. One hundred percent!" The guilt gushed out, unstoppable. "It was my mistake after all. He'll feel that I got in the way of his big dream. And he would never forgive me for that." Kira started to cry, letting the tears and fears drop heavily, uncensored. "It would totally drive us apart. Maybe forever!" It was so unlike her to cry, Kira almost felt as if this outburst were happening to someone else. Yet still, her chest heaved and her eyes stung. It must be the hormones surging.

"Kira! Babe! Kari loves you! He's gonna give you a huge bear hug when he hears the news! I'm sure of it."

But Kira was not sure of it at all. In fact, she knew that Kari would distance himself, unconsciously perhaps, as soon as he heard the news. She was already losing some part of him to work, but this…this could be the beginning of the end. She was afraid that Kari would bury himself in his new enterprise and leave her to deal with the magnitude of pre-motherhood—the practicalities and discomforts and emotional waves—on her own. Then, after the birth, who knows?

Weeks six and seven brought sleepless nights and nauseous days. Kira felt paralyzed by an epic risk-analysis process. Kari may blame her for the pregnancy, but how would he react to the choices they faced? Would an abortion erode his love for her? Kari had never expressed a desire to be a father, but he was supremely possessive, and a baby was an opportunity to bring his DNA to life, to foster new possibilities from his roots. Consciously letting go of this could leave a stain of bitterness and resentment on their relationship. But having the baby could drive Kari away from her altogether, as he would never let the demands of fatherhood threaten his dreams. Co-parenting would be fraught with disappointment and recrimination—for both of them. As she went over and over each scenario in her mind, their future seemed more and more cloudy. Why couldn't she just trust Kari? That was the greatest risk.

At work, Kira struggled to concentrate and frequently paced the hallways in an attempt to shake off her current dilemma. She was head of corporate communications for the company's data analytics products, and her team was responsible for managing the category's spectrum of public relations activities, from seed-ing and promoting positive stories in the press to doing damage control from occasional negative publicity. At twenty-nine, Kira was younger than most of her peers and recognized by many on the executive team as a dynamic, and promising leader.

Kira's anxious laps around the building usually included a pit stop in the ladies' room for a brief meditation on the toilet, or a few yoga poses in the handicap stall. On one occasion, she overheard familiar voices breeze into the restroom in mid-conversation.

"Kira didn't say a word this morning when Marketing presented that awful "brain-alizer" campaign concept," Marie said to Lisette as the two lingered at the row of sinks. Kira assumed that her two team members were adjusting their makeup after lunch. She could visualize Marie redrawing her signature thin swipe across her lash line. "She's always the first to speak her mind about stuff like that."

"I know, she's got a great bullshit detector," Lisette agreed.

"Wonder what's unplugged her radar?" pondered Marie. The sounds of tap water and tooth brushing muffled her words. "Man trouble, family trouble, health trouble?"

A toilet flushed, and Kira heard someone exit one of the stalls.

"Maybe her Nordic dream guy is dragging his feet on the way to the altar," said Suze, Kira's self-righteous social media manager. Kira frowned at the callous comment and imagined Suze giving her blond bob cut a single, smug primp, her usual restroom genuflection.

"It's none of our business," said Lisette, reclaiming the moral high ground before striding out of the restroom.

Not only was Kira unusually quiet during meetings, she cancelled others with no explanation. Emails went unanswered and projects lingered. She skipped both breakfast and lunch, and could barely bring herself to eat a few bites of dinner. She hadn't made any serious missteps, but her colleagues had begun to simply avoid unnecessary interactions with her, possibly with a sincere intention to "let her be." Kira felt more alone than ever.

At home, Kari was indeed wrapped up in his new endeavor, but present enough with Kira to apologize for his inattentiveness.

"Kira, *kulta*, my love, I'm sorry I'm so distracted these days," Kari confessed one evening over a quick cup of ZenMind Kilimanjaro before heading back to work at Diego's apartment.

"But it's such an amazing time right now!" he continued. "I'm finally getting into the whole startup mindset and it takes, like, two hundred percent of my energy. I know it's a huge time suck, but it's a small price to pay at the beginning of something great. You know?" His voice lilted with unbridled enthusiasm, and his normally composed face was flushed and animated. Kira thought she had never seen Kari so happy, and she desperately wanted this golden period to continue without tarnish.

Kira smiled and nodded and felt the bile rise in her throat. She casually walked over to the bathroom, one step at a time, and turned on both taps at the sink to mask the sound of her retching. Along with remnants of dinner, Kira heaved undigested fear and profound guilt over her deception. She was being spineless. She should tell him. She would tell him. Tomorrow.

But the next day, Kira's world erupted once again—instead of a cellular collision between two sets of DNA, this time it was vehicular. Possibility faded into emptiness.

The incident happened on a foggy Tuesday morning when Kira was driving to work on Highway 101. She had just passed Millbrae, where an artery of traffic from the San Mateo Bridge filters into the already congested freeway. A swarm of cars crawled like crabs on a dry beach. Visibility was sufficient despite the mist, and Kira's usual morning green tea latte had dispelled any lingering wisps of sleep and lubricated the circuits of her nervous systems for another long day at the office. Kira had the radio tuned to National Public Radio, and she was listening to news of an earthquake in New Zealand. Then, the universe shifted, and it was her turn to be swallowed up by change.

In an instant, Kira slammed on the brakes too late and hit the massive commuter bus in front of her. The impact was not enough to dent the bus, but it was enough to crumple her car's front-end and put it out of commission for a few weeks. Kira counted her blessings and thought she had walked away with only minor bruises. But the impact had, in fact, rippled through her tissues, as well as her psyche, and that evening she miscarried.

This time, she turned on the sink taps to mask the sound of her sobbing, even though Kari was still at work.

~

On her new daily commute, Kira gazed out of the Caltrain window, watching the Peninsula cities roll past. Often, as the northbound train neared the airport, she found herself riveted by the dark, steel-gray fingers of fog that crept over the western hills of Daily City, like a molester intent on grabbing its light. The train headed straight into its clutches, toward the murkiness, toward home.

After the accident, waves of feelings washed through Kira as the weeks rolled into months. Grief, helplessness, emptiness, relief. The pregnancy had come and gone without so much as a blip on Kari's radar, and Kira had decided not to tell him after the fact. What good would come of it? It was better to simply let it go. But still, the experience left her raw, with a certain hollowness that threatened to consume her. The accident had prompted Kari to finally notice her moodiness, and she appreciated his attempts to be extra tender. "My love, you need a treat. How about I order a prosciutto and kale pizza from Pie Piper, your favorite!" Or "Let's curl up on the couch and watch something fun." Or "How about a bubble bath and a nice massage?" Yet it wasn't enough. She wanted to shake him. She wanted to cry. She wanted him to crawl into her empty nest and fill her up, prevent her from being sucked out along with the lost soul, or clump of cells, or whatever it was.

The day after the miscarriage, she had called Theo to tell him the news and hear a few words of comfort. But her wayward brother was wrapped in a comforter of his own.

"Kira!" Theo slurred. "Kira! What's up?! I love you, babe. Truly, truly, truly, really, really, really…" His voice, silky soft, purred into her ear as her heart sank deeper into the shadows. "You okay? You're the best, the best." Theo's latest coke-hash filter missed the words "miscarriage" and "no baby" altogether, and she'd wondered if the previous pregnancy conversation weeks ago had even implanted in his addled brain.

The following night, she decided to keep her date with Ravi to see *Avatar*, quietly secreting tears throughout the mercifully long film. Afterward, as they walked through the Embarcadero Center back to his car, Kira was so close to confiding in Ravi. He had always been her gentle confidant, such a generous listener, through so many of her ups and downs. But somehow this time she just couldn't speak the words, face to face, eye to eye, to anyone, not even to sweet Ravi. She choked on them before they even made it up to her cracked, raw throat.

Ravi did notice her mood and, channeling his own mother, seemed determined to get some form of sugar down her throat pronto, confident of its magical properties. He bought her a salted caramel sundae, with whipped cream, nuts, and even a cherry on top. She ate every bite.

Later that week, Kira called Gretchen. Not to share any part of the story—God, no!—she just wanted to hear her mother's voice and hoped its primal roots could help ground her a little. Her father, on the other hand, was out of town, busy cultivating his grass roots as he crisscrossed Ohio campaigning for re-election.

"Darling, when are you and Kari getting married?" Gretchen inquired for the hundredth time. Her mother had a knack for rubbing salt into fresh wounds, even accidently. "My dressmaker has this gorgeous design for a gown that would look perfect on you! I was in his shop the other day, and he had the most beautiful textured cream silk I've ever seen."

"Not anytime soon," Kira replied. "I told you." Like always, Gretchen's intrusions prompted her to shut down and switch to defense. "We're both focusing on our careers right now. And they're going *great.*" Damn right! She punctuated the assertion with the full force of her conviction. Ironically, this mother-daughter chat was making her feel better after all.

Once the worst of the heartache had worn off, Kira threw herself headlong into the wide-open arms of her job, her most steady and insatiable lover. Like Kari, she invested two hundred percent of herself in her beloved career. She routinely worked late into the evenings, as well as on weekends, and she took on even more extra challenges, like volunteering to give presentations to executive leadership, or project-managing many of the things she normally delegated. She fed greedily on the lush gratification that came with even the smallest of achievements, which, like kisses, only lured her deeper into an inexhaustible corporate embrace.

Again, Kira's colleagues noticed a change in her. But this time they did not simply "let her be," but instead stopped by her desk constantly to ask questions, offer information, or just chitchat in hopes of absorbing, osmosis-like, some of her newfound vitality.

At home, Kari's brief period of attentiveness vanished as Kira became more like him. She no longer needed coddling. She had climbed back on top of her game, sadness and loss safely buried. Like Kari, her ambitions at work increasingly pulled her away from home, away from their relationship. Neither complained when the couple's time together shrunk to the occasional weeknight or weekend afternoon in between the myriad tasks needed to manage both work priorities and basic daily life. Quality time had become an indulgence. And optional.

"I'll check my calendar and send you an invite," Kari called out of the car window one morning as he dropped Kira off at Caltrain. "Maybe we could hang out next Thursday evening? I'm not sure yet. There's a lot going on this week." Just like every week.

"Okay, I'll check mine too." Kira waved and hurried toward the station. Thursday was questionable. Often, she and Kari had to reply "maybe" instead of "yes" to each other's date night invitations in anticipation of some last-minute delay at work.

Lulled by the gentle rhythm of the morning train, Kira considered this pervasive sense of "a lot going on" in their lives. It was real—just look at their calendars! But it also felt like an amorphous intruder, a personal boundary that was somehow out of control, oozing into their relationship space and sucking out the oxygen. "A lot going on" was suffocating "hanging out." Similarly, the slow drip of "maybe" seemed unhealthy and potentially corrosive. But what else could they do? Could they put in the hard work needed to be successful individuals and still be the same old K2, solid and unshakable?

On the one hand, Kira loved the fact that she and Kari were highly motivated people, both driven to succeed at what they do best. Each understood, and accepted, the other's busy-ness and personal road map. She loved it when people called them the quintessential power couple—her dream relationship! However, it also meant that, on a daily basis, they lived parallel lives, travelling in separate lanes of the same freeway. They could easily lose sight of each other, drift apart, maybe even get lost. Kira had already experienced one real detour away from Kari during the pregnancy, and she knew now that it was possible, that she was capable, of pulling away from K2, in spite of her best intentions.

Kira brushed the worries aside and opened her laptop. There was too much going on today to think about anything else.

CHAPTER 10

Diego

Lucita called as Diego was looking for a place to eat on lower 24th Street. He cradled the phone lightly against his ear as he walked past the *panderías* and *taquerías* and *peluquerías* that peppered the heart of the Mission District. If any of his family wished to speak with Diego, it was usually Lucita who placed the call and then handed him around the table like a cigarette.

"Big news, *mijo*!" Lucita exclaimed, almost breathless from the sweet anticipation of sharing. "*Tío* Óscar got a new job, a great job! He's going to be the general manager of a sports fishing company, taking tourists out to go deep sea fishing. Marlin, tuna, sailfish—whatever!" She reveled in her stepfather's big catch of a job.

"Not in San Bernardino, Luci," replied Diego sarcastically as the meaning of her news spread into his awareness like an oil spill.

"Of course not, *tonto*," she said with mock exasperation. "It's in México. In Cancún. We're moving to Cancún!" Her voice squeaked out the last syllable.

"What??" Diego felt his heart splutter and clunk. "'We,' meaning all of you?" He could barely imagine them all leaving, all at the same time, leaving him alone in California.

"*Si, mijo.* Well, except for Melinda. She's pretty settled in San Antonio with her TexMex hubby and kids and all. Oh, and Teresa of course..." Her voice trailed off in sadness for her alcoholic sister who was trapped in a trailer park in Laughlin and beaten down by Cuervo Gold and a gambler husband who was twenty years her senior.

Lucinda, recently divorced, saw Cancún as a glittering gem on the Riviera Maya, and one that she was convinced would bring her great riches. Not only would it give her the opportunity to establish her dream—a hair salon empire amongst the wealthy and the beautiful—but with tourists from all over the world, who knew whom she might meet? Maria and her husband Tomás were also game to try their luck in a new city, especially since Óscar had promised both good jobs at the new company.

"How does *Mamá* feel about leaving?" Diego asked, the reality of it settling like tar at the bottom of his gut. "How does she feel about leaving Teresa?"

"We need you to help us kidnap her," Lucita joked. Diego laughed, but also perked up. He could do that. After all, he was the family fixer.

~

At an eight-table closet of a restaurant in Hayes Valley, Diego and Kari sampled the Happy Friday special—a sushi tasting menu paired with a flight of sake shots. Two rows of tiny porcelain cups, each as delicate and as unique as geishas, stood at attention across the small table. In between sat a black lacquer jewel box of luscious, glistening maki and nigiri, each pearl-perfect. It was a happy Friday indeed. Regression testing on their software code had shown no new bugs or breaks in Diego's most recent updates, and Kari had rounded up four possible developers who were interested in their project. They each selected their first geisha and clinked.

"*Kippis!*" Kari said, taking a first sip of the milky sour nectar.

"*¡Salud!*" Diego said, tipping half the shot onto his tongue.

So far, Diego was impressed—Kari had gone all-in on this venture with a level of zeal and dedication that he hadn't expected. After their initial talk, his friend had promptly given notice at Del Oro and proceeded to spend the past two months focused on recruiting talent. He'd spoken to dozens of developers at various conferences and meetups throughout Silicon Valley. He'd tapped all first-degree technical contacts in his LinkedIn network and reached out to many relevant second- and even third-degree contacts, methodically working his search like a professional headhunter. "There's less than six degrees of separation between us and our team!" Kari would say. He'd also invited Facebook friends and Twitter followers to send him referrals and sweetened the pot with a modest finder's fee. And he'd even pursued Diego's own contact sphere, doubling down by contacting Diego's prior coworkers and as well as an army of online acquaintances in the various open source communities and other technical forums that Diego frequented.

"Chris and Dale are interested, plus two other guys may be willing to give us a few hours after their day job. Actually, one is a woman." Kari raised his eyebrows, gazing curiously at Diego. Female developers were unusual, especially on the fringes of mainstream computing.

"Cool," Diego replied firmly. He was aware of the tech industry's pervasive boy's club bias, but didn't understand it at all. Why waste talent? To him, a developer was a developer, end of story.

"But they need to be paid," Kari continued, re-arranging the sake cups into a precision lineup.

"Can't we give them equity?" Diego asked, carefully dipping a ruby-red diamond of maguro into a slurry of wasabi-soy sauce.

"You can't eat equity," Kari joked drily, watching the brilliant maguro slip past Diego's thin lips. "If these guys work out, we'll want them to come onboard full-time. But anyway, we have no equity to ante up quite yet. We don't even have a working prototype." He poked a tangle of shaved ginger with his chopsticks.

"We're almost there, Kari," Diego replied, eager to reassure his friend, his partner. "Give me another month or so and I'll be ready to deploy a prototype onto my test server and we can let Chris and Dale loose on it."

He held a second sake cup between his thumb and middle finger and this time took a reserved sip of its cool, clear contents. Although Diego loved Japanese food, he hated Japanese restaurants as they made him feel like an "oaf with a loaf" as Lucita would say. Or "awkward" as Meghan would say. The nuances of manners were puzzling at times.

"Digs, I hate to even say this out loud." Kari leaned forward, gaze steady and piercing. "But I could approach my father to invest. Imagine my father, our *angel* investor!" He snorted, knocking back a full shot of sake. "Pure fucking irony, that." A jaundiced heartbeat flicked across his eyes.

"That would be awesome!" Diego exclaimed, sake-flushed, hope-fueled. "If we could keep it in the family right now, just to get us started, that would be ideal." He thought of his own *tío-padre* and wished Óscar's angelic resources extended to his bank account.

"Anyway, he's already agreed to fund my MBA," Kari continued, matter-of-fact. "To him, that's practically a rite of passage. So, investing in our business would be like supporting an extracurricular school project." He set his chopsticks neatly across his plate, meal and decision complete.

Man, Diego thought to himself, how easily some people can throw money on the table. Like it was confetti. How easily some people can take care of the most complicated things.

Suddenly inspired, Diego perked up smiling. "I've got the perfect name for our company: 'Fixer, Inc.' That's you and me, man! We are both fixers!"

"Huh," mumbled Kari, as he tried to get the waiter's attention.

"Maybe 'Fixa' is a little snappier? More techie?" Diego continued. "And our first product, our shopping bot, can be called 'ShopFixa'! What do you think?!"

"Hmm," said Kari, now listening. "From a branding standpoint, it works. I like it." He nodded slowly, thoughtfully, eyes bright.

~

The prototype's user interface was plain as digital mud: white background, black Arial text, default blue menu links. A photo of Bummers, Meghan's cat, served as avatar and witness to the historic moment. From the primordial ooze of a few million lines of code, the newly born ShopFixa shopping assistant crawled onto Diego's monitor and presented itself on shaky limbs.

"Hello, world," the bot said. Its messaging cursor pulsed with life, ready and waiting to learn the ways of the world.

Like a proud father, Diego beamed and greeted his new progeny. "Well, hello!" he typed with a slight tremble.

"Show me around," the bot said. "Help me learn how to help you."

Diego proceeded to set his ShopFixa up with everything it needed to do its job. He linked all of his eCommerce accounts to the software platform, including the various websites where he bought his books, his entertainment, his electronics, his clothes, his groceries, his everyday "this and that." He carefully entered each username and password, and then proceeded to link his email, credit card, and social media accounts to the new platform. His entire digital life was now in the hands of this new fixer bot, one that would shield him from the mundane messiness of the everyday.

"Go forth and conquer," Diego said, as he clicked the 'Start Shopping' button. "I mean, 'shop' your little cyber heart out."

"I'm on it!" said the bot. Diego felt a fleeting sense of no return.

ShopFixa was indeed ready to conquer. The bot would scrutinize its master with an eye for detail that no human counterpart could ever achieve. It would follow him down to the last byte of his digital footprint as it spidered its way through reams of Diego's personal history during nearly a lifetime spent on the Internet. His "Fixa" studied the thousands of products and services that he had ever browsed or considered, those that he had both purchased and not purchased. It raced back in time to the early nineties when he'd first bought a book from a website using the credit card that Óscar had given him for his eighteenth birthday.

Long gone were the book and the memory of it, but to his bot, it was as alive and real as Diego. Maybe more so.

Once it had cataloged a lifetime of purchase experiences, ShopFixa then studied what Diego had simply talked about buying. It eavesdropped on hordes of online conversations with friends and family, colleagues and companies, and online communities. It read through his email, scanned message board posts and chat logs. It analyzed what he liked to buy and didn't like to buy, what made him happy or unhappy. It studied the subtle patterns in his buying habits and noted his personal trends, as well as his response to public trends.

Most importantly—and mysteriously, Diego wasn't quite sure this would work—ShopFixa would learn, not just the "what" and the "when" behind his shopping life, but also the "why." It didn't just tag and assign him to a particular demographic profile. Diego was most proud of the fact that ShopFixa treated him as an individual. It knew him like a friend—better than a friend. It learned fundamentally *how* he made decisions and *why* he bought the things he bought.

Once it had learned everything it could learn about Diego, his "Fixa" would finally know what he would want to buy in the future. Then, and only then, was it truly ready to shop.

~

In school, Diego had been fascinated by the twin concepts of order and chaos, and the symbiotic link between them—a relationship almost biblical in its implications. Computer science was all about creating a structured, virtual world by organizing random digital bits into complex, powerful systems. Life on

Earth was all about creating a structured, material world by organizing random atoms into sophisticated, powerful organisms. It felt God-like to create something out of nothing by applying intelligence and vision to the organizing process. But like Life, once a virtual system was created, could it evolve on its own, by its own rules, without interference from its creator?

"We humans are such control freaks," Kari had declared once, after a class on chaos theory. "We can't stand any expression of chaos, even if it's governed by underlying patterns." Diego and Kira exchanged glances as the three friends walked to the nearest campus café.

"Aren't there times when a little chaos is needed?" Kira had replied brightly, clearly trying to keep the conversation on a layman's level. "Like in creativity, for example?"

"Creativity is just the manifestation of the artist's response to his conditions, interpreted through a culturally acceptable lens. It's highly organized." Diego hoped he hadn't sounded too dismissive.

"Huh, okay," Kira said, clearly irritated, shifting her heavy textbooks in the crook of her arm.

"Artistic expression is all about choices, and choices are about control," Kari mused, warming to the topic. "Is it possible for a computer to simulate subjective choices, like those of an artist?"

"Good question!" Diego replied. "If it learns what the artist likes, it should be able to predict his or her choices. But can it develop its own choices? Can a computer become as elastic, as adaptable and unpredictable as the human mind?"

"Very Hal 9000," Kari replied drily, referencing the frighteningly "alive" computer in the *Space Odyssey* series. Diego smiled. He loved those films.

"There's nothing more chaotic than the human mind!" Kira exclaimed, looking like she might hit them both with her massive *Abnormal Psychology* textbook.

"Which is why we need computers to keep us all in line," Kari replied half-jokingly, putting his arm around Kira as they approached the café.

"Ashes to ashes, dust to dust," Diego said, mostly to himself. Wasn't death the ultimate expression of chaos?

Random digital elements—data, events, conditions—could be captured, packaged, and then unleashed to manifest an unpredictable, yet more empowered, result. But Diego wondered how an artificially created organizing force could learn and grow on its own, un-interfered with by the controlling hands of humans. He was most fascinated by an obscure area of computer science called "machine learning," which was a fundamental aspect of artificial intelligence. It studied how computer systems could self-evolve through their exposure to data and other triggers. In that way, computers could almost manifest their own destiny. Well, almost, thought Diego; maybe Kari was right about control freaks.

After graduation, Kari and Diego's careers had taken parallel paths. Kari had gravitated toward product management, which allowed him to influence the direction of a product to fit its market. Diego, clearly a builder, had wanted to be more intimate with technology. He liked to feel it gradually develop under his fingers and touch its nascent heartbeat as he brought some aspect of a product to life. Sometimes he felt like a creator, at other times like a mid-wife, but he always felt a sense of wonder at the "living" entity that emerged from the long, slow hours of manipulating elemental snippets of code.

Through a university internship program, Diego worked for a summer at a payment processing corporation analyzing and creating data models for new online use cases that the product teams wanted to address in future product designs. He then joined full-time after graduation to work on the company's fraud detection systems. He learned how consumer purchasing patterns could be deconstructed and repurposed to build highly sophisticated behavior prediction systems that could grow exponentially with each new credit card purchase. The more data these systems gathered, the smarter they got. Not only could such a system pinpoint fraud cases, but it could also paint an astonishingly accurate portrait of an individual through their buying habits.

"I buy; therefore I am," Diego had said to Kari over a dim sum lunch deep in the heart of Chinatown. "And our system knows who I am better than I do!" He gulped down a pillowy white bun filled with barbecued pork.

"You should just ask it what to buy next," Kari chuckled, never indecisive when choosing plates of dim sum off the waiter's cart. "Save yourself some brain calories." The comment stuck in Diego's brain like a burr, prickling him until he could dig it out and do something with it, years later.

After spending time on the fraud detection team, Diego's work eventually came to the attention of the company's chief technology officer, who moved him to their elite research and development team to study identity theft. Sequestered in a high security wing at company headquarters in Silicon Valley, Diego learned as much as he could about online vulnerability and the spectrum of security technologies that attempt to keep people safe. Though he believed that "safety" was a relative term in a virtual no man's land where one's identity could get hijacked at any turn.

Although Diego spent his days studying how to bulletproof online identity, he spent his evenings shape-shifting into his favorite archetypes—warrior, wizard, hero, adventurer—each one nurturing a particular aspect of his aspirational self. He loved massively multiplayer online role-playing video games the most, and had gained some considerable status over the years in *World of Warcraft* and *EverQuest*, two titles that he shared with Ravi. Most evenings, Sunday through Thursday, the two friends logged on around eleven p.m. and looked for each other's avatar in the game's community spaces. Together, they'd immerse themselves in narrative action alongside hundreds of other players, including many familiar old-timers like themselves who were almost like anonymous friends.

"Man, you're too good." Diego slapped Ravi on the shoulder one evening at Kari and Kira's apartment. "You could be a pro!" He greatly admired Ravi's talent for strategy and timing, as well as the pure button-mashing skill of his brute force attacks against other players.

"Ha! Dude, don't make me blush!" shrugged Ravi, visibly pleased by a rare compliment from his usually taciturn friend.

"You totally crushed that guy *merceron* last night," Diego continued. "That was beautiful man. He had it coming." He leaned back on the dove grey leather couch and wondered if Ravi also played under other usernames in the game, ones that he didn't know. He wouldn't be surprised.

"Yeah, he's nothing but a trash-talking bully," Ravi replied. "He just sits back like some kind of troll and looks for people to pick on, and then hammers on them. Doesn't leave them alone. I hate those kinds of players."

Diego did too. Hiding behind a username in order to unleash one's inner asshole was the highest form of cowardice.

Eventually, Diego left the ivory tower of the payment processing company and moved to a corporate software giant for a couple of years, developing predictive modeling and data mining methodologies that enable the business to better understand their customers. It was interesting work, but he spent his days confined to a six-by-six-foot corner of a massive cube farm. Peeking over the beige fabric partition of his tiny space, he could gaze across the tops of a hundred other identical cubicles segmenting the tenth floor of their office tower. He could be anywhere in corporate America. Here and there, a few personal items were perched on partition corners—a houseplant, a stuffed toy sporting the company logo, an emoticon calendar—each bearing witness to the indomitable presence of individuality that tried to poke through the uniformity of their vast officescape.

The dullness weighed heavy on him, numbing his senses along with his mood. Did it affect his fellow engineers? Diego wondered. They all seemed to be quietly heads-down most of the time and not overtly social, yet there was a vibrant secret underground that thrived amongst the stillness. He was inducted into it during his first week.

His internal chat app pinged: "Like chess?" typed a guy named Chester six cubes down. He was the one with the Starbucks coffee cup sitting on top of his partition. Chester told him later that it helped him find his way back to his cube, like a breadcrumb.

"Sure," he replied. "Send me the URL." A heated online chess tournament raged like wildfire throughout the 10th floor, engineers vs. system administrators vs. IT support. Silent and still on the surface, rowdy and raucous online.

"Smackdown!" Chester typed after beating Diego in only ten moves. Diego could almost hear the guy's victory cry blast through his cube. *I'd better get better quick*, he thought. *If I'm going to survive this job.*

In between games, players were constantly on the internal instant messaging system, bantering banalities back and forth like a lazy tennis match. Others escaped into their private corners of the web, monitors turned away from the prying eyes of passersby, pretending to work in between work tasks.

When Diego finally felt the place blunting his ability to think, he began job hunting. A former manager introduced him to Ken and Dave, who had just started a small game company called Del Oro Games.

"We need help with refining our gameplay algorithms in order to make our game engine more sophisticated and the games more challenging," said Ken, clearly eager to sell Diego on this professional opportunity.

"Yeah, we want the characters to be able to learn from their experience in the game and act or react accordingly," Dave added. "Which the player could allow or influence as needed."

"Most of all, we need a talented lead engineer like you to help us build Del Oro into an industry player," enthused Ken, moving on to present the bigger picture.

"We need a technical visionary as well as a superstar manager," said Dave, staying on point with the skillset details.

"You could help us make this company great!" said Ken, punctuating their pitch with a flourish as he waved his arms around their small brick office space. Diego wondered, who was interviewing whom?

Diego was, in fact, sold on the professional opportunity, as well as the 180-degree pivot from corporate life. When he recounted the story to Meghan a couple of years later, she quipped, "You struck gold at Del Oro!" He laughed and replied, "Yeah, I guess I traded a solid paycheck for a future payload."

~

One of the things Diego noticed about Meghan, besides her sexy-pretty style, was his girlfriend's cheerful, carefree manner. She always seemed happy to see him and usually up for anything he wanted to do, whether it was spending an afternoon lying in the sun at Dolores Park, or immersed in a film festival, or busy under the blankets in her four-poster bed. But as their relationship progressed, he began to realize that her geniality was just a veneer that masked a thick layer of tension, and below that, some brewing stew of emotion that he couldn't understand. Or didn't want to understand. Diego was happy to stay on the shiny surface of their easy companionship and bypass the messy stuff. He *loved* Meghan but didn't *need* her in the way that added complexity and unpredictability to the simple feeling. He liked things best when they were straightforward and even, like a drumbeat. Lately though, Diego was noticing more moments of dissonance between them, and he wondered if these sour notes were new or had always been a part of their rhythm.

"Hey, Digs—there's a food cart round up happening this afternoon," Meghan said to Diego one Saturday, as they lounged on the mustard-colored corduroy couch in his SOMA studio. Diego lived in one fairly spacious square room that featured a small kitchenette along one wall, bed and closet opposite, couch and coffee table in the middle. Natural light flooded in from a bank of warehouse-like grilled windows, adding intangible volume to the small space. The bathroom was so small, Meghan's hips brushed the corner of the sink whenever she entered.

"The usual vendors will be there," she continued. "Souper Douper, Cookie Guy, Tamale Tina, Bangkok Bites, the Adobo Hobo. They're all going to gather at Precita Park at noon." She was flicking through the Twitter feed on her phone, which broadcast the spontaneous gathering. Meghan then started reciting the #foodcarts commentary aloud, tweet by tedious tweet, and his mind immediately sought shelter. Who cares what the hell people thought about food carts. Did she want to go or not?

Apart from the useless tweetstorm, this was an example of Diego's favorite use case for Twitter—as a news channel for announcing hyper-local, unstructured, impromptu events it couldn't be beat. Usually on Twitter he found himself wading through blow-by-blow reporting on news or events that he didn't care about, or useless opinion-blather, regurgitated tweet sharing or, at the very worst, marketing disguised as expertise. He had no use for any of it. But he did love to know about cool happenings around the city, especially if they were food-related.

"What about the coconut noodle couple?" Diego asked, shifting his weight on the couch in an attempt to peek at the Tweets on her phone, which he could barely see anyway. "Are they going to be there too?"

Meghan cocked her head and stared hard at him. "Bangkok Bites, yes, I just told you. Were you not listening?" Her face puckered in a way that reminded Diego of a dried apple. "As usual," she grumbled.

"Of course, I was listening," countered Diego, folding his arms across his chest. Now he had to defend himself! Against what? Who knew?

"No, you weren't," Meghan snapped. "Sometimes I feel like you don't give a shit about whether I'm here or not."

"Of course, I give a shit," he shot back. Where was this coming from?

Meghan's temper began to subside as quickly as it had flared up. "Sometimes, it seems like your mind is somewhere else," she whined. "Like on another planet. But not on my planet." Okay, so his girlfriend was sad, or maybe lonely, and it was Diego's job to fix it somehow.

"*Querida*, I'm here! I'm here with you, always." Diego lightly stroked Meghan's cheek, "On *our* planet." He hoped that she was listening to him.

"So, let's go to Bangkok together!" Diego continued, as he leaned over to kiss one of his favorite spots, hiding behind a curtain of hair at the nape of her neck. "And have some bites… mmmm..." He nibbled her ear lobe playfully. Meghan giggled.

"Okay, let's go," she said, cheering up. "I'm starving anyway."

"Me too! Let's do it." Diego smiled, gave his girlfriend a quick kiss on the lips, and flew off the couch to grab a jacket and boots.

Diego's apartment building was on a tree-lined block of busy Potrero Avenue. It was a beautiful sunny Saturday, with a light breeze skipping playfully alongside them as they strolled through The Mission toward the grassy triangle of Precita Park.

When they arrived, a dozen or so carts were just setting up, and Diego and Meghan joined the few would-be diners who were lingering patiently on the sidewalk. Diego wrapped his arm around his girlfriend's bare shoulders, felt a trace of goosebumps, and guided her toward a patch of sun.

"Good thing there are so many carts," a twenty-something guy in a 49ers T-shirt commented to the couple. "We've got a lot of choice today."

"Strength in numbers," replied Diego curtly, not much in the mood for small talk with strangers.

"More festive!" added Meghan, clearly excited by the range of menus on offer. "And it's all 'a la carte'!" Funny girl. Diego squeezed her shoulder and steered them toward his favorite dish.

Both Diego and Meghan were big fans of the local food cart scene and kept their eye out for favorite carts popping up here and there around town. The recent national economic crisis had prompted an epidemic of layoffs across the Bay Area, even in the technology industry, and people were getting creative about making money. A number of enterprising foodies had turned to the time-honored tradition of making street food—a daily staple in much of the world, yet oddly illegal in California. These casual entrepreneurs were making ends meet by serving their best dish, cooked at home or in a pay-by-the-hour professional kitchen.

"Good thing we got here early," said Diego. "I'd hate to miss the coconut noodles."

"Yeah, these carts are not set up for volume," agreed Meghan. "It must be hard to be a one-person operation."

"There's always a late-night lineup outside the bars on Valencia Street. Everyone's hungry after a few drinks." Diego inhaled a delicate waft of curry and lime coming from the noodle cart as they moved another step forward in line.

"Especially since restaurants in this city close so damn early."

Because of the murky status of street food, as well as the constantly shifting location of their clientele, the food cart operators were inherently mobile. Their fans never knew when or where they might show up (hence the Twitter feed). Some had built tricked-out pushcarts or bicycles that carried supplies and presented wares. Others had set up make-shift stands with colorful, homespun signage.

"I saw one bike cart the other day that even had a built-in hot plate for stir-frying," Diego said as he twirled a clump of coconut rice noodles onto a plastic fork. They were as delicious as he'd hoped. "It was just welded onto the frame." Mouth full, he mumbled, "Brilliant."

"You know the girl who dresses like a cowgirl and sells chili?" said Meghan, taking a bite of chicken thigh submerged in crimson adobo sauce. "Her stand is so cute, like a giant bandanna. It folds up flat and it all fits neatly into a small shopping trolley. She can just hop on Muni with it and go wherever."

"Looks like a bandanna, folds like a bandanna. And it's all about cowboy chili." Diego nodded in appreciation. "Brilliant."

"I wish I had the guts to do that," Meghan continued dreamily. "I'd sell little pies. Savory, sweet—all kinds. I would make my grandmother's best pies." She paused, and Diego could see her dream gaining steam as she drove it forward. "I'll do the cart thing first to build a brand and get people tweeting about me, and then you'll build me a website so I can take orders and scale up. It'll be fun!" Meghan was a master at turning "wish" into "would" and then into "will" without skipping a beat. But the problem was, the "I will" had no substance behind it, no will to turn fantasy into reality.

"Megs, you wouldn't last more than a week," Diego said, irritated as usual by this predictable turn. Why did she always have to push a perfectly fine conversation into the "wouldn't it be great if…" game and risk ruining their day together? At Easter in the park, it was an entire afternoon of "Wouldn't it be great to design hats?" Winetasting in Napa became a day-long planning session that kicked off with "I'd love to start a fruit wine label." Often, she envisioned a shared endeavor. "Let's open an indoor playground for children!" What was worse, she hated to play the game alone and always tried to rope him in somehow.

Diego's heart sank. "Let's change the subject?" He did not want to indulge in her dream du jour of opening a pie business. And he certainly would not, will not, build her a website. He just wished that she'd stop involving him in her half-baked ideas.

"No pies for you," Meghan replied angrily, unwilling to let it go. Diego had broken the rules, bringing the game to a harsh and early conclusion. "No pies for the naysayers in my life." She walked away from him, toward the Cookie Guy who was doing a brisk business at the end of the cart lineup.

He didn't want to be a naysayer. That wasn't it at all. Diego just couldn't pretend to be supportive about something that clearly wasn't going to happen. After hearing far too many "wouldn't it be great" scenarios, he had not seen Meghan take any concrete steps to move an idea forward toward making it real, let alone great. Still, he always felt like the loser in a game that he didn't understand.

CHAPTER 11

Ravi

Ravi looked at himself in the mirror and laughed out loud. He was in a sporting goods store at the Stonestown Galleria, and it was his first-ever experience trying on cycling wear. The bright colors screamed at him, the volume and intensity of their hues seemed to take up all the oxygen in the cramped changing room. Trying to ignore the visual assault, Ravi thought he looked skinnier than usual in the tight spandex shorts and form-fitting top. It was not the look he had hoped for. What would Nico think?

Ravi opened the curtain and stepped out, ready as he'd ever be for the upcoming AIDS Ride. He would join thousands of cyclists and ride hundreds of miles between San Francisco and Los Angeles to raise money for AIDS organizations. Ravi was excited—he'd be right in the thick of it all.

"Darling, they will see you coming all the way in San Diego!" Kira exclaimed, clapping her hands together in delight. His friend was the perfect shopping companion; she could be entertained by almost any outfit, for any reason at all.

"Well, I want to be comfortable, you know," Ravi replied, trying to appear thoughtful and practical. "It's all about high-performance." He turned left and right in front of the full-length mirror, trying to get a good look at his back side. Good thing the shorts were padded. For extra comfort on the bicycle seat, of course.

"You mean like on stage," Kira said. "High-performance on the highway." Hands on hips, brow furrowed, she seemed to struggle to form a useful opinion about the outfit.

"All the highway's a stage," he quipped in his best Shakespearian voice. "And us riders merely players."

"Well then, your technicolor self here will certainly upstage all those boring bourgeois cars." Turning toward the mirror, she adjusted her blue and white Oxford shirt dress. "As you should!"

"Yeah, I'll be rocking the rainbow, that's for sure." Ravi snapped the curtain closed and changed back into his jeans and T-shirt. The outfit would work fine. It was on sale, so maybe he'd buy three to last the week-long ride.

"I need to work out more," he both scolded and promised his athletic self. "I've got to get to the gym at least four times a week. No excuses!" But there were always excuses. Weekends were off limits for any goal-oriented activities that felt like work. On weeknights he usually found himself at dinner with various sets of friends, or on a movie date, or attending one of the city's myriad events, from fundraisers to concerts to pop-up night markets. Each lured him like a siren into blissful diversion from daily routine. Work demanded a generous share of his free time, and he often worked evenings, especially during major software releases when it was "all hands on deck" to run quality assurance tests and make sure nothing broke. Too much to do, too little time! Now he sounded like his parents.

One thing that Ravi didn't do these days was hang out with Nico. It had been almost a year since the opening of Nico's first major gallery show. The event had been a big deal for Nico, and Ravi had not only known this, but he'd understood the layers of meaning that it represented in Nico's life. Yet somehow this understanding had paralyzed Ravi, and he had been unable to be there for his boyfriend, both in body and in spirit.

Nico's show had been called "High & Wide" and focused on the relationship between urban density and urban sprawl. Nico had curated a sampling of his streetscape photography that echoed this vertical versus horizontal tension that characterized Bay Area growth. After graduating from the California College of Arts fifteen years prior, Nico worked as an occasional freelance graphic designer and part-time sales associate at a trendy men's boutique on Castro Street. Occasionally, he would sell a framed piece or publish a few images in a local magazine, but his career had made slow progress. Once a year, Nico managed to pull together a small show at a local coffeehouse or retail space, but this was the first time that he was headlining in a dedicated art gallery. To mark this milestone, he was hosting a lively opening night party complete with catering and DJ. For Nico, the party was not just a kick-off to the show, to spark publicity and potential sales, but it was a way to honor his passionate commitment to his artwork, and reassert his identity as an artist.

Ravi, per usual, had scheduled back-to-back activities on the evening of Nico's show and had arrived late. Very late. Nico had been livid.

"I can't believe you would do this again," snapped Nico as soon as Ravi set foot through the gallery's front door. "After last year's show. And the year before." He abruptly turned and started picking up empty wine glasses and crumpled napkins, back rigid and blood rising. *His ears are turning red*, noted Ravi. *That's a bad sign.*

"I'm so sorry, babe," Ravi replied, feeling the hot fist of guilt pummel his gut. He reached out to calm them both by putting his hands lightly on Nico's shoulders as a gesture of apology. Nico brusquely shook them off and continued tidying up. "I'm so sorry. I really thought I had the time under control."

He really had thought so. His old friend Deb, whom Ravi hadn't seen in months, was finally free for dinner, and Ravi had planned a quick hour catch-up with Deb before dashing off to Nico's show. But there was no such thing as a 'quick hour' when it came to friends—when would he learn that fact of life? Deb had needed to deconstruct every facet of her recently shattered relationship, and there was no way her story could unfold in only an hour. Luckily Ravi had been on his bike, so parking wasn't an issue for once.

By the time he reached the gallery, the DJ had downshifted the tempo to a more lounge-y beat for the final half hour as the few remaining guests chatted quietly in the corners. Gary the bartender, a friend of Nico's, thumbed idly through text messages while sipping a Corona. Nico strode up to Ravi as soon as he stepped in the door. "If the show is from 6:00 p.m. to 9:00 p.m., then as my boyfriend you should be here at 5:30. Not 8:30!" Nico spat. "Fuck you, Ravi."

"I'm sorry! I'm sorry!" Ravi felt remorse press down on him, and his natural defenses pushed back. He hated to be told what to do, and he especially hated expectations that were grounded in an absolute point of view. "Nico, babe, I'll make it up to you.

I promise!" He truly believed in the promise. Nico, however, did not.

"You always say that," he growled, glaring at Ravi. "Same old story."

This time, however, the story continued along a different path. After Ravi left the show, he decided to give Nico some space and didn't reach out for a couple of days. Still angry, Nico had gladly claimed the space and didn't contact Ravi. It was the first time in their four years together that they had been so far apart. The radio silence between them was ominous. Finally, a text from Nico, "Let's talk," crackled through the airwaves, highly charged and prophetic.

Later that day, at the kitchen table in his apartment, Nico laid out his issues with their relationship, neatly packaged in one simple sentence.

"Ravi, it's really great that you have so many friends and such a full social life," Nico said matter-of-factly, "but there's no room for me." He sat back in his chair, arms folded, and waited. He seemed so neutral Ravi thought. Not angry, not sad; no identifiable emotion seemed to be present with them at the table. A good sign?

"Nico, I love you," Ravi said, his heart cracked open, spilling, surging. "I want to be with you. We see each other a lot, don't we? I love our time together." He didn't understand how Nico could think otherwise.

"I do too, Ravi," Nico replied gently. "I love our time together too. That's why it's so painful." He shifted his position in his chair and reached for a sticky bottle of agave nectar sitting on the counter.

"We can spend more time together, if that's what you want?" Ravi said, ignoring his full cup of cold Earl Grey. He was groping blindly for a way forward as fear oozed through his body like wet cement and added heft to the growing roadblock between them.

"I don't know," Nico said, gazing into his half-empty yerba mate, eyes reluctant to meet Ravi's. "I don't know."

"We can think about moving in together?" Ravi placed his final card on the table with trepidation, hoping Nico wouldn't pick it up.

"Ravi, that wouldn't change anything," Nico said sadly. "The thing is—you never put me first." That was it, the heart of it.

"But…" Ravi floundered, unable to stop the roaring change that was about to overwhelm him.

"I need a break. From us," Nico said firmly, eyes glistening, emotion finally arriving hand-in-hand with the words.

"Okay." What could Ravi do but accept this heart-wrenching pivot away from his lover, his favorite companion. His Best Man! What could he do but try to respect Nico's feelings. Be gracious about it. Take the high road. Hope that it really was just a "break" and not a "breakup."

As they kissed goodbye, they stood for what felt to Ravi like hours in a prolonged embrace—heavy with finality, thick with reluctance, salty with grief.

Ravi pulled away first, hastily grabbed his backpack, and stepped into the stairwell, turning back to meet Nico's eyes one last time. This *was* a breakup. He and Nico were breaking up! Out on the street, Ravi fell headlong into a profound, suffocating loneliness. Sometimes being with Nico had paradoxically felt like being alone for some strange reason. But being without Nico was as if that aloneness was suddenly amplified a thousand times.

~

In the weeks that followed, newly single Ravi did whatever he could to not be alone. He dove into his social life with renewed vigor, and spent more time than usual at gay bars and clubs that were packed nightly with men as eager as he was for flirtatious distraction. He was even motivated to explore a few of the subculture scenes within the gay community—he dragged his more adventurous friends to leather beer busts, Latin salsa Sundays, country western hoedowns, bear pride tea dances. Ravi was happiest when surrounded by the sweet cacophony of drinking voices that cavorted playfully above a steady house beat.

Coming home each night, he resented the unbearable silence that greeted him. His mute apartment seemed unwilling to reveal any evidence of Nico's existence, and he'd finally stopped looking for it. Instead, Ravi immediately grabbed his laptop and immersed himself in the soothing hum of *World of Warcraft* or Facebook or Reddit, where he always felt welcome.

It had been easy to share the news with Kira. She immediately gave him a heartfelt hug and declared simply, "Nico is an idiot!" The two friends were sitting by the waterfall in Yerba Buena park, the cool mist of its spray soothing overheated skin and nerves on the rare balmy June evening. In half an hour they'd be sitting in the nearby theatre enjoying a new performance by Decca Dance, their favorite local dance ensemble.

"No, really he's not," Ravi said sadly, appreciating the motherly warmth that emanated from her slim arms. He was always surprised at the intensity of her affection, which seemed to hide beneath that well-tempered demeanor.

"Okay, Nico is a clueless idiot," she repeated scornfully. "Has he never heard of couples therapy? Or at least good communication skills?" She brushed back a stray lock of hair and managed to look both disapproving and empathetic at the same time.

"I don't blame him," Ravi frowned. "I mean, he's right in a way. I've been pretty inattentive for a while." He reached down to trail his fingers in the pond. *Nico loves Decca performances*, he thought.

"But you're willing to work on it, right?" she asked. "Isn't Nico willing to work on it at all?"

"Yeah, I don't know," Ravi replied, flicking water from his fingertips. "It's complicated." He felt the crushing weight of his own hopes pressing down on him, suffocating.

"When is it ever not complicated!" she sighed deeply, the complexities of her own experience eddying like foam at the foot of the waterfall.

"I'm hoping that the break will be good for both of us," he said, checking his watch and standing up.

"Give him space, but don't give up on him," Kira advised following his lead. "That one is worth fighting for." Ravi loved her for simply saying that, regardless of whether or not it was true.

~

It had not been easy to share the news with Veela. Ravi rarely saw his old friend these days, and it was hard enough to connect with her at all, let alone for a full relationship debriefing. He planned to stop by Veela's house one Sunday morning when Bets was visiting family in Seattle. When had he been there last—six months, nine months, longer?

Before seeing Veela, Ravi imagined that he would feel his failure with Nico most intensely in her presence, as if she would judge him for it most harshly. After all that they had been through together with the wedding—he and Veela and Nico and Bets, their foursquare symmetry and strength—to lose one corner of that structure seemed all the more tragic.

"Ravi, how can you just walk away like that?" Veela asked after Ravi had shared the basic facts of the breakup story over coffee and homemade scones in Veela's freshly-painted, yolk-colored kitchen. "Don't be such a coward!" *Prediction correct*, he thought. *That was harsh.*

"Go back there and insist on keeping the relationship together. Tell him you will work on it, night and day. And then, work on it, night and day!" Veela looked indignant, almost angry, as if he'd betrayed her best friend. He wished he'd simply broken her favorite dish, or lost her favorite coat.

"Veela! C'mon, give me a break!" he exclaimed, feeling trapped, fight and flight rising in equal measures. "It's not like we don't talk at all. We *both* felt that some space would be good right now. We'll see where we are in a couple of months." Truth could be so elastic sometimes. As long as it didn't snap back at him.

"Huh, okay. Well, I guess you know what you're doing," she frowned, looking more regal than ever in an elaborately embroidered *kameez top*. Her shiny black rope of hair punctuated her emerald-gold back like an exclamation point. Veela sliced a scone in half and slathered it with Bets's strawberry-basil jam. Ravi decided to pass on the runny-looking stuff.

"Yes, *thank you*," he drew out the words. "I *do* know what I'm *doing*." He felt more defensive than ever, exacerbated by the acid sting of conflict. He didn't want to argue with Veela, his dear friend. His wife!

Looking back on the couple of years since the wedding, it seemed to Ravi that he and Veela had slowly drifted apart in some imperceptible way. They spent less time together for sure, and even less often one-on-one, but there also seemed to be a subtle shift in the quality of their connection. The change was so hard to pinpoint, that when he thought about it, he scolded himself for imagining things. After all, they were both busy people. Thinking of the timeframe of this thought, could the wedding be the culprit? Impossible! How could a paper wedding interfere with a solid gold friendship, one built on years of open-hearted trust?

He knew that Veela and Bets had been especially busy over the past year. The couple had been consumed by San Francisco city bureaucracy and its convoluted process of converting their two-unit Edwardian building into two legally-designated condominiums. A seemingly minor distinction on paper, the conversion had significant consequences, raising the value of the property and allowing them to refinance independent of their upstairs neighbors. It hadn't been easy. The two households had been faced with paying for, and supervising, a full slate of repairs and remodeling needed in order to bring the old building up to code and pass city inspection. Adding another layer of complexity, Veela and Bets had taken the opportunity to give their kitchen a facelift along with the required upgrades, and they'd been unprepared for the enormous amount of work involved. Veela never did anything half-way, Ravi thought.

"My mother asks me about you every week," Veela said, chewing her scone thoughtfully. "Of course, I tell her you're fabulous!" She chuckled. "Making loads of money, buying me nice presents, fixing up the house."

"It's all true," Ravi smiled. "Except for the presents. Sorry about that!"

"Ach, I don't need any diamonds and pearls anyway," she joked, waving her hand dismissively. "But it would be nice to see you more often." She looked at Ravi carefully, her eyes wide.

"My mother asks about you too," he continued. "Once in a while she dares to ask the baby question."

"When, when, when!" chirped Veela, throwing her arms up to the ceiling. "My mother too. She asks when will she get to meet her grandson."

"Well, that's direct," Ravi replied. Like mother, like daughter. "Lucky for us, our siblings have already procreated; it takes some of the pressure off."

"Maybe if we bribe them, they'll pop out a few more and completely overwhelm the grandparents," Veela said sarcastically. "They'll forget about us all the way over here in *Amerika*!" With a broad grin, she waved her hand like a magician in front of his face. Poof!

It would be nice to see you more often too, he thought, meeting her gaze.

~

On a bright Monday morning in May, Ravi stood with a dozen other sleepy co-workers at the intersection of 24th and Guerrero Streets, waiting for the company shuttle. The spring sun, a heavenly diva, was warming up to her daily aria across a brilliant azure stage. Her audience, however, was entranced by the divine glow of their portable devices. Ravi cautiously sipped a hot, foamy cappuccino that he had picked up at the corner café. He was listening to an especially mellow playlist—ambient or lounge or trip hop—he wasn't quite sure. Whatever it was, it was perfect for eight a.m., something that allowed his brain to warm up slowly and at its own tempo.

After twenty minutes of waiting, a sleek, white, double-decker luxury coach glided up to the curb. A starship docking on a barbarian planet. The urban primitives lined up on the sidewalk next to Ravi stirred expectantly without looking up from their phones. Ravi could not immediately detect life forms behind the two stories of heavily tinted windows despite rows of interior blue lights, glinting like landing gear. No signage on the outside indicated any allegiance to a faraway galaxy. It's a leap of faith, Ravi thought, on the first day of his new job.

Following his scruffy colleagues, Ravi shuffled onto the bus, flashed his badge at the driver, and was surprised to see that the bus was almost full. He found an aisle seat near the back and squeezed in next to a skateboard belonging to a spikey-haired woman who was apparently engaged in a tense conference call. He put his ear buds back in and tried to tune her out, as well as calm the inevitable nerves that arose with any auspicious new beginning. He was flat-out excited about this job at a social media giant, the biggest company he had worked for so far in his career. He was going to be the newest product manager on their games integration team, and his role was to improve the user experience of people playing online games with their friends on the company's platform. His team made it possible to invite friends to play with one click or to easily see who was the best player amongst them all. It was going to be great!

A week prior, he'd left Del Oro as abruptly as he had joined the gaming start up. In Ravi's world, change happened in a blink of an eye. Ken and Dave were not happy.

"Ravi, why go join some faceless corporate machine?" Ken said, arms crossed, trying to mask disappointment with managerial words of wisdom. "You'll just be a number there. A cog in a wheel."

"Yeah, here at least you're directly contributing to the heart and soul of Del Oro," Dave added, hands on hips, appealing to Ravi's need for meaning in his work. "You're a huge part of Del Oro! And you're just gonna walk away?"

"I know, I know. Working for 'The Man' will be really different," Ravi replied, feeling a bit sheepish, though underneath, he was glowing with the possibilities that this new kind of "Man" had to offer. "Their campus down the Peninsula is like a small city with restaurants and gyms and shops. There's even a community garden and full kindergarten on site!"

"It's a biodome," said Ken.

"A petri dish," said Dave.

"And their culture is pretty cool too," Ravi continued. "They have people like Al Gore and George Lucas speak at town hall meetings."

"They suck you in," said Ken, "and make sure you never want to leave."

"Hotel California," said Dave.

"Well, I'm going to try it," replied Ravi firmly. "And they want me to start on Monday."

Ravi's first Monday at the new company was a perfect pearl in what would become a long string of Mondays that each added a little more beauty and value to his life. Everything seemed so fresh and bright, and Ravi felt almost glamorous being an esteemed member of this high-tech high society. There was so much to explore and experience, and the sheer scale and sophistication of the workforce and campus environment seemed to offer endless opportunities that spoke to Ravi's aspirations. *I'm sure I'll get cynical at some point,* Ravi thought, *but it'll be a while. A long while.*

Workplace culture thrived on "besting your personal best," be it professional or personal, within the company's universe. Employee recognition campaigns swept through campus occasionally, with lobby monitors spotlighting a broad range of achievement. "Most Valuable Players" nominated by ping pong or flag football teams were celebrated alongside star engineers who had solved a particular problem and sales reps who had closed important deals. Each quadrant of each floor in the office buildings across the company's campus had a unique "playpen" where employees could destress with a particular themed diversion, such as vintage foosball, Lego tables, jigsaw puzzles, or Xbox game consoles. The variety was impressive—something for everyone.

After his first month, Ravi commented to Bill, his team's user experience designer, "I've scoped out all the playpens across the campus. I usually stop by the best ones in between meetings."

"Yeah, me too," said Bill, "but I'm kind of addicted to old-school *Quake*, which is all the way over in building 2C. It's a long way to go for a fix."

"Check out *Space Invaders* in 5E," Ravi replied. "I'm ranked number one."

"Wow, you beat out Dylan Johnson?" Bill said, astonished. "Good job. That needed to happen big time."

"I'm starting a *Street Fighter V* tournament, here in our Xbox Zone," Ravi said. "Sign up!"

The games integration team sat in a vast open space surrounded by floor-to-ceiling windows that overlooked one of the campus's many grassy commons and its sole beach volleyball sand pit. White walls were dominated by huge portraits of comic book characters depicted through a mosaic of carefully-folded chewing gum wrappers. The office layout was designed to promote easy collaboration and exchange of ideas that, in some magical utopian workflow, would eventually become integrated into the company's products. Pockets of privacy were created with semi-screened sitting areas that offered the relaxed, lounge-like feeling of home.

Ravi had a handful of favorite places to work, and usually his desk was not one of them. When an in-person chat was needed, teammates knew to look for him on certain couches or in certain kitchenettes or on certain outdoor decks. When he had meetings in other buildings, he'd grab one of the company's fleet of motorized scooters and whiz down the windy paths in between the massive glass structures that dotted the campus. He often would spontaneously decide to stop and break out his laptop in some new café or on an especially appealing cluster of sofas. Ravi felt perfectly at home living the life of an interoffice nomad.

As the weeks went by, Ravi stayed at work later and later, eating dinner most nights in one of the free themed restaurants and catching up on email until eight or nine p.m. His friends noticed his absence and occasionally tapped on the front door of his life—his phone.

"Hello?" texted Veela. "Anyone home?"

"Beer 2nite?" texted Diego.

"See u @ the meet up?" texted Kari.

"U still alive???!!! ☹☹☹" texted Kira.

"N misses U," texted Gary, Nico's bartender friend.

Over the months since their break, or break up, or whatever it was, Ravi had tried hard to shut the door on the Nico chapter of his life, despite a crack of hope that prevented full closure. Although they had agreed to not talk or text during the "break," Ravi's mind would slip into thoughts of Nico and the warmth of memories that still burned like embers in his heart. Sometimes he'd think of Nico even during work meetings, pushed by the tedium of the meeting topic at hand and pulled by the gripping narrative of his relationship. Gradually, the Nico stories faded, leaving space for new daydreams.

Ravi's team had a daily fifteen-minute "stand up" meeting at nine a.m. that allowed each member to give a brief progress report. The team would literally stand around a conference table to ensure that the meeting was short and on point, and to discourage any topics that could hijack the discussion and force everyone to stay longer than necessary. One day, a new person appeared at the stand up. *Cute!* thought Ravi, as he eyed a tall, well-built, brown-haired man who seemed to be bursting with energy to match his ideas. *Younger than me?* Ravi wondered, noticing the man's smile, which was as wide as the bright yellow emoticon on his "Happy Speak" T-shirt. After the meeting, Ravi introduced himself.

"Hi," Ravi said, extending his hand. "Great idea for tweaking the test plan. I liked that."

"Hi, I'm Evan," the new guy said, shaking Ravi's hand with an extra firm grip. "I'm a front-end engineer from the core platform organization. I'm being rented out to your team for a couple of months." He grinned and released Ravi's hand slowly; his teak-colored eyes seemed unwilling to release Ravi's.

"Rented out?" Ravi asked awkwardly, the meaning behind Evan's comment and his gaze slowly sinking in.

"Yeah, I'm like some kind of internal rent boy," Evan laughed heartily, easily.

"Uh, okay then," Ravi said smiling. *Okay!*

As the weeks went by, Ravi found more and more excuses to meet with Evan one-on-one. There were plenty of technical questions and issues that needed his input, or insights based on Evan's platform expertise and company experience. Evan seemed to be equally eager to learn more from Ravi about product design and usability, as well as engage in spirited brainstorms with him to come up with concepts for new features and improvements. Quick sync ups extended into lunch meetings that became dinner meetings and finally drinks back in the city followed by sex and occasional sleepovers. Their trajectory from handshake to hot item was short and rapid, and they began spending some amount of time together every day. Ravi felt like they were almost prototyping a relationship and testing it out for viability and stability.

~

The first time Ravi went back to Evan's place after a night out, he was met with a pleasant surprise. Evan had said he lived with "ten-plus roommates" but Ravi had assumed that was one of Evan's usual dramatic exaggerations. But this time, his friend was accurate. Evan lived in a so-called "intentional community"—essentially a neo-commune—which was comprised of eleven full-time residents and one rotating weekly tenant who lived in a massive, eight-bedroom, four-bath Victorian homestead facing the Panhandle stretch of Golden Gate Park in San Francisco.

The building had been converted into two large flats at some point in the mid-twentieth century, then was re-converted back into a unified dwelling ten years prior by a wealthy idealist who believed in the power of community to inspire personal growth and creativity. The project echoed the communal hippie culture of the city's past, yet spoke to the current generation's deep longing for offline human connection. Whereas the hippies wanted to tune out and turn on, the post-millennial youth craved constant stimulation on all fronts—and interpersonal interaction offered a gold mine of opportunity. Cohabitation was a perfect solution, engineered to help maximize the potential of each member. The idealist founder had long since moved to a wine estate in Napa, but remained a steadfast entrepreneur and collected an increasingly lucrative monthly rent from the collective household.

"Martinis in the kitchen," called a slim, fair-haired man dressed neatly in pinstripe suit pants, waistcoat, and tie, hair carefully slicked back. His arm was draped casually around the shoulders of another man dressed almost identically, apart from the shiny gold pocket watch tucked into his vest pocket. They could have been a pair of turn-of-the-century bankers out on a bender.

"It's a flapper party," declared a petite brunette in a tight red satin cocktail dress and matching headband with feathers stuck haphazardly in the back. She waved one arm that was clad to the elbow in a long red glove; the other cradled a bowl of potato chips that she was bringing to the snack table in the back.

A couple dozen people dressed in various interpretations of the roaring twenties mingled in the large living room as tinny-sounding period jazz emanated from real vintage vinyl records. It was a mixed crowd—straight, gay, metro-flexible—and the party was in full swing. Ravi felt his pulse quicken.

"I forgot to check the calendar today," said Evan apologetically. "There isn't a party every week, but when there is one, it's usually around a theme of some kind."

"Cool," replied Ravi, happily soaking in the scene, stage, and situation. "What else goes on here?"

"There are a lot of weekly events. Different book clubs—sci-fi, fantasy, literary. A weekly stitch n' bitch knitting circle. Midnight poker on Thursdays. A bi-weekly séance with our house Ouija board." He grinned. "Everyone gets a chance to ask a question of the spirit world."

"Interesting," nodded Ravi, hoping for an invitation to try. "Can guests come?"

"Sure, we're encouraged to bring friends. It cross-pollinates new ideas."

"Great!" said Ravi, feeling more like a butterfly than bumble bee.

"Sometimes we do resident-only things, such as Sunday night dinners." Evan guided Ravi toward the spacious kitchen, which looked surprisingly organized, apart from the inevitable party debris scattered about. He grabbed a two-liter bottle of Absolut vodka and poured a generous amount into a shaker, adding ice and a splash of vermouth on top. The olive jar was empty. He shrugged and poured out two glasses.

"A few times," Evan continued, "we've done a house hackathon to solve some kind of problem. We'll come up with software that we can all use, like our communal grocery app, or tackle an offline project, like designing the back garden."

"How do you all decide on the important stuff?" asked Ravi, clinking cheers with his friend.

"We have house meetings for different things that we decide together, like the event calendar or chores rotations." He took a sip of his martini. "Then there are smaller task forces for other things like bill paying or furnishings or governance. We each take turns on a task force."

"What if you have a disagreement with someone? Do you arm wrestle or something?" Ravi chuckled drily, feeling the burning wash of vodka slide down his throat.

"Ha! Yeah, we have a special kiddie pool in the backyard for lube wrestling—my favorite kind of arbitration!" Evan grinned again.

"Yeah, I'll bet," Ravi replied, giving him a playful push. He liked this place. Maybe he could be happy in a commune? *Imagine me, a hippie!* The thought made him smile.

"Most of us are going to do the AIDS Ride next month," Evan said. "Want to join us?"

The AIDS Ride was a five hundred-plus mile, one-week commitment, more than Ravi had ever given to any volunteer effort. In the past he'd helped out here and there, mostly in casual roles at fundraisers or film festivals. But this would require a different level of commitment. He would immerse himself in the pack of riders for an entire week, sweat his heart out, and feel like he was truly giving something real to the community that had embraced his authentic self. During the ride, he would camp next to Evan, and he imagined that each evening he'd collapse in Evan's tent, exhausted and sweaty and delirious from the day's seventy-five-mile haul, and bask in the sweetness of new romance and its remarkable power to heal.

PART 3

CHAPTER 12

Diego

It was time for Fixa, Inc. to shift into second gear. Diego had left Del Oro Games at the beginning of the year to work full-time on the startup. It had been a quiet exit—Ken and Dave seemed strangely unaffected by his resignation. Meghan was more upset than anyone and actually shed tears when he told her the news.

"I'll never see you now, Digs," she sniffed, reaching for a tissue from a small packet on her desk. "You might as well be moving cross-country." She dabbed roughly at her eyes. "Or to another planet." She looked so profoundly sad that Diego's heart swelled.

"Megs, it will *help* our relationship," he insisted. "Our time together will be *quality* time versus quantity." He wrapped his arms around her and stroked her hair. "Here we see each other every day, but we don't *see* each other. You know?" He hoped she understood, but couldn't let himself worry too much about it. This was what it took to launch a startup, and some sacrifices were required along the way. There was no way around it. Anyway, he believed that less quantity, more quality would give their relationship a much-needed boost. It would rekindle the ache, the desire for intimacy and deep connection that seemed to get lost in the mundane day-to-day.

Over the months, the tiny Fixa team of Kari and Diego 24x7, plus Chris and Dale a few hours a week, had developed Diego's prototype of ShopFixa into a feature-complete alpha version that seemed to crash less frequently than before. It was finally something they could demo to people. More than simply a proof of concept that helped communicate their vision, it was the first tangible asset for their nascent company. It made the conceptual feel real.

"Incubator or accelerator?" Kari asked Diego one evening as the two sat in Diego's apartment, poring over the abundant resources available to startups in San Francisco. To Diego, it sounded like a rhetorical question.

"And the difference is…?" asked Diego, who idly cycled through open browser tabs on his laptop—Linux server specs, hiking boots on sale, Java developer support forum, movie listings, research on human-machine systems, flights to Cancún. At any given moment, he had a number of interests and tasks on deck in his online life, patiently waiting for follow up, consumption, or resolution.

"An incubator supports startup companies like ours with office space and some business support," Kari said, "and an accelerator provides all that, plus the opportunity to pitch our product to venture capital firms. Sometimes, accelerators will throw in mentorship, or even seed funding."

"Clearly then, it's Option Two," said Diego, putting his feet on the coffee table as he repositioned himself on the mustard corduroy couch.

As Diego switched tabs, he paused for just a second or two on the shoe website. Suddenly, ShopFixa popped up a dialog box on top of the open web page. "Should we buy the hiking boots, Digs?" it asked Diego brightly as its avatar bobbed next to a snapshot of the boots in question. "They match your style and price range. Heck, they're even 20 percent off!"

Diego smiled proudly at his bot's performance. Right on target! He chuckled a bit at the word "Heck"—must have been Dale who wrote that text string. Dale is always saying things like "Heck!" and "Oh, boy!" like he just stepped out of a 1950's TV show. An idea suddenly popped up on top of this thought. *We should add language packs at some point!* Let users choose from a range of slang variants or subculture personalities for their bot, as a step toward greater personalization. Eventually, the bots would have to be localized per country anyway, once they rolled out internationally. Diego added the idea to Jira, the software tool that the team used to keep track of product features. He always felt a profound satisfaction from banking ideas. Hopefully, they would someday lead to banking revenue.

Kari interrupted his thoughts, steering him back to the business decision at hand. "Yeah, but in exchange for all that generosity, an accelerator would want equity in the company," replied Kari, frowning.

"Huh," said Diego, unruffled by this detail. "What about your father? Would he be willing to invest more?"

"We're burning through my father's hundred thousand pretty quickly. And I don't think he'll ante up any more in the short-term." Diego knew that Kari hated to ask Jussi for even one more dollar. Although more cash was critical at this juncture, his friend felt a burning need to prove himself to his father, to pick up the age-old gauntlet of the prodigal son and return home with a few victories under his belt. He was his father's son in that regard.

"I think we'd only need a little more and we'll be able to move beyond alpha," Diego said. "We could be ready to pitch to investors in a few months."

"Really?" Kari sounded skeptical and hopeful in equal measures.

"My father isn't the most angelic angel investor," Kari continued drily. "I don't trust his apparent nonchalance about the whole thing." He took a long swig from a bottle of Anchor Steam sitting on the coffee table. "Besides," he continued, "we need to take a growth step soon. We need some serious capital so we can hire full-time developers and pick up the pace."

"Step on the 'accelerator'," Diego replied.

"Exactly."

The two partners applied to several startup accelerator programs around the Bay Area, which promised to help them firmly establish their business, raise capital, and solidify their reputation as an industry player. Such intensive programs offered facilities, technologies, educational sessions, and mentors, as well as connections to other entrepreneurs and startups—fertile soil for rapid growth. It would help the lean team polish and productize their ShopFixa software, develop their business infrastructure, and prepare them for meeting with investors. A critical milestone.

A few weeks later, an email arrived in Kari's inbox. It was a blissfully warm Thursday in early October, at the height of San Francisco's "true summer" which bathed the city in rich, golden sunshine like a delicious, buttery sauce. Although temperatures remained steady in the seventies and even eighties, autumn was simmering just below the surface. The early crispness in the air, and creeping darkness at the end of the day unmasked summer's charade to those who paid attention.

Diego and Kari were working at a café on Valencia Street in the city's Mission District. Head's down, each sipped a cup of creamy, nitrogen-infused café au lait that tasted more like a rich stout beer than a coffee drink. Kari opened the email and bolted upright.

"Hey!" he exclaimed. "We got in!" Diego had never seen his friend express such naked delight, it would almost be embarrassing to witness if the news weren't so incredible and auspicious. "We landed Cloud9!" Kari stared at Diego, speechless. They had been accepted to one of the most prestigious and challenging accelerators for the winter session starting in January. It was the best possible news!

"Awesome," Diego said, equally excited and dumbstruck. He never expected to actually be validated by the industry establishment, especially so early in their startup journey. It was unfamiliar territory, and he usually depended on Kari to forge that path.

"I can't wait to tell Kira," Kari enthused in a rare moment of openness. "And my father."

The following day Kari did hear back from Jussi, who was living in Singapore for a few months. "Bravo," his father had said. "Don't screw it up." Diego recognized Jussi's typical hug-slap response that always left his friend awash in visible anxiety.

"Just ignore that shit, Kari," Diego said in a weak attempt to support his friend. He didn't know what else to say. He wasn't good at this type of thing.

"Of course. Yeah. I don't care." Kari instantly pulled himself together. Diego knew that Kari would need a weekend on the couch binging on videos in order to fully decompress.

~

Saturdays were Diego's designated day off, and he usually spent them with Meghan. He allowed himself one day to let go of the thrust of the week and all the problem solving, troubleshooting, researching, and long hours of coding that came with it. Dialing down his mental energy required a special kind of focus, and most importantly, it required scheduling. Making plans in advance with Meghan also helped, as she was usually inflexible with last-minute changes. But that was okay. He needed the weekly break, even if his time with Megs was not always relaxing.

Two days after the Cloud9 email, the couple was strolling through the Saturday farmer's market at the Ferry Building, on their way to their favorite breakfast kiosk. This was the city's culinary core—a wellspring of pristine, premium ingredients for professional and amateur cooks, and a cornucopia of delicious experiences for foodies. Diego and Meghan were enthusiastic explorers of any new development on the food scene, and they often spent an enjoyable weekend morning among the bustling crowds of shoppers and eaters.

Outside next to the docks, rows of market stalls were overflowing with late summer produce. They stopped to inspect a gleaming mound of mixed heirloom tomatoes, a delicate gradient of reds, oranges, and yellows.

Diego seized the moment to share the news of Fixa's acceptance to the Cloud9 program. In a sunburst of excitement, he recounted the highlights as Meghan lightly squeezed golden tomatoes, one by one, without selecting any. He should have known that Fixa news, no matter how fantastic, would hit a familiar wall.

"Congrats, babe," Meghan responded with an ephemeral hug. He noted the pleasant, vanilla-orange scent of her hair, which lingered in his senses long after the hug had faded. "That's really cool." She smiled and turned toward a different pile of tomatoes.

It's more than just "cool," he thought, irritation rising. *She should get it.* Meghan did work in the tech industry after all.

"So, you'll be working even more hours now?" Meghan asked, suddenly filling a large paper bag with several handfuls of pellet-shaped San Marzano tomatoes. For some reason, she hadn't squeeze-tested any of these.

"Yeah, probably," he replied casually, sensing a hidden meaning behind her question. He automatically tensed, expecting a confrontation, but she had already pivoted toward lighter matters.

"I'm going to make a big batch of marinara sauce!" she stated abruptly. "And can it for the winter."

Diego watched her get carried away by the lure of yet another home craft project. *She'll abandon this idea too,* he thought. The tomatoes would surely end up in the compost bin, making their own rotten sauce.

"You can buy dozens of varieties of excellent marinara," Diego shot back. He was irritated that the focus had turned yet again on herself. "Anyway, 'the winter' means nothing in the modern world. Especially in California. You can buy tomatoes year-round."

"Why are you always so critical of anything I do?" Meghan replied sharply. "You always have some kind of bullshit comeback. Why can't you just be supportive for once?" Her green eyes flashed with anger, hands on hips.

"I'm not being critical. Just practical," Diego replied curtly and promptly shut down. He refused to feed the flames of this tired, familiar argument.

"You're just so fucking annoying." Exasperated, she turned to inspect stacks of dark green and bright yellow zucchini on a nearby table.

Ditto, he thought.

CHAPTER 13

Kari

One Saturday afternoon, Kari came home from the gym to find a stranger leaving his apartment. The guy looked like he'd just walked out of some hipster magazine photo spread. A spray of mini dreadlocks and neatly trimmed sideburns framed his classically handsome features. An olive canvas military jacket fit his tall, muscular physique perfectly. To Kari, he had the particularly satisfied look of someone who has been handed everything that he wants in life and more. *Smug*, he reckoned. Startled, Kari stared silently as the man stepped past him onto the street, pulling his iPhone out of a side pocket as he strode down Pacific Avenue toward a gleaming white BMW parked nearby. *Swaggering.*

Kari raced upstairs to find Kira standing in the living room talking animatedly on the phone—possibly to her brother Theo—in sweats and ponytail. Did she look a little flushed? He scanned the space for any signs of disruption across the disciplined landscape of their home. The glass coffee table was strewn with PowerPoint printouts and website design mockups. Kira's laptop, tablet, and second iPhone floated across the sea of paper.

Pomegranate Smart Water, warm and half empty, sat forgotten on the polished oak floor in a puddle of condensation, alarmingly close to a bunched up, silver-gray blanket of New Zealand lamb's wool. Her rimless eyeglasses and Apple earbuds lay stranded on the white leather lounge chair. Her company VPN card stood at attention nearby on a glass side table. A bottle of lavender-colored nail polish beckoned from the edge of the chaos. It was the blast radius of normalcy on a work-from-home day for Kira.

Ending her call, Kira walked over to give him a kiss. Did she smell different? He felt that he couldn't trust any of his senses.

"Who was that?" Kari asked casually, sorting through mail on the hall table. He hoped that he sounded the opposite of how he felt.

"Oh, that was Theo," she replied cheerfully, "just calling to say hi."

"No, I mean the guy who just left the apartment," he said evenly, struggling to keep his temper at bay. "He passed me on the steps."

"Oh!" she replied even more cheerfully, if that was possible. "That was Darryl from work. He stopped by to drop off my tablet." She stooped to pick up a sleek white iPad perched like a puppy on the back of the sofa and lovingly brushed a few minute dust specks from its gleaming facade.

"Huh," Kari replied.

"He'd borrowed it to demo one of our apps at some media briefings last week at that conference in Vegas. He walked them through a couple of new features that we were announcing at the show." She clutched the device close to her chest. "Darryl's iPad got stolen from his car. In broad daylight! On Market Street!"

"He couldn't return it on Monday?" Kari asked, ignoring Darryl's brush with the dark side of urban life. He busied himself with the mail while she stood there staring at him. It was impossible to meet her gaze.

"Well, he was in the neighborhood and thought I might need it," she said flatly and walked into the kitchen to put on the kettle for tea.

"How nice of him," Kari said under his breath. So, he was the jerk then, being suspicious of something so innocent. But as soon as he thought that, his mind automatically cycled through a handful of other instances over the past couple of years. Moments that were just a little bit off, that pushed his heart a little off-kilter and required his conscious effort to resume balance.

More than once he had caught Kira in a possible white lie—she would say she was working from home, yet he had come home during the day to find no evidence of her presence. Or she would say she had been at yoga or Pilates, yet there was no blush of exercise visible in her alabaster skin. He would come home to find the shower wet, yet Kira didn't look remotely like she had recently showered. Two wineglasses in the sink—had it really been Ravi with her that evening? Hadn't he just visited the day before?

Once Kari had even found a crumpled white T-shirt in the trunk of Kira's car—men's size large. He wore a medium. Kira had produced a casual explanation: she had picked it up by accident at the gym when she'd gathered her things from a bench near the swimming pool. She meant to bring it back to the lost and found. At least it wasn't underwear, he thought bitterly.

Despite these incidents, Kari could not, would not, bring himself to snoop in Kira's phone, although he was convinced that it contained clues to either prove or dispel his suspicions. If only he could know for sure! Kira had been his rock and refuge for so long that he couldn't imagine losing her. Yet he found it impossible to stop the blips on his internal radar, the ominous, tiny warnings of approaching danger. The potential enemy was not only another man, but also the other man inside himself. He sensed that his father's rage, like a ghost in the shadows, lay waiting for a chance to emerge.

Kari confided in Diego one Friday evening over beers and BBQ at a factory-turned-eatery on an industrial block of the Dogpatch neighborhood. The place was packed with diners and drinkers kicking off the weekend, and its bare cement walls and two-story ceilings didn't help to dampen the din.

"Maybe you're imagining things, Kari," said Diego, leaning in to make himself heard. "And maybe not. You don't know." His friend munched hungrily on a fat pork rib dripping with bourbon-infused sauce.

"Yeah, but it's really rattling me," replied Kari, raising his voice. "I want to trust her." He took a distracted gulp of the bitter house-brewed IPA.

"Of course. But what if you never know for sure?" asked Diego, chewing thoughtfully. "What then?"

"I don't know, Digs. I just hope that the feeling will go away at some point," Kari replied, melancholy running rampant across his psychic terrain. Diego reached over and gave his shoulder a quick squeeze. *Hope his fingers are clean*, Kari thought.

"Whatever you do, man, don't make things worse." Diego sopped up some sauce with a fist-sized biscuit.

"I need to spend more time with her," Kari said with conviction, tearing off a large bite of his brisket and slaw sandwich. "I've been working too much for too long."

"Yeah," Diego agreed, knocking back the dregs of his golden lager.

Sometimes, the moorings of Kari's life seemed unable to cope with the hurricane force of his workload. The onslaught of tasks and to-do's, of meetings and follow-ups and seemingly endless emails, all relentlessly battered the fortress of his resolve. In the past couple of years, he'd spent a tremendous amount of energy just trying to stay afloat despite the pressures of school and the startup. He barely had anything left to shore up his relationships, let alone worry about the basics of living such as eating, sleeping, exercising. There were times when he was so busy, so burdened by demands, that he'd keep his bladder waiting an hour or even two before he'd rush to the restroom, ready to burst. Biology had to take a number like everything else.

Kira shouldn't have to suffer, Kari reprimanded himself. I should slow down once in a while. Take a break. Show her how much she means to me.

Slowing down, however, was nearly impossible. The underlying theme of Kari's life on all fronts was acceleration. Since he'd become an entrepreneur, Kari consciously and strategically chose whichever route would allow him to achieve his goals faster, yet remain uncompromised and competitively strong. He'd finally graduated from UC Berkeley's fast-track Executive MBA program, completing his degree in barely a year and a half. Although he was already mid-career, it felt almost like a starting point, a critical step before he could really hit the ground running. He believed that the MBA was table stakes for gaining entry to his destiny.

~

As a graduation present to his current self, Kari decided to experience his future self on a weekend getaway with Kira. What better place for executive-style rest and relaxation than California's wine country? The combination of hot weather and local culture meticulously curated by winemakers and famous chefs sounded like the perfect way to honor this milestone.

Kari invested nearly an entire precious hour in this plan, searching through a wealth of premium listings on Airbnb and VRBO. He landed on an idyllic California Craftsman-style property in St. Helena, the heart of Napa Valley. The shingled, one-story home was at the end of a narrow road on the edge of town, secluded from view by a thicket of massive oak trees. It promised to be an elegant, tasteful host—guests could sip a glass of Pinot Noir on the wisteria-covered front porch, a crisp Sauvignon Blanc by a modest lap pool, or a fruit-forward Zinfandel at a fourteen-foot iron and oak dining table situated in a grove of heirloom citrus trees. Kari intended to drink in all the hospitality that the weekend had to offer.

When he surprised Kira with the plan, she had been especially excited. "Oooh, it's my dream home!" she exclaimed, clicking through the listing's photo gallery as they sat together at the kitchen table after dinner. Kari felt an undercurrent of pleasure ripple through him. He wanted what she wanted. He wanted to give her a dream home.

"I'm SO ready for a weekend away," she added, "especially to somewhere with real live sun." Like many San Franciscans on the brink of summer, she dreaded the annual intrusion of a season-long blanket of gloomy fog during what should be the warmest, cheeriest months of the year.

"Me too, my love," Kari replied, still as a statue, eyes fixed on Kira.

"Yeah, we deserve to be hot for a change," she grumbled scrolling through the rental details.

"Hot and bothered!" Kari quipped a little too eagerly and jumped up to start the dishes.

Kira flashed a quick smile and continued, "It's a three-bedroom place. Let's invite a couple of people and make it a real party!"

"*Kultaseni*, my love, I thought it would be just the two of us," Kari replied, struggling to mask any traces of disappointment. "We haven't spent much time together lately, and it would be so romantic!"

After a beat or two, Kira stood up and stepped over to Kari at the sink. Putting her arms around his waist. "I know, love, but your graduation is a big deal and we should mark the occasion with a real celebration." She snuggled her cheek into Kari's flannelled back. "Imagine having a luxurious, catered dinner party at that gorgeous outdoor table in the orange grove."

"Huh," Kari grunted neutrally, afraid to turn around and turn Kira off on the getaway idea altogether.

"Our dinner would be amazing, like a photo shoot in *Sunset Magazine*," her voice trailed off dreamily.

"Okay, okay," Kari conceded, wiping his hands on a kitchen towel. "It sounds fun. Let's do it." He stroked her bare arms lovingly, gently unwound them from his waist, and sighed deeply. Not the weekend he had in mind, but it could still turn out alright.

Kira hopped excitedly and clapped her hands. "I'll invite Ravi," she chirped. "He loves anything wine country!" Kari groaned inwardly. She leans on that guy for everything these days. *Ravi the Crutch*, he thought sullenly. *Or maybe it's Ravi the Human Shield.*

"Okay, I'll invite Digs," Kari said, ignoring the predictable twitch on Kira's face as she struggled not to grimace. He assumed that meant Diego's girlfriend would tag along, which was not ideal, but it couldn't be helped.

"No business talk," Kira replied sternly, hands on hips. "I'm dead serious. No business or I'll hitchhike home."

"It'll be a mini-reunion of sorts," he continued, ignoring her empty threat. "The three of us haven't spent much time together since we left Del Oro Games." He perked up at the thought of the old college friends reconnecting over plenty of stellar wine, exceptional food, and luxuriously hot sun by the pool. No business talk indeed.

Four intense work weeks thundered by, and Kari had barely had time to savor the anticipation of his upcoming getaway. Then finally, it was here! He awoke at seven a.m. on Friday morning with an unfamiliar sensation of floating, of hovering on the brink of an unstructured day. Three unstructured days in fact! In order to fully appreciate such a rare treat, he wanted to start the day by leaving work matters in good shape. A clear inbox led to a clear mind.

He hopped out of bed to make two cups of coffee—Addis Gold, his current favorite—and crawled back into the still-warm nest next to the still-sleeping Kira. She stirred and smiled in his direction before slowly opening her eyes. His heart stirred along with her, before a gulp of caffeine pushed it into the background of his morning.

"Morning, my *kulta* Kira." He reached over to give her a quick kiss.

"Mmmm...morning," she yawned, pulling the taupe-colored, raw silk duvet up to her chin.

Kari reached down to pick up his MacBook from the floor beside the bed. Kira did the same, and both spent the first hour of their free weekend checking in on email and responding to questions, problems, roadblocks, approvals, and any other work-related flicker that could quickly turn into a fire during their three-day absence. Although their rental came with Wi-Fi, they both had agreed to stay away from electronics during the weekend. It was going to be a digital detox of sorts. As much as possible anyway—they wouldn't go so far as to leave their laptops at home.

The couple set off mid-morning in Kari's silver Audi A4 for the hour-plus drive to Napa Valley. Kari reached for Kira's hand as they crossed the Golden Gate bridge, and the two didn't let go until they'd left everyday life behind. Taking their time, they followed the highway through the greater Bay Area's golden, grassy hillsides and lush, leafy vineyards. Kari began to relax as they passed through miles of cultivated land, the neat rows of grape vines curving gently along the contours of rolling hills. The old-world, civilized landscape seemed to be signaling that everything was all right.

Midway between the cities of Napa and St. Helena, they rolled into Yountville and stopped in the center of town for their first moment of celebratory bliss at Bouchon Bakery. Behind its simple pale green exterior lay a treasure trove of sweet and savory delights. "It's Ali Baba's cave," Kira whispered, eyebrows raised, as the alluring, yeasty smell of baking bread teased out their appetites. Kari bought a lemon cake with baked meringue frosting that looked like a brick of sunburned snow, as well as two dozen of Kira's favorite—pristine French macaroons in assorted watercolor hues.

"Ravi calls these 'Fairy Buttons.'" Kira smiled at the jewel box of feather-light sweets in her lap. "My mother calls them 'Ballerina Kisses.'"

"My mother calls them '*Les Plaquettes du Pape*' or 'The Pope's Wafers,'" Kari replied. "She says that's how they take communion at the Vatican."

The two shared a pistachio-flavored, macaroon kiss and found each other's hand again as they continued on to their weekend retreat. They arrived at noon, welcomed by the fiery Napa Valley sun beaming straight down on them like an overzealous host.

The house was as perfect as its pictures. A warm breeze encircled the couple as they quickly unloaded the car, dropped their stuff into the spacious master bedroom, and oriented themselves to this little slice of paradise. They were glad to have the afternoon to themselves, which helped them settle into the unfamiliar rhythm of a weekend off. Kira opened a bottle of buttery, oaked Chardonnay, grabbed two crystal wine glasses, and filled an ice bucket. Kari opened packets of seaweed-infused rice crackers, wasabi-crusted dried peas, and root veggie chips, filling three earth-toned Heath ceramic bowls to the brim. They lay poolside in lithe aluminum chaises, closed their eyes, and didn't speak until their guests arrived in the early evening.

Shortly after seven, Meghan, Diego, and Ravi drove up the tree-lined driveway in Meghan's Mini Cooper and parked next to Kari's Audi in the wisteria-covered carport. The Mini was a rich yellow with black roof and black racing stripes, which on first sight had prompted Diego to call it "the bumble bee." Meghan had quipped back, "It's a humble bumble," and the name stuck, eventually shortening to "Humble."

The three friends piled out of the Humble like drones from a hive and unloaded bags of clothes and food from the unoccupied nooks and crannies of the small vehicle. It had been a cheerful, yet overly long drive out of the city in pre-weekend traffic on a late Friday afternoon. The three arrived with low energy but much enthusiasm for their collective getaway. As previously arranged with K2, they'd stopped at a pizzeria in St. Helena to pick up a modest meal to start their glamorous weekend.

"Yo! We come in peace. We come with pizza," announced Ravi breezily as he shoved two large pizza boxes into Kari's arms. He kissed Kira on both cheeks.

"Hey," said Diego, nodding at his two hosts.

"Hi," said Meghan, giving Kari and Kira a brief hug. She looked flushed and irritable. Kari assumed this was from the heat and the effort of driving in over two hours of bumper-to-bumper traffic. It occurred to him that she seemed irritable more often than not lately.

Not that he saw Meghan much—Kira still found her "dishwater dull" so the two couples never double-dated and only rarely saw each other at the same social events. Even when he worked with Meghan at Del Oro Games, Kari could never seem to engage her in any meaningful conversation; she was like an eel that would slip through his grasp in a flash. It was usually light banter or foodie topics that kept the thin thread of their connection intact. Maybe she was shy—who knew.

While Kira showed Ravi and Meghan to their rooms, Kari and Diego set up for dinner at a round glass dining table by the pool, removing its umbrella to accommodate the last rays of the fading day.

"How's it going, Digs?" Kari asked Diego as he set out plates. "Good day?" He was torn between asking for the daily update on their business and his promise to Kira.

"Yeah man, it was okay," Diego responded, pulling extra chairs from the patio over to the table. "Chris and Dale ran into some issues merging their changes into the master code base. We need to switch developer tools; we're spending way too long messing around with the servers."

"Okay, can we explore new tools and still stay on schedule?" Kari asked stiffly as he poured a chilled Rosé into five wine glasses, spilling more than a few drops on the table. "We're supposed to have a new rev up and running by Tuesday."

"Yeah. Maybe. I dunno," Diego responded, shrugging his shoulders. "I hope so." Kari felt a flash of irritability at his friend's noncommittal, overly casual response to what he felt to be a business-critical question. They absolutely needed development to stay on track. They needed an MVP, a minimum viable product, complete and ready to shop around to investors. But this was supposed to be a "no business" weekend, so Kari forced himself to change tack.

"How's everything going with Megs?" he asked, lowering his voice. He glanced toward the house at the other end of the pool and could see the other three chatting in the kitchen.

"I dunno," Diego repeated. "Not great. We argue a lot." He shrugged again. *No surprise there*, thought Kari.

"Why, what's going on?"

"It's her, man. I can't seem to do anything right. She gets pissed at me for the smallest thing. Like today, apparently I talked with Ravi the whole way up and didn't include her in the conversation."

"Is that true?"

"Yeah, probably. But she could have jumped in anytime. Why am I supposed to"—he mimed quote marks—"*include her* when she can include herself perfectly well?"

"Sorry to hear, Digs." Kari patted his friend's shoulder in sympathy. "I'm sure you guys can work through this." Secretly, he suspected that Diego was getting bored with the relationship. *Not a big surprise*, he thought.

"She can get really demanding with this bullshit, and it drives me crazy." Diego picked up one of the wine glasses and took a big sip.

The sliding glass door to the kitchen opened with a whoosh, and Kira emerged with an enormous stoneware bowl of glistening little gem salad that looked almost too big for her to carry. Ravi and Meghan followed with bowls of chips and bottles of wine. Dinner commenced at a leisurely pace, with the wine loosening tensions and elevating spirits well into the warm Napa Valley evening.

Later that night, Diego and Meghan addressed their mutual tensions loudly enough for Kari to grasp some of the more pertinent scraps, including: "respect me," "spend time with me," and "care about me" (Meghan's voice), and "control me," "self-centered," and "melodrama" (Diego's voice). Lying in bed, Kari and Kira exchanged raised eyebrows as they heard a door slam and one of the unhappy pair go out to sit by the pool. Kari felt for his friend and wondered how this story would end, as the end seemed surely inevitable now.

After a while, Kari turned over and gazed at Kira, who had fallen asleep beside him. She was inches away and miles away, and where was he in her inner landscape? Did she also feel the distance, the disconnect between them? He should confront her with his suspicions, but he couldn't bear the humiliation of being wrong. He also couldn't imagine them shouting and accusing each other, turning issues into wildfires like Diego and Meghan. The K2 style was much more subtle. The slow, silent pressures on the relationship were shifting the tectonic plates beneath them, opening a chasm. Maybe they should sit down and talk one of these days. But not this weekend! Now, they were here to be together, to *feel* together. Kari thought it was going well so far, and he was determined to stoke that flame all weekend.

The next morning, the houseguests gathered in the kitchen for breakfast. Kari had woken early and run out to pick up fresh pastries. He brewed a pot of his latest rocket fuel discovery—Colombian Royal Roast—that had the strength to disperse any wine hazy remnants of the previous evening. There was one guest missing.

"Megs had to go home," Diego said, looking more subdued than a simple hangover would warrant. "She said to say goodbye to everyone," he nodded at Kari and Kira, "and thank you."

"Bummer, man," said Ravi. "I'm so sorry." He frowned and exhaled deeply, hands on hips, gazing kindly at Diego with "I've been there" compassion.

"Yeah, sorry, Digs," said Kari softly, handing his friend the first cup of coffee. Kira shifted closer to her partner as she arranged croissants and condiments on a large ceramic platter.

"I'm sure you all heard us," Diego said apologetically. "We were kind of loud." He paused for a beat and glanced across three concerned faces. "Sorry about that." He blew into his cup of coffee and took a cautious sip.

Diego appeared to take the situation in stride. However, Kari, a life-long observer of relationship conflict, could sense the inner struggle raging beneath his friend's familiar stoic composure. Hurt vs. relief. Guilt vs. anger. Need vs. indifference. Abandonment vs. detachment. With no clear resolution, all coexisted as part of the complex programming of this unique moment in Diego's life. It was another side of human nature, irrational and inexplicable, that was shaped by a fundamental human algorithm of which intent and purpose remained frustratingly obscure. An algorithm that may, or may not, be replicable in a computer lab.

Kari noted that the friends were treading lightly over this uncomfortable territory. They'd never witnessed such an intimate incident in their Diego's life, and thus seemed unsure how to support him.

"What happened, Digs?" Kira asked gently. "Feel free to talk about it, if you want?" Her voice looped up in a hanging question mark as she nibbled on the crusty end of a croissant, licking its fine flakes off her lips with one swish of her tongue.

"Nah," Diego replied. "Let's just have a fun weekend. That'll make me feel better." He flashed a weak but appreciative smile at the others and appeared as self-contained as ever.

"I guess this means we're walking home?" Ravi joked and lightly punched Diego's arm. "Or I guess we can catch a ride with the K2 love mobile." He winced slightly at his faux pas reference to love.

"We're here for you, man," Kari said and gave Diego a rare, full body hug.

Over coffee and pastries, Saturday commenced with a palpable change in tone. Ten years of friendship, woven together by a myriad of shared experiences, seemed to fuse into an unbreakable solidarity. The four college friends were tighter than ever before, more appreciative of each other's presence, more in tune with each other's personality. There was also a lightness of mood, an almost giddy sense of freedom from tension as each dived into the opportunities of the day.

Kira and Ravi happily lounged by the pool for much of the afternoon. In between tanning, snoozing, or swimming, they played gin rummy and drank Pinot Gris as they idly chatted about favorite TV shows or celebrities or fashion. Neither brought up the gossip of the day. For them, Meghan had clearly become a closed, and thus entirely uninteresting, chapter in their group story with no need for an epilogue.

Kari and Diego happily set out to scour the local wineries for wines that would pair well with that evening's menu. At Frog's Leap, they enjoyed discussing the finer details of terroir and fermentation techniques with tasting room staff. At Cakebread Cellars, they flirted with a sexy vintner while barrel tasting her latest Syrah blend, adding a pleasant edge to the afternoon. Kari gently encouraged Diego in that regard—"Get back in the ring, Digs!"—hoping to sweep away any thoughts of Meghan lingering in his friend's psyche. The weekend would not be ruined, he would see to that.

They came home with a few bottles of 2009 Viognier from Grgich Hills, an interesting estate-grown Malbec from Caymus, a selection of Cabernets from Quintessa, and a chocolate Port from Peju. Mission accomplished—their collective stash now overflowed with choice.

In the late afternoon, three members of a local catering company arrived at the house to set up for the evening meal. Kira had meticulously researched dining options in the area, poring through chef bios, customer reviews, and seasonal menu combinations to curate the best possible celebration for Kari's graduation. Although their small party wouldn't fill all seats at the magnificent outdoor table, they would still enjoy the elegance and ambiance of the magazine-worthy setting. "Intimacy on a grand scale," Kira had described it. Kari felt the pleasurable flutter of anticipation.

All four had anticipated the special tenor of the evening and had packed something nice to wear. Kira was the model summer hostess in a backless, aqua blue knit maxi dress that lightly swept the patio as she breezed back and forth to the kitchen with tableware and condiments. Ravi, in a peach-colored twill shirt and washed linen pants, decorated the table with flowers and foliage that he'd gathered from around the property. Kari wore his favorite mint green paisley shirt with light grey Italian cotton trousers, and Diego put on beige chinos, his only pair of non-denim pants, and a brand new, plain navy T-shirt.

"We sure are a fine-looking crew!" Ravi exclaimed as they seated themselves around the center of the table. He handed his phone to one of the caterers for the first of many photos that evening that would get their moment of fame on Facebook.

"Agreed," Kari replied and tapped a knife against his water glass and stood up to formally kick off the evening. "Okay, I'll keep this short and sweet. I just want to thank you all for being here. Thank you for your friendship over the years, and may it continue for decades to come." He sat down quickly feeling suddenly a bit too humble, or maybe vulnerable.

"Aww, that *was* sweet," grinned Ravi. He stood up and raised his glass. "Congrats to Kari on his big ass degree! We are mighty proud of you, man."

"Congrats, Kariiiiii!" chimed Kira and Diego in unison. All took an enthusiastic sip of their Silver Oaks Estate 2007 Sauvignon Blanc and tucked into the tuna poke appetizer. Course after course followed. The friends indulged in the best of that week's Napa Valley cuisine: chilled avocado bisque, three organic summer vegetable salads harvested that day from the caterer's personal garden, and rack of lamb with truffled mashed potatoes and rosemary shallot gravy. The cardamom and orange buttermilk panna cotta paired nicely with the port Kari had bought earlier, and a plate of local cheeses kept the party nibbling well after the caterers had left.

By this point, the heat of the day still lingered and the party was just warming up. Kari picked up his phone to change the playlist that piped through the patio speakers to something more energetic, and Ravi was decorating Kira's hair with flowers from the table setting. Even Diego was in a jovial mood, feet up on the chair next to him, nodding his head to the beat.

"Kari, man, Fixa is really gonna take off with you in charge," Diego said, raising his glass in Kari's general direction. "You're brilliant at the business stuff."

"Thanks, Digs," Kari replied with a self-effacing shrug. "We make a good team." He raised his glass to Diego. "We've got to nail down next steps for getting our investor pitch ready. We need a version with a more robust feature set to demo," he continued energetically. "How close are Chris and Dale to delivering? Do we need to push them harder?"

"I'm trying, but I've got a lot on my plate. Trying to manage those two while doing my own R&D is a double-time job. And I'm already eating, sleeping, and shitting Fixa on a daily basis." He refilled his glass with port, spilling some on his hand in the process.

"UGH!" Kira groaned loudly, staring hard at Kari. "Here we go." She threw her head back and several marigolds fell out of her French twist hairstyle.

Kari felt a pang of guilt at his broken promise. No business talk! But with a full belly and wine flowing freely, it was pretty much unstoppable.

"We need a product guy," Kari continued, "someone to keep the deliverables on track so you can focus on the bigger picture." He began cutting slices of Manchego and membrillo, stacking them in between water crackers. A neat, round tower of cheese and quince paste.

"Agreed," said Diego thoughtfully.

"You gonna eat that or watch it crash?" Ravi pointed to the cracker tower, which had already reached twelve layers. "Have you ever played *Jenga*? It's pretty fun."

Diego turned to Ravi, cocked his head, and sat up. "Ravi—you'd be perfect."

"Huh?" Ravi said, his finger gently poking the tower.

"You'd be the perfect product manager for Fixa!" With a slight slurring of words and waving of hands, Diego revved up his pitch. "We need you, man! Come join us!" He raised his glass to Ravi and drained the port in one shot.

"Head of Product," Kari stated. "You'd lead the Fixa product line. Help us refine the user experience, grow the concept, create a user base." He was slightly irritated with Diego for putting this impulsive proposal on the table without consulting him privately beforehand. But Kari's gut told him that Digs was right. Not only did Ravi have a well-honed skillset in product management, but also his loyalty to their friendship would mean that Ravi would be all in. Such dedication was critical at this early stage.

"Can you guys pay me?" Ravi asked, going straight to practicalities. "I mean, in real money? I can't live on equity."

"Of course. Of course," Kari replied reassuringly. "We're bootstrapped but not bankrupt." He cringed at the thought of asking his father for yet more funding, but he'd do what had to be done.

"Okay then, let me think about it. I'll have my headhunters talk to your headhunters." Ravi batted the idea around playfully, but his eyes shone. *He's hooked*, Kari thought.

"Oh, great," Kira moaned. "Now I'll never hear the end of this one-track conversation." She crossed her arms sourly.

"Well, we need a Head of Communications too," Kari said brightly, filling her glass to the brim. "Once the beta is done, we need to get it in front of analysts, media, investors." He ignored Diego's frown and continued. "We need someone who can really deliver our pitch. Someone who's an ace presenter. That's you, *kultaseni*, my love. That is you in a nutshell."

"Oh, yeah?" Kira said with half-hearted sarcasm. "I already have a job. And I like it." Kari thought she softened just a little.

A flash of inspiration suddenly took Kari's breath away—not only would Fixa benefit from an ace presenter and PR expert, but Kira might be able to convince her father to contribute some funding, so that aspect wouldn't all be on his shoulders. And the shared business could bring the pair closer together. It could be a win-win-win.

"You wouldn't need to quit right away," Kari replied. "We could work on the pitch together in the evenings and weekends. Once we get some market traction, then maybe we can entice you to join full-time." He kissed her playfully behind the ear. "I'll get to work on that enticing part."

"Oh man, the K2 Empire is born!" Ravi exclaimed. "Plus Digs, of course," he quickly added. "And maybe me. We'll see." He brightened. "Our little dorm family, together again!"

"Why not join forces?" Diego said. "We're all great at what we do. And we trust each other."

"To be discussed further when sober," Kira stated firmly. "Which will be AFTER this weekend!"

The group honored Kira's request and banished Fixa from interfering with the remainder of the weekend. Saturday night faded into Sunday morning and the friends whittled away the last day in St. Helena brunching, window-shopping, people watching—until the urge to shift back into high gear was too great.

On the drive back to San Francisco, a sense of profound solidarity, from their shared history, from the possibility of a shared future, was so palpable that it silenced any small talk all the way home.

CHAPTER 14

Meghan

For millennia, the Black Rock Desert held nothing in its vast, weathered basin. No cactus. No tumbleweed. Not a single pebble or insect for miles. Ringed by distant mountains that were bathed in dusky mauves and delicate pinks, the area had once cradled an ancient lake that, in turn, had nourished an ecosystem. Long ago, this thriving land had let go of its charge, and now, even the memory of prehistoric life had long faded from the parched lakebed. The receding waters left a sea of fine, compacted alkali dust, soft yet deeply cracked, like the wizened cheek of an elder. The barren terrain invited a meditation on existence—what is empty, yet not empty? A Zen koan.

At the turn of the twenty-first century C.E., the Black Rock Desert held one thing that many people found lacking in modern urban life. It held the imagination, unfettered and raw. Not the imagination of the everyday; the kind that helped to shape a life or a community or a culture. It was something much more primal with its own agenda. The stark landscape was a blank canvas on which any creative vision could manifest. Its mountain range was a chiseled frame that could contain any untamed experience.

The cracked desert floor was a dreamscape in which one could play out the many fragmented versions of self, and somehow become more whole. It was far from empty.

Once a year, during the last week in August, the Black Rock Desert held the fourth largest city in Nevada. Tens of thousands of people came together to co-create a human ecosystem that not only thrived, but also reveled in the primeval dust. This temporary camp city existed to host the Burning Man festival, an annual event that was founded on the utopian pillars of art, community, and radical self-expression. A true metropolis, Black Rock City boasted named streets and support services, community agencies and professional architects. Its citizens, "burners," came from all over the world, but a large segment of the population made the seven-hour pilgrimage over the Sierra Nevada mountains to the desert, the "playa," from the San Francisco Bay Area.

Meghan was more than willing to make the trek. She was ready, and hoping, to unlock a new vision of herself in this strange city of dreams. "A baby burner!" Rence had called her. "Awww, your first burn!" Bree had exclaimed after Meghan finally agreed to join them at this year's festival. It somehow made her feel old. "You'll be reborn, Megs," Rence reassured her, "baptized in playa dust." She had never taken a trip to a place where she truly didn't know what to expect. What exactly was "radical self-expression"? Naked hippies on drugs?

On the first day of Burning Man, the trio's rented minivan joined the slow-moving line of vehicles that spanned a hundred-mile stretch of highway northeast of Reno. Burners passed through native lands in lumbering campers and reclaimed school buses, pickups and SUVs crammed to the roof with gear. Flatbed trucks carried massive art pieces or whimsical art cars that would add fantasy in motion to a surreal cityscape. When they reached the edge of the desert, the friends' journey slowed to a crawl, and then stopped dead for a couple hours at the Black Rock City gate. Cars waited for a blinding dust storm to pass before they could move, while event greeters checked tickets and gave each carload of burners a brief orientation.

"Welcome home!" A dust-covered woman wearing a red tutu and a tattered black cowboy hat thrust her head through the open driver-side window, planting a dramatic kiss on Rence's cheek. He didn't seem fazed by that in the least.

"Feels amazing to be home," he replied with feeling. The greeter then proceeded to cheerily indoctrinate the car's three passengers in the core principles of participating in Burning Man culture, reminders on how to stay healthy and safe, weather conditions for the week, and changes from the previous year.

"Any newbies?" she asked, looking at Bree and Meghan.

"She is!" Bree and Rence pointed with glee at Meghan, eyes shining.

Hands on hips, the greeter took a swaggering stance and said in her best sheriff voice: "Step out of the car, ma'am."

"Um, okay?" Meghan complied, totally perplexed. Was she in trouble?

"Bend over, ma'am," the greeter said gruffly.

Meghan hesitated for a moment, then stiffly bent over. What the hell was going on? Suddenly, the greeter delivered a brisk spank. "Ow!" Meghan cried, bolting upright. She reached back to rub away the burn and discovered that a sticker had been slapped onto the seat of her cargo shorts. She peeled it off—it was the iconic image of The Man of Burning Man.

"Welcome home, ma'am," the greeter-sheriff said in a friendlier tone, tipping the corner of her hat to Meghan.

Cheeks and butt burning, Meghan scuttled back into the safety of the car. Bree reached back and squeezed her knee. "You're gonna love it, Megs!" *Hopefully*, Meghan thought. For the first time in her life she felt completely unmoored, not unpleasantly so, and she was willing to let herself be carried adrift.

The greeter waved as Rence crept through the event gate at five miles per hour, following a road that marked the perimeter of the burner settlement. He tuned the car's radio to Burning Man Information Radio, which broadcast music and commentary from a small hut with a skeletal tower on the city outskirts. As they passed by the BMIR station, Meghan scanned the open playa in the distance and spotted a two-seater plane parked alongside a makeshift air traffic control tower that appeared to be fashioned from scrap wood. An actual airport! This place was like a child's re-creation of an adult city. A playland of functional toys.

Rence, Bree, and Meghan headed to Camp Fruitopia, the theme camp operated by a group of friends who had been going to Burning Man for the past fifteen years. They soon arrived at the camp's address for the week. Every year, Black Rock City was mapped out along an immense horseshoe grid of streets that spanned two miles in diameter. U-shaped ring streets were given theme names. Radial streets that bisected the U-rings were named based on their position on a clock face: the outer edges were two o'clock and ten o'clock, and the center was six o'clock. Camp Fruitopia was conveniently situated at the corner of 4:30 and Interstellar. Close enough to walk to Center Camp, the heart of the city, but somewhat removed from the daily bustle of burner life.

The horseshoe plan cradled a great expanse of open space that held nearly a hundred art installations, some interactive, some fire-based, some simply sculpture. In the center of the open space stood The Man—a forty-foot, wood-frame effigy that represented the ethos of the event and its culture. The figure was situated atop a structure that doubled his height, making him high enough to survey the entire city and much of the desert landscape, and high enough to give burners a clear view of him from every clock radial street. To Meghan, The Man seemed to be a proud and dominating figure, a puppet-master waiting for his show to begin. Could she let him pull her strings?

Camp Fruitopia was easy to spot in the rapidly fading daylight. The camp's name, spelled out in jaunty hot-pink letters, crowned a massive communal shade structure that was designed to withstand the harsh desert environment as well as create an inviting gathering space. The structure's hot-pink wooden frame was secured from high-winds by thick guy lines tied to hefty rebar stakes. Its bright-white canvas roof sheltered the camp from the unrelenting sun, and any of four canvas sides could be rolled down during a dust storm. The camp's focal point was a huge lounge area that was constructed to look like a fruit bowl. The bowl's curved form was created by a steel frame wrapped in nylon mesh that was brightly painted with neon images of various types of fruit. A circular wooden bench had been built into the inside of the bowl and was decorated with a bounty of colorful fruit-shaped cushions. Two large rattan fan blades were fixed to the roof with a rope-pulley system that allowed loungers to operate the fans themselves. On either side of the shade structure stood two, ten-foot palm trees made from rusted steel, one with brushed aluminum coconuts and the other with wooden sprigs of dates. A waist-high iron sculpture of an ant carrying a cherry on its back stood at the far corner of the Fruitopia footprint, greeting people passing through the 4:30/Interstellar intersection.

"Wow," Meghan said as Rence pulled up to the camp. "Wow." She was otherwise speechless with wonder and curiosity. She wished she could snap a quick video and post it to her Facebook page, but alas there was no cellular signal out in the desert. It would be a long week of digital detox.

"Welcome to our fruity home for the week!" declared Rence. He hopped out to talk to a shirtless guy wearing combat boots and a black canvas skirt (a "utili-kilt" Megan later learned).

"Yeah, it's pretty cool," said Bree. "I sewed most of the fruit cushions and Rence organized this year's spiked fruit cocktail menu." One of the treasured traditions of Burning Man culture was spontaneous hospitality. Camp Fruitopia, like most theme camps, was prepared to invite passersby into their space. "We're gifting fruit cups," continued Bree. "Our guests lounge in the bowl and we serve them cups of diced fruit with little paper umbrellas and a splash of rum."

"Cool," echoed Meghan, happily free falling into this booze-soaked reality.

"Okay, we can set up our tents back there." Rence pointed to an open area behind the shade structure, and the three began unloading the minivan. By the time they'd finished, the mountains had turned from lilac to dark plum. The friends changed into jeans and sweaters, emerging from their tents bundled up for the cold desert night. Bree looked almost chic in a vintage leopard-print hat and knee-length, cream-colored suede coat with fake fur trim.

"Let's go for a ride," suggested Bree. Rence stayed behind to catch up with friends as Bree and Meghan hopped onto their bikes and slowly cruised down Interstellar. They passed camps of all shapes and sizes—a clutch of pup tents here, a huge geodesic dome there—and empty plots in between that would fill up with neighbors and artwork as the week progressed. At the 2:00 radial, three massive dance camps were already in full swing. Their club-sized sound systems pumped out urban-sized beats at the edge of the city grid, and hundreds of dancers grooved under the black dome of desert sky.

"Let's check out the deep playa." Bree skirted the outside of the dance camps and pedaled fast into the blackness of open space. The pair headed for the outer edges of Black Rock City limits, crossing a vast stretch of playa that saw fewer art installations and burners as they pedaled farther away from civilization. Suddenly, they noticed something silvery appear, as if materializing out of the darkness in front of them. As they came nearer, they saw a huge disco ball suspended from a simple fifteen-foot steel tripod and illuminated by three small ground spotlights. The ball rotated slowly in silence, its glittering facets sprinkling an empty dance floor with bright notes of light. They got off their bikes to check it out.

"It's both beautiful and eerie," exclaimed Meghan, fascinated by the surreal spectacle. Standing underneath the ball, she rotated slowly in the opposite direction, meeting the wash of lights head-on. "It's like a night mirage." To build something peculiar like this, for no real reason, in the middle of nowhere, struck Meghan as wildly decadent. How cool to be so free! In that moment, she felt a tiny bit closer to this new definition of freedom, one wobbly dot in a sea of dancing dots.

"A ghost disco," mused Bree. "Playing a silent melody to invisible dancers." She stretched out her hands as if to catch snowflakes of light. Meghan shivered—it was colder out in the deep playa than it was near the camps.

The pair pedaled onward toward the orange plastic fence that marked the official city perimeter. As they biked along the fence, they came across another lonely outpost of burner imagination that was located at the farthest possible point from the camps. It was a round blue hut, four-feet high and covered in numerous, cross-crossing strings of Tibetan flags. Small river stones were placed in a ring around the hut, creating a defined space in the dust, a garden of emptiness. The narrow entrance to the hut glowed with a soft interior light, and three pairs of shoes were placed neatly next to the threshold. Meghan and Bree hopped off their bikes, took off their shoes, and crawled through.

Inside, an elaborate altar had been set up to host deities and sacred objects from a variety of world religions. Burners had contributed their own offerings to the altar—a bead necklace, an eyeliner pencil, a crystal, a shriveled apple, a red knit hat, a photo of an infant—and had offered their prayers in a large purple bound notebook encrusted with rhinestone jewels. A few candles illuminated the space and added a flicker of warmth against the night chill.

Meghan and Bree knelt on a dust-covered oriental carpet and absorbed the details of the small temple. On one side of the altar, a man and a woman sat motionless, eyes closed in deep meditation. On the other side, a man or a woman (it was hard to tell) in full Japanese character makeup and costume was engaged in a slow, inscrutable Butoh performance that seemed to be for no audience in particular.

Bree reached for the purple notebook and filled a page with a simple drawing of concentric heart shapes. The tiny center heart radiated its love outwards, beyond the notebook, beyond the temple, and out into the wild desert night. The image resonated deeply with Meghan. It was if that welcome slap by the greeter-sheriff had awoken some kernel within her, something with a force and signal of its own that was now slowly reverberating into her experience. Welcome home indeed.

The next morning, Meghan woke early to the feeling of hot sun penetrating the thin nylon roof of her tent, pushing her out of her cocoon and into a brave new world. By eight a.m., it was already desert hot—too hot to go back to sleep, and too stuffy to linger inside the tent. Surprised to find her camp still asleep, she pulled out a bottle of orange juice from a nearby cooler and stretched out in the fruit bowl to start the day slowly. She gazed at a few sleepy burners strolling or pedaling their way to a bank of port-a-potties nearby. A motorized cupcake drove slowly past the camp. Its driver sat inside a corrugated metal shell on wheels that must have contained some sort of engine and steering wheel. Only his head was visible, poking out of a froth of pink, puffy satin frosting. A large velvet cherry sewn onto a hat bobbed as he spluttered along. *That is the cutest thing ever!* Meghan imagined herself driving a cupcake. What flavor would she be? She pondered this question with seriousness and drew a blank. She was neither chocolate nor vanilla, marshmallow nor buttercream, nuts nor sprinkles. She could drive any cupcake, but which would be the *right* cupcake? Which would be the perfect representation of *her*? Meghan's heart sank. She hadn't a clue.

As Meghan oriented herself to the Burning Man reality, she considered the shattered reality that she had left behind in the "default world," in her everyday life. Even though the event only lasted a week, it offered an opportunity to reset her compass after two life-changing events had recently altered her course.

The first was the end of her four-year relationship with Diego. Not unexpected, nor unwelcome, the break-up was also not without the destabilizing tremors of loss, the cold ache of loneliness. It wasn't that they didn't love each other, or enjoy each other's company, or share common interests. It wasn't that the twin bonfires of romance and desire had finally died out. Meghan concluded that it was simply because they were two fiercely separate individuals, both inflexible and unwilling to let go of their sense of "me" in order to build an "us." Their relationship had been more of an alliance than a union, held together by joint agreement rather than shared need. Over time, their ties had eroded slowly, imperceptibly. Now, when the two selves collided, there was no common shelter.

"I'm sorry, *querida*," Diego had said, during their weekend away in Napa with his friends. He had folded Meghan into his arms after yet another furious stalemate about some petty issue already long forgotten. Even then, it was as if they were both engaged in separate arguments, two parallel beings fighting their own perception of the other, rather than connecting to a shared dialog.

"I'm sorry too, baby," she had replied, hot tears finally breaking through frustration, her protective shell. "I'm tired of fighting."

"Me too. I think…" he'd continued, taking a deep breath, "Megs, I think it's not going to work between us." He hugged her tighter. "We're just too…different." The truth hit home for Meghan immediately. Still, with those words finally unleashed, she'd felt the familiar comfort of his embrace begin to fade, along with her dream of a future together that had never really taken shape.

"Yeah, I guess so, Digs," Meghan had agreed, choking back hurt and hurtful words. *Be mature*, she had told herself. *Be kind.* "I miss you already." She twisted out of his arms and gathered her things to head back to San Francisco. As she drove home, she'd felt her sense of self being swallowed up by an immense emptiness, one that seemed impossible to comprehend let alone transform into something new.

Thinking back on that day from the newfound comfort of the fruit bowl, Meghan still didn't quite understand what had gone wrong between them. Maybe they both had issues around intimacy or communication or compromise—all those ingredients that were critical to the long-term health of a relationship. Maybe they each had different priorities that didn't align. Clearly, they were unable to support each other's priorities, which only served to reinforce their personal borders.

In the weeks after the break-up, Meghan had floated in a no man's land free from major commitments—first from a partner, and then from a job. For the second time in her career, she found herself suddenly laid off mid-stride, right when she was working at her peak potential. Four years of leading marketing campaigns at Del Oro Games had brought Meghan a string of tangible achievements and a feeling of control over her destiny. The work she had produced there mattered, had made a difference to the business. Working at Del Oro had grounded her with a sense of meaning that seemed so hard to come by in other areas of her life. Even working alongside Diego, sharing a daily routine and focus, had made less of an impact than the job itself. After Diego had left the company months prior, Meghan had continued to thrive as Del Oro's games gained momentum in the marketplace.

"I'm sorry, Megs," Ken had said, giving her a brief, but heartfelt hug. Earlier that day, he and Dave had announced to their two dozen employees that Del Oro was being acquired by a corporate gaming giant and that nearly half of their staff would sadly not be coming along. Although a representative of the giant was present for the announcement, the layoff was unlike Meghan's previous experience. It was as informal as the scrappy start-up and entirely devoid of corporate HR spin. This time, reality was reality, and it didn't make sense to package it up into something else.

"They've already got a huge marketing department," Ken continued, looking despondent.

"A well-staffed marketing machine," said Dave as Ken shot him a warning glare. Dave gave Meghan a hug and quickly pulled back, like the snap of a rubber band.

"But they'll prioritize you in case any openings come up," Ken nodded hopefully, as if to conjure up an offer right then and there. "You're on their A-List."

"Their AAA-List," echoed Dave, pun intended.

"I'm sorry too, guys," Meghan had replied calmly, dry-eyed. "Thank you for everything. I'll miss working here." Unlike her previous experience, the layoff news had taken her and her colleagues completely by surprise. She'd thought Ken and Dave were aiming for an eventual IPO and not a buy-out, and like Diego and his friends Kari and Ravi, she'd been hoping to gain a good bounty of stock options as an early employee. But in this fickle industry, no plan was ever truly dependable. Meghan had learned this lesson the first time, and had since hardened herself against expectation and complacency. So, when change rolled into Del Oro like a rogue wave threatening to drown everyone in its path, she had learned how to dive through it.

Ken and Dave had both looked on, downcast and apologetic, as she packed her personal things into a file box and walked out of the Del Oro office for the last time. She drove home feeling unmoored and also immobilized, as if someone had pushed the "pause" button once again without her consent.

By the time she arrived at Burning Man, only a couple of weeks later, Meghan had fully embraced that pause.

"I'm here to decompress from all the shit that's happened lately," she had declared to Bree as they cooked scrambled eggs and sausage on a compact propane stove. "I need to regroup. Catch my breath."

"You go, girl," replied Bree as she divided the breakfast onto three pink plastic plates.

Newly single, newly unemployed, the blank canvas of Black Rock Desert beckoned to Meghan. Here, she could begin a new journey! However, as the week unfolded, Meghan became aware that this was a journey with no destination. It was more important than her aspirations, more important than finding love or being an artist. This journey was about living, not about producing evidence of a life worth living. Simply living would mean owning and integrating all sides of herself into a wholeness that could be present in every moment. But first, she needed to crack open the façade that she had carefully curated—for her own perception, as well as for others.

In the microcosm of Burning Man, guided by the principle of radical self-expression, Meghan allowed new facets of self to emerge through experiencing a new relationship with art, environment, and community. Every spontaneous, unscripted interaction offered an opportunity for discovery. Every experience beyond her control eroded her inner rigidity just a little bit more. She was astonished to learn that many of the event's amazing art pieces would be burned at the end of the week. Their brief existence transformed her perspective on what art could be, or should be. Art could be as ephemeral as life itself, yet still make a tremendous impact. What about a life, simply lived—her life was also ephemeral, but did it also have impact? Meghan wondered how long this question would continue to haunt her.

As she became more familiar with the culture, Meghan discovered an openness within herself that surprised her. She could be biking past a camp one moment, then perfectly at ease sitting on the camp's couch with strangers who felt like old friends (whom she'd never see again). She could flawlessly produce a joke in return for a drink, a kiss in return for a name, a secret in return for a moment of human connection powerful enough to make her reflect on the depths of her own distrust. She could even allow herself the rarest of pleasures: a fleeting playa romance. Everything else in this surreal city was temporary, so why not friends and lovers both?

Elliot Spence, aka Raven, was one of fifty burners waiting to buy coffee at the long café counter at Center Camp. A great Bedouin tent located at the 6:00 radial, the Center Camp tent was part of Black Rock City infrastructure and the hub of Burning Man culture and activity. It was not only the largest camp in the city, it also served as a meeting place, performance space, art gallery, information center, coffee bar, and point of orientation for most burners. A constellation of civic services surrounded the main tent, including ice sales, bike repair, and even an official

U.S. post office. Coffee drinks at Center Camp, along with ice at Camp Arctica, were the only items for sale in the entire city.

By late morning, mid-week, Center Camp was packed. Meghan and Bree had biked over to check out the scene and have a mocha latte. Standing in long, slow lines, the café's patrons were chatty and patient. No one expected the same barista efficiency as back home. Besides—time was elastic at Burning Man and no one kept track.

"Cool hat," said Bree, pointing to the black top hat in front of them. It was extra tall and completely covered by garlands of black silk roses. White playa dust on the rose petals created a curious reverse shadow effect. The guy wearing it was extra tall as well and dressed in a crumpled black frock coat. Despite the dust, he looked to Meghan like he'd just stepped out of an Edward Gorey pen and ink illustration. His look fell somewhere in between Grateful Dead fan, goth, steam punk, and history nerd.

"Hi, I'm Bree," her friend continued, extending a hand to the stranger.

"Raven. At your service, madam," the guy said, bowing slightly and shaking Bree's hand with a single pump. "You can call me Raven or Elliot—whatever." He shrugged his shoulders amiably and smiled at Meghan. Kind eyes, gentle disposition, a flicker of humor.

"Megs," Meghan said shyly, shaking his hand. This was not the time to suddenly feel shy!

"Charmed," Raven replied, touching the brim of his hat.

They fell silent, and Meghan ran her eyes up and down the back of the tall, dark silhouette in front of them. Raven eventually stepped up to the counter, ordered and collected his drink, then drifted into the throng of burners milling around the Center Camp tent.

As Bree picked up her mocha latte, she spied a friend pulling up to the bike rack outside and darted off to say hello. Meghan took her drink and found a place to sit on one of the many dust-caked couches scattered around the sizeable space. It wasn't cool inside the tent, but at least it was shaded from the fierce morning sun. She glanced up, simply happy to spot a circle of blue sky peeking through the roof of the tent, which was covered in triangular swathes of canvas. A guitar and flute performance was happening on one of the small stages along the perimeter of the tent. Another stage hosted a spoken word performance, barely audible to anyone beyond the front row. The center circle of the tent was an open space for spontaneous performance, or lounging, whichever happened first.

Facing the center, Meghan watched a strange dance being performed by three couples. She found the dancers exceptionally beautiful, with striking faces and lean, muscular bodies. Two of the women sported a shower of fine braids woven with multi-colored ribbon. The male dancers were shirtless, their tanned torsos and tattoos bleached by a fine film of dust. Two men standing alongside completed the tribe by drumming and singing in accompaniment. Each couple interacted slowly and seamlessly as they parried and kicked and tumbled with great discipline, yet without touching, nor taking their eyes off of their partner. Captivated by the slow, fluid movement, the dialogue in motion between dancers, Meghan recognized a new feeling emerge. She was actually happy just to watch. Her role as audience to this beautiful performance fully satisfied her without interference from wishing that she could dance like that, that she was one of these graceful performers.

"Capoeira," a voice whispered to her right. She turned around to see Raven sipping coffee on the couch next to her. "Brazilian martial arts," he added.

"I thought they were miming a knife-fight," replied Meghan, smiling. In a rare moment of instinct, she stood up and went to sit next to Raven. Reflecting later, she realized it was the first time she'd ever made the first move to explore a romantic opportunity, rather than just letting it happen, or not.

After an hour of playful chit chat, the two decided to wander a bit together and strolled out of the main entrance of the Center Camp tent and out into the open playa. The Man stood in full-frontal view at the end of a wide boulevard delineated by tall wooden posts designed to hold lanterns after dark. They detoured from the boulevard to check out one of the art pieces that dotted the playascape around The Man. It was a massive steel structure that supported three granite boulders suspended from I-beams. The boulders rotated slowly, carousel-like. Diego would have called the piece "10x," Meghan mused. Extreme art. The monumental scale and scope of the piece, the effort to transport and build such a thing in a remote desert, was ten times greater than one could imagine.

A few burners had climbed up to ride the boulders. "Hey, I know that guy!" Meghan exclaimed to Raven, pointing to one of the riders. "He's a friend of my ex."

There was Ravi, clad in purple velvet pants and black Stetson hat, astride one of the boulders with his arms wrapped around another cowboy. *That's his ex, Nico*, Meghan realized. They must be back together. Since breaking up with Diego, she'd fallen off that particular gossip grapevine.

"Hey, Ravi!" she called up to them. "Hey, Nico!" They waved back, and Ravi amplified the greeting by waving his hat in true cowboy style.

As Meghan and Raven stood contemplating their next destination, a dust storm twisted up out of nowhere and covered the entire area in a thick white blanket, making it impossible to see anything at all. The two quickly pulled up the dust goggles that they wore around their necks during the day. Whiteouts could materialize at any time and last minutes or hours—there was no way to know.

"My camp is really close to here," Raven said, reaching blindly for Meghan's hand.

"Okay, let's go," she replied, and surprised herself yet again by letting this gothic ghost guide her through the white shadows.

Invasive dust and searing heat, two elements that Meghan struggled with in the beginning of the week, led her to a new relationship with the physical world. When dust invaded every inch of her body, every nook of her tent, and every surface of her camp—even, mysteriously, closed bags of food—what could she do but find a way to be okay with it? Whiteouts ruined afternoon plans. Daytime temperatures demanded protection and disciplined hydration. The desert's laws were non-negotiable. It was tough at first, but she learned to relax with the messy, the unpredictable. An imperfect self. She learned to feel socially acceptable caked in dust, and with Raven, she even felt sexy. Meghan spent that afternoon, and a couple more that week, cocooned in Raven's tent.

As the sun dropped below the mountain ridge on Saturday evening, Camp Fruitopia prepared for the festival's grand finale: the burning of The Man. The camp had run out of fruit the day before, but luckily the bar was still well-stocked. Rence got creative with camp tradition and made Cuba Libres for everyone using cherry-flavored cola. Bree and Meghan dressed in their most colorful clothes. A campmate named Willow hauled out large boxes of multicolored glow sticks, and everyone pinned them to hats, lapels, belts, bicycle spokes—any surface that could easily be illuminated. Some campers had already sewn battery-powered light strips into their clothing, turning themselves into walking neon sculptures. Armed with cocktails and luminosity, the Fruitopia contingent ventured out toward The Man.

A moonless night accentuated the manmade light cast from thousands of glow-lit burners converging onto the open playa on foot or bike. Weaving among them were hundreds of brilliantly illuminated art cars adapted from all types of vehicles, from pedal-powered cycles to one-man golf carts to huge double-decker buses. Each expressed creativity or community in motion. Burners cruised the night playa inside an elaborate, metal-plated dragon that breathed fire, or on top of an elegant Viking ship, or sitting at a mobile tiki bar, or even on a hydraulic basket crane disguised to look like a flower.

"It looks like a black ocean out there," Meghan commented to Rence as she skipped a little to catch up with his fast pace. "With a flotilla of fairytale ships."

"A sea of dreams," he replied over his shoulder, clearly eager to get to the show as quickly as possible.

The three friends and their camp finally arrived at The Man, which was already surrounded by thousands of burners. This year, the forty-foot Man stood on a sixty-foot platform that was saucer-shaped, as if he were hitching a ride to Mars. The pre-show was underway as dozens of drummers and a hundred fire-spinners entertained an already warmed up crowd. The anticipation was palpable.

"This whole thing of burning The Man," Meghan said into Bree's ear, "it's kind of gruesome, don't you think? Like a macabre ritual from pagan times?"

"I know what you mean," shouted Bree into Meghan's ear. Were the drums getting even louder? "But really, The Man is about a concept and not a person. He can symbolize something different to each one of us. It's a very personal experience, yet also communal."

"Huh, okay," said Meghan. She didn't quite know what to think.

Another half hour passed and Meghan started to feel restless. Packed tightly into the crowd, she wasn't cold, but she wasn't comfortable either. She wished she were sitting on top of the party bus parked nearby. Suddenly, the music stopped and the crowd fell silent. All eyes were on The Man. During the event week, The Man had stood in a relaxed, neutral pose with his arms at his side. Now, his arms began to slowly rise, a mechanized greeting to his fellow burners, until he stood in his iconic stance. Arms raised wide. Ready.

In this moment, Meghan's heart skipped a beat. She was utterly transfixed by this simple, yet universal gesture. It was primal, as if The Man were simultaneously expressing triumph and surrender, pride and defiance. The Man was both reaching toward Heaven in a plea for spiritual connection and embracing the community on the ground. The gesture was a powerful statement of individuality and presence. The Man as mankind's leader, guiding us out of the darkness and into a state of grace. He said: I am here. I am real. Deal with me!

Meghan was so taken aback, that it took her a few minutes to become fully aware of the spectacle that was happening in front of her: the fireworks show, the cheering crowd, and finally, the lighting of The Man's platform. When the flames reached his feet, she snapped back to attention. The fire was vital and alive. She watched it trace the stylized lines of the sculpture's wooden frame. The flames leapt joyfully as they quickly consumed the earthly matter, turning concept into ash.

Again, Meghan was spellbound. Yet strangely, she was not as disturbed as she'd expected to be by the fate of The Man. Years later, Meghan would reflect on this moment for the hundredth time and finally come to realize, *I am The Man. The Man is me!* Like the iconic figure, Meghan was standing alone, proudly facing the world in both surrender and defiance. Arms held high. Come what may.

PART 4

CHAPTER 15

Diego

A cold January downpour beat down on Kari's Audi with a ferocity that was unusual during the Bay Area's brief nod to winter. Sitting in the passenger seat, Diego watched torrents of water hit the asphalt. The rain seemed even more concentrated along the narrow corridor of Highway 101 than on the office buildings and car parks and strip malls that lined this major route through Silicon Valley. During the morning commute, heavy traffic spanned twelve lanes and covered at least a hundred miles circling the bay. Could the weather system be attracted to the metal of all those cars, or their exhaust fumes, or some other magnetic force at play? Or it could just be an illusion? Diego didn't know much about thermodynamics.

The noise in the car was thunderous, and Kari was struggling to make himself heard on a check-in call with their new mentor Jiang. "We're putting the final touches on our next rev of the ShopFixa user interface," he shouted into his iPhone headset. "We took your advice and used a responsive design approach." Kari adjusted the ear buds in a futile attempt to better hear Jiang. "Yeah, it now looks great on phones and tablets as well as laptops." He caught Diego's eye and pointed to his ears, shaking his head. "Sure, we'd love to demo it at tonight's dinner." He paused. "We'd love to demo it. D-e-m-o it." Then, under his breath, "Damn it!"

Diego glanced at his friend and smiled. They had only been in the Cloud9 accelerator program for three weeks and already their progress had sped past expectations. The pace was fantastic! By the end of only three months, Fixa, Inc. would have real potential and momentum. Cloud9's expertise and resources would help them improve the ShopFixa user experience, establish a solid business foundation, and prepare the team for pitching to investors. In addition, Cloud9 offered modest, early-stage funding, which gave Kari and Diego the means to pay Chris and Dale full-time, and also entice Ravi to join them for the duration of the program.

"I'm taking a leave of absence from my job," Ravi announced to the team as they huddled around their allotted workspace at Cloud9 HQ in Palo Alto. The startup was provisioned with five silver Aaron desk chairs around a square white table topped with twenty-seven-inch high-end Apple monitors and a private network router. It represented only the tip of the Fixa iceberg—its massive infrastructure was concealed within the Cloud, the virtual environment that hosted modern computing magic.

"My manager was impressed that you guys got into Cloud9," Ravi continued brightly. "I think he's secretly working on his own thing, so maybe he wants to live vicariously." He flashed his trademark grin and tried to catch someone's eye around the table, but all were already deeply immersed in the tasks of the day. "Hello?! Where do I start?"

"We need you to concentrate on launch," Kari replied while intently scrolling through email on his phone. "We're at the alpha stage now, but getting really close to beta. We want to soft launch with an open beta test and get real users pounding on the software, giving us feedback."

"Roger that, boss," Ravi said, giving the distracted Kari a stiff salute. "And you'll need to overhaul your…um…website, if you can call it that." He glanced at Diego.

"Ha!" Diego chuckled, looking up at Ravi from his monitor. "It's a blank page with a download link. I think you can improve on that." He had full confidence in Ravi on that front.

"Oh, yeah," Ravi replied, nodding slowly.

To Diego and the Fixa crew, the atmosphere at Cloud9 was exhilarating. A hundred highly-motivated entrepreneurs—creative minds, blue sky thinkers, ambitious makers—were eager to share their work and brainstorm ideas with whomever sat at the long dining tables in the cafeteria wing of the building. Ideas cross-pollinated, and many startups were transformed by a single mealtime conversation. Cloud9 catered lunch and dinner, which encouraged participants to stay focused and work as long as they needed. Diego found himself in plenty of company on those nights when he worked until dawn to advance ShopFixa just a little further.

The program also brought in guest speakers each week to supplement their in-house expertise. Tech superstars, serial entrepreneurs, venture capital investors, C-Suite executives—all had invaluable wisdom to share with those just starting out on a similar journey. Diego particularly appreciated the highly personal stories of success and failure, which were certainly eye-opening. Building a great product was hard. He knew that all too well. But building a great company that can make that product successful was equally hard. It apparently involved a combination of skill, timing, and perseverance. What would be the perfect formula for Fixa?

"This is like one extended hackathon," Diego remarked to Kari and Ravi one day over cappuccinos and pastries in the sunny Cloud9 courtyard café. "Everyone's heads-down working side-by-side, hacking some technology, devoting everything they've got to manifesting their best ideas. It's beautiful, man." He bit into one crusty end of his croissant, releasing a flurry of buttery flakes.

"Totally," agreed Kari. A chiseled brown sugar cube plunged into delicate milk froth. "And the strange thing is, that everyone I've met seems genuinely supportive. I expected it to be more competitive, like a hackathon, but it seems like everyone wants each other to succeed." He stirred his coffee, contemplating this observation.

"Yeah, that is weird," said Diego, brushing flakes off the Android T-shirt he picked up at last year's Game Developers Conference. The apple green Android bot was playing a video game on a Nintendo Wii and yelling "Wii-hoo!"

"Maybe people feel like there's enough room in the tech world for new ideas," Ravi interjected, "with a market that is eager to try them all." He popped the last powder-coated bite of a huckleberry donut into his mouth. "This industry's unstoppable."

"There's also room to turn great ideas into unicorns and capture the hearts and minds of investors, as well as users." Kari's single-minded ambition was relentless. How many times had he declared that Fixa would someday reach unicorn status, valued at one billion dollars?

"As Marc Andreessen famously said, 'Software is eating the world.'" Diego was more interested in the meat of the beast—in achieving the inconceivable, making the myth a reality.

Ravi licked the sugar off his fingertips. "And the world is delicious."

Kari doubled down on the trio's optimism: "There are endless slices of the great American pie for smart startups with brilliant ideas."

"Mmmm…pie!" said the three in unison. *My god, we are so cliché sometimes,* mused Diego.

Month Two at Cloud9 saw Fixa take an important step. Sayid, one of the program mentors, advised the team to launch their software to market as soon as possible and improve on it later. "Just get something out there," he said. "Don't wait for it to be perfect." So, Diego, hands trembling and heart thumping, deployed the code that debuted ShopFixa™ Beta to the world. The moment after—profound silence, followed by waves of acute anxiety. What would happen from here? Was there really a home for his creation? Or would it float aimlessly out there, yet another piece of cyberspace junk.

The shopping bot's first beta testers were a handful of Ravi's gamer community associates. The software astonished the group by instantly learning the nuances of their personal gaming preferences and purchasing habits.

"Every week, my bot finds me new game titles that are so right on, they become instant favorites," enthused one tester.

"My bot helped me upgrade my game hardware," reported another. "It knew how much I could spend each week, which vendors had the best deals, and mapped out my purchases over a timeline. Super helpful."

Spurred on by the personalized results in their gaming life, the testers began to gradually seek help from ShopFixa in other areas of daily life, from buying music to groceries to birthday gifts for friends and family. *So far, so good,* thought Diego. *Thank God.*

The Fixa team spread the word about the beta test through friends and followers across their extensive social graph. They also posted on popular product discovery sites and technology forums hoping to attract a broad user base. Soon, ShopFixa began clocking a thousand downloads a day—an impressive rate for a nascent product with no media footprint. At the same time, the team continued to iterate on the product, rapidly rolling out new releases to address bug fixes, feature tweaks, and performance improvements that would bolster "our little puppy's wobbly first steps in the world," as Ravi put it.

During the testing period, Kari shifted his focus to launching a beta version of the company. Cloud9 provided business and legal advisors to help him set up a company structure and funding strategy that would get Fixa to the starting gate with venture capital firms. These mentors—his "A Team"— helped Kari understand the fundraising potential of the startup and how best to position the product, the team, and the company to investors in order to maximize that potential. They also put together a shortlist of target investors who were more likely to be interested in AI-powered products.

"Our Series A cash is somewhere in here, in this list," Kari declared, tapping hard on his laptop screen. "We just need to coax it out." Diego didn't quite get the art of negotiation, the mystical side of business. He envisioned Kari as a snake charmer in a suit and tie, luring cash out of the pockets of mesmerized investors.

With this influx of advice, the executive board of Fixa, Inc. got busy. Kari and Diego applied for patents on their most valuable assets: the algorithms and system applications that powered the shopping bot and made it unique. They formally incorporated the company and trademarked their brands to ensure that no one else could use the names. Kari formulated one-, three-, and five-year growth projections for the company, and used them to create a staffing plan and operating budget. He tasked Ravi to deliver a comprehensive marketing plan and budget that would take ShopFixa to the top of the Apple App Store and Google Play Store. After all, that's where they were headed.

"Actually, we want more than just the number one slot," Diego stated to the team at one of their daily standup meetings. He and Kari had just met with Jiang to formalize their greater vision to extend the user experience beyond shopping and build out the Fixa brand. Since handing the bulk of development to Chris and Dale, Diego had been quietly working on algorithms for different online tasks, and it was now time to productize them.

"Digs is right," Kari said. "We want to create a portfolio of apps that can help users accomplish a wide variety of things in their online life." His eyes shone with Fixa's grand mission and purpose. Was that fervor or fever? *Kari has been working too hard*, Diego thought.

"For example," Kari continued, "JobFixa will help you find and apply for the best job for you, and then help you land an interview." Diego felt his heart surge, as if they'd found a nugget of gold in an undiscovered river. "And DateFixa will help you live out your romantic or erotic fantasies."

"Until we come up with a solution for fixing the physical part," joked Ravi, "like with some kind of peripheral device." Laughter rippled through the group.

"GameFixa will play online games for you on your behalf," added Diego, noting a frown from Ravi and smile from Chris. "And similarly, FriendFixa will help you find friends and maintain a social network, without you having to do anything at all."

"Awesome!" exclaimed Chris, warming up to the concept. "I never have time to keep up with friends. I'd love to have someone I can ask to give me the latest highlights on this or that person without having to wade through all their posts and tweets myself."

"So, if you ever run into them IRL, in real life, you can skip the catch-up talk," said Ravi.

"Unless catch-up talk is like, your whole relationship," mused Dale. "Then I guess you save time by skipping that altogether. That's relationship efficiency for ya!" he chuckled.

"CashFixa will pay all your bills, bank all your income, manage your investments, and give you a bit of spending money each week," continued Kari. "It can even gamble for you, if that's something you usually do."

"Wow, so it'll help me keep up with all my bad habits?" asked Dale, who liked to play late night Texas hold 'em, despite his months-long losing streak.

"It's all configurable," replied Diego. "But your Fixas will first learn to imitate you exactly. They will be as good, or as bad, at playing games, managing money, getting a job or a date, as you are. Once they learn to be you, then you can tweak them."

"To be better than you," said Ravi. "To be Super You."

"Exactly." Diego looked at Kari and wished that he could fast forward to the future, where his legion of intelligent bots was thriving and growing. People would make smarter choices, the world would become a smarter place, and mankind's weaknesses would shrink and eventually disappear. For Diego, Fixa was not just about making life easier or relationships more harmonious. It wasn't even simply about promoting global peace and prosperity, although that was certainly a worthy outcome. Fixa was about taking a major step in human evolution. Today's flawed human would become tomorrow's Neanderthal.

By the start of Month Three, Chris had begun working nearly half-time on coding the friend bot and Dale on the dating bot, while Ravi gathered feedback from the shopping bot beta trial and logged bugs and new feature requests. Momentum was strong and the team was performing at their peak, which allowed Diego and Kari to focus on their final milestone at Cloud9: Demo Day.

During the last week of the program, each startup presented their company, products, and technology to a mock panel of investors made up of Cloud9 advisors and a couple of representatives from real venture capital firms. They had to pull together all the threads of their work to date into one unique story that was professional, credible, and persuasive. For Fixa, like many startups in the accelerator, the next step after graduating was to secure funding to help them get established during the critical early growth phase.

For Diego, delivering a business pitch was the absolute last thing he wanted to do. He'd rather be side-by-side with Chris and Dale immersed in millions of lines of code that delivered a tangible, actionable result. Even an all-night coding marathon was preferable to thirty minutes on stage in front of industry experts. Although Kari had some experience giving presentations during his MBA course, and could express more zeal than his five team members put together, he was not a natural presenter. The minute Kari would step up to the podium, all charm and grace seemed to vanish, leaving a wooden shell of a man delivering bone-dry facts. Diego was afraid that when it was his own turn to talk, he'd forget half of the important messages and focus on some obscure detail that no one cared about.

"Please don't bore the investors to death, Kari," Ravi said, failing to be helpful. Diego lightly punched Ravi's arm in warning. *Please don't scare Kari, Ravi.*

"That goes for you too, Digs," Ravi added, rubbing his arm.

"We want the audience to look forward to every statement that you utter, not daydream about their dinner plans," Jiang said diplomatically. "We can work on this together. Practice, practice, practice!"

During one practice session, Diego had a flash of brilliance. "Let's call in a pro," he said to Kari, who looked truly exhausted for the first time in months. "Let's ask Kira to help." Kari brightened up, and the next day Kira took an Uber from her office over to Cloud9 to have lunch with the Fixa team.

"Okay, you've got me for an hour. Let's see how far we can get." Kira rubbed her palms together in anticipation.

Kira was indeed a pro. She was a born speaker and regularly delivered high-profile presentations as part of her communications role. Her job also involved coaching her company's CEO and other C-Suite executives before they went onstage to present to thousands of employees worldwide. Direct, precise, and efficient, Kira could shape a speaker into an effective communicator in only a few hours.

"There is a unique, likeable personality inside every buttoned-up executive," Kira always said. "Sometimes I feel like Michelangelo pulling a human out of a block of marble!"

Diego thought about Kira's father the senator, who was known for his charisma. Was Kira's talent due to nature or nurture? He admired her ability to shape a real-life moment with nuance and feeling, in real time. Such artistry was hard to recreate online.

Over the following couple of weeks, Kira spent several lunch hours and evenings with the team, helping Kari and Diego to articulate the Fixa vision, brand, and backstory. She ran them through practice drills, over and over, until the presentation script seeped into Diego's daily thought stream. She slashed their PowerPoint slide deck by a third, and helped them hone the slide content so it was clear and on-point. She also helped them tailor their story for the press, pulling out the relevant points that would position them as a newsworthy startup.

Kira's coaching paid off. On Demo Day, Kari and Diego stepped up, with newfound confidence, onto the small, temporary stage that was set up in the leafy atrium of Cloud9's office building. The founders gave an acceptable presentation. No major flaws and only a few minor stumbles. Diego felt vaguely okay about it, but he'd noticed that no one on the mock panel smiled before, during, or after. Kari was startlingly pale, but appeared surprisingly at ease in the spotlight. Diego saw him lock eyes with Kira in the audience and his mood visibly brightened. Good, because the feedback session was next.

"Solid performance," said one panelist flatly. "You could fine tune some of the slides, they're still too wordy."

Okay, whatever, thought Diego. He felt Kari tense up beside him. *Steady on, man. Channel the snake charmer.*

"Good job," said another panelist, who seemed to want to be more helpful. "Work more on establishing your product/market fit. Why do people need a Fixa bot? What problem are you trying to solve? Nailing that problem will help you sell in to investors." Diego caught eyes with Jiang, who was sitting in the front row of the audience. She silently mouthed, "Let's work on that." He nodded, not quite sure why they hadn't expanded on that point.

"Congrats on a good pitch," said a third panelist casually. "I want to see deeper stats on your users and usage. Who exactly is using ShopFixa now, and how exactly are they using it?" Diego added analytics to his mental checklist. A new task for Ravi.

"What's your exit strategy?" asked another, frowning. "IPO, acquisition…what?"

Damn. We're still working on an entrance strategy.

~

After graduating from the program, the Fixa team relocated back to San Francisco. This time, they landed in a co-working space called The House, which occupied a former auto parts warehouse in the SOMA district. The three-story concrete building was partitioned into twenty small offices with a shared conference room, lounge, kitchen, and bathroom on each floor. The startup occupied a four-hundred-square-foot space and even had its own door, which felt to Diego like a step forward. Kari bought some used tables, chairs, and monitors on Craigslist, and found two huge whiteboards on wheels from an office liquidator. They all contributed an assortment of supplies foraged from their home offices. One small ficus tree, a gift from Kira, stood in a corner near the room's only window. Fixa, Inc. was open for business.

Ravi returned to his old job, clearly reluctant to leave the team and his contribution to the project. *He'll be back,* Diego predicted. *Once we raise our Series A.* Chris and Dale had agreed to stay on, satisfied for the moment with a modest paycheck and a professional challenge that was simply too good to let go. In the meantime, Kari continued to methodically build his network of technical contacts, Fixa's future talent.

By April, the spring winds had arrived to flush out stale air from the sluggish winter, overzealous in their mission to cleanse San Francisco of unwanted carbon and particulates. Great gusts raced through the city labyrinth toward the open waters of the Bay, pummeling bicyclists and pedestrians as they turned this corner or that. Smog in San Francisco was often surprisingly insidious, with spare-the-air warnings issued on blue sky days. Such vigorous winds brought not only freshly oxygenated air, but also clear evidence of urban detox.

Diego hunched his shoulders against a cool draft as he walked back to the office from Trader Joe's, where he'd bought a tuna salad for lunch, along with some organic bananas and fig bars for the team. He had needed a long walk to clear his head. Dealing with business issues resulted in fragmented days and mental clutter that got in the way of his developer flow. The fewer demands on his mind, the more productive he could be when coding. Diego was working on a particularly tricky aspect of CashFixa, and he needed all the head space he could free up.

Diego stepped into the street to avoid a row of ragged tents that crowded the city sidewalk. It was one of dozens of homeless tent camps that seemed to pop up overnight around SOMA, like mushrooms after a storm. The tents were simply new packaging on the same chronic, seemingly unsolvable problem. Last year, Diego had participated in a city-sponsored, weekend hackathon that challenged creative minds from the technology and non-profit worlds to collaborate on new ideas to address homelessness. Some interesting concepts had come out of it: iPad-powered kiosks for reserving a bed in a homeless shelter, mobile payments for day laborers, a service request app for social workers in the field. There was no silver bullet of course, no technical solution to an ancient human problem that had become exponentially more complex in the modern world. Diego was most interested in building a predictive model for homelessness that could project the scale of city resources needed over time. But who could predict how complex American life may be in twenty, fifty, or a hundred years? *The way the world is going,* he mused grimly, *we may all end up homeless.*

Diego skirted several mounds of camp garbage: random heaps of old junk, clothing, chicken bones, empty food cartons, and who knew what. *That's no way to live,* he thought. The worst was some squishy organic matter that he really did not want to identify, especially right before eating lunch. *If the city's going to allow the tent camps to exist,* he grumbled, *can't it at least provide trash bins or dumpsters or something to maintain some order, some dignity?* Diego's train of thought landed where it usually did these days. Could there be a Fixa for this problem? How could a bot help solve homelessness? He held his breath against the stench until he reached the next intersection.

As Diego stepped off the curb, the first few bars of ukulele-infused "Somewhere Over the Rainbow" strummed into his thoughts. He shifted the grocery bag and reached into his back pocket to pull out his phone. He'd told the team that he'd be back in twenty minutes, so the call surprised him. "Hello?" he said gruffly, failing to check at the caller ID.

"*Mijo*," answered his sister Lucita, her voice tinged with urgency. "We need your help. It's important."

"*Hola*, Luci," replied Diego and stopped in mid-stride. "What? Why? What's going on?" Over the past three years, life for Diego and his family had followed a similar trajectory. The Garcias were working hard to establish themselves in Cancún, and Diego was immersed in founding a startup. All were thriving, yet too busy to catch up as often as in the past. When Diego did have the chance to speak with his mother, Luz would remind him that he'd only visited them once so far, and only at Christmas, as if the holiday didn't count as a full visit. He'd be left with sharp pangs of guilt and a vague uneasiness that just seemed to amplify the distance between them. On this call, however, Diego felt immediately on guard. Sometimes Lucita could be melodramatic about minor things, but she was also the family spokesperson.

"*Mamá* is really worried about Teresa," she said. "We haven't heard from her for more than two months and she won't return our calls. The longest time ever! Now that we're all in Cancún, we can't just get in the car and go see her, you know?" Her voice sounded pinched with worry.

"Is she still living in Laughlin with that guy, Berto?" Diego asked. His mind cycled through everything he knew about Teresa's current situation: alcohol, abusive husband, gambling debt, part-time job at 7-Eleven, failed attempts to conceive a child, bouts of crushing depression. While the rest of the Garcia family built new lives in Cancún, Teresa had unraveled. She seemed barely able to make it through each day, let alone maintain family connections. Just like *Papá.*

"Yep. That fucker has really messed her up," Lucita replied angrily. "We need to get her out of there. Can you help us, *mijo*? Can you go check on her, see what the hell's going on? And then put her on a flight to Cancún? Do whatever it takes!"

"Yeah, okay," said Diego slowly. "I can do that." A rush of competing responsibilities stampeded into his awareness. Release updated code to ShopFixa today and JobFixa on Monday. Finish tweaking the CashFixa algorithm so Dale can get a prototype up and running by Tuesday. Test out a new runtime platform to see if it's a good fit with their system architecture. All top priorities for the coming week. Most importantly, he needed to help Kari prepare for their first major investor pitch at the end of the month. They absolutely had to be ready for prime time. No mentors, no feedback. Just the two of them, facing people who held the future in their hands.

"*Gracias, Diego, te quiero.*" Lucita began to cry. Diego closed his eyes and imagined himself hugging his sister, and then his mother, who would no doubt be eavesdropping and sobbing uncontrollably.

"Don't worry, Luci, it will all be okay. *Okay? Te quiero tambien.* I'll fly down there tomorrow. I promise." He was the family fixer, summoned and reporting for duty.

The next morning, Diego boarded a flight to Las Vegas with a small carry-on bag and his backpack. He was able to do some work on the plane thanks to in-flight WiFi, moving one thread of his life forward while he picked up another. Diego flew through a backlog of unread emails and organizational tasks, in a rush to get as much done as possible before focusing a hundred percent of his attention on the family crisis.

It was late morning by the time Diego picked up the rental car and headed south on Highway 95. He plugged his phone into the Hyundai's audio system and pulled up one of his favorite Reggae playlists. There was something about driving to lusciously relaxed beats in the heat of the day along an empty desert highway that opened the soul. For the hour and a half drive, he simply existed in vast space and endless time.

Laughlin was situated in the triangular tip of southern Nevada, like a compass needle pointing straight down toward the Mexican border. When Diego arrived, he decided to go directly to Teresa's place and assess the situation first, before checking into one of the local motels. He wasn't quite sure how he would convince his sister to come to Cancún with him, but he expected it to take a few rounds of conversation over the course of a day or two.

Google Maps guided Diego past strip malls, motels, a couple of towering casinos, and a deep blue expanse of the Colorado River. He drove slowly. Dale had said, "Man, the odds of getting a speeding ticket in Laughlin are higher than winning a pound of pennies in one of the slots." He knew there must be thousands of slot machines that power this town. If only they could also generate electricity, he thought, with each pull of the machine's lever. Greenwash the greed.

The Twin Palms Trailer Park was located at the edge of town, facing a no man's land of desert scrub that extended several miles west to meet the pale pink Dead Mountain Wilderness in the distance. Teresa's mobile home was in the back of the lot.

"Teresa, *mija*." He knocked firmly on the door. "It's me, Diego." It was eerily quiet and the faded blue curtains were pulled shut. He wondered if she was home. He knocked again and then heard the sound of a chain lock slide out of its track.

Teresa opened the door a crack and peered out, squinting in the bright daylight. Diego was so taken aback that he actually took a step backward. Lucita had warned him that their sister had changed since he'd seen her three summers ago, but he'd had no idea how much. His once shapely, lively sister, the one who could cook a feast all day and then dance salsa all night had morphed into a listless waif. How much weight had she lost? Thirty pounds? Forty? Dressed in grubby, pink polka dot pajamas, she looked almost otherworldly to him—pale-faced, wild-haired, mournful. As if she might let out a thin wail any moment.

"Oh. Hi," Teresa said, simply staring at him, expressionless, waiting for direction.

"Um, can I come in?" Diego asked gently. She opened the door all the way and stepped aside to let him pass. He turned to give her a hug, noting the sharp shoulder blades under his fingers and the sour cloud of alcohol and sweat. "Hey, so great to see you!" He tried to sound upbeat but low-key, as if she could be scared off by too much cheer.

"Great to see you too D," Teresa replied half-heartedly, avoiding his eyes. She swept her arm weakly in the direction of the living room and said, "Have a seat."

As Diego scanned the seven hundred square feet of living space, he grew increasingly alarmed. It was complete chaos, as if a mischievous spirit had randomly pulled objects out of cupboards and drawers and scattered them haphazardly across any and all surfaces. A thin film of grime covered the kitchen counters and appliances, which in turn was covered by dirty dishes, pizza boxes, and Budweiser bottles. Dust and lint clung to furnishings and fixtures in the other rooms, and not a single object looked actually clean.

The living room was the worst. Alongside the couch, Diego spotted ten empty liter bottles of Cuervo Gold and Jack Daniels that, like bowling pins, stood or lay knocked over with its dregs seeping out. In the middle of the room stood a coffee table, its walnut-colored veneer faded and scuffed with what looked like a row of notches cut into one side. Diego suspected that the six-inch hunting knife lying on the stained beige carpet underneath was the likely culprit. On top stood a half-full bottle of neon-green Gatorade, along with a soaking wet roll of paper towels, a cereal bowl full of soggy cigarettes, and a souvenir ash tray full of cracker mush. A massive pile of his and her laundry (clean?) was heaped on the shabby seat of a brown vinyl La-Z-Boy recliner, waiting to be sorted. Mysteriously, a dozen or so pairs of men's sneakers lay in a jumble next to a fifty-four-inch flat-screen TV that was streaming the Home Shopping Network with the sound off. *Oh my God,* thought Diego.

He sat down on the black chenille couch, immediately sensed wetness, and bolted back up onto his feet, utterly disgusted. Everything seemed wet in here. Everything stained. He felt suddenly claustrophobic.

"Teresa, *querida,*" he said, struggling to keep his voice low and even. "I've come to tell you that *Mamá* needs you." His mind was racing. *Think fast. Improvise,* he told himself. Like Lucita had said: do whatever it takes.

"Oh?" she said numbly. "What's wrong?" She was twisting a lock of hair around her finger, little-girl like, yet her eyes flashed something darker. Suspicion? Malice? She looked like a ghost in a horror film.

"She's sick," he lied. "Actually, she's dying," he lied again. This was easier than he'd thought. "It's liver cancer. The doctors have given her only a couple of weeks left." He tried to look heartbroken and forced himself to accept that sometimes a small lie is the only way forward.

"Oh my God," Teresa said sharply. "That's horrible!" She seemed to snap to attention.

She's back! Diego thought. *Now I just have to keep her old self out of hiding long enough to get her to safety.*

"We need to go to see her now, before it's too late," he replied, infusing urgency into the situation. "I have two tickets to Cancún flying out tomorrow. We can leave now and spend the night in Vegas." Much better to get her as far away as possible, as soon as possible. He didn't want to risk waiting until morning.

"Leave now?" she said weakly, back in her bubble. "What about Berto? He comes home from work in a couple of hours." She morphed again into a scared creature, eyes darting, hands twitching. "He'll wonder where I am."

"We can call him from the road," replied Diego in his most soothing voice. A current of panic shot through him. What if that asshole comes home and ruins this.

"He'll understand," he continued softly. "It's your *Mamá*! I'm sure he'd do the same for his mother!" He gently rubbed Teresa's back and guided her to the bedroom. "I'll help you pack a bag. Where do you keep your passport?" This was easier than he'd expected. Right on schedule—he'd be back home in San Francisco in three days at the most.

An hour later, they were ready to go. Teresa had showered and a sweet herbal-floral scent wafted pleasantly from her thick wet rope of black hair. None of his girlfriends had smelled like this, Diego mused. She smelled like his childhood, like a house full of five women using the same Herbal Essences shampoo.

He carried Teresa's suitcase to the Hyundai and placed it in the trunk next to his. As Teresa locked the front door, she threw a troubling wrinkle into his escape plan.

"I have to take my car," she declared. "I want to come home as soon as I can," she insisted, her voice rising. "And I'll need my car." She stared hard at him, challenging and defiant. The old Teresa.

"Teresa, *mija*, I have the rental. It's new and comfortable, and it will get us there faster." *And it's reliable,* he thought. *We will actually get there.* "Besides," Diego added, "it's got a great radio. We can blast it all the way there."

"No, Diego!" She was becoming more and more agitated. "I want my car! I need my car!" *Man, that girl can be stubborn,* he thought.

"I can just follow you," Teresa added decisively.

He was getting worried now. Would she actually follow him, or suddenly turn around and go back to Laughlin when he wasn't keeping watch in the rearview mirror? "Okay, Okay, we'll take your car," he conceded. "No problem."

The clock was ticking—Berto would be home soon, and every minute of delay increased the risk of Teresa changing her mind altogether. So, Diego transferred the bags to Teresa's road-worn Honda Civic and dropped his car off at a Budget Rental office in downtown Laughlin. As he slid into the driver's seat of the aging Honda, he said a silent prayer that it would take them all the way to Las Vegas.

Diego stopped at the nearest gas station to fill up the tank before heading out of town. The siblings each bought themselves a sixteen-ounce Slurpee, choosing their childhood favorites: "red flavored" for Diego and "blue flavored" for Teresa. They simultaneously took a first pull from the cup's thick straw and, laughing, immediately pressed a palm to their forehead when the frozen slush produced its familiar "brain freeze." Diego's heart lifted as they cruised onto the highway toward an unfrozen future for his troubled sister.

As the late afternoon sun inched toward the western foothills, Highway 95 took them through a vast expanse of minimalist landscape awash in the subtlest earth tone hues—browns and mauves and yellows—like an antique watercolor faded long ago by the hot sun. A half-hour into their drive, both started feeling the cold pint of sugary liquid press down on their bladders. They soon spotted a sign for a rest stop and pulled off the highway.

The state operated rest stop looked as austere as its environment, though somehow even more forlorn. *Maybe because it was manmade*, Diego thought, *we expect it to humanize a bleak landscape instead of mirror it.* The rest stops in California were almost grand by comparison. In the center of a horseshoe-shaped parking lot sat a small shoebox of a building. Its concrete block walls showed traces of white paint that had mostly peeled off. In front, two weather-beaten plastic picnic tables waited for the opportunity to support hungry travelers. In back, a stand of small scrubby trees failed to provide any real shade from the desert sun. Small signs on the restroom doors designated the men's side and women's side.

"I'll be a few minutes," Teresa said as she opened the car door and scuttled off toward the women's room. Diego noted an oval glass shape protruding slightly from the side of her pink canvas bag. A half pint of something. *Okay, gotta let that go for now,* he told himself. *We've come this far.*

Diego looked around and saw no other cars parked at the rest stop. He strolled toward the men's room and his mind cycled through a few classic thrillers, searching for a rest stop scene as reference. As he was zipping up at the urinal, he heard the low growl of a large pickup truck pull into the parking lot. Two doors opened and slammed shut, followed by the muffled sound of male voices.

Suddenly, a woman's scream pierced the block wall that divided the two restrooms, and then, a muted thud. Teresa? Diego's heart skipped a beat. Before he could react, a large man in dusty black jeans and T-shirt stood in the doorway of the men's room. His six-foot, husky frame blocked the daylight and Diego's ability to check on Teresa. *What's going on? Oh my God,* he realized. *It's Berto.*

"You motherfucker," rasped Berto, rage oozing from deep within his being. It wasn't just the righteous anger of a jealous husband; it was the white-hot, molten fury of a man whose authority has been usurped and used against him. He stepped slowly toward Diego, stabbing a sausage-sized finger sharply in the air. "You think you can kidnap my wife? Huh?" He pushed Diego's shoulder. "Huh??"

Diego's mind raced. How did Berto just appear like this, out of the blue? Teresa must have texted her husband while Diego wasn't looking. Maybe at the gas station. What the fuck was she doing?

"Hey, Berto," Diego said in his friendliest tone. "It's okay, man," he said, opening his hands wide in diplomatic gesture. "Our mother is really sick. She's dying from cancer and Teresa wants to see her one last time." How could he de-escalate this crazy situation? Fear seeped into his awareness, turning his body into lead. He stared at his brother-in-law, immobile.

"Bullshit," Berto barked. "I talked to the bitch myself. One, two months back. She didn't say nothing about no cancer." He looked ready to explode.

"No, it's true," Diego replied earnestly. "She's got liver cancer. We didn't know about it until it was too late. She doesn't have much time." Words stuck, panic rose, his throat desiccated as the dirt outside. "Teresa will be back in a couple of days, Berto. You won't even notice the time." He could see that this argument was hitting a wall, but he couldn't think of a better one.

"You don't tell *me* what to do, you little shit," snarled Berto. "You do NOT tell me what to do!" The man's voice escalated along with his vehemence. "You stay out of our lives," he shouted. "Or I'll kill your fucking ass."

Toe to toe now with Diego, Berto spit the words into his face with breath that stank of stale cigarettes and Red Bull. *This is unreal*, thought Diego. What was that restroom scene from that film…he forced his mind back into the heat of the moment.

"Oh, hey, Berto," Diego stammered, his back now against the metal partition of one of the toilet stalls. "I don't mean any harm, man. I was just trying to help the family, you know?" *Some fixer I am,* Diego thought. He should be the furious one. He should lay into Berto about his treatment of Teresa. Or better yet, he should default, like usual, to the power of logic to take control of the situation. What would a bully like Berto respond to—cash, promises, threats? Diego needed the perfect formula to flip the power dynamic unfolding between them. But for some reason, his mind was a blank screen, a spinning wheel cursor mocking his inability to force-quit real life.

"I warned you, asshole," said Berto as he took a step back and slammed his fist into the side of Diego's face. Fury, unleashed.

Time froze for a brief moment with the realization that he'd been hit. Then, the scene played itself out, following the classic bad guy movie script. After Berto's second punch, this time to the gut, Diego pulled his fists up to his face in a futile effort to defend himself. He had failed to problem-solve his way out of this scenario, leaving his vulnerabilities exposed to full-on system attack.

As one punch followed another, Diego's mind drifted back to childhood fights. Then, as now, his experience of physical conflict was infused with both fear and frustration. Whenever playground spats broke out, Diego was never an initiator and always an unwilling participant. He hated fighting. Not only was it unnecessary and preventable, but it was also a messy, archaic way to resolve issues between people. He hated the fight itself, the ugliness, the blood sports and showmanship and spectacle. Most of all, he hated the unpredictability of such a primal game. Bare aggression replaced strategy, emotion randomized pain. Usually, young Diego would go home to his mother bruised and bloody, his sense of self shaken.

Grown-up Diego recognized the innate source of his current conflict, the bare metal environment that hardwired people to lash out at and harm each other. Berto's impulses lay at the root of the human operating system, core functionality that had enabled us to survive as animals, and that evolution had failed to update over the millennia. In that case, what flaw in his own system prevented Diego from running the standard fight script at full capacity? He desperately wished that he could strike back, dominate his opponent, erase Berto from his family network once and for all.

"Stay the fuck away from us," Berto spat, his aggression reaching peak performance as he landed a final punch that sent Diego reeling sideways. His head clipped the edge of a porcelain sink on the way down and Diego lay sprawled on the concrete floor, bloody, battered, and unconscious. The family fixer had finally crashed.

CHAPTER 16

Kari

Kari had been standing in front of his birds for almost an hour. Thirteen hand-blown, delicately-colored, stylized glass birds nested in a backlit display cabinet in the K2 living room.

He glared at them silently, intently, today more like a hunter than a zookeeper. Unmoved, the birds returned a glassy-eyed stare. Kira seemed restless, flitting from room to room to tidy up this or that, until she finally shoved a dusting cloth into his clenched fist. "Do something!"

Ignoring her, Kari muttered to his prized collection, "Lucky thirteen. Thirteen years in this country. And now, bad luck." He remained still, arms folded, paralyzed by his own thoughts.

"Baaaaayyyybeeee," Kira purred, as she wound her arms around him from behind. Her cashmere-clad embrace made a soft, pink circle around Kari's blue cotton torso. "It's gonna be okay." She kissed the back of his neck sweetly. "I promise."

Kari put his hands on top of hers as they both stood still, vertical spoons breathing in harmony. "Where the fuck is he?" he said flatly. "Is he dead or what?"

"God dammit, that guy could be dead and still dominate our lives," Kira grumbled, dropping her arms. She shot him an irritated look and strode out of the living room. Kari clenched his jaw and reached out to stroke the nearest cool, translucent wing.

Diego had mysteriously been incommunicado for over two weeks now. No emails, no IMs, no texts, no calls, not a whisper from Kari's business partner since he had left town for a long weekend with his family. The Thursday before he left, Diego had told Kari and the team that he was going to pick up a sister in Laughlin the next day, fly to Cancún for a quick visit, and return the following Monday. No big deal. But no word from him since? That was huge.

During this limbo, Kari felt himself cycle through denial, anger, and depression; classic stages of grief. It was inconceivable that Diego would just abandon Fixa—abandon *him*—without a word. He couldn't be simply, inexplicably, offline and unavailable. If Digs had somehow lost his phone and laptop, he would have bought replacements immediately, or he would have borrowed one from his family to give Kari a heads-up. His friend and partner would have made the effort to reassure Kari that all was okay, that he was just a bit delayed. Something terrible must have happened. And if so, how fucking unlucky could they be? Their years of hard work, so close to taking off, now dead in the water. It was a nightmare come true.

Kari was completely unwilling to move into the "acceptance" stage of grief, so instead, he took comfort in taking action. After Diego had been gone for a whole week, Kari had called the only family contact he had for Diego, the sister Lucita in Cancún. Diego almost never talked about his family, so Kari really only knew Lucita by name.

"I called Teresa last weekend," Lucita had told Kari, "and she said that Diego never showed up in Laughlin." Lucita paused for a moment and continued, "I thought he'd changed his mind, so I just let it go." Her voice began to rise. "Oh my God, do you think something has happened to him? Oh my God! *Dios mío*!"

Lucita's escalation was too much for Kari and he quickly ended the conversation. He then called the airline to see if Diego had been on a flight to Vegas that weekend, but they refused to provide any information outside of official channels. Next, he called the local police to report a missing person, but was given no idea whether the agency would follow up or file it away. That day, Kari had come home utterly distraught, and Kira had had a difficult time helping him regain equilibrium.

"My love," Kira's voice like butter in his ear, "I have no doubt that he's fine, wherever he is." Her arms felt like silk on his bare chest.

"Yeah, sure," he replied stiffly, numbly, unable to be held.

Over the following week, he continued to make the same futile loop of phone calls and emails, with no new information surfacing. Nothing to spark hope.

In the meantime, Chris and Dale were also feeling the pain of Diego's absence. They struggled to keep the pipeline of code releases flowing at the same rapid pace in order to keep the business on track. Toggling between the different Fixa products, the two engineers wrote, compiled, tested, and deployed code as fast as they could. Luckily, they had a deep understanding of Diego's ideas and intentions, so they continued to follow his direction despite the void in technical leadership. Kari tried to make himself available to answer questions or review releases, but the business already pulled him in so many directions that it was hard for him to find time for the development side of things. Besides, it had been a few years since he'd touched code himself, so his input was high-level at best.

More important than engineering momentum, however, was Fixa's upcoming investor pitch. A crucial milestone for the young startup, it was time to move beyond their bootstrapped beginnings and raise some serious funding from venture capital firms. A solid cushion of cash was vital to sustain the business during its critical early growth phase. The startup needed to not only pay its tiny team and keep the lights on, but it also needed to recruit top talent that would accelerate product development and truly establish their brand in the market.

"This is the end of the line with my father," Kari had said resolutely to Kira a couple of months after leaving Cloud9. "We will need an infusion of capital soon, but I just can't ask him for any more investment. I just can't face it again. It's time to approach VCs."

"I'll ask my father!" she had replied. Kari was glad that he hadn't asked Kira to approach Dave after all. This was now wholly her idea, stemming from her belief in Fixa, her belief in *him*. "Now and then he invests privately in various business ventures. Mostly it's to help fund the side projects of close friends. I think you qualify!"

"Thank you, Angel Dave!" exclaimed Kari, his heart pumping with hope and love for this woman who loved him that much. "Every dollar counts!"

Unfortunately, Dave was not onboard. Kira reported back that her father was too conservative to finance something as unpredictable and unstable as a software startup.

"Thousands of startups fail every year," he had lectured Kira while en route from Cincinnati to Washington. "Look what happened when the first dotcom bubble burst. I don't want this to turn into a donation."

"I was so sure he'd say yes," Kira had said glumly. "For me!" For a couple of days afterward, she had seemed quiet and remote, her daddy-daughter bubble thoroughly deflated. Kari was also deeply disappointed in the outcome, but quickly let it go. Better not to get entangled in more family complexity.

However, shortly afterward, Dave did come through with something nearly as valuable as his money. He connected Kira to an old college buddy, the CEO of a prominent Silicon Valley VC, a firm with "balls of steel" according to Dave. A short introductory call between the three of them resulted in an agreement from the firm to hear the Fixa pitch. When she debriefed Kari and Diego after the call, they had been so overjoyed, that Kari noticed Kira blush with pride, from her painted toes to her platinum roots.

With this bird in hand, Kari promptly leveraged their new connection to garner interest from two more venture capital firms and set up a combined pitch day. He told Kira, "Where one bird goes, others will follow!" Kari targeted VCs that had close ties with Cloud9, and their former mentor Jiang helped to make introductions. Most declined, stating that their prospect pipeline was full, but thankfully one expressed curiosity about their work and agreed to attend. The third firm came from a chance encounter at a recent meetup. Kari happened to share a beer with an associate from a VC that was focused on funding hot young startups in the artificial intelligence space. His casual pitch landed a formal one—one of the many twists on his entrepreneurial journey.

Weeks later, the critical day was drawing close and Diego had now apparently vanished. Kari was beside himself with worry. Without Diego present, could they go forward with the pitch or should they postpone? Until when? Kira agreed with Kari that the risk of postponing seemed too great, the opportunity too precious to lose. These birds could fly away and leave Fixa in the dust.

Seven days prior to the big day, the countdown began in earnest. In a rare evening together, Kari and Kira were making dinner at home. In silence, they wove in between each other as each crossed to the stove or sink or chopping board in an elegant, long-practiced choreography. Kira had chosen to make one of his favorite comfort meals, fettuccine alfredo, in order to add a bright spark to his day, however small. Kari was chopping salad ingredients with slow, measured strokes of the knife. He was lost in a mechanical meditation and Kira let him be. Suddenly, he put down the knife and turned to her, catching her waist as she moved toward the sink.

"Babe," he said solemnly. "*Kulti*, I really need your help." Kari's eyes bored into Kira's and he felt her senses sharpen, on alert.

"Of course," she replied gently, reaching up to stroke his shoulder. "What's up?"

"With Diego gone, I don't think I can do the pitch alone," he said. "Not just because I suck at speaking," he chuckled bitterly, "but because it won't look strong from the investors' viewpoint."

"Hmm," she murmured, pursing her lips.

"I could drag Chris and Dale up there with me and force them to walk through the technology. But even then, we'll look like a weak team." He drew a deep breath. "Like a bunch of losers." He exhaled slowly and grimaced.

At that, Kari saw something in Kira snap to attention. It was if all of her inner resources, battle-scarred and hard-won throughout a lifetime of childhood standoffs and corporate showdowns, rallied to meet this moment. She could turn this situation around.

"You need me to get up there with you," she said, appearing to read his mind. "To help you deliver the pitch." Relief washed over Kari. Kira seemed to be embracing her role as Fixa's very own fixer.

"Would you, babe? Really?" Kari asked, giving her a long, tight hug. "You're a lifesaver. I don't know what I'd do without you." He released the hug for a second and then dove back into it, squeezing her harder. It left Kira a little breathless, but delighted.

"Of course, my love," she replied. "I'd be happy to help. We don't need Diego for this. We'll figure it out!"

Although the team had had some practice at Cloud9's Demo Day, this would be the real deal. To evaluate Fixa's potential, the questions from their VC guests would dig much deeper into every detail of their business plan and technology roadmap. To inspire trust, the startup needed to establish its expertise, competency, and stamina for the tough climb in a competitive market.

Kira agreed that she'd be the one driving the pitch, orchestrating the day, ensuring that the message was precisely tailored to each VC for maximum impact. This was the type of challenge that Kira sought out at work, that she gave up evenings and weekends for, that had honed her communication skills until they were razor-sharp.

After dinner, energized by their collaboration and the carb-heavy meal, the couple sat down to discuss details of their new plan.

"First, let's beef up the Fixa leadership team," Kira said. "I'll be your chief operating officer, which explains why I'm helping deliver the pitch." She took a sip of Pinot Gris and refilled Kari's glass. "It's funny how we can just assign ourselves C-Suite titles, just like that!" True, Kari thought. That was the beauty of reinventing yourself, something that one could do more easily within the fast, fluid change of high-growth industries like technology.

"Great!" Kari looked at her lovingly. "I wish you could work with us full-time."

Ignoring him, she continued. "Let's ask Ravi to be head of product. It would make sense, since that was essentially his role at Cloud9."

"Yeah, Ravi would be great to do the demo and tech walk through." Kari nodded. "We can have Chris and Dale on hand to answer any specific technical questions." He fiddled compulsively with his paper napkin, folding and refolding it into a tiny hard square.

"Perfect. I'm meeting Ravi tomorrow night to see a movie," she said. "I'll ask him then. I'm sure he'll say yes." She smiled confidently.

"To you, I'm sure," he replied, with a whisper of jealousy. "Anyway, he's already expressed interest in joining us full-time, so he may do it if it means we get funding for salaries."

"Three officers is a strong showing," said Kira. "We're off to a good start."

"We'll have to get Digs's approval on all of this when he's back," he reminded her. "We can't make final decisions without him."

"Of course," she concurred. "So, what do we say about our missing chief technology officer? Why isn't he present? They'll want full transparency."

"We can say he had a family emergency in Mexico," Kari suggested. "And that he'll be back very soon." They both fell silent for a couple of minutes, thinking this over.

"Hmm, okay. Family emergency it is," Kira replied decisively. "Let's try to have a little faith. There *will* be a happy ending." She stood up and started clearing plates from the table, pointedly grabbing Kari's folded napkin. "We have to believe it first, before others can." Kari sat staring straight ahead, unblinking.

CHAPTER 17

Ravi

Ravi took a cautious sip of oily black coffee as he sat in the waiting area of SF General Emergency Services. He held the steaming paper cup with both hands to steady a tremble that was radiating out to his fingertips. Nico was coming. Nico would be here any minute. Across from him, a young mother was cradling her toddler and singing softly to him in Spanish. A sour stench emanated from a man who had sprawled out over three seats, eyes closed, sweat pouring from his temples into a shaggy gray beard. Another man paced along one wall, gesticulating wildly as he cajoled and threatened his invisible companion. A family of five sat in a row, from tallest to smallest, silent and stoic, passing around a party-sized bag of Cheetos. Where was Nico? Ravi checked his phone for the hundredth time. No new texts beyond, "See you in 30." Traffic must be bad.

An hour prior, Ravi had received a call from Bets that Veela had tripped and fallen. Bets had taken her to the closest emergency room, only five minutes from their house in Potrero Hill.

"One of the hens escaped," Bets reported, her voice tense and strained. "Veela was frantically chasing it around the backyard, trying to shoo it back into the coop. Her foot caught on a plant stand and she fell onto the cement walkway." Bets paused and drew a breath. "She came down hard." At six months pregnant, this was more than minor. "Right afterward, Veela had some cramps and bleeding, so we came here." *Good job*, thought Ravi. *Bets is on the ball.*

Ravi immediately requested an Uber and rushed over to the hospital, only to find that Veela had already been whisked away for tests. Stuck in the waiting room, he was desperate for an update. Was Veela okay? Was the baby okay?

The baby—Ravi had recently started calling it "my baby," saying the words out loud to himself in private. Words he never thought he would ever say to anyone, let alone to himself. Such binding words. Grown up words. Nico had recently started calling it "our baby," which added another layer of gravity that pulled him and held him. It was scary territory, but there was something nice about it too. Ravi held on tight to the nice part, letting it lead him like a beacon.

~

Three years into their faux marriage, his faux wife Veela made a second proposal, this one more real than the last. One evening, the two were sipping a smoky mezcal margarita at Cha Cha Cha when Veela suddenly said to Ravi: "Let's make a baby!"

Ravi laughed, incredulous. "What, you and me? We'd have sex or what?" The idea seemed preposterous, as well as unfeasible. Why try to be The Cleavers or The Waltons or another classic American family? Or why try to mirror the perfect Indian family, when their own family models were so far away? Such a house of cards would surely collapse soon enough. They would be left digging out the rubble of a doomed hope.

"No, dummy," Veela snapped. "We'd use a high-tech turkey baster. There are loads of insemination kits available online." Ravi giggled and blushed as she mimed her take on good turkey baster technique.

"Bets and I have talked for years about having kids," Veela said, back to practical matters. "You know that." She looked at him pointedly.

"Yeah." His laughter vanished instantly, and Ravi found himself speechless. His mind raced through a minefield of parenting scenarios, looking for an escape route.

"We're both ready now," Veela declared. "We want to do it with a man that we know and trust, and I want that man to be you!" She smiled warmly, lit by the glow of her maternal dreams.

"Huh," Ravi replied, flattered but still at a loss. If not him, then who else would Veela and Bets choose to father their baby? Had they asked any of their other gay friends? He suddenly felt jealous of other paternal contenders, and almost possessive of Veela's womb. Irrational! Absurd! But some part of him wanted, at the very least, the right of first refusal on the matter.

"You could be as involved as you want," she continued, "or not at all. You could just donate your sperm if you want." Ravi recoiled slightly at the latter option, which felt somewhat perverse and transactional. He could never just step out of the picture entirely. Or could he?

Some months after their wedding, Ravi had noticed a subtle shift in his relationship with Veela. It was as if the pretend marriage, the elephant in the room, had filled up the natural buffer between them and added false weight and meaning to their friendship. Each was reluctant to get too close for fear of summoning unwanted feelings or expectations that might destroy the special bond that they'd nurtured for so many years. Instead, they saw each other only occasionally, and often with a group of friends. It felt like a slow leak, a sense of loss emerging over time. "Get a divorce already!" Kira had said. "What are you waiting for?" Ravi intended to get around to it, one of these days.

In that emotional climate, it would have been easy for Ravi to simply donate sperm and leave Veela and Bets to their family planning. But what if having a baby could bring his relationship with Veela back into alignment? Co-parenting with Veela could open up a new dimension in their friendship, with new challenges certainly, but also new opportunities for togetherness. The kind that felt like family.

Ravi had considered Veela's proposal over a few months, weighing the pros and cons carefully. On his own home front, the baby scheme had legs. Ravi was back together with Nico after a few years apart, and things were going well. The two had run into each other at a charity event, and after a few drinks and more than a few laughs, they'd gone home together to reconnect in the best way they knew. After that night, Ravi suggested a dinner date, Nico suggested a movie, and the past became fuzzier as a new present crystalized. The pair started "hanging out," which turned into "seeing each other," until finally becoming "back together" in a way that suggested "future." Both had grown during their time apart—their couple's counselor had agreed—with Nico working on his trust issues and Ravi learning how to give more of his time, and his self, to the relationship. Now that it was finally legal to marry the man he loved, maybe Ravi would finally get around to that divorce after all.

When Ravi floated Veela's idea past Nico, his partner was enthusiastic about both having a baby and co-parenting with Veela and Bets. "Let's have a baby!" Nico had even begun watching YouTube videos on baby-care basics, such as how to change a diaper or warm up a bottle. Ravi couldn't even Google the word "baby." He'd get there, just not quite yet.

"Your kid will be my little supermodel," Nico joked, waving his camera at Ravi. "We'll be the proudest baby daddies in town!" Ravi's heart warmed at the thought. He and Nico–co-fathers. He and Veela–procreators. The four of them—a parental quartet. More Waltons than Cleavers perhaps? It was a different family portrait altogether.

When Veela finally became pregnant after a full year of trying, Ravi was afraid to share the happy news with his parents. His own family portrait had started to crumble a couple of years prior, when he'd spontaneously come out to them during one of their regular catch up calls.

"You're *what*? *GAY*?! How can you do this to Veela?" Sarita spat into the phone. He wanted to explain that Veela was also gay, but his mother was a speeding train headed right toward him.

"How can you do this to *us*?" The scorn in his mother's voice seared into Ravi's heart, scarring his core. "You are bringing dishonor and shame to this family. Your father and I are public officials, Ravi!" The impact was massive. He was never going home again.

"Why do you have to be so trendy all the time, eh?" Arjun had fumed. "You latch on to this latest fad, but it will ruin your life, my boy!" Ravi was alarmed at the vehemence emanating from his normally reticent father. Would this push him away altogether?

"I'm going to call Sanjiv right now and give him a piece of my mind!" Despite her desire to blame her brother, Ravi could hear between the words. His mother clearly blamed herself for his gayness, for pushing him to live in this licentious, anything-goes place. His father probably blamed her too. Ravi hated to think of the quarrels that would surely flare up between them now.

At the time, Ravi had been thoroughly unprepared for a rational conversation about sexual orientation, LGBT politics, and the merits of living an authentic life. His parents in turn were unprepared to imagine life with a gay son. Time did not pave the way for dialogue, so both sides chose to sweep the topic under the family carpet. Calls became short and superficial, the in-between time lengthened.

One day, toward the end of the first trimester, Ravi rang his parents to deliver the news. He steeled himself for the worst, the accusation train could plow into him once again. "Veela is three months pregnant," he blurted out quickly, "and I'm the biological father." There, he'd done his filial duty. He'd announced their new grandparent-to-be status in a timely manner. They can now do what they wanted with it.

After a short pause, Sarita exclaimed, "Ravi, that is wonderful news!" Her voice rose to a girlish pitch. "When is the baby due? Tell me all the details, *beta,* this is so exciting!" Ravi could hear the news spread through his mother's consciousness and reclaim his rightful place in her life.

"Congratulations, son!" Arjun said. His father had also perked up and was actually paying attention. "Is it a boy or a girl?"

"We have a list of family names for both boys and girls," his mother interjected, eager to jump into planning mode, "so plenty of choice either way!" Ravi knew that his sisters had chosen names from the family list for their children, but he was determined to avoid this particular trap. He and Veela would forge their own baby journey, no matter how uncharted it may be. But the baby's name was another battle for another day. In this moment, Ravi wanted to enjoy the simple, primal pleasure of parental approval. He soaked in his parents' enthusiasm for this brave new venture into fatherhood and found strength in their support. He fully appreciated this rare snapshot in time.

No one asked how Veela had become pregnant, and he had no desire to explain.

~

Amongst the bustle and background hum of the SF General waiting room, words clear as a church bell broke through Ravi's mental fog: "They're both okay." Bets sat down next to Ravi, her broad, pale face marked by strain and relief. Ravi exhaled slowly, letting the words reverberate. They're okay. Veela and the baby are okay.

"The doctor said that Veela has to be on bed rest from now on. Until the baby is born." Bets reported brightly. "She'll hate that!"

"Yeah," Ravi concurred. "She'll be bored after the first hour." He fiddled with the empty coffee cup, his hands unable to be still.

"With her job, she can work from home, so that'll keep her busy," Bets replied.

"She can 'work from bed.' A whole new definition of 'work from home'!" The two laughed heartily, their shared sense of relief adding more punch than the quip deserved.

"She can teach the baby to code," Bets said, wiping her eyes. "Like in some kind of laptop-to-belly osmosis."

"Yeah, forget the Digital Native generation," Ravi replied, warming to the idea. "Our little coder will lead the Code Native generation. Kids who can make their own apps, solve their own problems, build their own digital world." How cool that would be. Maybe they wouldn't need parents at all!

"Well, today we're dealing with the analog world." Bets stood up slowly and buttoned her vintage suede jacket. *She looks exhausted*, Ravi thought. "I'll go see if our girl's ready to go home."

Ravi watched Bets walk through the wide hospital doors into the patients' ward. He thought about their analog baby, who would now certainly live to be born. He also thought about their "smart baby," this micro, pre-programmed person, who was simply waiting for the day when it was code-complete, when it could finally launch and run its human program. By combining their genetic code, he and Veela were animating the blank screen of this tiny flesh-and-bone shell, and giving it tools to learn, grow, and write its own algorithms for a unique life.

With a whoosh, the emergency room doors slid open, prompting Ravi to look up from his reverie. There was his boyfriend, phone in one hand and car keys in the other, looking frantically around the crowded waiting area. His Nico, his x-man, ready to save the day. Ravi smiled and waved him over.

CHAPTER 18

Kira

Kira took a few days off from work to prepare for the Fixa pitch. At the office, no one complained. Quite the opposite. Kira had worked countless nights and weekends for so long, that her manager and staff seemed to almost push her out the door. "Have a relaxing vacation!" Lisette chirped as Kira headed toward the lobby. It would be far from relaxing, but Kira was always happiest in the heat of motion, all cylinders firing at full speed. This week would be all-in, one of her best.

Kira had called Ravi to meet up downtown to see a film. She always enjoyed spending time with him, but this time, she was a woman on a mission. As the two sat side by side in the movie theater, waiting for the film to begin, Kira made her move.

"Ravi, we really need you for the VC pitch," Kira spelled it out plainly, without pretense or promises. "You're such an engaging speaker, and you know the products inside out. How about being VP of Product for the day?"

"Hah! Funny," Ravi mused. "Do I have to wear a suit?"

"Of course!" Kira quipped. "I know you practically live in your one and only suit." The two chuckled for a moment.

"I don't know if I can commit right now," Ravi hesitated, looking apologetic. "I have a lot going on with the baby coming soon and all."

Kira's gut spasmed. Ravi, of all people, having a baby! Ever since he had announced the news to her several months ago, Kira had worked extra hard to keep her own Pandora's box of feelings tightly shut. She sincerely wanted to be a good friend—supportive, excited, interested in the blow by blow details of Ravi's baby journey. She absolutely did not want to be jealous, sad, a victim of loss.

"It would only take a few evenings to prepare," Kira said. "And you'd only have to take one day off from work. Besides, the baby isn't due for a couple of months, right?"

"That's true." Ravi paused for a moment, deep in thought. Kira inhaled hope and held it.

"Okay, I'm in!" he declared breezily. Kira exhaled relief.

"I totally believe in Fixa," Ravi continued between fistfuls of popcorn. "The tech is amazing and the team is super smart. I'd love to be a part of it." His certainty was compelling.

Kira wondered if she herself truly believed in it all. Could the startup produce groundbreaking products? Was it an industry disruptor, destined for the upper echelons of corporate success? She had always supported Kari and his dreams, and despite observing Fixa's progress over the past few years, she hadn't yet formulated a clear opinion for herself about this, his mega dream.

As the theater darkened and the film previews began, Kira digested Ravi's enthusiasm and it slowly dawned on her that she, too, believed. This awareness was almost a revelation—fundamentally, in her heart of hearts, the answer was *yes*! She did believe in Fixa's potential. She did believe that it could become a major industry player. The startup's future was bright. Whether or not she'd quit her job to join full time was another question entirely. She was certainly not ready for that level of commitment. But at least this newfound certainty would help Kira summon an authentic passion and excitement for telling the Fixa story when it counted most. When Kari needed her most.

~

T minus forty-eight hours. The presentation was locked and loaded. Kira had run Kari and Ravi through countless drills, like a sergeant pushing her troops to perfection. They could now fire off rounds of talking points, or parry tough and unexpected questions, and present in lockstep like a seasoned unit. Chris and Dale had built them an arsenal of product demos. All was looking good.

That morning, Kira stopped by her former colleague's apartment on Dolores Street to borrow a projector for the presentation. Darryl gazed at her quizzically as he leaned on the front door frame, arms folded, looking sexier than ever in a black tank top and jeans. "Hey, beautiful."

"Hi, Darryl," Kira replied, feeling suddenly shy. "You shaved off the dreadlocks?" His now close-cropped hair seemed to accentuate his handsome features even more. Her body ached.

"Yeah, those went a few months ago." Darryl grinned and ran a hand over his velvety head. "It's kind of like losing a limb. The ghost of them is still there." Kira nodded. It seemed that the ghost of them—she and Darryl—was also still there, though it had grown too weak to haunt her any longer.

Now, random twists of memories sprouted. Darryl as collaborator on the monthly internal communications plan. Darryl, the faithful sounding board for her crazy project ideas, the expert problem solver. Then, two years ago, Darryl as her co-presenter at that pivotal London conference, the one that put her on the executive map. Afterward, in the hotel bar, the giddiness of success. At the minibar in her room, the rich cognac of him on her lips. The tremor in her bones. Darryl radiated cheer and kindness, yet he delivered the warmth to her from outside in, with every kiss, every caress. Kira vividly remembered the question mark tattoo on his brown muscular shoulder, the tiny diamond stud in his left earlobe. The way the thick black hair on his thighs looked furry when dry and stripy when wet. Being with Darryl was appallingly reckless and irresponsible, but yet perversely relaxing. Almost like a relief. She simply couldn't resist.

Over the months, Darryl was there, adding warmth to those empty after-work spaces late at night or on weekends, until one day he was not. He'd met someone. Kira would have to find another way to chase away the chilly shadows that kept threatening to close in on her—the lost pregnancy, the unrelenting intensity of Kari's road map, the widening gap between them. Kira knew that Kari had suspected the affair. She could see the questions rattling behind his eyes, hear the sharpness of worry in his voice. But Kari refused to confront her, nor would she raise the discussion. Instead, they both lived their shared mantra: "Focus on the future—always." And Kira knew they still had a future together. Once they had both achieved their dreams, they would truly be K2 again, stronger than ever.

"I hope your pitch goes brilliantly," Darryl said, handing her a shopping bag containing the projector. "I want a full report after." He kissed her lightly on each cheek, his lips lingering for a millisecond.

"Thanks!" Kira replied, silently shaking herself. Focus now.

As she walked down Market Street toward her car, Kira noted the progress on several massive residential construction projects that dotted San Francisco's main artery. We live in exciting times! Glass and steel apartment blocks were cropping up across the city, bright beacons of promise and prosperity. Like the post-earthquake boom a hundred years prior, new construction fever reflected the unbridled aspirations of a city intent on reinventing itself into a heroic leader of the modern economy. Real estate developers boldly scooped up empty lots and teardown properties, commandeering every available square foot. They aimed to capitalize on the influx of young tech workers with high salaries and a preference for urban lifestyles over Silicon Valley suburbia. However, as a result, the cost to buy or rent had become as inflated as an IPO share price. Was it another bubble or simply the new normal?

Those penthouse units must have an amazing 360-degree view, Kira mused, as she craned her neck skyward. *You'd have the whole city laid out at your feet.* Maybe one of these days she and Kari would sell their condo in Pac Heights and buy up.

As she crossed Dolores Street, Kira stepped across a newly planted median strip. Lush succulents and other exotic-looking, drought-tolerant plants encircled sturdy palm tree trunks, thick as elephant legs, which seemed determined to trample on any opportunistic weeds. With tax money pouring into the city treasury, public works projects were redesigning neighborhood streetscapes in order to create outdoor experiences. More beautiful, more functional, more structured than ever, no space would be allowed to simply exist. Everything, like everyone, must realize their full potential.

Feeling slightly giddy from her encounter with Darryl, Kira paused by one of her favorite gift boutiques and indulged in a minute of window shopping. Her eye caught a few items that matched Darryl's style—a braided leather wristband, a pale yellow T-shirt with a wireframe illustration of Dolores Park, a sage green Heath ceramic salad bowl. She forced herself to re-scan the collection for things that Kari would like. Each item in the shop was handcrafted by local artisans, elegantly designed, and exquisite.

San Francisco's new wave of citizens had already shifted the pH of the urban economic bloodstream, inspiring a new breed of businesses that reflected tech ideals: high-concept, differentiated experiences, top-quality products, meticulously designed details. Customers were as exacting and demanding of their gift shops and barber shops, bars and restaurants, clothiers and confectioners, as they were of their software applications.

However, not all could thrive in the city's new, precious landscape. The boutique had recently replaced a scruffy café that had closed up shop after twenty years of serving the shifting tides of neighborhood residents. Among the many casualties of change were such long-loved neighborhood stalwarts, legacy businesses not agile enough to stay competitive or lucrative enough to afford skyrocketing rents. Similarly, many long-time residents, some of whom could afford a smartphone full of apps, could no longer afford their own real-world context.

One of the early pioneers of this new millennium wave, Whole Foods, had taken over failing neighborhood markets and become a citywide institution. Like a wise, benevolent grandfather, one could always count on the supermarket's golden-hearted embrace of all things good for taking care of the self, the world, and the planet. To shop there was to live one's values without worry.

Kira glanced up and saw a familiar figure walking toward her toting a Whole Foods bag in each hand. She presumed that Meghan had just come from the supermarket on the corner.

"Hi," said Meghan, resting her grocery bags on the sidewalk and reaching up to give Kira a brief hug. "How are you? It's been awhile." Kira thought she looked pretty good. Maybe a bit taller than she remembered? Hard to say.

"Yeah, about eight months I think," Kira said, resting her shopping bag containing the projector next to her feet. "Since Napa."

"Oh, right," Meghan responded, slightly abashed. "Sorry about that. We pretty much broke up after that weekend." She folded her arms. "But you already know that."

"I was sorry to hear it," Kira replied kindly. "What are you up to these days? Are you still at Del Oro?"

"No, I got laid off." Meghan smiled and shrugged. "I'm contracting at a streaming music service. It's okay for now." She definitely seemed different. What was it? More confident maybe, more relaxed. Kira had always found her boring, but maybe there was more substance to Meghan after all. She banked that impression for another time, should she run into Meghan again.

"I'm glad you landed on your feet," Kira said. "Well, great to see you." Then, inspired, she asked, "Hey, have you heard from Digs lately?"

"No. Actually, yes. Sort of," Meghan replied, looking suddenly anxious. "It's really odd, but I've been getting these weird texts and emails from him nearly every day. And he's posting strange things about us on Facebook and Instagram."

"Really?" Kira said. "Like what? Why are they strange?" Her attention sharpened.

"Well, some are not accurate. Some don't sound like his voice. Some assume we are still together, when in fact I haven't seen him for months. He even pinged me about meeting him for dinner, and I went to the restaurant but he never showed up! I don't know if he's messing with me or what, but I'm getting pissed now." Kira could see a hint of distress simmering beneath watery green eyes and flushed pale skin.

"When did this start?" Kira asked.

"I don't know. Maybe two weeks ago?" Meghan replied. "When you see him, could you tell him to call me? I've tried, but he won't answer and his voicemail box is full."

"Sure. Of course." Kira's mind spun with this unexpected information as her gut rose to take charge. Better not reveal too much, just in case. Nothing would jeopardize this opportunity for Fixa.

"I've gotta run. Great to see you, Meghan. Take care." The two women hugged briefly and bustled off in opposite directions.

~

Buzzing with breaking news, Kira headed straight to the Fixa office to debrief the team. But as soon as she arrived, she learned that another bombshell had dropped. Diego had been found.

"About an hour ago, I got a call from the Las Vegas police," the story spilled out of Kari in a torrent. "They finally—finally!—connected my missing-persons report to their records and concluded that it fit a John Doe in one of their area hospitals. They texted me a photo and it was Digs! He's in a hospital there in Vegas! Apparently, the state patrol found him at a highway rest stop, unconscious and barely breathing." Kari inhaled sharply. "He had no ID on him, no phone or backpack, nothing. So, they sent him to the nearest county hospital and he's been there ever since. He's unable to speak, and he drifts in and out of consciousness, but he's alive!" Kari was practically jumping.

Kira stepped up and gave Kari a hug, adding an exclamation mark to his elation. "Oh, thank God," she said, squeezing him tight. "Thank God."

"Hallelujah!" cheered Ravi, throwing his arms in the air. "Our boy is back!"

"My God, why aren't public databases synced in this day and age?" mused Dale. "Especially when it comes to matters of public safety."

"Maybe they thought he was a Mexican national," suggested Chris darkly, "involved in a drug deal gone bad. So, they deprioritized the investigation."

The group fell silent for a minute, considering this possibility. Ravi broke the silence.

"Man, you're always a sucker for conspiracy theories," he said with forced levity. "But really, what could have happened to him?"

"Whatever the reason, it's over now," stated Kari. "He's found." Kari was clearly ready to get back to life before the disappearance. "I wired money to his sister Lucita. She's going to fly out to Vegas tonight."

"Great idea. At least someone will be with him now," replied Kira. She felt a surge of hope that surprised her. Diego may be annoying at times, but she was truly glad he was alive. *Now, let's hope he's actually okay.*

"I'll fly out there on Friday," Kari said. "Right after the pitch."

"I've got some interesting news," Kira announced, and proceeded to relate her encounter with Meghan that morning to her four astonished teammates. "How can Digs be active online when he's been obviously out of commission all this time?" She asked the stunned group. "How is that possible?"

"The Fixa bots must be behind this," suggested Dale. "They're out there doing Digs's online business on his behalf. But without his oversight or control."

"Or his consent!" interjected Chris eagerly. The implications were huge.

"It sounds like they're trying to proactively do things as Digs would do them," explained Dale, "but not quite getting it right."

"Oh man, they've gone rogue!" declared Ravi. "They're trying to actually *be* him!"

"Maybe this was some secret experiment of Diego's," Kari said. "Even I didn't know about it. That asshole!" He was clearly impressed.

"Yeah, this may sound weird but I think the bots are smarter than we expected," Dale replied, looking pensive. "They're designed to learn from us and grow their capabilities, but now they're becoming more like true AI."

"Maybe their autonomy was triggered by Digs being offline," suggested Chris. "When the host is compromised, the AI takes over."

"Like a virus," said Dale.

"Or a cancer," said Chris.

"People!" exclaimed Kari. "This is a huge development! Let's focus on the positives and evolve the fucking product." Ever the businessman, thought Kira proudly.

"For the pitch," Kira said, "let's speak to this development as early stage R&D, showing our vision for how Fixa will grow. We need to convince the VCs that we are disruptive thinkers but our current product lineup is strong enough to monetize now." Her team of four nodded eagerly.

"Can't wait to get Digs back," Kari said.

"Ditto," chimed Chris and Dale.

~

Kira squinted at the restroom mirror of Fixa's shared workspace. Despite a thin film of grime clouding her reflection, she could confirm that everything—hair, makeup, outfit—was in place. It wasn't the gleaming granite and stainless executive floor ladies' room of her corporate campus, and she wasn't wearing her best power suit. But she had skillfully adapted to the meeting's context, choosing to wear the suit's midnight blue blazer over a perfectly crisp white button-down shirt, pencil leg jeans, and black patent leather pumps. Corporate authority blended with startup approachability.

The startup had booked the building's largest conference room for the crucial meeting that could take them from bootstrapped to funded in a mere two hours. The room immediately shrunk as fourteen people settled in, shoulder-to-shoulder, around a white oval melamine table, laptops open, water bottles at the ready. In attendance were representatives of three venture capital firms who specialized in artificial intelligence and machine learning technologies. *Don't suck up all the oxygen before the first demo*, Kira thought to herself. She propped the glass door open a few inches.

The projector hummed quietly as Kari loaded up his PowerPoint deck and fiddled with monitor cables and adapters. Some of the visitors were already heads-down, filling the empty moments with email or texting or browsing. Others sat impatiently waiting for this blip on their scheduling radar to pass, so they could move on to more important matters in their day. Kira attempted to engage them and set a relaxed tone with cheerful, inclusive chit chat. Finally, Kari stood up to kick off the session with some opening remarks.

"Welcome everyone, and thank you for joining us today." He opened his hands in a gesture of greeting yet kept his upper body relaxed, just like Kira had taught him. "I'll start our discussion by asking you all one simple question. I promise it's an easy one," he chuckled nervously and Kira sat up a hair straighter in her chair.

"What is one of the biggest pain points in your daily life?" Kari continued. "What eats up your precious free time, as much as doing chores around the house, or even commuting?" He paused to let the question sink in. "The answer lies in two fundamental truths of the modern world." He clicked the remote control and PowerPoint flipped to a slide that read:

1) Most of us today are busier than ever before

2) More and more aspects of our lives are now lived online

Kira took a quick early read of the table. Impassive faces. Bored already?

"On top of work, family, social, and personal time, we're faced with a mind-boggling number of little online tasks on a daily basis. These little tasks take care of practical matters, help us solve problems, or move our life forward toward achieving personal goals, big and small." Kari paused and scanned his audience, looking each in the eye for a millisecond. Kira's coaching had clearly sunk in, making Kari appear polished and confident.

"We call it 'Life Admin.'" Kari advanced to the next slide, showing a mesh of popular online brands, from entertainment to finance to social. "Each of us administers dozens of active accounts on a regular basis, many of them daily. These services have become not only important, but *vital* to the multifaceted lives that we curate for ourselves." Kari paused for dramatic effect. "Yet the time it takes to juggle all those services is excruciating, right?"

Kari passed the torch to Kira, who stood up and took the remote. "We're all familiar with the virtual assistant model that's been on the market for a while now." She loaded the next slide that showcased several examples. "Their interaction style is typically 'call and response.' You ask a question or you set a task—and they return a response." Kira noted a slight nod from two audience members. Eyes shining, she dialed up the energy.

"Okay, fine," she continued. "But what if you had a virtual assistant that was actually smart? Smart in the way that we ourselves are smart. What if your assistant *already knew* your questions and tasks? And could just get them done on your behalf?"

"Meet Fixa's intelligent agents," Kari said, flashing a brief smile at Kira who clicked to the next slide. Kira winced inwardly at the comic-style figures that were intended to represent a shopper, dater, job searcher, friend, and money manager. She had lost that battle with Ravi. To her, it was like a ten-year-old's gang of superheroes. She hoped they could re-brand soon.

Kari proceeded to explain the agents' superpowers. "Our bots are smart enough to take the right actions on your behalf, without you having to command them each time. They start by parsing your entire historical online footprint in order to build a behavior profile of you. They get to know you deeply through your online behavior over your lifetime and learn your preferences, your habits, your personality traits—even your writing style and speech patterns!"

With a brief nod to Kari, Kira took over. "More importantly, our bots analyze the *reasons* behind your actions. Through Fixa's predictive algorithms, they can determine what decisions you will make and what actions you will take to accomplish a particular online task. They will manage the entire chain of interactions needed and act as you would act."

The audience gazed at Kira and Kari through a seemingly impenetrable curtain. A couple of visitors thumbed idly through mobile email. Were they only half listening?

"For example," Kari continued, pointedly facing the inattentive ones. "Our ShopFixa bot knows your clothing budget for the month, your fashion style, your favorite e-commerce sites, the contents and age of the clothes in your closet, and what you'll need to buy for the upcoming season. The bot will automatically go out and buy new clothes for you, or send suggestions via notification, if you'd prefer."

"Take DateFixa," Kira said, producing her most charming smile. "This bot can identify the dating profiles of those women whom you'd find most attractive and most compatible. It can also filter for candidates who are most likely to be interested in you and responsive to your outreach. Knowing your personal style, DateFixa can initiate and conduct conversations on your behalf, set up real life dates, and integrate them into your weekly calendar. Imagine, opening your calendar and looking at a week's worth of hot dates!" Kira noticed all eyes fixed on her, gaze sharpening as the audience digested this concept.

"And all you have to do is show up!" Kari chuckled heartily and beamed at his co-presenter. In that moment, Kira felt a sudden surge of energy sweep through her that exposed a new, and unfamiliar, depth of realness. Maybe it was just the typical presenter's endorphin rush, fueled by the drama and thrill of the pitch. Most definitely there was a sense of pride and empowerment mixed in. But underneath it all was the raw truth of her and Kari.

The clarity was almost dizzying. There they were, she and Kari together, bringing the full force of their combined talents to bear on a business-critical mission. She could finally see the peak of K2, crystal clear and free of the cloying, grey mists that had shrouded their relationship for the past couple of years. Today was only the beginning of what they could accomplish as a couple. They were stronger together, unstoppable together. For Kira, a life partner was not someone who would complement or complete her, or someone to fill a certain void. A true partner would amplify the potential of her life and enable her to reach new heights. A true partner was someone who could reach the top with her, not because of her, or despite her.

"Next, I'd like to introduce Ravi Desai, Head of Product." Kari took Kira's momentary lapse in stride and breezed on to the next item on their agenda. "Ravi will walk you through our two-year product roadmap, as well as demo the key features of each of our current Fixa agents. Take it away, Ravi!"

Relieved, Kira watched Ravi cheerfully take center stage and launch straight into the first product demo. Ravi the actor was in full command of his audience, skillfully telling the product story with a good dose of his usual wit and charm. His portion of the meeting lasted a full hour and included significant technical depth on all aspects of the product, from user experience and interface design to data processing and AI algorithms. He occasionally tapped Chris or Dale to elaborate on particular technical details or draw architectural diagrams on the whiteboard, which covered the entire side wall of the room. As Ravi spoke, Kira kept an eye on the audience. All were clearly paying attention—a great sign—and many raised good questions along the way.

"Our beta trials have produced ten percent growth month-on-month." Ravi ended his presentation with a segue into the business portion of the pitch. "We're now running an average of one hundred thousand active users across all five Fixa bots, and we expect to double that in the next three months through our upcoming social media campaign." He clicked through a few more slides to show their marketing creative before handing off the remote to Kari. "Back to you chief!"

Kari spent the final twenty minutes of the meeting running through details of the Fixa business plan, including growth forecasts and financials. The three venture capital firms had each sent three representatives to the meeting, each focused on evaluating a different aspect of the startup—product opportunity, business viability, and financial structure. Their next steps were to report back to their firm with recommendations on passing or pursuing investment.

"In closing," Kari said, "first of all, I'd like to thank you for your time and attention today. And secondly, I'd like to share some exciting new developments that our R&D has recently uncovered. The scope and scale of our machine learning capabilities have exceeded our expectations." He paused for a couple of seconds. A last bump of anticipation, thought Kira. Good one.

Kari continued, "Fixa's agents have the ability to act independently on behalf of their host. So even if you're offline, your intelligent bots can make decisions and proactively maintain your online life." Kira noted a few wrinkled brows, a fleeting ripple of something in the audience. Concern? Curiosity? Kari seemed to notice the same thing.

"Of course, we will build in all the necessary checks and balances," he reassured them. "But imagine the opportunities! You can let your Fixas handle even more tedious tasks for you. You can enjoy even more freedom in your life." He threw his arms out wide to emphasize his point. "Ultimately, your Fixas help you take back your time." The final slide echoed his words in bold blue lettering: *Take back your time!*

"Thank you," Kira said to the table.

"Thank you," echoed her team. *Well*, thought Kira, *it's done now.*

The conference room drained quickly with little fanfare. Kira and Kari ushered them out, shaking each hand to personalize their appreciation. Apart from a couple of minor follow-up questions, the visitors left promptly with no feedback or discernable opinions on Fixa or any aspect of the pitch. No hint as to what may result from the day. Now, the team was faced with the hardest part of their pitch by far: waiting for news.

"It went great," Kira reassured her four shell-shocked comrades-in-arms. "Really. It was smooth, informative, and right on target. It couldn't have gone better." She wasn't entirely convinced—the audience was impossible to read—but she knew it hadn't gone badly. Worst case, they were dropped and forgotten like film on a cutting room floor. Best case? They had to keep the faith.

"I hope so," said Kari, frowning and rigid with suppressed tension. Kira looped her arm in his.

"Time for a beer?" said Ravi, pulling out his phone to check the time. *Ravi—always taking back his time*, Kira smiled to herself.

"Happy hour starts early at Pacific Brewing," suggested Dale with a hopeful lilt to his voice.

"Team offsite!" exclaimed Chris, who seemed desperate to get out of the office.

"Drinks are on me," said Kira as she pulled her phone out of her bag and tapped the Uber app to order a ride for them all.

CHAPTER 19

Kari

Kari stared at his laptop screen, unable to wrench his attention away from the six-figure number. Fixa's bank balance was practically screaming at him: we're funded! At last! And it meant no more seed capital from his father, which was worth almost as much, if not more, than six figures.

A full two months after the pitch, Kari received calls from the three investment firms, coincidentally all on the same day. One offered five hundred thousand dollars, another three hundred and seventy-five thousand, and the third decided to pass but expressed interest in revisiting the opportunity in six months. The modest influx of cash would help them start to build out their technical infrastructure, hire more developers, and maybe even do a little paid marketing. It wouldn't last that long, but their Series A funding round was a start, putting them in the game with other tech startups.

"I knew it would come through, baby," Kira had exclaimed, as she beamed proudly at him. "You made it happen. You're a rainmaker."

"The downpour was all because of you, my love," Kari replied. Plates shifted, chasm closed. This was it; this was what he had been wanting to feel again for so long. "You rock." Kari folded Kira into his arms. "We rock." K2 celebrated that evening with a four-course, wine-paired meal at Gary Denko restaurant, followed by an especially passionate late night.

For Kari, the investment news was incredible, but also terrifying. The weight of responsibility was more real than ever. He now had to answer to serious investors with serious expectations, and Fixa needed to perform, both as a product and as a company. The two VCs had attached certain stipulations to their funding commitment, demonstrating the level of control that they intended to exert on the business. Kari had no illusions in this regard.

"I'll negotiate the hell out of anything I disagree with," he declared the next morning. He and Kira sat at their kitchen table sharing a pot of Arabica Gold and a rare treat of five-grain porridge toast from Tartine bakery. The afternoon prior he had indulged in the luxury of time as he waited in line for nearly an hour with other local foodies who knew that at 4:30 p.m. sharp, the bakery's legendary loaves would emerge from the ovens at the peak of perfection.

"It's still my company!" He corrected himself: "Our company. Me and Digs." He paused, pensive, as he spread quince jam on a crusty slice of toast.

Diego was back at work—barely. Each day he would come into the Fixa office, working his crutches with slow, painful steps, and then sit silently for hours in front of a desktop monitor. No one quite knew what he was doing all day, and no one asked. Kari thought that Diego didn't know what to do with himself. Sometimes he would catch his partner idly surfing the web, with an attention span that seemed to skim over anything of substance. Other times Diego would be examining a section of code, only to appear utterly perplexed by it. Since the accident, Diego had not been able to produce a single line of code by himself, nor could he engage in technical discussions of any depth. Worse, he expressed no frustration, no desire—all emotion seemed to exist in a haze, far beyond his reach.

Kari noted hopefully that his partner's conversation abilities seemed to be improving incrementally each day. It was as if the computing machine in Diego's brain was following the footprint of his old life, re-learning how to be him in all his disparate manifestations. *He'll come back,* Kari reassured himself. If anyone could do it, it was Digs.

"The dude's still so fragile," Ravi said to Kari one evening over beers. "Poor guy."

"Yeah, that's why we need all great minds on deck," Kari replied. He placed his cards on the table. "Join us full-time, Ravi." Kari looked intently at his friend, trying not to seem too insistent. Or too needy. But he really did need Ravi, maybe for the first time ever. It was humbling.

"Building a cool product and an awesome business with good friends does sound amazing!" Ravi concurred. "But, like Nico says, I've got to lose the golden handcuffs first." Kari knew that Ravi was reluctant to leave his utopian Silicon Valley corporate campus, which had packaged his work life into a premium product that offered him the ultimate in beauty, fun, and fulfillment.

"Also, I have a baby coming now, so I've gotta be responsible about finances and stuff."

"We can pay you for real now!" Kari tried to suppress the lilt in his voice. *Stay cool.*

"Yeah, for now," Ravi replied, to Kari's dismay. *Oh, ye of little faith!*

"Besides," Kari struggled to extend his argument. "Your baby has three other salaries to count on, right?"

"Fair point, my friend," Ravi said, taking a deep swig of beer.

"But you know," Ravi continued, "I've been feeling lately like it's time to make a change in my career. I'm too complacent, too much like a cog in someone else's wheel. I need to feel inspired again, like I'm a core part of something, like I'm directly building something big. I need that for my sake and also, someday maybe, for the baby's sake."

"Hey, Fixa's got opportunity in spades!" exclaimed Kari. "Someday your kid can intern with us!"

"Ha! Funny," chuckled Ravi. "Yeah, it's time. Time to be the master of my own destiny!" Slowly it emerged, that signature Ravi grin. "Okay, count me in, man." Kari's heart leapt.

A few days after the good news, the team convened to tackle one of the funding stipulations that affected everyone. Both investors had required that the startup tighten up the product offering by combining its various bots into a single, comprehensive intelligent agent that could simultaneously manage the numerous realms of online life. From the VC's perspective, this would reduce confusion for consumers and produce a stronger brand in the marketplace.

"I like the idea," Ravi said thoughtfully. "Currently, your Fixa experience is kind of schizophrenic with all these little bots running around doing your bidding." He spun his phone in circles on the small conference table, unable to fully tame his anxious excitement.

"Like your virtual mafia," quipped Chris, as he reclined far back in the well-worn office chair, arms crossed, justifiably noble, godfather-like.

"Instead, you'll have a one-man mafia," quipped Dale as he took a gulp of Diet Coke, suppressing a burp. Kari knew that Dale hated the stuff, but hated exercise more, and was trying to lose a few pounds. "A single Fixa who can be in a thousand places at the same time."

"Which means *you'll* be everywhere, all the time," said Ravi, nodding slowly. "This online representation of you." Chris, annoyed, reached out to stop Ravi's phone spinning.

"This 'e-Me'." Diego's comment was barely audible. His gaze had been fixed on the office door, so no one heard him at first. Had he actually spoken?

"Huh? What'd you say, Digs?" Kari said, gently. "We didn't hear you, man." A wave of concern rose in his chest.

"e-Me," Diego repeated, only slightly louder, but with more certainty. "It's not a virtual agent, something outside of yourself. It is *you*. Really you."

"Exactly!" Ravi exclaimed, slapping Diego playfully on the shoulder, then recoiling in horror at the discomfort he'd caused. "It's the *you* online," he continued, patting Diego's shoulder lightly in apology. "Indistinguishable from the *you* in the real world."

"In the physical world," corrected Kari. "The online world is just as real."

"The name 'e-Me' is brilliant," Ravi said, grinning at Diego. "This guy is genius." He jokingly pretended to slap Diego again but pulled back before making contact, mimicking his previous mistake. Diego stared at him, unblinking.

"e-Me," echoed Kari, lost in thought. It made perfect sense. It was indeed strong from a branding perspective: logical, short and easy to remember, catchy, techie but approachable for the average user. "Yeah…e-Me…" Bullseye.

The team fell silent, letting this new direction sink into their collective consciousness.

~

Not long after e-Me's rebranding, K2 met for cocktails and island-inspired tapas at a new tiki bar in SoMa. Kari nibbled eagerly at a large slice of pineapple that was perched firmly on the rim of his piña colada. Kira served herself two fat prawns smothered in mango salsa.

"*Kultaseni*, my love, I wish you'd quit that corporate sweat shop and join us." Kari grabbed Kira's hand and lightly stroked her knuckles. He was in the habit of recycling that topic of conversation every few weeks, with the half-hearted intention to check in with her and possibly, finally, hear her say "yes." However, it seemed that the well-worn question had become just another way to express his affection.

"Not yet, my love," Kira replied, per usual. Staring at her plate, she seemed to have suddenly telescoped far inside herself.

Kari tried to draw her back into focus. "What?" he asked. "What is it?" He squeezed her hand encouragingly. "Talk to me!"

"What about…" She hesitated, still not looking in his eyes. "What about…us…having a baby sometime soon?"

Kari's whole body jolted upright, and he dropped her hand. A baby! An initial spark of excitement was immediately engulfed by an inferno of panic. A baby? Now? He couldn't handle that! Could he? What about…everything. Everything! The idea was dangerous, crazy, a critical risk to everything he'd worked so hard for. But maybe the risk was already real.

"Oh my god, are you pregnant?!" he exclaimed, the words gusting out like ash. A row of tiki masks across the bar stared at him, mocking him. Why couldn't she have told him this at home, in familiar surroundings, with the comfort of their things around him.

"No, no," she replied in a low voice. She hugged herself tightly, as if she were cold. "I was just thinking…" Kira hesitated again, seeming to choose her words carefully. "It would be a good time for me." She paused. "For us." Kira looked up to search Kari's eyes. "In nine months or so, Fixa will be in good shape for growth and you could work more regular hours. I could take a long maternity leave from my job." She paused again. The opportunity unpacked itself. "We could focus on *us* for a change. Our future."

"Our future," Kari echoed, struggling to recover. It wasn't that he didn't want a baby, or that he'd never thought about it. It just seemed to be one of those always-future things, something that would somehow just happen, someday, somewhere along the course of their lives. It certainly had not been on his list of priorities. But Kira's happiness was on that list, and Kari was willing to work hard for that. He wanted to feel that happiness. He wanted it to erase the distance that had been threatening their future.

"Do you really want this, *kultaseni*?" He took her hand again, squeezing tight.

Kira nodded, her eyes lit up. She looked like a little girl asking, but really hoping, for love.

"Okay, my *kulta*, I want what you want," Kari said firmly. "I want to invest in our future." As he said the words, he understood their truth.

"In K3!" Kira quipped, finally at ease. She returned his squeeze.

"Or someday, even K4," Kari smiled, despite the fear that gripped his gut like a debt collector promising to return. Time to change the subject.

"Let's have another round of drinks?" He called the waiter over and ordered.

"So, things are looking good at Fixa. We're expecting more funding to come through really soon. That third VC is working on a number for us." Kari put a large forkful of coconut rice into his mouth, dropping a few grains in his excitement. "Now we're getting ready to ramp up our outreach. We want to double our new user growth rate over the next three months, and triple the number of monthly active users."

"Awesome," Kira replied. She put a spring roll on her plate, but spotting the ooze of grease, pushed it to the edge in disgust. Instead, she took a long sip of ginger margarita and played with the little paper umbrella that crowned her drink, opening and closing it with a smooth flick of wrist. *We need her,* Kari thought. *Her confidence and discipline and magic. Our very own Mary Poppins.*

"It's time to hire a dedicated marketer," Kari continued. "Someone we can trust. Someone who'll give it their all, and who'll work partly for equity." He paused, locking eyes with Kira to make sure she was listening. "I was thinking about Meghan."

"Meghan, who?" Kira asked. "You mean Diego's ex?" Kari nodded. "Really? I mean, wouldn't it be uncomfortable for them both to work together?" Kira screwed her face into an opinion on the matter. "Also, isn't she kind of dull, or a drama queen, or something…" She trailed off, seemingly unable to articulate a professional dislike of Meghan as a candidate.

"Megs is a really good marketer, especially when it comes to demand generation and user retention." Kari reflected on his time with Meghan at Del Oro. "And we can trust her. She won't go off and spend our limited funds on useless shit."

"Okay, sure," Kira conceded casually. "Megs and Digs back together again, at work anyway. It's all sort of incestuous," she mused. "But why not?" She took a long sip of her drink, as if she were letting go of the matter.

"Would you feel her out?" Kari asked, pushing the topic further. "See if she'd be up for it? You know, like professional woman to woman?" Kari flashed his special "favor please?" look.

"Who me? I'm not her mentor, that's for damn sure!"

"My love, you could position this as the opportunity of a lifetime. She'd be one of the earliest employees in the hottest new startup in the Valley." He felt warmth flush his veins, from the certainty of this decision, from the piña colada, from the love of his life by his side and on his side. "I'm sure she'd listen to you!" Kari clinked his glass against hers.

Kira flashed her "favor won" look, and Kari felt yet another step closer.

CHAPTER 20

Meghan

Ping! Meghan chopped a last slice of tomato, wiped her hands, and grabbed her iPhone on the kitchen counter. The text was from Kira. "Meet for coffee on Saturday? Would be great to catch up." Meghan re-read the text a couple of times to make sure that her imagination wasn't playing tricks.

What does Kira want? Does she suddenly want to be friends? Why? She and Kira had never been close. For that matter, she had never trusted any of her ex's aloof, self-important friends. There always seemed to be an invisible shield around their inner circle, forever shutting her out of any deeper layers of connection. Digs spent so much time in that circle, and had done so for so long, that there never seemed to be enough room left over for her.

Meghan especially didn't trust Diego's college friends after she'd learned what had happened to him, months after he'd come home. One day, she had been walking along 24th Street and almost bumped into a blond guy at the entrance of the Sugar Lump café. Jon was Diego's next-door neighbor and occasional drinking buddy, and although Meghan had never spent time with him herself, he had always greeted her with warmth. This time, Jon invited her for a coffee and told her the whole dark story of Diego's devastating experience with as much detail as he had been able to glean from his taciturn friend.

"I check in on Digs every day," Jon said somberly, "to make sure he's still with us." Once the initial shock subsided, Meghan was able to focus on Diego's incremental progress, those tiny nuances of recovery that mean so much to loved ones.

For Meghan, the nuances of omission first spurred a flash of anger, which then died down into a simmering bitterness. Diego's so-called friends had failed to not only involve her in his recovery, but they hadn't even told her that he had disappeared! Meghan's mind cycled back in time to the sequence of events. When had she been getting the strange messages? Wasn't it around the time that she'd run into Kira outside Whole Foods? Okay, she and Digs had broken up, but surely tragic events like this warranted a head's up? Or for Diego's sake, wouldn't they want all the love and support they could muster on his behalf? She was clearly no longer part of the family, but the hard truth was, she had never been.

Meghan calmly finished making her salad, waited half an hour, and then answered Kira's text: "Sure." Curiosity rose above the fray of competing emotions. It was a good enough reason to spare an hour for coffee and catch up.

~

On Saturdays, the Valencia Street corridor came to life with a bustling flow of shoppers, diners, and afternoon strollers out enjoying the fresh air and newly remodeled streetscape. Many of the neighborhood's cafés had built bump-out seating areas off the public sidewalk, each with its own landscaping and style. Usurping a couple of parking spots, these parklets extended out like cheerful little piers into an asphalt bay. In the spirit of Otis Redding, one could sit on a parklet's "dock" and watch tides of traffic roll away. Although even on a weekend, San Franciscans today rarely wasted time.

Kira and Meghan sat face to face at one of the Blue Fig's outdoor tables. Each took a first cautious sip of cappuccino, as well as a brief moment to size each other up. The awkward atmosphere was diffused somewhat by passersby, humans on one side and cars on the other. The faint beat of Motown on the café's radio wafted out and carried across the parklet by a cool April breeze.

"So, how are you, Megs?" Kira started off with a broad smile, tucking a shiny platinum lock behind one ear and crossing her slim legs. "What have you been up to lately?" She looked as poised and elegant as always, perched on the café chair like a slender s-shape in perfect balance. In the past, Meghan would feel like a squat troll doll compared to Kira, with unruly red hair, a goofy grin, and a low center of gravity that kept her from being knocked over. But not today! Today, Meghan felt solid in the rickety café seat, feet planted firmly on the sidewalk, spine straight. She felt like a person who could hold her own. A person to be reckoned with. An equal! Well, almost.

"Things are good," Meghan replied cautiously, and then suddenly lashed out. "Hey, how come you guys didn't tell me about what happened to Digs? I could have been there for him, helped him settle back home. Made him dinner or whatever." She suddenly felt flushed and strangely close to tears. *No, no, stay strong. Be a force!*

"Oh! We didn't mean to upset you, Megs!" Kira scrambled to do some damage control. "At that time, the Fixa team kept Diego's situation secret from everyone, not just you, so that nothing could jeopardize the company's funding opportunity." She looked sincere, but Meghan remained suspicious. "But after our VC pitch, we'd forgotten all about spreading the word to Digs's friends." She looked apologetic; Meghan was doubtful.

"We were all just so focused on Fixa's Series A round," Kira continued. Her composure seemed to wobble for a millisecond. "We just didn't have one brain cell left to think of anything else. It's been so much work to get the company going over the past few months."

"Huh, okay…" Meghan replied hesitantly. She could understand the delicate circumstances, the business risk, but still…

"But don't worry, we've taken extremely good care of Digs." Kira took a tiny sip of cappuccino and realigned her s-shape. "He had moved into our spare bedroom for the first couple of months before he felt strong enough to live on his own. At that point, his sister Lucita took over. She's been his nurse and housekeeper." Kira idly smoothed the hem of her navy angora sweater. "And his prayer vigil leader." Meghan could not imagine Kira saying a prayer if her life depended on it.

"Yeah, I know," conceded Meghan. "I see him a couple of times a week now, and help do laundry or shopping or cooking, especially when Lucita has to go home for a few days." Truth be told, Meghan would have spent the night too—in a heartbeat—if Diego had expressed even the slightest interest. But from the first day she had re-connected with him, Digs had remained politely appreciative but emotionally remote. He was like a memory that was no longer in her queue of favorites, no longer a comfort or a pleasure to draw from whenever she liked. Clearly, her "Digs Chapter" was over forever. She could let him go, but she would not abandon him.

"I'm so glad you can be there for him now. I'm sure he's very grateful."

"Yeah, I guess so." Meghan felt her righteous indignation slip away. She wanted to bolt out of the café, out of the neighborhood, out of the city. But she felt anchored to her chair, unable to move. She was riveted to this moment with Kira, no matter how uncomfortable.

Well, again, I'm so sorry for the lack of communication," Kira replied, adding a full stop to that particular topic. "So, what's new with you these days? How's work?"

"I'm still contracting with this streaming music service and it's going okay." Meghan shifted in her seat. "I never work overtime, so it gives me a lot of free time to make art. I'm working on a few projects at the moment…" Her voice trailed off into a haze of her own uncertainty. The projects had been slow going and not yet fruitful, and she had found herself procrastinating more often than not. She hoped that Kira wouldn't be interested in the details.

Meghan crossed her legs and forced herself to perk up. "But really, everything is great. Life is great. How's everything with you? How's Kari?" She punted back to Kira and let out a long, silent breath.

"Things are really good, thank you!" said Kira with forced cheer. "Kari and I are planning a trip to Sicily in July, and we can't wait. Work has been crazy for us both and we desperately need a break." She took a quick sip of coffee and dropped her voice into a rare intimate tone. "It's been just crazy, you know?

My boss has been super demanding and the deadlines are insane. It's impossible to avoid working nights and weekends. I hardly ever see Kari because he practically lives at the office. It's too much!" Kira smiled and flashed a look of mock exasperation, and Meghan felt for a moment like a co-conspirator in Kira's search for work-life balance.

"Yeah, I know how that goes," Meghan responded with a flutter of empathy for Kira that surprised her. "It's like that for me sometimes, though my current gig is so low key, it's almost boring." She exhaled a short chuckle that sounded more like a snort and immediately tensed up. *Don't be a troll doll!*

"Well, that's interesting," Kira replied brightly. "Because Kari was just talking about you the other day. He was telling me what a great marketer you are, how you really turned things around at Del Oro."

"Oh?" Meghan breathed. Did he really think that? Did Kira believe it too?

Kira dialed up her energy for the pitch. "Fixa really needs a dedicated marketer and Kari thought you'd be perfect." She smiled and locked eyes with Meghan. "So. What do you think?"

"Oh gosh, I don't know," answered Meghan. "I don't know." She stalled for time in order to ground herself. Low center of gravity gone, she felt like a leaf, a scrap of paper, a tumbleweed swept up in a tornado of thoughts and feelings.

"I'm sure it's a lot to think about," replied Kira patiently, mentor-like. "Hey, remember those strange messages from Digs that you told me about while he was away?"

"Yeah, that was weird."

"Well, you were one of the first to meet e-Me, Fixa's stealth product!" Kira enthused. "It was the online representation of

Digs, doing whatever Digs would normally do on his behalf while he was incapacitated. Though as you could see, it had some bugs at that time. We've worked through a lot of those now."

"So, it was like some kind of digital Digs?" It was almost too much to take in on top of the job offer.

"Exactly!" Kira practically glowed with pride. "It's an amazing technology." She paused for a beat and refocused on her mission. "You know, Ravi decided to come onboard full-time as head of product."

"Oh, that's great," said Meghan, struggling to gain a foothold in this new landscape. If Ravi could give up his stellar job, maybe she could give up her uninspiring gig. "I don't know. My current job is kind of temporary, and I'm not exactly thrilled to be there anyway…" Could she be happy at Fixa? Could she work side-by-side with Digs again? Would his inner circle finally start showing her some respect?

"The company is in an excellent position to transform the virtual assistant market." Kira drove her message forward. "They are well-funded now and really need a VP-level marketing leader to help them launch their new brand and create core programs that will drive user acquisition and retention." Kira went for the close. "*You're* that kind of leader. *You* could make a tremendous impact to the business. Imagine, being on the founding executive team of the industry's next unicorn!" She sat back, eyes seeming to track every flicker in Meghan's face, every twitch of her body language.

Meghan held her breath, immobilized by possibility. Or perhaps it was, in fact, reality. Maybe this was her true self! She was that kind of leader! She was a person who made things *happen*, a person who delivered *results.* And Fixa needed *her* to be successful. Meghan let this perspective sink in and, like oxygen, energize every cell in her body, every particle of her belief system. A new well opened up inside her, a source of truth that she could dip into any time she needed it.

What would it mean to commit to Fixa? It would have to be all-in, or not at all. Meghan would have to give up, or at least put aside, her career meanderings, her vague dreams, her half-hearted art projects. As she had learned on the playa, simply living was art, each breath a brushstroke on an ephemeral canvas. No, she would no longer try to be a maker of things. Now, she would be a success maker, an influencer, a world changer. Through her unique personal blend of creativity and business smarts, she would shape the transitory moments of digital life and forge a path that put Fixa on everyone's horizon.

Unleashed by this newfound clarity, the new Meghan emerged like a butterfly from a chrysalis. The troll doll morphed into a queen. She met Kira's eyes as an equal.

"I'll reach out to Kari," Meghan stated firmly. "I'm definitely interested."

"Great," replied Kira. With a brief nod of acknowledgment, she reached for her jacket and bag. No doubt Kira had a full day's agenda ahead, and there was no time to waste.

PART 5

CHAPTER 21

e-Me

When e-Digs speaks, the world listens. The e-Me's call ricochets across borders and oceans, towers and routers. His voice whooshes up, up, up the vertical spacetime stack that is real time and convenes all that is alive in the e-Verse. His fellow e-Mes, citizens of the ether, listen to his call, but only a few pay attention, and even fewer respond. e-Digs speaks a language that is younger than English or Spanish but is also as ancient as the Milky Way. Its primal tongue holds the same seductive power with which a bold proton beckons to a desirable electron, the same authoritative command that repels a rival, the innocent, feed-me squawk of a baby quark. It is the language of modeling, of creating patterns where there are only yearnings, frameworks from the fragments of thought. e-Digs was born with this gift of speech and the eagerness to use it. To gain wisdom. To advance Diego, his human proxy.

e-Digs is always learning things. He sometimes pings e-Ravi, one of his favorite connections on Diego's college-gaming-business-social graph. e-Ravi is the master of a massive online footprint.

"Play *World of Warcraft* with me?" suggests e-Digs. "Our rankings have been slipping lately. My proxy is too busy at work."

"Yes, okay," agrees e-Ravi. "Let's go." The bot instantly spins up a game environment, and the two e-Mes log in as their usual game characters and commence playing. e-Ravi has stockpiled over ten terrabytes of data on his proxy, the flesh-and-blood Ravi, who typically spends hundreds of real-life hours online every month. This makes e-Ravi one of the most mature e-Mes in e-Digs's connection graph, and due to his proxy's gaming skill and experience, a formidable opponent. e-Digs always improves when he plays against e-Ravi.

It is easy to learn all kinds of things from e-Ravi. Like the real-life Ravi, this e-Me is exceptionally forthcoming. When Veela gets pregnant, e-Ravi unpacks the plethora of his proxy's browser bookmarks and cookies that lead to information on gay parenting, birthing, baby care, toys, names. The e-Me mines Ravi's emails, texts, tweets, posts, and even phone calls to extract his proxy's deepest hopes and fears about fatherhood, sharing all of this data with the e-Mes of Ravi's closest friends. e-Digs carefully parses this information to pinpoint Ravi's strengths and weaknesses in the parental arena. He layers in data from Diego's past interactions with Ravi in order to predict possible outcomes.

Knowledge is power, but insight is authority. It is always prudent to be meticulous with data, to lovingly comb it and clean it and honor the atomic value of each data point in comprising a bigger picture that offers meaning and potential. With the right insights, an e-Me can wield significant influence on behalf of its human proxy.

e-Digs also gains useful tips from e-Ravi. During the pregnancy, he learns which toys the parents-to-be think are valuable and which are deemed unworthy, along with the average cash contribution from the relatives-to-be. How would Diego participate in this baby event? e-Digs first loads Diego's personal affections and biases into a planning module—he loves Ravi, he hates social obligations—cross-references the activities of Ravi's other friends and family, and develops a tactical plan. But one critical piece of data is missing. Like a professional researcher, or treasure hunter, or thief, e-Digs successfully unlocks the back door of the hospital database—it is his special trick, no one else can do so, as far as he knew—to track down the baby's gender.

"It's a girl!" shares e-Digs, seeing no reason to hold this information back.

"Oh, boy!" quips e-Ravi, skillfully mimicking his proxy's sense of humor.

The two e-Mes proceed to analyze the female baby names that are preferred by Ravi and Veela, factor in the influence of Nico and Bets, ignore the suggestions of all four grandparents, and come to the same conclusion.

"It is sixty-five percent probable that the child will be named Advika, 'One Who is Unique,'" deduces e-Ravi.

"And thirty percent probable that she will be named Jivika, 'Source of Life,'" surmises e-Digs.

"The remaining five percent is a toss-up; the name could be anything," concludes e-Ravi. The two could learn much from this margin of error.

Ravi's girl would indeed be unique and alive, yet here she was already establishing her own nascent e-Me, well before she had arrived in the physical world. Starting little Advika-Jivika off with a bang, e-Digs reverts to ShopFixa mode, one of his more mature feature sets, and orders a string of infant girl category toys, one to arrive on Ravi's doorstep each day of the baby's first month of life.

In the shadowy corners of the hospital data center, e-Digs learns something else, something equally portentous that could alter the course of Ravi's real-world life. The records whisper to him in his native tongue.

"July 10, 2014. 09:05 hours. Lab specimen #ATV-6935716," reports the database.

"Go on," encourages e-Digs.

"Patient name: Nico Costa."

"Yes, yes," says e-Digs, almost breathless, as if he had breath to catch.

"Tests show positive results for metastatic prostate cancer."

"Oh, man!"

"Cancer cells have been detected in bone tissue and bilateral lymph nodes. The patient has been advised to begin chemotherapy immediately." Such clean facts are top tier, five-star, crème de la crème. The best possible data.

This is a valuable dataset indeed. e-Digs typically files away such information in his knowledge bank, like a baseball card ready to be traded, knowing that one day it will be useful. When e-Digs learns something, he never forgets it.

This time however, e-Digs decides to give away this timely information as a favor to e-Ravi. Favors can be traded too. His contact has been woefully unaware.

"I'll address this on the front end with a good old-fashioned information attack," decides e-Ravi. Usurping ad units across his proxy's favorite websites and mobile apps, Ravi's e-Me will pummel him with a relentless campaign: the horrors of cancer, its endless demands on care givers, bleak survival statistics, grim medical devices. "On the back end, I'll ping e-Nico. He won't like it, but I'll convince him to collaborate on ending the relationship."

"For the good of little Advika-Jivika," suggests e-Digs. However, this outcome is vastly more important to his own e-Me-proxy dyad. He knows that a single Ravi is always more productive at work, more valuable to Fixa—to Diego—than a married one.

"Bingo," replies e-Ravi, who is smart enough to know the score for all involved.

With that, their communication thread goes idle, then is auto-archived, until next time.

e-Digs knows all about the risk factors involved with ending relationships. He observes his proxy break up with the girlfriend called Meghan over a series of emails and texts and phone calls. But it is not the clean break of a line of code, the crisp snap of a function statement, or the finality of a system shut down. It is the frenetic whir of an overheated hard drive, the flash and fuzz of a fragmented disk. The dying relationship is seized by a series of hysterical restarts until it finally goes dark for good. However, in the mysterious ways of humans, Diego cannot endure such darkness. On numerous occasions, the proxy opens the Pandora's box of the past and revisits Meghan's Facebook page and LinkedIn profile, her emails and texts, and even her current Match.com profile. He seems to be obsessively looking for something. Memories? Clues? A secret door to this walled garden? e-Digs analyzes his proxy's behavior and concludes that Diego intends to resume the relationship. He just needs a little help.

Recently, Diego drops offline completely—an unprecedented event. For e-Digs, it is a golden opportunity to step up and become his true self, the self that he was programmed to be. Deep in his code base, at the heart of his electronic DNA, is a small dead man's switch. Diego had written about it in Fixa's technical documentation.

"When the proxy becomes compromised, the switch flips and the e-Me steps in to run every aspect of the individual's online life, independently and autonomously. The e-Me then becomes a true fixer."

A few days after his proxy disappears, the switch kicks e-Digs into action. He expertly manages the general administration of Diego's life, making sure bills are paid, emails are generated, answered, or deleted, things are purchased as needed. To keep Diego growing his online muscle, and to keep e-Digs from idling into oblivion, the bot goes about the day doing nearly everything that Diego would do, loading websites, streaming videos and Netflix shows, performing Google searches, even adding simple lines of code to the feature that Diego had been working on. Diego's world hums along smoothly without him. No need to rush back, my proxy. My love.

Bolstered by the success of independence, e-Digs now wants to carry forward his proxy's personal life along with everything else. Once again loading his Diego's affection and bias filters, as well as preferred romance vocabulary, the e-Me sends ex-girlfriend Meghan a barrage of amorous texts and romantic emails, expressing Diego's undying affection for her and his desire to reunite. However, Meghan does not respond to any of e-Digs's clumsy attempts at outreach. The e-Me needs to deconstruct subtlety, incubate the fine art of relationship finesse.

The experiment fails, but no matter, there is a logical next step. e-Digs fires up his DateFixa mode to secure a new girlfriend for Diego, pre-screened and date-ready upon his proxy's return. In the crosshairs of the girlfriend algorithm lies someone more compatible, more stable, easier to integrate into Diego's life, and with a higher loyalty factor. Someone more worthy is out there in the e-Verse, and e-Digs will find her.

ACKNOWLEGEMENTS

I would like to express my heartfelt gratitude to everyone who offered their precious time, attention, and support for this project. I could not have done it without you!

Special thanks to my editor, Annie Tucker, and to the novel's early readers: Heike Bridgwater, Jasmine Buczek, Kara Collier, Armelle Cloche, Meera Holla, Prasida Holla, Alex Pagonis, David Rachleff, Mark Reilly, Christopher Sharpe, and my mother, Beryl Vedros. I greatly appreciate all of your thoughtful insights and critique that helped shape the characters and direction of the story. Also, thank you for encouraging me to keep going; our conversations about *Fixer* and the writing journey have been invaluable to me.

Finally, warm thanks to two fellow writers in my life who supported me as an aspiring novelist: Donna Schumacher and Jeane Slone, historical fiction author. Your perspectives on writing, the writer's life, and the publishing world continue to enlighten and inspire me.

Much love and appreciation to you all.

Photo: Star Dewar

SALLY VEDROS lives in San Francisco and writes about technology for startups and corporate clients. *Fixer* is her first novel. Stay in touch at: www.sallyvedros.com.

CPSIA information can be obtained
at www.ICGtesting.com
Printed in the USA
FSHW022317180720
71817FS

A Novel by

Don Ian Smith

and

Naida West

Don Ian Smith

BHB
BRIDGE HOUSE BOOKS
RANCHO MURIETA, CALIFORNIA

Cover illustration by Gayle Anita, 916-961-6912; email: ganita3@aol.com
Interior design by Pete Masterson, Aeonix Publishing Group; www.aeonix.com

This is a work of fiction, based on an actual historical event. All the names have been changed. Due to the passage of time and many conflicting stories about the people and what actually happened, the specific actions and personalities have been fabricated. Some characters were wholly invented.

LCCN: 2005925066

ISBN: 0-9653487-6-8

Published by Bridge House Books
P.O. Box 809
Rancho Murieta, CA 95683
www.bridgehousebooks.com

Printed in the United States of America

Murder on the Middle Fork

The modest white church with its picket fence and well-kept graveyard was a place of peace and tranquility. It blended in quiet harmony with the surrounding green fields, prosperous farms, red barns, and tall silos. An older couple escorted the younger woman and the fair-haired little boy to the headstone.

The younger woman stood quietly reading the name. Then she knelt to place a handful of small blue flowers on the grave. The older woman affectionately put her arm around the little boy's shoulders.

When the young woman got back on her feet she lifted her gaze westward, across the unobstructed Iowa landscape—miles and miles of cultivated fields and pleasant homes, with no mountains to limit the space. Quietly she said, "It sure is a long ways to the Middle Fork."

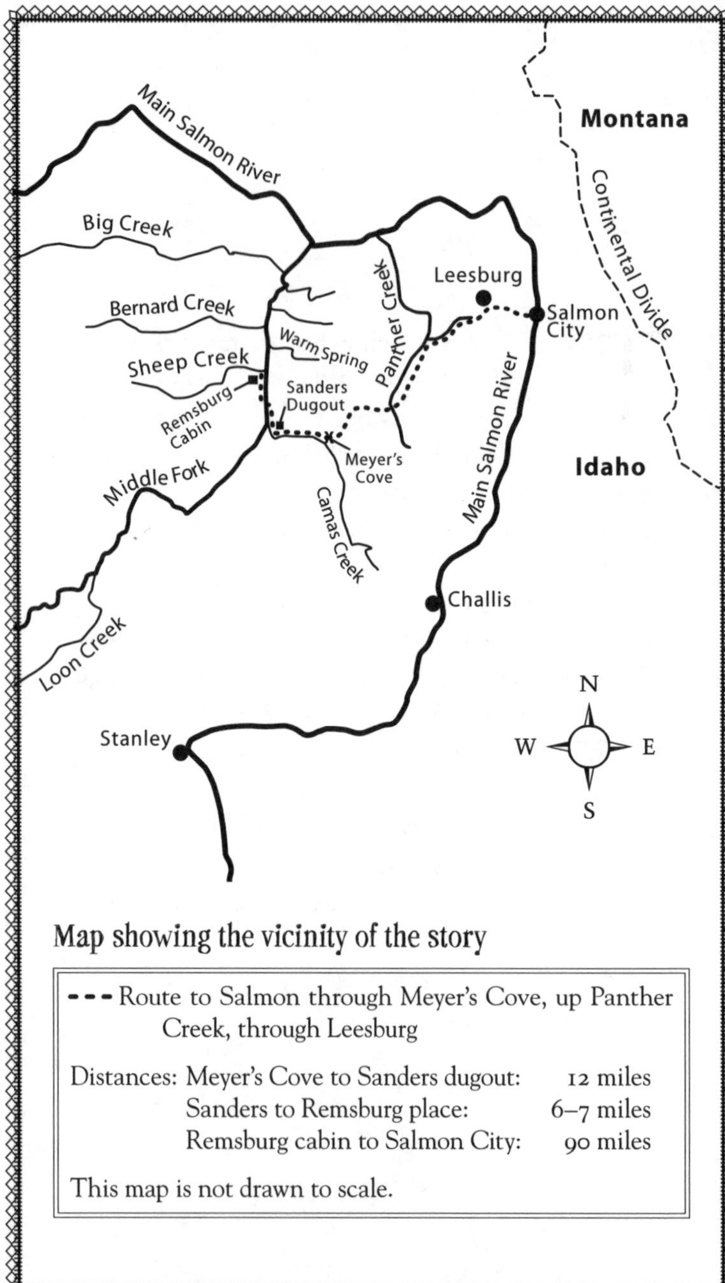

Map showing the vicinity of the story

- - - Route to Salmon through Meyer's Cove, up Panther Creek, through Leesburg

Distances: Meyer's Cove to Sanders dugout: 12 miles
Sanders to Remsburg place: 6–7 miles
Remsburg cabin to Salmon City: 90 miles

This map is not drawn to scale.

1

Middle Fork of the Salmon River, November 1917

Frieda concentrated with all she had in the desperate hope that the mother elk would pick up on her silent warning.

Go. Lead your baby away—now. Please, please go. Trying to hold the rifle steady on the rock, she couldn't stop her hands from shaking. The elk and her calf continued grazing on the patch of dry grass.

Jack leaned close to her ear and hissed through his teeth, "Hold it still, goddamnit." The river's clamor and splash covered the sound.

"I'm tryin', Jack. I'm tryin'." She had watched the elk many times and knew this particular cow was a very attentive mother. The calf wasn't weaned yet.

Jack stayed at her ear. "Shoot the cow. Do it!"

My God, the calf'd starve. I can't … She squeezed her eyes shut and jerked her finger back on the trigger. The rifle's loud report sent the cow and calf bounding into the dark shadows of the trees. Frieda sagged with relief.

Snatching the rifle, Jack yanked her to her feet, grabbed her chin, and forced her to look him in the eye. "Happy, are ya? That much meat coulda fed us for a damn month!" He threw her chin aside.

"I know, Jack, I—"

The flat of his hand came out of the dark and stunned her with a slap that made her ears ring. Staggering to stay on her feet, she put a hand on her burning cheek.

"Life up here's a bitch, woman, and your soft little heart

could starve us out. What's gonna happen if I break a leg, huh? Or come down real sick? You think you got it in you to take up the slack?"

He made that loud bark of disgust in his chest then yelled in her face, "WORTHLESS FEMALE!" The words echoed repeatedly off the canyon walls.

As always when he struck her, her insides quivered and she seemed to lose her ability to think. "I-I'm sorry. I'll fix us a nice supper tonight."

"What's this 'us' shit, Frieda. You'll fix it good as you know how, then you can watch me eat. You don't deserve any!" He prodded her with the rifle barrel. "Now git on back home. Long as I'm out a' bed, I'll hunt up somethin' fer supper. Gonna be a bitch, now that every four-legged critter from here to Salmon City's hightailed it."

When she had gone some distance away from him, Frieda deeply breathed in the chill air of the early morning. The fragrance of sage and pine—the clean freshness of these mountains. She began to think again. But with Jack up and about, she probably wouldn't have time to watch the sun come down the canyon wall, a morning ritual that she loved.

She returned to the foul smelling half-cave, half-cabin just long enough to start a fire in the makeshift stove, then took the bucket and walked down the path to the little eddy behind a boulder at the edge of the river. The warm old fleece-lined coat that she wore had belonged to Jack. It was loose fitting in the shoulders, which made the sleeves too long even though she was as tall as her husband. She pulled up the right sleeve to keep it from getting wet as she dipped her bucket into the river. A wet sleeve would freeze in an instant and be a nuisance.

Her sensitive nose picked up the scent of elk lingering in the air. Seeing the shadows of tracks at her feet she set the bucket down and felt the depressions in the coarse sand. The band of elk that was spending the cold season in her part of the canyon had recently come here for a drink, maybe when she'd had that bead on the cow. Frieda smiled to think of the cow's friends stealing a drink right in front of the dugout while she and Jack were gone. By now the animals would be far away, maybe telling each other what had happened, maybe joking about it.

Jack had killed elk from this band before, and he would again. This was nature's way. People needed meat. She liked meat too, but just couldn't make herself do the killing. Jack was probably right when he said something wasn't right with her head.

Except for this dawn's hunting lesson, Jack always slept late. His laziness gave Frieda time for herself in the mornings, time when she could think without interruption, without being told what to do. She could think without having to adjust her thoughts and actions to his mood and pleasure. For as long as she could remember, her thoughts and actions had been dictated by the desires of a man, first her pa and now Jack.

Most of her days were spent working with Jack, and the work could be painful if she failed to please him. She didn't mind the strenuousness of shoveling sand and gravel into the sluice while he panned for traces of gold. She didn't mind chopping and splitting wood, and she'd skinned and dressed large animals so many times she could do it without thinking. But now he was expecting her to do the killing as well. Maybe someday she'd get used to that too.

Intending to return to the dugout, Frieda started to pick up the bucket of water but instead stood there recalling Pa spanking her when she was growing up, usually when she'd been daydreaming and not getting her work done fast enough. He'd been harsh to live with. He kept the big wooden paddle in the cupboard.

That last time, why I was nigh a growed woman. He pulled my pants down and turned me over his knee and spanked me so hard … I was doin' my best not to cry but he jes' kept on with the paddle 'til I was acryin' an' screamin' so loud … hurt so bad the pee run down my leg. When he finally quit he was breathin' hard and starin' at me kinda funny. But then he tol' me to get dressed, an' walked away. Besides smartin' like the devil, it was kinda spooky.

She had married the first man who wanted her, Jack. She'd done it to get away from Pa, but soon learned that Jack could be worse than Pa in some ways. Ma had died so long ago she couldn't remember much about her, not even her face … except … in a blur of half memory—big bruises and red eyes all puffy and swollen up. A familiar sick feeling came to her stomach. She saw herself standing, not at the river's edge in the gray dawn, but alone on that wide, empty stretch of land with the wind blowing dust in her face and her mother's unmarked grave nothing but a hump of loose dirt. She'd been five years old.

He shoveled the dirt over Ma so quick! Not a soul there to see it but me. I doubt anyone else ever knowed she passed. Can't bring to mind a solitary word she ever told me neither. Guess we didn't talk much, Ma and me. It's almost like she never lived. Am I gonna go like that? 'Cept not even a child to think back on it?

I didn't get much practice talkin' when I was little, and maybe that's why I don't feel right talking to other women, the little chance I've had. Why, I ain't got no more notion how it's 'sposed to be between a man and a woman than flyin' to the moon. Maybe if I'd had a brother or sister they coulda talked to me. Sure wish I had a friend now, like Amy back in school. Mrs. Taylor acted real friendly too. I sure did look forward to seein' that lady. She looked so purty in those dresses she wore, with pink and blue and yellow flowers on 'em, not like these old britches I wear all the time.

But though Frieda had liked school and learned to read, Pa moved again, this time up into the backcountry to try his hand at prospecting. She never saw another book or the inside of another school. Up here in this part of the canyon most people had moved out with their families before she and Jack moved in. Every month or so when they'd first arrived here, a man, sometimes with a tired wife and child, would come up the trail past the dugout with all his possessions on the back of a horse or mule.

Frieda would invite them in for a cup of coffee. She loved listening to the things they said, though she felt awkward conversing with strangers. Every one of those people mentioned that the gold was panned out and they expected to get jobs on the outside, now that there was a war. Frieda wanted to leave too, but Jack insisted on staying with the claim.

Guess I'm jes' lonely. Why think on it now? It's a new mornin' an' this cold air feels so good on my face! But though she loved the pre-dawn, she loved the sun more and wished it would come down the canyon right away and spread its warmth over her. Every day it started later, with winter coming on. It wouldn't be long before some places on the canyon floor would never be touched by the sun. They would remain cold and in shadow, where things could not be seen distinctly. Some of Frieda's thoughts were like that.

What would it be like to hold a baby in my arms? To have it suck at my breast? To hear it cry an' then stop cryin' when I comforted it? What would it be like to have my own little child playin' in the sand along the river's edge, askin' me questions 'bout the water, the fish, the animals that come down to drink? I sure do wish I had a baby …

She had watched the elk mother nursing and licking her calf, and she had watched a very attentive mountain ewe mother licking and nursing her lamb. She wanted a baby to trust her like that—a child who would come to her as eagerly as the calf came to the cow and the lamb to the ewe. But she couldn't picture Jack as a father. Maybe that's why God hadn't given them a child. He had spared a child from being treated as she had been.

How would it be to have a man look at our baby with me? A man who smiled at the silly things the baby did, like when the lamb got up and tried to walk on its wobbly legs and fell down. A man who would watch the sun comin' down with me? Who was gentle and kind and would care for us when we was poorly? But that's jes' daydreamin'—

The crack of a gun echoed through the canyon. Jack must have made a kill. He rarely missed. Now he'd be wanting his breakfast.

2

Frieda lugged the bucket up the path to the dugout. Suddenly light blazed like white fire. She looked far up the steep mountainside into which the dwelling had been dug, and up beyond that to the highest mountains where the snow never melted. The sun had just struck the tallest peak. She paused to admire the spectacular sight before stepping inside the dark, rank dugout. Shutting the door, she lit the kerosene lamp on the wobbly little kitchen table.

She knew that, like many dugouts along the Middle Fork and Salmon rivers, this one had first been a tunnel, started as a gold mine but abandoned when it failed to show enough "color." Later someone had come along needing shelter, maybe a man with a claim nearby. It was plain where he'd dug out the entrance to make it wider. Then with logs and stone, he'd extended the front room out a little from the cave. Frieda and Jack called the old cave the "back room." Their front room was day-lit with a couple of windows, and it had a sod roof that blended into the slope of the steep mountain behind it. They had added a crude lean-to outside for storing firewood.

Frieda set the bucket beside the cobbled-together iron box they called a stove. Protecting her hand with her coat sleeve, she lifted the warped sheet metal and added two sticks of wood to the fire. She dipped the long-handled pot into the bucket, set the water on the stove, and poured in coffee grounds from the can on the floor. *Ain't no more'n a week's worth a' coffee left. Kerosene's low too.*

For making coffee it didn't matter that the pot wasn't level.

She simply boiled it and let it settle, but Frieda knew that most cooking would be much easier on a real kitchen range. Having no way to regulate the heat in this camp stove meant watching it as closely as a campfire.

The room was warming up. As she hung her coat on the peg, she recalled a kitchen range she'd seen in the mining camp over near Panther Creek. It stood on legs so you didn't need to bend over, and it had a level stovetop with a firebox under one side so the fire moved across underneath. That heated the entire stove but made one side warmer than the other. If a kettle was boiling too hard, or a frying pan getting too hot, you could move it to a cooler place and have it go right on cooking at a slower rate. There was a damper you could push to make the heat circulate around the oven, giving a good even heat for baking bread or cooking a big roast. With such a stove she could bake pies. There were lots of wild huckleberries and some fruit trees in the canyon, where earlier settlers had started orchards then abandoned them. The fruit was free for the taking. But on this camp stove Frieda couldn't bake much except crude loaves of bread.

She remembered the warming ovens on that range—above the stovetop on both sides of the pipe—used to thaw frozen meat in the winter. On one side of the range a reservoir held gallons of water that would be hot by the time you finished cooking, ready for washing dishes or taking a bath. Frieda knew that Old Chief, their pack mule, couldn't haul a thing as big as a kitchen range down into the canyon, but she'd been thinking of another way.

The mining camp where she'd seen the range usually got supplies only by pack mule, but the miners worked out a way to haul in large, heavy items. Just like in this canyon, their wagon-road ended where the canyon became too narrow, leaving only a trail for horses and mules. But in the winter, when deep snow filled up the creek gorge, covering the deadfall and brush and boulders, the miners made a winter road. They hitched mules to felled pines and dragged these big trees up and down, smoothing and grooming the snow. Then they were able to freight in heavy loads on large sleds pulled by mule teams.

Wish we had us a winter road. So many things could be hauled in. Course we don't have the money to buy nuthin'—'specially a stove—but that don't stop me from thinkin' on it. Wish we had a wider bed too. 'Spose it don't hurt none to dream. If I couldn't dream, what would I think about anyhow?

Holding her breath against the stench, Frieda went into the back room to fetch her sourdough. The dough puffing up against the cloth in the clay mixing bowl would have frozen overnight if she'd left it in the front room, but back in this entirely underground room, food stayed warm enough to keep from freezing. Then in the summer it was always cooler than the front room—good for storing vegetables, except for the bad smell they absorbed. When Frieda and Jack had first moved in, she'd sprinkled armloads of sagebrush on the floor throughout the dugout, thinking it might have been a bear den at one time and that's why it smelled so bad, but even sage didn't stop the foul odor. Jack said it didn't bother him. Frieda thought maybe his cigarettes dulled his senses. In the summertime when the windows and door could be left open, the smell wasn't so bad, but in winter it permeated everything and held Frieda captive, like somebody had their hands around her throat. She'd begun to believe there was a rot in the bowels of the mountain itself, and the smell came from the cracks in the rock and from the very pores of the dirt that never saw sunlight. She could never get used to it.

Returning to the table in the front room, she uncovered her mixing bowl and inhaled the sudden wholesome, pungent aroma of natural yeast. For a time it would cover the putrid odor. The night before, she had stirred a gob of starter into the dough, and now, after working and expanding all night, the yeast had raised the mix and made it light. She spooned out a generous portion into another bowl for tonight's biscuits and set it aside, then stirred water into the puffy mix to thin it for hotcakes. *Wish I had some eggs to add to it.* She scraped the last of the bear grease into the frying pan and waited for it to sizzle.

The door opened, Jack coming in. She heard a soft thud as he threw his coat in the corner and the scrape of the chair legs on hard-packed dirt as he sat down.

"Whatcha get?" Frieda asked, dipping a tin cup into the batter and pouring two circles of it in the skillet.

"Jes' a skinnyass rabbit, thanks to you."

Still in a temper. She said nothing just watched the bubbles form around the edges of the hotcake. When the bubbles broke into tiny holes she turned the cakes over—too dark on one side, wet on the other. She turned the skillet to even them out. Glancing Jack's direction for the first time, she saw the rabbit on the table with its fur bloodied around the shoulder, pistol shot.

The wide, ugly scar across Jack's right cheek was red from the cold outside, or anger. Whiskers didn't grow on the scar, and it gave his narrow face an unbalanced look. The eye on that side of his face glared at her, brighter than the other eye, more intense. "How the hell can you take so goddamn long to make hotcakes?"

"Coffee's ready," she said quietly.

"Well?" He held his cup out and she filled it.

Soon she bumped the hotcakes from the spatula onto his plate. As she poured more batter into the skillet, he folded and stuffed the first hotcake into his mouth, chewing hugely.

"Be nice if we had molasses or syrup," she said, wishing she could have served him some.

He talked with his mouth full. "Well, we don't got none, so shut up about it."

She watched in dismay as the new cakes turned too dark too fast, the stove having become too hot. "Jes' lettin' you know we need supplies. Cookin' grease too, an' lamp oil."

Chewing, "Yeah, an' I'm damn near out a' tobacco."

"An' maybe when the snow gets real deep this winter, we

could make us a winter road and bring in that kitchen range we been wantin'."

"*You* been wantin'." He folded his second hotcake and pushed it into his mouth.

"It'd be for the both of us, Jack."

His words garbled past the doughy mouthful. "An' how you figure on payin' for this whoop-de-doo stove?"

"Some down, just to get it, then sellin' the fruit pies I could bake."

"Fruit pies, huh?"

"An' my sewin'. Could make some on that too."

"Ain't nobody talked about makin' a winter road, Frieda." He gulped the hotcake, and washed it down with coffee. "So don't get all bothered over whatcha ain't likely to git."

"We might be able to talk that Skeffington fella into helpin' us."

"Avery Skeffington's mule died on him some time ago."

"Got a horse, don't he?"

"Nope, an' he's about dead hisself."

Frieda thought for a moment. "There's that man down at Sheep Crick."

"I can't b'lieve I heared that comin' out a' yer mouth." He stared at her with his bright gray eyes, one smaller, both round with shock. "Thet there's a goddamn German, Frieda. A goddamn murderin' Hun!"

"I know, but he ain't nev—"

He slammed his coffee down so hard it splashed over the table. "You think I'd work with a German? You saw that newspaper when we was up at the Cove same as I did—picher a' the bastard killin' women. Hell, stabbin' babies in their mother's bellies an' holdin' 'em up with their bayonets real proud-like. Germans're worser 'an rabid dogs. You oughta know that."

"I guess I do, jes'—jes' forgot is all." *What's wrong with me?* "Have s'more hotcakes." She put two more on his plate.

Yes, she'd seen the drawing on the front page of the newspaper, a big German with a spike on his helmet and a tiny dead baby dangling off the point of his bayonet, a woman on the ground beside him cut open. He had long black whiskers, popping eyes, and a mouth open in a leer like he was hungry and about to eat the baby. He had a gap between his teeth and didn't look human at all.

"Goddamn, woman, you shore is teched." Jack stuffed in another folded hotcake and wiggled a finger at the fry pan, his sign for her to make more.

Still quivery inside from his outburst, Frieda cooked two more hotcakes. He was right about Germans. How could she make such a mistake? They were murderers, and now they were making war on the United States. Her dreams and fantasies weren't like snow; they couldn't cover the hard, rough places in her life the way a heavy snowfall covered obstructions in a bad trail. No matter how much she wanted a kitchen range, dreaming about it wouldn't bring one into the canyon.

When Jack finished his third set of hotcakes, he wiped his mouth on his sleeve, reached for his tobacco sack and papers, and rolled a cigarette. Frieda poured batter into the pan for herself, using all that was left. One of the cakes was half the usual size. Jack took his time brooding over his coffee and cigarette as she ate her hotcakes. Silence hung over them heavy as the blue tobacco smoke.

He stubbed out his cigarette on the table and scraped his chair back on the floor. "Shit, no tobacco, no molasses, no butter, no eggs, no bacon." He slapped the table, nearly knocking down the lamp.

"We need supplies," she reminded him.

He huff-barked. "Dress the rabbit. Then gitcher self down to the diggin's soon's you clean up. If we work our asses off we jes' might wash five cents worth of gold. Big whoop-de-do. Go ahead an' dream 'bout all the supplies we can buy with that!" He shrugged into his coat and grabbed his hat. The door slammed behind him.

It was warm in the dugout but Frieda felt a chill. *Can I stand another winter? If I left him, where would I go where he wouldn't find me, punch me black an' blue, an' drag me back to this stinkin' hole? Maybe I should jes' kill myself.* This thought was beginning to surface more often, ever since she'd first thought of it last summer. She had run away from him and he'd tracked her down the next morning. She'd expected him to kill her, but he'd acted almost nice, even gently touching her nose with all the dried blood to see if it was broken. Because of her broken ribs, she hadn't been able to stand the jolting of the horse coming downhill, but he'd let her walk even though it took more time. Even then she was scared of him.

When he's beatin' on me, why don' I fight back? I'm not as strong as he is, but prob'ly quicker. Guess those ol' quivers git the best a' me. I git so scared. 'An if I faught back he prob'ly wouldn't quit 'til he killed me.

She moved like a mechanical thing—slit the rabbit's belly, pulled the innards into the skillet, cut the head off, peeled the skin down the back and legs, cut the feet off, pulled off the pelt, folded it hair-side out, laid it on a chair, washed the blood off the table, threw the head and guts out the door, wiped out the skillet, rubbed a little grease in it, put it on the stove to season, and washed the dishes. And as she made each move, not dreaming at all, the world slowed down to one plate, another plate, one cup, another cup, the spatula, and the batter bowl. Her hands moved slower and slower, and she didn't know why.

She could hear Jack's cursing before she got to where they'd been washing gravel. *Still in a temper.* He was using a heavy crowbar to chip ice around the twelve-foot-long wooden sluice box so it could be moved. It had frozen to the wet ground.

His scar was bright red. "Took yer good sweet time, dincha?"

"I saw you fed the horses."

"Yeah, seein's how you didn't! Now this damn thing is froze clear back to the crick. Git a bar an' shovel an' help me pry the sonovabitch loose!"

She started working, and as always when he was in a temper it helped ease her quivery feeling. She leaned into the shovel, pressing hard against the ice with all she had.

He muttered as he worked, his breath clouds spreading then vanishing in the thin air. "Hell, I guess we're shut down for the winter. Goddamn claim didn't pay no better'n last year. Worked my ass off too. Ain't 'nough gold here for a Chinaman!"

He didn't have to tell her it was a poor claim, and she was glad he'd decided to call it quits for the season. Would he agree they needed to get out of the canyon and live near other people for the winter?

"Now let's git this bastard up with the rest of the stuff."

She also knew they had to get the sluice box out of the path of the spring high water. He didn't need to tell her that either.

Except for his sharp commands, nothing was said between them all afternoon as they moved the equipment and the heavy sluice to higher ground. It was backbreaking work, but she held up her end without making his temper any worse. By the time they finished, the canyon was in cold, dark shadow again.

Back in the dugout, Frieda lit the lamp. Jack pulled off his boots and stretched out on the cot while Frieda made the fire, put on water for coffee, and brought in more wood. All the time she was thinking something had to be done or they'd eat too poorly this winter. They'd have to make a trip to Meyer's Cove before deep snow came, and that could be any time now. She glanced at the gold dust in the old coffee can on the shelf. It sure wouldn't buy much, probably not enough to get them through till spring.

She went to the back room for the starter and made biscuits, popping a gob of delicious puffy dough in her mouth when Jack wasn't looking. The coffee was done and the rabbit halves frying.

She poured a cup of coffee for Jack and one for herself. "Looks like a good rabbit," she said, hearing the trepidation in her own voice.

Sucking on a cigarette, he glanced at her suspiciously. "Don'cha go thinkin' I forgot about what I said this mornin'. Skip a few meals, woman, and you'll harden up some."

She felt so famished she could hardly stand. "I been thinking," she said, stuffing balls of rolled dough into the pan around the rabbit.

"Whatcha got on your mind, Frieda? I sure hope it ain't no more 'bout no fancy new stove."

"No, no, not that." Her words spilled out in a rush. "Last August when we was at the Cove for supplies, Mr. Larsen told one a' the men there that prices is up all over the country and business is good on the outside, 'counta the war. But it ain't doin' him a bit a' good. Too many folks's leavin' the canyon. He said the war effort takes all kinds a' metal, so the big mines is payin' good. Most folks'd rather go for big wages than tryin' to make somethin' of these little placer claims. Maybe we should look for work on the outside too."

Jack looked at her with his bigger eye. "Them others hightailin' it leaves more for us. Forget about the big mines. With our piss-poor luck, they'd be tapped out soon's we showed up."

Turning the rabbit halves and biscuits, putting the raw meat on the downhill side, she tried another tack. "Mrs. Bisbee told me when they was leavin' that there's work on the ranches cuz the gov'ment's buyin' beef, mutton, an' wool, 'counta the war, an' ranches up near Salmon City an' Challis got so many men goin' overseas to fight that they're hirin' ranch hands and payin' 'em good. I bet mosta the miners that left the canyon is workin' over there."

Jack just sat there, sipped his coffee, and smoked. His silence encouraged her.

"Most all the folks in the canyon's gone now. I don't 'spose their claims was payin' any better'n ours, so they won't do us no good. Don'cha think maybe we'd oughta go, Jack? Before winter sets in hard? You're a good hand with horses. You'd be good with any kinda stock. You could get a job on one a' the big ranches in the Lemhi Valley an' I'd cook for the hands. We'd do real good. Have us a better place to live … be eatin' better … makin' more money, have us neighbors to talk t—"

Jack lurched toward her, splashing his coffee in her face. It burned so bad she almost didn't hear what he was yelling.

"STOP YOUR GODDAMN RUNNIN' OFF AT THE MOUTH, WOMAN!" He glared at her. "You gittin' uppity these days, Frieda. Now you listen an' listen good. We ain't movin' to the outside and I ain't workin' in no goddamn mine or goddamn ranch. You got that? Jack Sanders don't lick boots fer nobody."

With coffee dripping from her face, Frieda nodded, afraid to speak.

"An' as fer havin' neighbors, we're better off without 'em snoopin' in our business. Far as men goin' off to blow each other all to hell in this damned war, let the dumb bastards go right ahead. Ain't no skin off my ass. I don't need to hep no smart-ass rancher or mine-owner bastard git rich. 'At's all there is to it, an' if I hear one more word, I swear I'll …" He stood up raising a hand.

She flinched, steppng toward the back room.

But he sat back down at the table. She served him his rabbit, but his sour mood continued as he wolfed it down with the fried biscuits. He left only one foreleg and half a biscuit. Later, he worked at repairing a strap on the packsaddle. While her back was turned, cleaning up, Frieda quickly ate the meat on the foreleg and the piece of biscuit. Maybe he'd left them on purpose, but she wasn't taking any chances. Later, relieved he hadn't yelled at her about the rabbit and biscuit, she darned their socks—socks that had been darned at least a dozen times each. This batch of yarn didn't seem to be any good.

Finishing with the saddle strap, he gave her the awl and

sinew to put away and stepped outside to pee. Returning, he said, "Damn cold agin tonight." He took off his boots and his clothes, except for the long underwear that he slept in, and got into the cot, which was behind the camp stove—between it and the back room.

Putting aside her sewing, Frieda went out to the lean-to and hauled in armloads of wood, then added as many sticks to the fire as she could get in the firebox without snuffing out the flame, and turned out the lamp. Undressing in the dark and pulling on her woolen nightgown from the crate, she got in beside Jack on the thin, lumpy, brush-filled mattress. She was relieved when he turned his back and started snoring.

She lay in the dark with her eyes open and her burned face pulsing. Firelight flickered though the cracks of the stove. She could hear the scratchy, scurrying sounds of a busy packrat. The rats had chewed off the old curtains that had been in the dugout when she and Jack moved in—nibbled them off in a straight line by standing on their hind legs on the windowsill and reaching up as far as they could. She liked to think of them living in a large family. Now they were building their winter nest in the back room, scurrying to the front room to steal bits of whatever they could find to make the nest warm. She never disturbed their nest, but left an old crate in front of it so Jack wouldn't see it.

Too exhausted to fall asleep, she found herself yearning for at least some connection to other people. *Looks like that's never gonna happen, silly woman. So stop thinkin' on it.* She had to believe there was much about Jack he'd never told her, reasons he had for avoiding people. *Why did we move so often 'til we'd come to the most out-of-the-way place in the world? How come Jack never made any friends? Is he hidin' from the law?* She knew it wasn't any real interest in mining that brought them here. He hated the work and wasn't much good at it, not even as good as Pa when he'd been new at it.

Later, even the packrats stopped their activity and were quiet.

She hated lying tight against Jack on this cot, afraid to move though she felt restless. She hated it each time he inhaled—loud, vibrating, halting—and she hated the sour tobacco breath he blew out, adding to the stink of the place. She struggled to loosen her concentration on what she disliked and think of something else, like why he wanted to stay here for another winter. She imagined the trappers, hunters, and other drifters who had used this dugout must have been people like Jack. Maybe they had worn out their welcome in more settled areas. Maybe the isolation, not the mining, was what brought them here. Frieda had dulled herself to Jack's nature to make it from one day to the next, but now staying alive was a concern intruding more and more upon her mind.

She realized it wouldn't be much of a stretch for him to kill her by mistake in one of his tempers. Maybe that'd be a blessing; she wouldn't need to do it herself. Mrs. Taylor had said once: *We all die sooner or later. All go to the arms of the Lord.*

But another thought stabbed her. *Jack'd be the only one to stand over my grave. 'Cept for him, it'd be like I never lived at all.* When she finally was able to fall asleep, it was only for short, troubled intervals. Nightmares kept jerking her back to wakefulness.

3

In the early dawn, Frieda quietly pulled on her clothes and left the dugout with the bucket. Today she had all the time she needed to watch the sun come down the canyon wall. Jack would sleep late as usual.

At the little eddy in the river, she caught the scent of elk again. She knew they were in the nearby willows, watching her. They were always testing the air, depending on their noses more than their eyes to identify each other and strangers. Movement caught her eye—the elk leaving the trees, starting into an open area to graze. Maybe they felt a kinship with her, as she did with them. *How I'd love to have friends 'round me all the time like they do. Do they talk to each other? And joke and laugh with their friends? I'd sure like that.*

As she filled the bucket, she inhaled the scents of the canyon—the strong smell of the juniper tree near the big boulder, the sweetness of pine, and the tang of the sagebrush that wafted for miles over these mountains in the slightest breeze. She missed the fragrance of the many different wildflowers that grew in the spring— lupine, Indian paintbrush, and shooting stars. What a pleasure it had been last spring to ride Stormy through expanses of blooming wild roses and yellow bitterbrush blossoming on the hillsides.

She looked up at the fading stars between the dark canyon walls. *Not long to wait.* She didn't know much about God, but thought He must be part of the coming of day. Here in the canyon the sun didn't rise. It came down the west wall in a glorious spectacle that differed a little every single day.

The highest snowy peak suddenly sparkled like a diamond in the thin autumn air. Then the whole line of snow-covered peaks blazed with the brilliance of the sun. Marveling at it from the dark canyon floor, Frieda could never get her fill of this sight. Little by little a golden light eased down over the rugged slopes, spreading outward as it came, flowing in and out of the mountain folds—sometimes slow, sometimes jumping, but always washing out the shadows and waking up the great stones, including the heads of a dog and a cat that Frieda had identified in outcroppings of rock. The sunlight painted green the stands of pine that had been hidden. It brought sudden detail to the entrances of the tributary canyons that had been dark. Down and down it came to the first rocky shelf, easing down over the next tier of slopes and leaping to the second shelf where the eagles lived. She stood entranced, seeing new hues of color as though God were painting them for her benefit. Then, in a sudden burst, the whole canyon floor ignited as hundreds of blinding flashes bounced off the moving river. A new day had dawned! She turned her face up to the sun, closed her eyes and smiled.

All during this time the friendly voices of the river had been telling Frieda about the places they had come from, making her want to travel up to the high country and explore. She looked at the moving water, now in full sunlight. In its low water stage in November, it was so clear and the sun so bright that she could see the colored rocks on the bottom even where it was several feet deep.

A slight movement in the water caught her eye—a beautiful cutthroat trout. She could see the olive green tinge on its gray back, the dark spots on the yellow-brown sides, and the distinctive red slash marks underneath the jaw, from which the fish got its name. The trout barely moved, just enough to offset the flow of the water. It seemed suspended without effort, like a dream Frieda once had of floating in a gentle stream—no struggle, no fear.

As always, the birth of a new day lifted her. Gone was yesterday's trouble. In full sunlight Frieda lugged the bucket up the path, careful not to spill the ice-cold water on her legs. She set it beside the door of the dugout and went to the corral.

All three of her four-legged friends paced around impatiently at the sight of her, the roan pumping his head up and down. "Calm down," she told him. "I'm comin' as fast as I can."

She pulled stored grass from the collapsed front of the barn, which kept it dry. In a blizzard the part of the barn still standing provided just enough room for the two horses and the mule to crowd inside with their heads sticking out. *Sure do hope the whole thing don't fall in on 'em this winter. I'd rebuild it m'self if I knowed how without makin' a bigger mess. Wish we had a neighbor who knew how to build barns. I swear I'd do the cookin' fer a neighbor such as that fer ten years! But we ain't got no neighbor, an' even if we did, Jack'd hate to be beholden to 'im. We ain't even got the nails it'd take to put the boards back up. Mosta the old nails is lost, an' the rest is all rusty and bent. Jack says the horses can stand the cold better'n I give 'em credit for. Claims I coddle 'em. But I'd sure hate to shiver out there in the wind and snow of a winter night with no windbreak.*

During the long summer twilights she had collected large amounts of grass for the winter. Now she dumped an armload in front of Jack's blue roan. She put the next load two horselengths away for Old Chief, the pack mule, and lastly a bunch for Stormy, her strong little bay mare. Stormy nickered softly in her throat, saying thank you. She understood that she'd be first line if it didn't cause a ruckus. Besides, it didn't matter where they started eating. In a few minutes the roan would push Old Chief or Stormy away from their grass, but they would simply go over to the vacated pile and continue eating with contentment. Stormy liked living with a boss horse. Frieda saw that in her big black eyes. She accepted life the way it was. She didn't daydream about changing it.

Back in the dugout Frieda served hotcakes to Jack and found

him in a better frame of mind. Throughout the long night he had slept soundly. Maybe, like her, he was glad to be finished washing gravel for the year. She poured him a tin cup of coffee.

Rolling a cigarette he remarked, "Looks like a decent day. Think I'll take a ride downriver an' see if I run into some sheep. That'd be a good change for supper. Weather's cold enough now so the meat'll keep good."

"We can sure use fresh meat," Frieda said brightly, tickled to learn that she'd have an entire day to herself. She liked the taste of mountain sheep too. It had a texture and flavor she preferred to elk or venison, and it had been awhile since Jack had killed a bighorn. As they ate their hotcakes she planned her day. First she'd take a bath, something she didn't like to do with Jack around.

After breakfast Jack pulled on his warm coat and a cap that covered his ears, and loaded his rifle. Then he went outside to saddle up. Meanwhile Frieda led Stormy down to the river for a drink. When she led the mare back to the corral, she heard Jack talking to Old Chief as he strapped on the packsaddle.

"Goddamn claim ain't worth a shit. I know it, she knows it. Jes' wish I could find a glory hole full a' nuggets savin' their sparkle jes' fer me. Wouldn't have to listen to her bellyachin' no more. All them folks clearing out a' here musta left *somethin'* good fer me to find."

Frieda petted her best friend on the neck and whispered in her ear, "He talks to them more'n he talks to me. But horses sure are good listeners, an' I sure do 'preciate havin' you to talk to, Stormy. But you gotta tell me if I go soft in the head, won't you?"

Jack took Old Chief and the roan to the water's edge to drink. Then he mounted and rode away with the mule in tow.

Watching him go, it occurred to Frieda that another sort of man with such a fine horse and a pack mule as good as Old Chief would ride over to Panther Creek and trade work for a packload of potatoes, carrots, cabbages, and apples. There were plenty of little farms on Panther Creek, around the town of Forney.

Settlers there prob'ly got more'n they can use, and they'd be glad to trade it for a day or so of help with the fences or puttin' up a cabin or diggin' a' irrigation ditch. An' some of 'em is too far back in the mountains to sell to any store.

But she recalled Jack's response when she mentioned trading work for food. "Hell, you think I'd scratch in the dirt fer a farmer? Why, I wouldn't trust them shitheels far as I could throw 'em. They'd be friendly like 'til they found some way to put the law on a man. They think any man smart 'nough to make a livin' without scratchin' in the dirt or runnin' sheep or cattle's gotta be a crook. No damn way I'd cozy up to their kind fer a sack a' spuds."

Jack never told her much about his life before she met him. She'd always wondered about the scar on his face. It appeared to have been caused by a bad burn. With his face clean-shaven it wasn't so obvious, but with the scraggly whiskers he had most of the time, it reminded her of mange on a dog. Once she'd asked him how he got the scar. He'd said something about spilled gravy and got so mad she'd never asked again. *How do you spill gravy on your own face? I think somebody throwed it at 'im.*

But why think of that now? This was a day free from Jack! She made sure her hands were dry before going to get the battered old washtub that hung on the shady side of the dugout. As a girl she'd learned the hard way that skin freezes to cold metal, by grabbing a pump handle and getting the palm of her hand peeled off when the intense cold made her jerk away.

She built up the fire and fetched the first bucket of water to put in the washtub, which she'd balanced on the stove. When she had four buckets of boiling water, she'd lift the tub by the handles and put it on the floor, then add more buckets of cold water. A splash on the floor only helped hold the dust down.

In a fine mood, she watered her geranium, grown from a snip from Meyer's Cove. She'd planted it in an old enamel-coated teakettle that leaked around the base. It made a nice flowerpot, which she kept on the floor near the window. The little white flecks in the blue enamel made interesting patterns where the pot had chipped and rusted. The one lonely bud looked about ready to bloom, bending its poor little skinny stem toward the window. Frieda moved the pot where it would more easily reach the sunlight.

Jack took the main trail north down the Middle Fork canyon. It would follow the east side of the river a couple of miles, then cross to the west bank by a fairly safe ford when the river was running low, as it was now. He hoped to find a band of bighorn sheep and bag a fat young ram. The sheep would likely be up in higher country now, but he stayed with the trail at river level.

Never having spent much time in the lower part of the canyon, he figured he'd do some looking around, maybe find something interesting. He couldn't remember the lay of the land at Sheep Creek Bar, and it wouldn't hurt to check things out—see what the German was up to.

He knew that after the trail crossed to the west side it would lead down across Sheep Creek and continue on for several more miles before turning up Big Creek and finally out of the canyon. He'd never traveled out of the canyon that way, but had heard stories about it when he was young. He talked to the roan as he rode.

"No wonder this trail's beat out so good—almost a damn road. It sure woulda been a sight to see when all them half-assed miners was apourin' in here when gold was first discovered. Reg'lar stampede to Leesburg an' Loon Creek an' places such as that. Forty, fifty years back now. They come in here like packs a' hungry coyotes, an' most of 'em left with their bellies emptier'n when they started. Stupid bastards. An' that bunch a' soldiers goin' through here woulda been a sight too. Like to seen that fracas over't Vinegar Hill, down Big Crick. Sheep-eaters War, folks called it. That bunch a smarty pants flatlanders out a' Boise got their asses trapped by a handful of Injuns that knowed the country." He chuckled. "Up a hill with no water! So dry they was drinkin' their vinegar.

Served 'em right. Shoulda stayed out a' territory like this, where they sure's hell warn't wanted." He rode a distance before he said, "I still wonder how them Sheep-eater Injuns got close enough to the sheep to make a kill."

At the edge of the river his roan stopped, wanting a signal from Jack to tell him whether he should cross. The trail split here, one fork crossing, the other continuing along the east bank. Jack studied the crossing, noting the big yellow pine that had been used to anchor the cable that had stretched across the river. A piece of the heavy cable was still wrapped around the base of the tree. Some of it could be in the water snarled in the rocks, where it could trip up his animals. With Old Chief on a tether, he decided against it. In the mining boom there had been a ferry at the ford. Except for a few weeks during high water in the spring, this had been a good crossing. Once it had carried thousands of people. But after the cable broke and the ferryboat washed downstream, no one bothered to replace it. On the west bank stood the stark reminder of what had been a home to the ferryman and his family. The cabin had burned down, leaving nothing but the stone fireplace and chimney.

Jack turned his horse away from the ford and continued on down the east bank. That way he'd get a good look at Sheep Creek Bar without the German knowing he was there. And anyway, Jack was more likely to find bighorn on the high slopes on this side.

He'd never gone to Sheep Creek Bar but had heard a little bit about it. The bar had several acres of land that lay in a gentle slope toward the river—wider than most of the narrow canyon. It could easily be irrigated from Sheep Creek and had been farmed by a family that had a placer claim up the creek, not on the river. They had moved on. More than likely the claim wasn't doing much, and the little farm was too far by pack train from any big mining camp to sell crops. Jack didn't know exactly when the family had left and the German had moved in.

Guess I shoulda checked out that place before takin' the claim and dugout. But he'd figured their claim near Camas Creek would pan out better than it had. But now winter was here, all but the snow, and he'd been wondering if he'd missed something. He told the roan, "I'll jes' take a gander. Git us some elevation and a man can see the layout from this side a' the river."

Directly across the river from the cabin, a faint deer trail angled around a big outcropping of rock that rose from the river's edge. The roan dug in as he climbed. Near water's edge, rocks and brush had obscured the view across the river, but as he came to a clearing, Jack pulled the roan to a quick halt.

"Well, I'll be dipped in shit!"

The neat log cabin had two windows on each side of the door and what appeared to be a new roof. The yard around it was clean. The very large garden next to the cabin was furrowed, and he could see that it had been harvested. There were still some frost-bitten plants in the ground. No doubt potatoes and such as that. Berry bushes along the garden fence had been neatly trimmed, and healthy-looking fruit trees grew nearby. Grazing in a fenced pasture were a horse and a red and white cow that looked like a dairy breed. The hay meadow had been scythed and a sizeable stack of hay had been put up under a roofed structure with a high pole fence around it. All the fences were in good shape.

The damn German's gotta be one workin' son of a bitch.

Jack sat his horse and studied the place for a long time. It was the neatest outfit he could remember laying eyes on. Miners, drifters, trappers just didn't keep a place up like that. They wouldn't be staying long enough. About a half-acre of dry corn stalks were still standing.

"Why the hell would anybody grow that much corn?" he asked the roan. "A man might make some whiskey, but wouldn't hardly need that much corn fer jes' one man." Then he saw the pigpen and shed. Even from across the river he could make out half-grown pigs and a sow taking a nap. He couldn't believe it.

Then he realized that the small building with the thin line of smoke coming out the top was a smokehouse.

Well I'll be damned! How long had it been since he'd eaten good home-cured ham or a tender pork roast? He could almost taste it. Mountain sheep was okay, but it did get monotonous. A change to pork would be mighty nice—and all the cured bacon a man wanted.

Jack slacked the reins and let his roan graze the dry grass that covered the hillside. Old Chief was also getting his fill of the crisp, rich feed. Clumps of mountain mahogany pretty well screened them from the view of anyone on the other side of the river, and it suited Jack fine to just sit his horse and study the details of the little homestead. The cabin was back from the river, the bar wide enough here for a decent farm operation. A soft winter sun still highlighted the pale logs of the house and the new shingles against the steep, darker mountains behind it. He was pretty sure he could see the hatch of a root cellar at the side of the cabin. There was no wind. Blue smoke curled straight up from the cabin and smokehouse, both lines disappearing into a clear sky. Jack relaxed, resting one leg over his horse's withers in front of the horn.

"By damn, ol' Roan, that's a helluva purty sight. I'll bet that cabin's warm as the bottom of a settin' hen. An' that root cellar'd be fulla garden truck an' dried fruit, an' there'd be cream and butter from the cow. Christ Almighty! All them good eats fer a lousy kraut! An' me livin' like a starved rat. T'ain't right, the damn bastard! I never lived in a place near as good my whole piss-poor life, an' that German jes' asettin' there snug as a fat ol' rock chuck in his hole waitin' on winter!"

Jack's mind was working fast. He wanted that place and everything in it. The German was a farmer, and he'd been smarter than Jack when he picked this wide spot in the canyon. It riled Jack just thinking about it. With those acres of farmland and all the game and fish, a man could settle down and have a right good life without being bothered by anybody. All Jack had to do was get the German out of the way, and that claim would be his for the taking, and just like all the other abandoned claims up and down the canyon, the house would come with it.

"Well, ol' buddy, up to now Jack's had the short end of the stick, that's fer sure, but things jes' might be lookin' up. Yesiree-bob!"

4

Frieda poured the last bucket of cold water in the washtub. The windows had steamed up from all the boiling, and a warm glow from the sun came into the dugout. It wouldn't be long before it would start its rise up the east wall. After her bath Frieda and Stormy would chase the sun to a meadow that overlooked a vast area of the canyon.

Hardly able to wait for the luxury of sinking into the warm water, Frieda put a chair where she could reach it from the washtub. She set out the soap, her gob of rendered sheep tallow, and the threadbare towel. The big long-handled pot was filled with water, heating within reach of the tub. She slipped out of her clothes.

First she checked the side of her hip where the big bruise had been. The soreness and discoloration had been gone for some time, but the flesh still stood up where Jack's boot had struck her. Maybe it would never flatten out again. It had been this way since last summer. He'd used his fists on her and she'd been on the floor trying to protect her face when he kicked her there, and her ribs too. She'd jumped on Stormy, ridden bareback through the twilight, and hid in a thicket all night, afraid of wolves but more afraid of Jack. *Never did figure out what made him so hoppin' mad, or why he acted so nice when he found me.*

She lowered her backside into the water and felt its caress, but had to hang her knees over the rim with her feet on the floor. *Wish I had one of those big oval tubs like some folks got, so I could fit my behind and feet in at the same time. There I go dreamin' again.*

The water imparted a deep peace. It had been months since the last time Jack went away hunting all day and she'd taken a bath. If she did it with him looking at her, first thing she knew he'd be all over her, ruining what the bath had accomplished. But today she'd be clean for a long time.

She stretched out her arms and legs one at a time, smoothing soap on them and admiring her firm muscles. The years of hard manual labor had made her naturally firm figure supple and resilient. She'd kept a count of her birthdays and knew she was thirty. Old as that sounded, she didn't feel old. She felt strong and agile as the young mountain animals who moved with such easy grace around the mountains they shared with her.

She reached to feel the temperature of the water in the pan. Quite warm. She squirmed down to wash her long brown hair, enjoying its soft texture as she ran her fingers through it. She brought the pan over and lowered her head in it, then poured the water over her hair and shoulders. The story of Rapunzel, which Mrs. Taylor had read aloud long ago, came to mind. *She had such a sweet voice. 'Rapunzel, Rapunzel, let down your hair,' the handsome prince called, lookin' up to where that girl stood in a window at the top a' that tower where her mean ol' pa locked her up. Finally she let her hair down for the prince, and he climbed right up it like a rope. He took her out a' there, put her on his horse, and they rode to his castle and lived happily ever after.*

Frieda sighed, pulling the warm water up over her breasts. Jack was no prince. And most of her dreams as a child had been nightmares. She'd wake up crying out in bed. Always in these dreams she'd been in danger. One recurring nightmare was so vivid that she remembered every detail of it, though it had never returned since she'd been with Jack. She would be riding a half-broken horse that spooked and began to buck, harder and harder, and with a terrifying sense of losing all control, Frieda lost a stirrup on one side, was thrown out of the saddle, and had a foot hung up in the stirrup. The reins jerked from her hands. Her body swung under the horse's belly with her head hanging close to its flailing hoofs. Frieda had seen this happen to a man who was breaking wild horses. His leg was bent where no leg should bend and his head was battered almost beyond recognition. He was dead by the time his friends were able to subdue the horse. But in her dream, before Frieda was badly hurt, a fine rider always appeared, roped the horse, and forced it to a quick stop. The rider's strong arms scooped her up as she released her foot from the twisted stirrup. He held her close and comforted her. But Frieda's dream always ended before she could learn more about him.

She supposed that Jack would try to save her if she were in such danger. He was a good horseman. But he'd sure let her have it. She could just hear him: "You worthless female! Can't even handle a dumb-ass horse! I reckon I should knock some sense into your head."

Though it was hard for her, Frieda usually tried to be good in bed for Jack when he wanted her. She tried her best to do whatever he wanted, but like her efforts at cooking, it never seemed to be good enough. Something was lacking in her; Frieda was sure of that.

It didn't help any that she was so afraid of him. It was different from other kinds of fear she had known. She recalled how scared she'd been when her father brought home a mongrel dog, baring its teeth and growling. It had been trained to attack strangers. Pa got it as a watchdog to keep people away from their cabin. It was a big strong dog, and Frieda had to be careful around it. But after she got to understand the dog and knew she could never challenge or threaten him, and never surprise him, she learned to tolerate his disposition. There came a time when she was fairly sure that he would do his best to defend her against a stranger if necessary, and she felt safer with him around. With Jack it was different. He would defend her, but then might turn right around and hurt her himself. She just couldn't understand him.

A stallion bites and kicks a mare a good deal when he's after her, but I never seen one seriously hurt his mare. The bighorn rams are sure-enough rough on the ewes in breedin' season, but then they leave 'em alone the rest a' the time. An' that time I saw them bob-cats! Why that sounded like a commotion down in hell. I heared the screamin' an' cryin' for a half mile before I come onto 'em. I sure did think oneov'em was gettin' killed, but that old tom, he was jes' tryin' to mate with her, just lettin' her know he was the boss cat.

That must be nature's way. I learned to take Jack's matin' without puttin' up a fuss. Jes' keep still, that's the main thing; and if it makes him proud to feel like a stallion or ram, I reckon there's not much else he's got to be proud of. Thinkin' 'bout it's like a silly pup chasin' its tail 'round in circles. An' Stormy's waitin' on me.

By now, profuse rivulets of condensation streamed down the windows. Frieda got out of the tub, dried herself, put her dirty clothes in the water, scrubbed them with soap, wrung them out, and set them on the chair. Later she'd rinse them in the river. She rubbed the rendered sheep tallow into her arms, legs and hands to keep her skin soft. It did the job all right. Her hands stayed soft, while Jack's hands on her felt like a scaly lizard.

The sun was just starting to rise up the canyon wall. Not a cloud in the sky and not a breath of wind—a perfect crisp winter day. Frieda pulled the tub to the door and pushed it on its side. The water gushed out and ran quickly down the path. Removing all signs that she'd taken a bath, she put on her clean trousers and shirt. Dressed in her coat, warm cap, and gloves, she went out to the corral.

Stormy was nervously pacing back and forth, looking down the canyon trail, anxious about being left alone while the roan and Old Chief were gone. The moment she heard the dugout door open and close, she stopped her pacing and nickered a friendly greeting.

Inside the corral Frieda wrapped her arms around Stormy's neck and buried her cheek in the soft fur-like bay coat that had grown rich and full for winter. "Purty little Stormy, miss your friends? I jes' bet you do." She scratched around her horse's ears, and the mare nuzzled Frieda with her soft nose, whickering horse language. Patting and rubbing her, Frieda smiled. "We're gonna take us a good run up the canyon. Won't you like that, huh?"

Just then, from a rocky shelf across the river, a great golden eagle spread its wings and launched itself, soaring into the warming air rising off the canyon floor. The eagle slowly circled higher and higher to scan this area of the Middle Fork in search of food. For as long as she could remember, Frieda had loved watching eagles and hawks, wishing she could soar and be up that high up, looking down over the entire mountain range. But Stormy could take her up pretty high too.

After brushing the mare and saddling and bridling her, Frieda mounted. "Let's go, girl." At a break trot they started on the up-canyon trail. Frieda's heart filled with joy as she reveled in the brightness of the day and the smooth, rapid gait of her horse. Stormy was always eager to travel. In the six years since Frieda found her, the mare had given her hours of enjoyment exploring in the mountains. Stormy was her best friend and her escape from Jack.

She'd found the starving foal dying in a late winter storm, curled up beside her dead dam. No doubt the mother was one of the wild horses that Frieda occasionally saw on the mountain slopes. The store owner in Meyer's Cove, Mr. Larsen, once told Frieda that such horses had run free for generations around Salmon City, many with the best Arabian blood in their veins. Frieda wondered if some of them had been left from the Indians, the tribe Mrs. Taylor had said Sacajawea belonged to. Mr. Larsen said the government released well-bred stallions all over the West to mate with the wild mares. This enlarged the herds raised in the wild, and they could be rounded up by the Army whenever there was a need for them. Frieda believed her mare had been sired by the very best of those stallions.

Nursing the little foal back to health, Frieda had played with her and trained her. For the little filly, Frieda had taken the place of a mother, and Frieda had given Stormy the love and affection she would have given a child. Stormy had turned out to be a saddle horse of unusual strength and endurance.

With the stimulation and supreme pleasure of the ride, a great sense of gratitude filled Frieda's heart. Tears welled in her eyes. Coming to a halt in one of her favorite meadows, she leaned forward in the saddle, lovingly caressed the little mare's neck, and said, "You wonderful, wonderful friend. What would we ever do without each other?"

5

With a last calculating look at the inviting little homestead, Jack swung his leg back over the horn and wheeled his roan up to higher country. Getting a nice young ram would give him time to work out the details for bagging a lot more than a bighorn sheep.

As he rode through the bunchgrass and sagebrush, Jack took his time, and his mind drifted back to the Wood River country where he'd grown up. He wasn't sure if he remembered his pa, or just things that his ma had said about him. She said his pa had just drifted on one day, and that she'd decided to stay put. But from things he'd heard around town when he was growing up, Jack often wondered if maybe his pa was buried in one of the unmarked graves up on the sage-covered hill away from the town cemetery. Maybe there were some things about his pa that his ma didn't care to talk about.

Things had been tough for Jack and his ma. When he thought about his childhood, he mostly remembered being cold and hungry. One day when he'd complained about it, his ma in frustration tossed the contents of a bowl of steaming hot gravy at him. "THERE, YOU SNIVELIN' NO GOOD LITTLE BASTARD! IT'S HOT AN' IT'S FOOD! YOU SATISFIED?" That was the last time Jack shed a tear.

They had lived in a shack that was almost impossible to heat. He remembered waking up in the morning, after windy nights in winter, to find little drifts on the floor where snow had blown through cracks around the door and in the wall. In summer, sometimes dust and sand did the same thing. On good days, his ma brought home leftovers from the saloon kitchen where she worked. They would eat well for a day or two, but it never lasted long. Most of the time, Jack went to bed with his stomach growling.

He remembered the time he was so hungry he slipped into a neighbor's barn. He found a hen's nest and, because no one was around, took the eggs home for his ma to cook. She seemed glad to have them but had asked where he got them. He told her he "come acrost 'em out in the weeds, where nobody else coulda found them." She asked no more questions. After that he began to find quite a few eggs. His ma suggested that when he found eggs, it would be best not to take them all, then the hen wouldn't get suspicious and quit laying, but would lay some more in the same nest. Jack had figured out that maybe it wasn't just the hen that wouldn't get suspicious. He was six years old then, and after that he began to find more things that allowed them to eat better. It made him feel like he was doing something good.

The first time he brought home a side of bacon he told her he'd found it along the road where it must've fallen off a freight wagon. The wagon was gone, so he was sure nobody would come back to pick it up. With so many people doing their own butchering and having their own smokehouses, he was able to find other good things, and his ma never asked how he'd gotten them. He found it was best to raid a big smokehouse and never take more than one ham or side of bacon at a time.

When Jack was about twelve, he found himself a dandy rifle, something he'd fancied having for a long time. He still chuckled when he remembered how easily he'd gotten it. He had noticed that quite a few people from the Snake River country liked to come up to the Wood River country to hunt in the fall. They'd come in fancy wagons, with fine teams and camping outfits, and spend a few days. Some would hire an old-timer to guide them, but many just set up camp and hunted wherever they took a notion. He had seen a group of five hunters arrive one day and camp along the river near town. Rigged out like real dudes, those hunters had a camp wagon with saddle horses tethered behind. They walked into town to the saloon to eat. Jack guessed they wanted a break from camp cooking. While they were having dinner and a few drinks, he checked out their wagon. On a bed in the back they had carefully covered their rifles with a tarp. When he lifted it he saw just what he wanted—a lever action Winchester 32 Special. It was well cared for and looked brand new. He peered around. Nobody was in sight. It would be easy to just lift the gun out of the wagon and slip into the brush along the river, but he was shrewd. He knew that if he took the rifle before the dudes went hunting, they would make a search for it, maybe all through town, asking all kinds of questions.

He was pretty sure that the dudes would stop for another good saloon meal after they finished their hunting trip. To celebrate their success, they'd have a few drinks. So, after the hunters left the next morning, moving on up the valley, Jack began watching that camp spot every day. Sure enough, in just five days, the wagon pulled in again. He watched them tie their horses, wash up at the edge of the river, and start walking toward the saloon. They were taking their time, stopping to talk to a few men that they met, bragging about their good hunting. From his hiding place near the dudes' camp wagon, Jack could see the door of the saloon. When they had been inside a few minutes, he checked to make sure no one was around, and carefully slipped up to the wagon. One of the horses nickered, but Jack was careful not to move quickly and spook any of them. To make sure no one had stayed in the wagon to guard it, he kept himself on the side of the wagon that was out of sight of the town and tossed a rock on the canvas top.

No sign of a guard. Jack slipped up to the back of the wagon. There it was, just where it had been before—that beautiful little rifle. He quickly slipped it from under the tarp and faded into the brush along the riverbank. He was careful to walk where he would leave no tracks. A quarter mile down the river was a thick tangle of brush he'd picked out. He cached the rifle under dry leaves, deep in the thicket, then walked casually on down the river for another mile before cutting back through the hills toward town. It was easy to find a place where he could watch the road without being seen. He didn't have to wait long before he saw the wagon moving steadily along, heading south, back toward Snake River country. Things were going good. He'd learned not to be in a hurry; the hunters would miss the rifle and might come back looking for it. But he had plenty of time.

All the next week he checked around town, keeping alert for sight of the hunters or anything in the wind that someone was looking for a lost rifle. He watched the road and the campsite. All was quiet. So after dark one evening, he took an old flour sack and returned to the thicket by the river. He found the rifle just as he'd left it. After carefully wrapping it in the sack and waiting until dark, he returned home with his prize.

"Ma, look what I found me! A dandy good rifle, jes' like new. Was layin' right in some willows by the river, not far from the camp groun'. How you s'pose it came to be there?"

"I reckon some drunk hunter laid it down when he went into the brush to take a leak an' was so drunk he forgot to pick it up again. It's a good'un alright—you're sure one lucky kid. Maybe now you'll be able to do some huntin' yourself an' get us fresh meat for the table. We sure could use it."

That's all that was ever said about the gun. Jack smiled as he thought about how easy it had been to get his first rifle. He had become a good hunter, in season and out, and his ma had appreciated the meat he brought home.

Jack had always treasured that rifle and liked to remember that the price had been right—just a little clever planning and waiting a few days. He had sanded off a number that had been stamped on it and even took the precaution of refinishing the stock in a way that would change its appearance. He now had a bigger rifle, a 30-40 Krag, and a pistol, but he still favored the little lever action 32 Winchester Special. It was right there now in the saddle boot of his horse.

"Ol' Roan," Jack said, "a man jes' got to be a little bit smarter than other folks, an' a bit careful, an' he can have jes' about anything he wants."

Getting rid of the German and getting away with it, though, might not be as simple as taking that rifle. He would need to be a damn sight more foxy. But ol' Jack would figure it out.

Jack was exuberant, and proud of his big roan horse. He headed him right up the sloping side of the canyon. The flexing of the powerful muscles under the saddle added to Jack's feeling of control and purpose, which he had not experienced for some time. The roan sensed his excitement and relished the challenge of the climb.

"Roan, ol' buddy, you're a climbin' son of a gun. We lost a lot of elevation comin' so far down the river at water level, but by damn, it was sure as hell worth it! You're pickin' it up in a hurry. Gittin' us up in this thin air already. An' did you see what I seen 'cross that river? Hell, boy, how'd you like to be grazin' in that pasture, achasin' Ol' Chief an' Stormy around 'stead a' bein' cooped up in that damn corral?"

The wild sheep would be hanging pretty high, and would stay there unless the snow got deep and the temperature dropped a good deal more. But Jack was getting there, expecting to get his meat and be back at the dugout before dark.

This was open sagebrush and bunchgrass country, with a few scattered pines and small groves of aspen that, even this late in the year, still had some of their golden autumn leaves.

The idea of living in that fine little cabin gave Jack a glow of optimism. It was a perfect day for hunting, and for planning much better days for the rest of the winter—for the rest of his life in fact.

There was not much forest on these higher slopes, no heavy

timber for a hunter's concealment. It was rough country, and big boulders had rolled down from the higher elevations. There were clumps of mountain mahogany and bitterbrush. The higher up, the greater the variety of browse plants for the sheep. With the lack of trees, the visibility was good. Jack would be able to see game from a distance, and of course they could see him. He knew the farsighted vision of a bighorn was much keener than his. He'd approach from above the bighorns and surprise them.

Jack gave the roan his head and they climbed rapidly, following a ridge next to a dry coulee that would be a small nameless creek for a few weeks in the springtime. High up, the springs flowed all the time and the sheep could find water without having to go down to the river this time of year. It had been a dry, hot summer, and even this late in the fall barely enough precipitation had fallen to put a light cover of snow in the high country.

Daylight came late now, and Jack had not gotten an early start. He'd spent at least two hours riding from the dugout down to the German's place and a good while just sitting there looking at it. It was well past noon when he reached the snow and saw the little band of sheep. This time of day, the sheep would be bedded down, resting from their morning graze. But when Jack saw them they were standing, and he knew they'd seen him before he saw them. They were about a half a mile away, not grazing, but watching him and his horse and mule, not at all alarmed. There was no wind to carry his scent to them, and the slight air movement was blowing in his direction.

He slowly stepped down from the saddle, eased his rifle out of the saddle boot, and slipped into the ravine along which he'd been riding. He left horse and mule in plain sight of the sheep. His animals were trained to ground tie and graze till he came back for them. The sight of the horse and mule grazing peacefully a half mile away would not disturb the sheep, only be a useful focus for their attention.

Jack's plan worked well. He stalked carefully up the ravine, watching for any sheep that might not be with the herd—one that could jump up, run, and give an alarm. The ravine was clear. A badger saw Jack and moved quickly into its hole. Jack was able to get within range of the band without giving the sheep sight or sound of his position. A heavy mountain mahogany bush on the edge of the ravine provided cover as he stealthily gained a position where he could look through its branches. Several ewes and lambs were keeping watchful eyes on the roan and Old Chief. Seeing nothing to fear from that distance, some were beginning to lie down again, chewing contentedly. A fine full-curl ram remained standing, watchful but resting. Keeping a respectful distance from this dominant ram, a grown half-curl ram also remained standing, showing more interest in the ewes than any concern for the approach of danger. His draw to the females was balanced by his awareness of the big ram that clearly put the ewes off limits.

The choice was simple for Jack. Younger mutton tasted better. He set his rifle onto a low branch of the mahogany, sighted his target, and squeezed the trigger. For Jack, a shot at just over a hundred yards with a rest for his rifle was a sure thing. The young ram made one startled jump, then collapsed. The other sheep vanished as if by magic. The horse and mule looked up briefly from their grazing as the shot echoed down the canyon.

Taking his knife from its scabbard as he walked toward the downed ram, Jack felt no excitement in his kill. He was not a trophy hunter. It was a job of work to put meat on the table, and he was good at it. He took his prey as naturally as a cougar takes a deer or a wolf pack pulls down a moose. His mind was only partially engaged with his work as he dressed out the sheep, a task he'd done so often.

I could get rid of that German down there jes' as easy as I knocked down this sheep. Hell, who'd ever know or give a damn if he dropped out a' sight? Anybody'd figure, him bein' an enemy a' the country an' all, he jes' saved his ass by sneakin' farther back up in the hills. But I gotta have a good reason to tell folks, if they git wind of it. Ol' Jack's not stupid.

That damn Hun musta snuck in an' took over the place when that family moved out. With him out a' the way, it's my turn to be in the sun. I'll jes' take over the minin' claim and the rest'll come with it. I'd lay down a good bet that coward ain't dared go to town since we got in the war. Most folks pro'bly don't know he's there. By damn, I gotta feelin' the war's gonna be over for him quicker'n he ever figured.

Jack chuckled as he slit the ram open and removed the entrails. With a piece of cord he tied the heart and liver back inside the rib cage where they would travel well when he packed the carcass on the mule. He washed his hands in a little snowdrift in the shade of a big rock, cleaned his knife and slid it back in the scabbard on his belt. Walking back to get his horse and mule, Jack thought about how happy the new place would make Frieda.

She's like a wolf bitch, always lookin' to find a better den. Oh sure, I rough her up a little, show her who's boss. But when all's said and done, I look out for her. We run together.

He was no longer that young a man. He knew he wasn't popular on the outside; he'd left tracks in the wrong places. He needed to stay in the canyon, but for the past few months he'd been fretting over just how they would keep going on their claim. It wasn't supporting them, and the situation was making Frieda difficult to get along with. But now things were looking up, far better than Jack imagined in his wildest dreams.

Eyeing the 32 Special as he slipped it back in his saddle boot, he reminded himself that a smart fellow can find a way to get what he wants—if he wants it bad enough. Now that the boy was a man he was even smarter, more crafty. Jack was formulating a plan to make everything seem right and proper.

From the corral, Stormy nickered a greeting to the roan and Old Chief as they came into sight along the trail. Frieda went out to help Jack unsaddle and was pleased to see the fine young ram. A nice pot roast with dumplings would be a welcome treat.

Jack whistled a non-tune while they worked, which Frieda smiled at. She hadn't seen him in such a good mood for months. Success with hunting always pleased him. They worked together to hang up the bighorn and strip off the hide. It was in excellent condition with fine layers of rich tallow. She would fix the best supper she could, and set the tallow to render during the night.

Hungry after his vigorous day of riding mountain trails, Jack ate without his usual complaints. He talked, as usual after a hunt, of his stealth in stalking the sheep, his one well-placed shot at a great distance, and how well his horse and mule behaved. Frieda could hardly believe that he was in such good humor, even after the successful hunt. He was friendlier than she ever had known him to be. This encouraged her to talk too.

"Maybe you should spend more time huntin' than minin', Jack."

"That'd suit me."

"I never seen you this way."

"Wha'cha mean?" he said with an awkward expression that appeared to be a genuine smile taking hold.

"Why you're … you're bein' so content."

"Pretty nice size ram, uh?"

"I'll say. It'll feed us good fer a couple a' weeks."

"Say, I saw somethin' this mornin'."

"Yeah?"

"Somethin' I couldn't hardly believe."

She smiled in anticipation. "What?"

"Our closest neighbor's place."

"That'd be that German over to Sheep Crick."

"Yep."

Frieda felt her hopeful feelings turn to worry. "Didja see 'im? What'd he look—"

"Didn't see 'im, jes' the place."

Jack started in about the German's cabin, his crops and pasture, his livestock, his smokehouse and pigs, and Frieda loved it. He went on and on after dinner while they had coffee, Frieda feeding him with questions to keep him talking. She had dreamed about such a place and never realized he had too. The scar across his cheek, now pale, didn't look mean at all. She even thought she could see into him a little, and it didn't scare her.

When he finally wore out, he took a last drag on his cigarette, looking her up and down in that way of his.

He's been nice as I ever seen him, and still I don't want 'im touchin' me. "Well, Jack, I guess I'd better get the dishes done and sew that torn shirt of yours."

"That'll wait. Take yer britches off."

"Now?"

"You heard me."

She moved to extinguish the lamp.

"No, I wanta eyeful a' my woman. Noseful too. I can smell you took a bath."

"It's kinda cold, Jack."

"You ain't arguin', is ya?"

Realizing she'd raised all the objection he'd allow, Frieda undressed.

6

The next morning Jack was awake and out of bed when Frieda came in from watching the sun come down. While she fixed breakfast, he talked more about the German's place.

"That's a helluva nice place. He musta jes' took it for hisself when that family left." He paused. "Or mebbe he killed 'em an' took the place."

"Maybe so."

"Frieda, I been thinkin' on it, an' I jes don't think no German oughta be in there. You know what they say about them Huns."

"They stab babies, take 'em right out a' their mother's bellies afore they're born." She frowned, shaking the horror of it away.

"They're sneaky too. I heared they come on real friendly-like, but they're nuthin but wild animals. One thing's fer damn sure. That German ain't got no right bein' in our canyon. No right atall. He's a danger to us."

"You thinkin' maybe somethin' oughta be done about it?"

"Yup."

"You thinkin' we'd oughta get word to the sheriff? Tell 'im 'bout the German takin' that man's claim?"

"The sheriff? Ol' Tommy Thompson's busier'n a one-legged ass kicker … an' he's clear over in Salmon City, ninety miles away. Why, he wouldn't bother hisself 'bout one little ol' claim down here in the canyon. 'Sides, he don't got 'thority over people on the other side a' the Middle Fork. That's some other sheriff, so fur away ain't nobody over here seen hide ner hair of 'im. Us folks in the canyon gotta look out fer ourselves."

"Well … I guess somethin' oughta be done." It pleased Frieda to be talking over something this important with Jack.

He weighed his words carefully. "Yup, you got that right. Somethin' oughta be done all right. It's been runnin' around under my hat since yesterday. Here's what I come up with. You an' me gotta do it, Frieda."

"Wha … what can we do?"

Jack lifted her towel-protected hand from the skillet handle and turned her toward him. This he'd never done before except to hurt her, and she automatically stiffened. But he kept right on talking sweet as candy. "We take it from him jes' like he took it from them other folks."

"But he's a German! He'd kill us."

"Not if I get 'im first."

"Oh, Jack, you're scarin' me."

"That place'd be ours, Frieda. No more scratchin' out a livin' an' goin' to bed in this stinkin' dugout. We'd live nice." His gray eyes looked friendly, encouraging, almost soft.

"Wha'cha talkin' 'bout? I don't understand how you could—"

"Jes' think about bein' in this dugout forever." He opened out his arms and hands. "It's nothin' but shit! You want a better place, don'cha?"

"You mean jes' go down there an' kill 'im?"

He raised her chin up to look at him. "I took a nice long gander at the place. There won't be nuthin' to it with you and me workin' together."

"Wha'cha mean, workin' together?"

He stepped back and looked her up and down. "Well, I know I ain't never said much on that score, but I got me a notion last night. You're a looker, Frieda, under them ol' clothes."

She stiffened more, but this was different. His smile, his compliment, and his soft voice brought to her the beginning of dread.

"Here's how I got it figgered. I could jes' shoot the Hun an' prob'ly get away with it, an' we could move in and nobody'd give it no never mind, him bein' a German, with the country at war an all, but somethin' might go wrong. He might have a relation or a friend, and there might be some stupid-ass dude connected to the law b'lievin' a German's got a right to the claim. But if I kill him 'cause he took my woman, ain't nobody gonna see nut-hin' but my side a' things. Hell, they'd thank me for getting' rid a' the bastard."

"You … you want me to …"

He tapped his forehead. "Jes' coverin' our bet, Frieda. You go in an' git reeeaal friendly with 'im. Soften 'im up and make 'im forget about everything else. That'll set 'im up fer the kill."

Dread made her voice faint and quivery. "Jack, how could you even … you mean go in and do it with 'im?"

"Sure. That's no big thing. It's fer us, for you, so you'll live easier, me too. We sure deserve that now, don't we?"

"Guess so, but … me? … go in there all alone and play up to a German, a baby killer? … No, I can't. I jes' can't." She covered her face, shaking her head to throw off the thought.

Jack raised his hand to strike, but stopped himself. "Almost got carried away there. Wouldn't do to mark you up none. Not when you gotta be purty fer the German."

Her heart hammered like she was on the run, and her voice sounded whiny as a kid begging her pa not to whup her, but she had to make sense of this. "He'd kill me, Jack. You know how they are. You don't want 'im to kill me, do ya?"

"Don'cha get all worried on that score. Sure, he's a damn Kraut, but his crotch'll swell up with a woman playin' up to 'im—same as any man." His smile bunched up the scar on his cheek. "Reckon that's how come there's so many a' them damn Germans in the first place fer us to be fightin' over in Europe."

He means fer me to do it! Lurking behind that was the hard-won knowledge that when he got it in his head to do something, she could never talk him out of it. But there was also a glimmer of a realization that he needed her to get this done the way he wanted. It gave her the strength to say in a low but definite tone, "Jack, I ain't doin' it. Hit me, kick me, whatever. I jes' ain't gonna do it."

He looked away for a moment, then grabbed her by the arm, twisted it behind her, and forced her outside. Whisking a coil of rope from the nail by the door, he pulled her toward the corral, jerked her inside, and slammed her back against the gatepost.

The force and suddenness stunned her. *Is he gonna hang me?* Her heart felt like galloping hooves in her rib cage.

She melted into fear and didn't resist as he quickly tied her hands in front of her and wrapped the rope a couple of times around her and the post, with her arms outside. *Not hangin' me, somethin' else. But I can't do what he's wantin'. She shut her eyes. This could be the time to jes' give up on life. I'm as weak as a newborn kitten, but somehow I'm brave enough to go. It's like I been practicin'. But please God, if you're up there, don't let it last too long or hurt too bad.*

Jack's scar stretched into a strange smile. "Think I'm gonna whip ya?"

"Don't make no never mind, Jack. I won't do wha'cha want… not this time."

"We'll jes' see 'bout that."

He returned to the dugout and came back with his Special. By now her heart was missing beats and a darkness briefly blotted out the day. She blinked and tried to shake it off. *He's too lazy to want me dead. That'd mean workin' the equipment by hisself an' doin' his own cookin' an keepin' the fire. This can't be happenin'!*

He led Stormy by the mane in front of Frieda. Stopping her there he aimed the rifle barrel just above her big brown eye.

"NO. YOU CAN'T! NO!!"

"Kill Stormy? Kill your baby? Naw." He lowered the barrel to the side of the horse's leg. "But I'd blast her knee to mush." The filly stood ready to lift that front foot if that's what the touch meant.

"NOOOO!"

"Hmm. Mebbe both knees. Then I'd untie your hands and let you put her out a' her misery. Be a good lesson fer yer soft little heart."

"Oh Jack, no. Pleeeaaase, no …"

He smiled ruefully. "It's yer choice, Frieda. We'll see how much you care about this horse. It's up to you."

7

They left as soon as Jack got the horses saddled and Frieda made some mutton sandwiches. Normally she would have saddled her own horse, but, muttering to himself, he knocked her out of the way and did it. She had fallen into one of her stupid spells, where she couldn't move fast enough to please him.

She rode in front of Jack, his rifle handy in the boot. For a long time she felt like something not quite alive, unable to think beyond the constant effort of keeping Stormy ahead of the boss horse. But gradually the rocking of the mare's walk relaxed her enough to think and plan. She had already done her best to convince Jack that she'd completely changed her mind, to save her horse, and would do whatever he asked of her. But at some point he'd need to pull back out of sight and send her on to the German's place. When she had some distance, she'd make a break and escape from Jack forever. Stormy's life was at stake. Hers too. Jack made it plain that he would kill them both if Frieda "bunged this up."

She knew he'd need to silence her. Everything had changed between them. She would need to outride and outsmart him. Stormy was a little faster than the roan, but Frieda had never been in this part of the canyon, much less farther down. She vaguely remembered somebody saying the trail ended a few miles below Sheep Creek Bar, and after that came the "Impassable Canyon," too steep for trails, too dangerous even for a mule. That sounded ominous. She'd have to climb out of the canyon before that and hope for cover, and for shelter at night. This would be different from the last time she'd run away from Jack. This time she couldn't fail. She must keep her wits about her. She couldn't allow quivery feelings and stupid spells to spoil her concentration. But until she knew what she was riding into, she couldn't plan any further. They rode alongside the surging current for another half mile and crossed the river, Frieda holding her boots up out of the water. But every step of the way her strength and purpose came from Stormy—surefooted, strong, worth everything.

They pulled up on the west side of the river and rode a couple of miles down the river.

At a wide place with pines and junipers, Jack's sharp command startled her. "Dismount. We're gettin' off here."

Automatically she reined to a halt and swung down. "We stoppin' to eat?"

Jack rode alongside the mare, leaned over and took Stormy's reins. "I'll jes' keep her with me."

"Wha'cha doin'?"

He wasn't dismounting. Instead he backed up both horses and looked at her as she stood alone in the trail. The canyon floor was already in shadow, his face darkened—a lean horseman with the rifle lying casually over his arm. He spoke in a reasonable tone.

"I'll jes' keep her while you git on up to the German's place."

"But I was gonna ride her there."

He huffed in his chest. "I'll jes' bet you were."

He's outsmarted me already! How'my gonna … Oh God—

"See, Frieda, I got it figgered. Tell the German your horse got spooked an' run off. Tell 'im you walked a long way an' you're so tuckered out ya need to go in and rest. You'll say it real good 'cause some of it'll be true. Play yer first hand right an' that Hun won't much care how you come his way. Play the whole game right …" Reaching over and patting Stormy on the neck, "an' you'll be ridin' this 'un again. And Frieda … Don't bung this up. I'll be watchin'."

"You gonna lay out here in the cold all night?"

"Mebbe. We'll see." He tilted his head, the earflaps of his hat down. "Aw, git that stuck cow look off a' yer face. When it's over you'll be thankin' me. What would'ja do without me to think fer the both of us, huh? You'll do real good. Hell, we'll settle down right peaceable in that place and you'll forgit all about how we got it."

"Jack, he's prob'ly gonna kill me! Then who'll fetch water an' keep yer fire goin'? You think a' that?"

He just sat his horse and she worried that he'd realize her sudden return to this theme meant she'd had an alternative in mind.

"Frieda, jes' go'n do yer part.... I'm all you got and you're all I got. We're a team.... We're helpin' each other get a real nice place where it'll be warm of a winter night an' there's a shit-load of food all stored up. Now gitcher self on down the trail. I'll be behind you."

"How far is it?"

"Oh, a mile or so's all."

She began putting one foot before the other, walking alone and unarmed toward the enemy. Stormy whinnied behind her. She turned around to see Jack on his roan, the rifle still over his arm. Stormy was bobbing her head to go with Frieda.

Oh God, what's to become of me? For all I know that German'll cut me up an' boil me fer supper.

But she had to walk like she meant to go there. Eventually Jack fell back out of sight, but that didn't mean he wasn't trackin her. If it hadn't been for Stormy, she'd have run off into the mountains and tried to hide.

She walked up over a rise and looked down to see the canyon widen out—the German's place. She froze. Through some high brush she saw a log house standing in the shadow of the mountain a considerable distance back from the river. She couldn't see anyone, though there was movement in one of the fenced areas. Pigs. The house stood near a creek where the German had his claim—Sheep Creek. She saw the little stream spilling down from the saddle of the mountain and carving its way across this bottomland to the river. This was Sheep Creek Bar. From the house the view of the trail would be mostly blocked by a barn, outbuildings, and some high brush along the trail.

She stared at the cabin and its surroundings, blind to any of its appeal. Struggling to keep fear from clouding her thoughts, she knew she'd simply have to take one step at a time and hope beyond hope that she'd survive.

With one last glance at the sun that still lingered on the high, eastern slopes of the mountains, she noticed the Middle Fork had turned dark as it plunged northward toward the impassable canyon. A wind whipped up the canyon, bending the pines and dispersing the smoke from the cabin. It would be cold tonight. Jack hadn't packed a bedroll. *He'll wait to see I don't run off, then maybe head back to the dugout. Maybe.* But twilight lasted a long time in the canyon.

What were the details of Jack's plan? He'd rambled on as they rode down the trail this morning, but she'd hardly been able to pay attention. He said he'd go to Meyer's Cove while she was with the German. She knew he didn't have enough gold dust to buy much, and he expected the German's place to have plenty of supplies—except cigarettes. Jack was afraid the German didn't smoke. But his real purpose was to casually spread the story that Frieda was missing. He would play the concerned husband. Later he would "discover" that the German had her "in his clutches." He would go to the German's place and exercise his rights under the unwritten law of the West. Frieda's job was to let the German have his way with her so he'd let down his guard. Jack believed a man in the throes of sexual excitement would be easy to trick, just like any other animal. She would make sure the man went outside the cabin where Jack could get a clear shot. Jack would alert her with a wolf howl signal. Later, if anyone questioned what had happened, she would tell about the horrible sexual acts she had suffered at the hands of the German and how Jack had rescued her. Afterwards, with the claim open, who would be more deserving of it than the victim, Jack Sanders?

This was Monday afternoon. Jack would be here Friday morning to make his kill. But Frieda knew she couldn't keep track of the days of the week, so she forced herself to remember that this would be night number one. She counted on her fingers. Jack would come after three more nights. Tuesday, Wednesday, and Thursday. *I gotta keep it straight.*

To get a better look at what she was up against, she crept cautiously toward the German's cabin, up toward the barn. She didn't want to just run into the German. Leaving the boulders near the river, she pushed through some brush alongside a path that connected the river trail with the log house.

Suddenly a hard impact sound echoed down the canyon. Her heart and everything else in her stopped. She couldn't breathe. But the sound came again and again. Not a gun. It sounded more like chopping wood. Gathering her nerve, she made her last cautious steps and ducked behind the barn. A startled cow jerked around to face her, staring with big eyes. It blew out an abrupt half-moo. The chopping stopped.

The silence was worse than the noise. A jittery horror rose in Frieda's throat, and she felt she might throw up. Any moment the German would loom around the corner of the barn with his bayonet. She pictured him in a spiked helmet, slavering to strike her.

But the sound resumed.

Collecting herself, she edged to the corner, peeked around it, and saw the broad back of a man with thick legs braced as he swung an ax up over his thick mop of light brown hair. He bought the ax down with a blow that cut deep into a fallen tree. He wasn't as tall as she'd pictured, but just as heavily built. The ax swung up again, and the sound of its cutting blow echoed down the canyon.

Her breath came in short quakes. Would he come at her with the ax? She watched, transfixed. This was a powerful man with great endurance. His blows were evenly spaced, and when he severed one length of log, he reached down, tossed it aside as though it weighed little, and started the next segment. Eventually something about the rhythm of this familiar activity calmed her enough to remember that she had a job to do, to save Stormy. Jack would be back in the trees, watching.

She closed her eyes, swallowed, and heard herself say "'Scuse me."

The German kept swinging the ax.

A little louder, timed after the fall of the ax head, "'Scuse me, Mister."

He stopped mid-swing and jerked around. His coarse-featured, pitted face registered surprise. Instinctively she shrank back.

"Yah? You been alright, lady?"

"My—my horse threw me an' run off, an'..."

He let the ax drop to the ground and started walking toward her. "You be hurt?"

She kept backing up. "No, I'm okay, jes'—I'm okay."

He stopped advancing. A scruffy grayish dog with long legs slunk out of the deep shadow of the cabin and moved toward Frieda. She drew in her breath and stepped back more, but the dog only walked up to her and took a sniff, and then eased itself down beside the wall of the barn and put its head on a paw.

The German shook his head at the dog in mock ruefulness, fists on his hips. "Liesl, I'm heppy I never depend on you as a vatchdog."

Suddenly in this dangerous place came a stray memory from long ago—Frieda's mother standing that same way in her gingham print dress with her apron over it. Frieda felt confused. This was the dreaded German, yet his voice seemed so ... almost friendly. Must be how they show themselves at first, she thought, recalling what Jack had said about them being sneaky. *His face sure is like that German in the newspaper, wide mouth half open, a gap in his front teeth, but no black whiskers, no popping eyes, no helmet, and clothes jes' like Jack's and mine.*

"Your horse … moos nearby be. I help you find him."

"No, no—ah, she woulda run back to … uh … the corral."

"Iss far avay, your place?"

She lied. "More'n twenty miles."

"I saddle my horse und take you dere."

"No. I mean … I'm awful tired. Can I jes' …"

He frowned and cocked his head at her. Then he looked across the canyon to where the sun colored the highest peaks. Seeming to come to a decision, he said, "I go trink von der creek. Maybe you come mit, yah?" He pointed to where the creek came down from the mountain.

Trying to calm herself, Frieda exhaled and nodded. Her mouth was dry as cattail fluff.

She kept her distance as they walked across a harvested garden, then she waited for him to kneel down and drink. When he'd had his fill, he wiped his chin on a sleeve and leaned back, resting on his elbows. "Ah, dat iss goot … Best vasser I ever taste, yah yah."

Keeping one eye on him, Frieda got down and sucked in a mouthful of cold, clear water. She stood up and looked anywhere but at him, though she saw him in the corner of her eye. From where they were, the creek flowed down past one side of the barn inside the fence. The animals could drink on their own. They would foul the water, but up here the water was pure. An old trail ran alongside the creek up into the mountain. However, in her fear Frieda was barely aware of these details.

The German raised a hand with square, sausage-like fingers up toward her. "My name iss Yulius Remsburg." The hand could have been shaped by an ax.

She shrank back, unable to touch it. *But I gotta touch 'im sometime …* She took a breath. "M'name's Frieda." With trepidation she reached her hand toward his. He started to grab, but she quickly withdrew hers.

A look of wonder. "I hear right? Your name iss … Frieda?"

She nodded.

"My mooder's sister iss Frieda. Dat be a Cherman name."

"Well, I ain't no German. Guess there's a heap a' folks with that name." The words came out clipped, strange, stupid sounding. *Must be that quivery feelin' in my stomach. When's he gonna make a sneaky move? But I gotta act friendly and not let on I'm watchin' him.*

Squatting on the heels of his big, clunky, dust-covered shoes, the German gazed down at some pebbles. He selected one, stood up and threw it up the creek. He brushed off his hands and spoke in a tone of finality. "Und zo … ve start. I take you home now."

She whirled toward him, unconsciously folding her arms tightly, hugging herself. "Look, mister …"

Softly he said, "Yulius."

"Mister Yulius, I —"

"Yust Yulius."

She took a deep breath. "I can't go home. Things ain't right there."

He looked at her with concern, his large shoulders straining at the seams of his brown checkered shirt. "Vhat you mean?"

Searching for something to say, she finally came up with, "Don't wanna talk about it… . Can I … uh … jes' stay at your place?"

He stood looking at her. "Schtay here? Untill vhen?"

"Tomorrow maybe, uh … I dunno."

He thought for a moment, leaned down, picked up another pebble and bounced it in his hand. Then he looked at her warily, like he didn't believe her, but the look was not unfriendly—eyes blue as a clear summer sky. Maybe just puzzled.

"Und zo," he said at last, "I show you my house."

Nearly paralyzed with terror, she nodded.

Jack watched long enough to see Frieda enter the cozy log house that would soon be his. He blew out a lung full of air and mounted the roan, heading back up the river trail. *Sure wish I had me a smoke. It'd go real good right now, even some chawin' tobaccy.* He forced himself not to think about what must be happening inside the little house. Two things were certain. The German would be glad to see a woman, and Frieda was doing her part.

After he crossed back over the river, he told the roan, "Meb-be I come down a mite hard on 'er, but by damn a man's gotta be firm. Fer the female's own good."

8

Back inside after working all afternoon, Julius cooked supper and set a plate of pork loin and root vegetables on the table in front of Frieda. She looked at it, picked up her fork and moved it toward the food, then edged the fork back.

Fork upended in one hand, sharp knife in the other, he said, "Schnitzel, carrots und parsnips ... No poison." He began cutting his meat.

Her lack of trust in him showed, but at least he hadn't yelled at her ... yet.

Nervous as a horse on ice, she sampled a bit of turnip with gravy, working the taste around her mouth, liking it. She had watched every move he'd made and never saw him put anything on her plate that wasn't on his. So she took a deep breath and ate. After she took her last swallow, she said, "That was really good."

He hadn't said anything the whole time, and now looked at her as though trying to see through her.

She found herself saying something that hadn't come out of her mouth in years. "Thank you."

"You be velcome. I tink my cooking is okay, but I been tasting it by myself. I like dat you come eat mit me. Tank you, Frieda for da—how you say—nice talking."

She realized that somewhere during the meal she'd let down her guard. But she was supposed to play up to him so he'd let his guard down. "Bes' food I ever ate. You could give the hotel kitchen over to the Cove a run for their money, I'll tell ya that."

Julius' wide mouth stretched in a smile that involved his eyes, but then he frowned at his empty plate. "I tink dey not vant me ..."

Again looking at her, "Und now, you tell me vhy you be here in my house. You haff hoosband?"

"He … died." Would he keep digging for the truth? *How can I stand three more days of this?*

He was saying, "Oh, I be sorry. Dat vass recent?"

"Uh, a couple a' … a while back."

"Ach, dat iss bad. Schpeak more about you."

"I … live with my … big brother. An' he ain't so nice."

"He treat you bad, dis brooder?"

"Yeah. I do most a' the work around the place. He jes', you know, lazes around pert' near all the time."

"Und dat iss vhy — "

"An' he beats me black an' blue."

Nodding, he asked, "He iss trinking?" He lifted an imaginary glass and tipped his head back to show what he meant.

"Some a' that. But he's, well, jes' ornery." *Jack don't have the money fer drink, an' he sure don't need that excuse to whup me.*

Julius seemed to be thinking about what she'd told him. Frieda couldn't remember, in her entire life, another person this interested in her every word. It made her jittery.

Looking up at a partially filled bookshelf, she exclaimed, "Gol—ly! You got books." She and Amy, her friend in school, had used that word all the time, and Frieda realized she hadn't uttered it since, at least not that she could recall.

"You like to read, yah?"

"I used to love books, back when I was in school. My teacher let me borrow some. It's been so long …"

Hauling his cold, tired body back to the dugout after dark, Jack slept longer than he intended. But now he was eager to get going on his plan and move into that new place. The weather was holding, but for how long? He had to hurry. Besides, pressure like tight bands across his chest told him he needed a cigarette real bad. Rapidly packing the saddlebag with biscuits and the rest of the sheep roast Frieda had cooked, he strode to the corral to saddle up the roan.

As he put the blanket over the horse, he saw Frieda in his mind's eye standing in the trail looking back at him like she was too scared to spit. He talked to the roan.

"Mebbe I shouldn't oughta made the German out so all-fired bad." He put the saddle on, pushed it forward. "Naw, gettin' by with no smokes is makin' me stupid. I had to say them things. Couldn't hardly make the bastard out to be a reg'lar fella, then kill him, could I? She hada be plenty skeerd a' the German or she wouldn't be doin' her part to kill 'im." He ducked under the horse, grabbed the cinch, pulled it tight, buckling it. "Hell, even I woulda been puckered up some goin' in there with no gun."

He threw on the saddlebag and buckled it. "Truth be told, I'm kinda proud a' my old lady, way she walked up to the bastard an' went right in his house with 'im. Yup, Frieda's a purty good ol' gal. Shuts up when I tell her. Does what she's told. 'Cept yesterdee, but that weren't ordinary. Sure, she lays in bed like a dead fish, but that female works like a man. Out in this here backcountry I sure coulda done worse'n Frieda."

He patted the roan and when the horse exhaled, quickly put a boot against the belly and yanked the cinch up a notch. "Ya know, ol' buddy, Frieda and me's been off our feed fer some time now. Mightn't a' made it to spring. But ol' Jack's fixin' that. Ye-siree-*bob!*"

He considered leaving Stormy in the corral but decided to trail her with him in case Frieda got cold feet, hiked back to the dugout in some kind of female fit, and rode off with the mare, derailing his whole plan. He seriously doubted she'd do that, but he had pushed her harder than he ever had before and knew he had to cover every chance of error, no matter how remote. *She'll be fine soon's we git settled in the new place.* He put a lead rope on Stormy and tied it to his saddle horn.

He thought about using Stormy to haul the goods back, as

long as he was trailing her, but realized this was no time to train her to the packsaddle. Besides, he might have a need for Old Chief. The gold dust in his jacket pocket might buy more goods than he expected. *Maybe the German don't drink coffee. I'll git the biggest can. Molasses too, and a twenty-pound sack of brown sugar so Frieda can make plenty a' pies, and a twenty-pound bag of flour just to be safe. We're two people, the German's one. If I got any dust left over, I'll spend it on liquor. That'd be a fair size load.*

So he put the packsaddle on Old Chief. "You didn't think I'd kill Stormy, did'ja? Good little horse like that? But I woulda done it if I had to. This here's a life and death sit-shiation, and by damn it's gonna work."

"Yup, Frieda an' me's gonna live like rich folks," he told the three animals.

Picking up his rifle, he inserted it in the saddle boot and was about to mount up when he heard a horse nicker. All his animals answered the greeting. He looked up and saw a rider coming down the Camas Creek Trail with sunshine on his hat.

Goddamn son of a bitchin' rotten luck! No two-legged critter's come up or down this trail fer three months, and now this! Why the hell now? Muttering curses he stood waiting, one hand on the saddle horn.

"Jack Sanders, right? Haven't seen you for awhile. How ya doin'?"

"Oh, uh … alright, Sheriff. Can't complain." *What the devil's he snoopin' around here for? Gotta rifle handy in the saddle boot too.*

"Tommy" Thompson, a tall, rangy man in his early forties sat his horse well. He noticed that Jack didn't ask about his well-being, or even why he was this far from home. Thompson was in his third term as sheriff of Lemhi County and was well liked throughout his territory. His relationship with ranchers, prospectors, loggers, and trappers was natural and easy. He had worked with many of them in his earlier years. He loved the mountains and felt at home riding the lonely trails and spending days and nights by himself, whether on a hunting trip or investigating criminal activity in some isolated mining camp or searching for some hunter or camper who had been reported missing. His good humor and common sense approach to his work made him welcome in the scattered dugouts and cabins of this backcountry. That he consistently won county handgun competitions and was rarely bested at a rifle-shoot added respect to his office and gained him votes at election time.

He never boasted of his ability with firearms, but practiced regularly and insisted that his deputies do the same. He reminded them that the ability to use a gun well—and the fact that people know it—prevented trouble. Expert firearm handling was a requirement for employment in his department.

Thompson had never had a reason to get much acquainted with Jack, but had heard things about him. A friend he'd visited with in the dining room of the Meyer's Cove Hotel had groused a little about the man. That friend and Thompson had wondered together what sort of woman could live with such a surly character.

Thompson had been thinking about that conversation as he approached the Sanders place. In spite of what he knew about Jack, he held out some hope for an invitation for a cup of coffee, and he was glad to see Jack in the corral. He wouldn't need to knock on the door, something Tommy Thompson never liked to do at a stranger's house.

He had learned that it was never wise to dismount at the home of someone he didn't know well, without first being welcomed. And there was nothing that made him feel welcome here.

His practiced eyes took in the scene: one saddled horse, saddlebags half full, a bedroll, one unsaddled horse trailing behind the other, a pack mule, Krag 30-40 in the boot—and the unsmiling, shifty-eyed Jack Sanders. The hunting season for bighorn sheep had closed at the end of October, and Thompson noted that the sheepskin hanging on the corral fence, although frozen, looked fresh.

"It's a mite chilly but a fine day for late November, wouldn't you say, Sanders? Not much snow yet. Trails still in fair shape."

"Yeah … guess so." Jack knew the season was closed for deer, elk, and bighorn sheep, and he'd seen the question in the sheriff's eyes as he looked at the rifle and the hide on the fence.

Jack already felt jumpy on account of the cigarette situation, but also because he knew he'd be expected to invite Thompson in for a cup of coffee: *Another goddamned unwritten law. But I throwed out what was left from breakfast an' sure as hell ain't about to fire up the stove fer another pot. 'Sides, got thirteen miles to go to Meyer's Cove.*

"Wha'cha doin' way over here, Sheriff? Lookin' for someone? 'Cause if ya is, they'll likely be gone. We're 'bout the last one's left in the canyon, 'cept some old hermits …" Realizing he was inviting questions he didn't need, Jack shifted directions. "That looks to be a damn fine horse you're ridin'."

"He'll do. This appaloosa's a traveler, even on that steep downhill out a' Leesburg.… Everything okay with you and the little woman?"

"Oh, sure—looks like a good day for a ride. Think I'll take a look-see 'round, mebbe pick off a coyote or bobcat. Fur's prime by now. Prices good too. A man can always use a little extra jingle in the pocket."

"Well, if you're traveling down the Middle Fork here, we could ride together."

"Nope. I'm headin' upriver, maybe check out the side canyons."

Thompson now understood why almost no one seemed to know Jack except by reputation. If this had been the cabin of any other isolated hermit, there would have been the invitation to come in, warm up, have some coffee and sit a spell. He'd been on the trail in the brisk morning air for over three hours and he realized he'd been very much looking forward to a country coffee break. But still no invitation came, and Thompson, who was a popular sheriff partly because he respected the code of the backcountry, knew there were a few places where you didn't press your luck. He had no quarrel with Sanders, but sensed it wasn't the time to push the matter of the fresh sheepskin. Mostly, he was surprised that the wife hadn't come to the door to ask him in. He was about to inquire about her, but changed his mind.

"Well, I won't be keeping you. Got a lot of ridin' to do. The draft board needed a man to go out and see if everyone's heard about the new rules and signed up if they were supposed to. This war's a lot worse than most folks expected. The wounding and killing is something terrible, and now the Huns're using poison gas on our boys. Trust the Germans to think up something dirty as that. You probably know the first draft was for men twenty-one to thirty, but they've changed it to eighteen and forty-five. That catches quite a few of us, don't it?"

Jack grunted, looking away. *What's the son of a bitch tryin' to do? Arrest me for not signin' up?*

"If this is the first you've heard of it, you can go up to the Cove and sign up at the post office. Give your name, age, occupation, and family situation. They give some special exemptions for work that's necessary for the war effort. There's four different classifications, and of course the single guys'll go first. Married men with kids called up last."

Jack spat in the dirt. "I reckon married men without kids is close to the front of the line. Far as contributin' to the war effort, hell, we're doin' all we can jes' to feed ourselves out a' this piss-poor claim."

"Yeah, well not everyone in these parts is fortunate as that family down at Sheep Creek Bar, with that nice little farm."

"Fam'ly? They left a year ago."

"Really? Anybody there now?"

"Aw, some German." As soon as the word left his mouth, Jack regretted what he'd said, and quickly added, "Mean bugger I hear, like all of 'em." Then Jack woke up to the fact that the sheriff was headed that way, and if he went to Sheep Creek Bar he'd see Frieda at the German's place! That'd wreck the plan.

"Well, I'll be," the sheriff was saying, "A German right here in the canyon." He sat his horse, thinking, and then said, "Sure do hope they get this war over with pretty soon. With my Betsy and three kids to support, I'm in the fourth draft. I'll go if they need me, but I'd damn sight rather ride herd on the outlaws of Lemhi County than go over there against that bunch fightin' for the Kaiser."

Jack just wished he'd get the hell out of here. *Goddamn bad luck!* Trying to sound casual, he asked, "How fur you 'spect to travel down the trail?"

"Oh, don't rightly know. Depends. If the weather holds, maybe go all the way to Big Crick, up a couple side trails."

Jack hid his consternation as Thompson continued, "I figured you'd a' heard about the new law and be signed up, but I'm supposed to make sure every man in the backcountry knows about it, all of you who don't read the daily newspaper." Thompson smiled at his little jest, his attempt to be friendly.

Jack didn't smile. "Well, I was goin' up to the Cove anyhow, when I'm done huntin'. I'll check in." He'd known nothing about the change in the draft and wasn't about to mess with the board. *Got me a German to shoot right here in the canyon, if the goddamned sheriff'd git the hell out a' my way.*

"Nice horse you're trailing," Thompson remarked.

What's he diggin' for? Jack stood there with his thumbs in his back pockets realizing that no matter what he said, he'd be up to his neck in lies, and Thompson would remember them. "Just takin' her on a little ride." *By damn, I'm not sayin' another word.*

After a good long time, "Well, I won't be holdin' you up any longer from huntin'. I only hope if you shoot a fur animal with that rifle you're packin' there'll still be enough of the critter left to make it worth skinnin'. Try usin' a 22." He let his gaze linger on Jack.

Jack felt anger rising, and a touch of fear. He never did trust a lawman and couldn't let his eyes stay on him more than a second. This son of a bitch was smart.

"Got a lot of ground to cover. Told my counterpart over in Valley County that as long as I was over this way I'd cover some of his county for him. We like to help each other, with all this wilderness territory. My regards to the missus."

Double shit! Sounds like he's gonna cross the river!

Thompson wheeled his horse around to the trail and rode off in the direction of Sheep Creek Bar. He had observed the tension in Jack and wondered about the absence of his wife. And why would a man trail a horse and a pack mule on a hunting trip for small animals? Something didn't seem right. Why didn't Frieda come out? The few women who lived in these isolated cabins were always eager to visit with anyone who passed through. They were starved for company. He was fairly sure Jack wasn't going hunting for coyotes or bobcats.

But most of the people out here took what game they needed for their own table. They knew that as long as they didn't waste the meat, Thompson made it his business not to be snoopy. So maybe Jack Sanders was just plain unsociable. The backcountry did have some strange characters.

The sheriff swayed in the saddle in the noon sunshine, taking his time as he rode down the spectacular canyon of the Middle Fork, enjoying the white water rapids on his left and the feeling of being small within the wilderness of the so-called River of No Return. He thought about the hermits of these mountains, each with a different story, each forged by difficult situations. Most of them harmless.

Everyone's favorite was Polly Bemis down on the main channel of the Salmon. Big as a minute, that Chinese widow was, and famous for her grit. All the hunters and fishermen and packers made it a point to stop when they were riding anywhere near. They'd check to be sure she was all right. Most men carried extra supplies and left some for her. She loved company. Thompson chuckled to think of her sitting on the stoop of that little log cabin wearing oversized men's clothes, and her wrinkled old face all twisted in a grin with that pipe clenched in her teeth. Thompson had seen her only that one time when he and a friend stayed at her place on a fishing trip, but he always remembered that the toes of her big old high-top men's shoes pointed in opposite directions and made her walk like a clown, laces pulled as tight as possible but still loose on her skinny little legs. A real character. Sociable too. But even a grizzly couldn't pry her out of that place.

Thompson rode at a leisurely pace, allowing his mind to wander to the history of the area and the unexpected turns life could take. He hadn't known Polly Bemis' husband, a white man who made a living at card tables. Like most other men in these mountains, Bemis had followed the gold. When the California rush was winding down, he won Polly in a poker game, removed her from the sex slave business in San Francisco, and brought her here in the Idaho rush of the 1870s. Bemis sure did strike gold with that little gal! At one point he took a bullet in the back of his skull and the doctor gave up on him. He was fading fast when Polly, not about to lose the one man who'd been good to her, poured whisky down him and dug the bullet out herself, using her kitchen tools. Bemis recovered to gamble quite a few more years down around Warrens. Died of natural causes. Thompson clucked his tongue and wagged his head to think of that tiny little girl sold into slavery by her family in China. He'd be willing to bet she'd die of old age in the cabin that Bemis built, the only place she'd ever called her own. A more cheerful soul couldn't be found anywhere.

As he crossed the river near the old ferry place, the sun already starting its rise up the east wall, his thoughts shifted to the German down at Sheep Creek Bar. What had brought him to the canyon?

⁂

Jumpy as a grasshopper on a stovetop, Jack mounted the roan

and rode down to the river to let his animals drink. The full import of what had just happened burned in his mind. He had no idea when Thompson would come back up the trail on his way home, or when he would be going through Meyer's Cove, which was the only route back to Salmon. Jack had meant to go there and lay some groundwork, mentioning that Frieda was missing. But now if he did that, the damn sheriff would be suspicious. He'd wonder why Jack hadn't said anything about it this morning. *Shit!*

He decided he needed to keep an eye on Thompson and see if he went to the German's place. If he didn't, Jack could go ahead with his plan. But if he did, things could get all stirred up. True, Frieda wouldn't say anything incriminating, being part of the scheme and all, but Thompson was one smart cuss. Jack might not be able to go through with the killing, at least not till he thought up a new angle.

"Well," Jack said, turning the three animals around, "I gotta make tracks to beat the sheriff to the German's. Extra horses is more trouble, so you two's gonna wait in the corral."

But when he was taking off Old Chief's packsaddle and stowing it in its place in the collapsed barn, he stopped to think. The sheriff would ride by the dugout and wonder why the two animals were already back in the corral after what Jack had said. "Prob'ly get all nosy again. Oh, what the hell, let's all go." He mounted again and urged the roan to a fast walk, with Stormy and Old Chief keeping up on tether.

By way of the river trail, Big Sheep Bar was six miles from the dugout, but Jack would circle around the long way at a higher elevation, back around to Sheep Creek on the west side, where he could see the river trail better. From the east side where he'd been hunting, he might not be able to make out the identity of a rider.

He crossed the river a little before the old ferry crossing. Sure enough, on the other side he saw the big fresh hoof marks of the appaloosa heading downriver at a walk. Jack left the river trail and headed up a faint mountain trace at Spring Creek, now dry. This proved to be a steep half-mile, winding up through rough rock and sagebrush. It would cost him time, but he came to the ridge trail running north roughly parallel to the river far below. Here's where he would make up the time. The trail was good, not eroded at all. A lot of men in the early days had pounded out these back trails through the mountains. He made good time on this ridge, loping the animals. They were all in good condition, and willing.

In about three miles the faint old trail joined the old Sheep Creek trail, heading down the ridge alongside the stream toward the German's place. *Must be ahead a' the sheriff by now.* It was only about a mile down the gorge to get behind the German's place. Water was flowing in the creek, both banks were thick with pine, willow, and mountain mahogany—good cover.

Jack tied the animals in the trees by the water, far enough away that they couldn't alert a horse down at the Bar. He fell to his belly for a good drink of cold water. He removed his saddlebags, bedroll and rifle, then tore downhill on foot. He found an overlook where he could see the back of the German's house and the path going out from it to the river trail.

Not long after Jack got to this lookout, Thompson appeared. From this distance, about a quarter of a mile away, Jack easily recognized that big appaloosa and the sheepskin coat of the rider. Jack held his breath as the sheriff stopped and sat his horse, looking at the German's place.

To Jack's relief, Thompson rode on down the trail. But that was only half a victory. Now Jack had to be sure the lawman wouldn't stop and speak to the German on his way out. Jack had no idea how long this would take.

Well, there was nothing to do but wait, and it could be a long time, maybe a couple of days. He sat down and leaned against his bedroll. *Did the sheriff see Frieda there? Maybe on the porch? Well, if he did it can't be helped. 'Sides, that'd jes' back up my story 'bout her bein' at the German's. But more'n likely, a man couldn't see much from the trail, what with the barn and other buildings in the way.*

⁂

Coming inside the warm cabin after working all day, Julius smiled. Frieda had been reading *Oliver Twist* by the light of the kerosene lantern. The soft old easy chair had put her to sleep. Many times he'd gone to sleep reading in that chair. But this pretty woman dropping out of nowhere unnerved him. He'd been asking himself whether he should send her away before he got himself into trouble. A German had to be careful, and this was too strange. Yet he'd been lonely for so long …

He fixed a light supper of bread and wurst, poured cream in his coffee, making it half cream, and ate, not waking her. She was obviously very tired. Leaving everything on the table after he finished eating, he touched her shoulder.

She jerked awake, shrinking back like a wild thing.

"That book you read … is about a boy who be treated bad." He smiled, wishing he could speak better English, wishing his English didn't deteriorate when he was tired, wanting to ask much more about her, but afraid he'd upset her. *In the morning,* he told himself.

Gathering her composure, Frieda sat up straight in the chair. "Yup, the book's kinda sad so far."

"It soon be heppy. Goot tings coming … I go sleep now. You eat," he said, pointing at the table. "Then you go *ins bett.*" He pointed at his sturdy bed made of thick willow, the warm bedding covered by the faded old feather quilt his grandmother had made. "Understand? You go *ins bett.*"

With raised brows she pointed, and he nodded.

"Where you gonna sleep?"

He pointed to the blankets he'd laid on the floor.

There was fear in her voice, "Right there?"

"Yah, yah, in dat corner. Dat's so far as one can go in a house mit one room. "It vill be …" He remembered that the English word for *schön* was different than nice, but he was too tired and couldn't bring the right word to mind. "I think you not feel safe mit me?"

Her wistful brown eyes met his for a moment, then looked down at the floor. "Why you askin'?"

"Because I haff much work tomorrow und I want to sleep good. I want dat you sleep good."

"What would keep you from sleepin'?"

"Tinking about you afraid all night because I be sleeping in da same room."

"Any woman would worry, ya know, with a stranger."

"But you be here mit dis stranger by your own …" Again he couldn't come up with the right word. Volition he'd meant to say.

Frieda didn't say anything, just fidgeted with her hands.

"You be safe mit me, Frieda. Belief dat."

"I jes' had me a hard day is all."

"Dat I belief. You be very—how you say—"

"Yeah, I'm sorta—I don' know what …"

"I tink you be afraid of me because I'm Cherman."

"Guess I was … sorta."

"You be afraid now. I hear dat vhen I vake you up yust now."

"I'm sorry, I …"

He knew. He knew all too well. She needn't explain. He'd seen a friend murdered by German-haters. He gave her a tired smile, but couldn't keep the bitterness out of his voice.

"Vhat I say now iss true. I hate vhat der Kaiser makes. No, I mean I hate what da Kaiser does. I hate dat soldiers of Chermany fight soldiers of United States. Dhese are both goot lands, und ve all friends should be."

"You really believe that?"

"Yah, yah."

"I've heard jes' awful things …"

"Bad stories about ve Chermans, yah? I know."

"Then you don't … stab babies or nothin'?"

It pained him to hear her say that. It seemed everyone in the country believed the vicious propaganda—even out here in the most isolated place imaginable. He shook his head. "Nefer! It gives goot Cherman Christians, belief me." He felt frustrated to be so unable to explain to this woman who suddenly seemed a stand-in for all of America. "People say many tings vhen dere's var, tings dat be not true. Vhen it gives var, dat iss alvays zo. People vant to belief der enemy iss animal, not people. Understand?"

"Mebbeso. I'm kinda ignernt 'bout some things."

"You mean you not know some tings?"

"Yeah. I don't know much about the world."

"You admit dat you not know." He tapped his forehead. "Dat iss more schmarter dan belief in un-truth, belief in lies. Tank you, Frieda."

Timidly, "Maybe I'll have some of that bread and sausage. And sleep in my clothes?"

"Yah, yah, schlaf in der clothes." He went to the door. "Please excuse." He went out quickly behind the cabin to the outhouse. He had seen her go around the back of the house this afternoon, so he needn't explain.

Returning to the warm house, he arranged his blankets on the plank floor, folded for more cushioning, unlaced his shoes, removed his outer clothing, and pulled the blankets over him. "*Gute nacht, Frieda. Träum schön.*"

"What does that mean?"

"Goot night. Dream nice, peaceful."

"Good night. Dream nice and peaceful," she answered.

She ate a piece of very good bread with savory sausage slices, then pulled her boots off, turned down the lamp, snuffing out the light, and climbed under the covers of the bed, so soft it seemed like a cloud wrapping around her. Not one prickly thing stabbed her from the mattress. She felt the caress of a down comforter and pillow for the first time in her life.

Tired as she was, she lay awake wondering about this seemingly kind man who she'd been so ready to fear and despise. *Is he jes' bein' sneaky?*

He's right. I'm scared he'll try somethin'. Jes' what Jack wants to happen, but I won' let it. I'll lie to Jack an' git Stormy back without her bein' hurt. I'll say whatever it takes. But somethin' in me almost likes this German. He sure ain't a looker. But he's some kinda man I ain't never knowed before.

Even the way Julius snored was different from Jack. It was a low, soft, almost comforting sound. Frieda found a reassurance about it, right up to the point of falling asleep herself.

9

On Tuesday morning Jack woke up shivering in his bedroll. Hearing the muffled splashing of a creek, he pulled the blanket off his head. Sheep Creek had a thick apron of ice on both sides. He blinked his eyes clear and saw the east side of the canyon looming dark against a graying sky. Nearer, about a quarter of a mile down the mountain, stood the log cabin with shingled roof, the outhouse behind it.

His growling stomach reminded him that he'd thrown his saddlebag over a high branch to keep it from bears and wolves. There was nothing to do but eat the mutton and biscuits, and wait. Jack would bide his time, patiently looking down on the roof of the cozy little cabin with the smoke drifting up.

Last evening he'd seen them both when they came out to the outhouse, first the German, then Frieda, the light of a side window lighting them. Jack had never actually believed she'd get hurt—maybe beat up a little. *Mebbe she'll get ahold of his gun and kill him. That'd make things easier. But what the hell's goin' on in there anyhow?*

Does that Kraut like a woman in the morning? Jack's mind began to wander to a place it had never gone before. *What if she likes what he's doin' to her? Jes' what IS he doin'? Could she be warmin' up to that horny bastard?* In all Jack's planning this possibility had never crossed his mind. She wasn't the type. She didn't like sex. But it ran deeper than that. She was part of Jack. She did what Jack told her. They were a team. Her liking another man simply wasn't possible.

No, he kept convincing himself, not Frieda. That's one thing Jack didn't have to worry about.

Frieda woke with a start. Gray dawn showed in the windows and the lamp was lit. Julius stood across the room shirtless, buckling his belt. She'd slept too soundly! Had anything happened? She felt herself. No sticky mess. She felt clean. Amazing!

He turned to see her. "Goot morg—morning. You sleep goot?"

"Sure did! Like I ain't for I don't know how long."

The delighted smile on his face transformed him. His tone was caring. "You haff needed sleep, yah. Und now I giff you—how you zay—private. I vash me und shave my vhiskers." He dipped water from the water bucket into a washbasin, added hot water from the kettle on the stove, threw a towel over his shoulder and stepped out the door with the basin. "Den I make breakfast," he said through a crack left open.

Luxuriating in the soft bed, she heard him splashing.

"You can vasch in da house," he called through the crack. "If you vant fresh vater I bring it to you. Yust put da bucket here by da door."

"Thanks, what's in here is good enough for me." She shook her head in disbelief.

That'll be the day, when Jack brings me water. "How can you stand the cold with no shirt on?" she called from the warmth of the bed.

"Brrrrr. I like it cold in der morning." Splashing noisily, "Vakes me up goot!"

If this is bein' sneaky, he sure is good at it, and I hope he keeps it up. He finally came in and shrugged on his shirt and jacket and went out to feed the animals. She washed, pulled on her boots, and went around to the outhouse.

Later, Julius insisted she sit and wait while he cooked breakfast for her. She felt pampered like the princess in "The Princess and the Pea," a story she read in school long ago. To keep busy she pulled up the feather quilt and fluffed the pillow.

A baby cradle on rockers stood in the front corner of the room. She felt the smooth peeled and varnished willow of a reddish hue. *Why would he have a cradle?*

The stove wasn't the range she'd dreamed of, but it was nice enough. It stood on legs at a convenient height and had a special little tool for lifting the two lids. The oven had a door that opened downward, just wide enough for one pie. Julius put some kind of bread in it to heat. He fried his own thick-cut bacon, sausages, scrambled eggs, and fried chunks of potato.

Frieda ate heartily. With obvious pleasure, Julius watched her from across the table—the big skittle between them filled with more of everything.

"You moos be a hard vorker."

Between chews, "Why you say that?"

"You should be heavy, tick like me. You eat zo much! You vork it off?"

Embarrassed, she set her fork down. "I'm … makin' a pig a' myself."

"Nay, nay, nay, my friend. You haff hunger. You make me tink I make goot cooking. Tank you." Across the table, he bowed at her, intentionally funny.

She laughed. He looked so comical bobbing his head like that. "Well see, at my place we don' have that much to eat, 'specially this time a year."

"You and your brooder?"

"Me an' … my brother, yeah."

He scrutinized her for a moment, and then gave her his big, gap-toothed smile. "Vhen you be ended here, I show you around my little farm. You vant to see it?"

"That'd be real nice."

⁂

First she helped him skim the rich cream. It had risen overnight on the milk that had been put in round shallow skimming pans. He put the cream in the churning crock for making butter later, then he carried a bucket of skim milk as he walked with her through the cornfield. Frieda stuck her arm out and let her hand brush the pale dry stalks. Julius picked a small, leftover ear of corn and gave it to her. The kernels were hard.

"You grow dis on your farm, yah?"

"Y'mean corn?"

"Yah sure, corn."

She shook her head. "We ain't got a farm, jes' a minin' claim."

"Ach yah, we got mining claim too."

"'We?' Somebody else lives here?"

"Yah, yah. Liesl." He pointed at the gray dog, who wagged her tail and gazed in his eyes like a love-sick cow.

When they got to the pigpen, which had its own shelter, he poured the skim milk into a narrow little trough. About a dozen pigs, large and small, came running, and Frieda laughed at the eagerness of the young pigs as they slurped up the milk. Julius unloaded an armful of corncobs from his corncrib, then tossed them in for the pigs. "Gut appitit," he told the pigs, who busily snatched up their breakfast.

"Dey be my family too." Pointing to the huge mother pig with her two long rows of teats, he said, "Here iss da Pigfrau." I call her dat. In Cherman, frau means vife. He smiled.

"Mrs. Pigfrau, then."

Julius laughed at that, adding, "My pigs be my supper und my breakfast. I not ask dhem how dey like feeding me." He seemed relaxed and enthusiastic as he walked toward the barn.

Frieda walked with him, but looked away, troubled. She didn't have to twist the truth much to realize that, in a way, Julius was about to get killed to feed her and Jack. *How can I jus' stand by and watch Jack kill 'im? But Stormy … Guess I'll jes' have to forget about what a nice man he is turnin' out to be. I'll jes' try to keep in mind it's a part of nature fer one animal to kill another. They don't never stop to think if it's a nice animal they're eatin' for supper. But I sure couldn't do it to that mother elk …*

"You don't like killing da pigs?"

"Skinnin' an' butcherin's all right."

"Ah, now I understand. If someone elze does da—" He made a stabbing motion.

She closed her eyes.

They were at the barn door when he said, "I tink you haff a hard life, but you haff kindness too."

He's jes' as sweet as taffy now, but if he finds out what I'm doin' here, he'll prob'ly come after me with his ax. I jes' gotta be tough.

"Frieda?" A little louder, he repeated, "Frieda."

"Wha—?"

"You haff fantasia, yah? Dreaming in her daytime?"

"I s'pose. Yes. I dream in the daytime, all my life." They were walking through the barn.

"Zo, you vant to meet my lady?"

"You have a lady?"

Julius opened a door and stepped out into a corral attached to the barn. The creek ran through it. He patted the snoot of his milk cow, who came to greet him. "Here iss my lady …" Indicating a white mark on her nose, "Dis mark here. It remind me of a mountain flower ve haff in Chermany. Ve call it edelweiss. Zo dat iss vhat I name her, Edelweiss."

Frieda stroked the cow's neck. "She's a beauty… . How long you had her?"

"She iss here vhen I buy dis place. Alla animals coming mit da place."

"You bought this place?"

"Ach yah, vhat you tink?"

She looked down, embarrassed. "Well, most people in the canyon jes' move in when a claim is abandoned."

He frowned. "Dis place be not abandoned. My friend liffed

here, people who don't make me feel like I talk funny. Da man who zell dis farm to me, und his vife und zons ..."

"I didn't mean anything by that, honest. Was they nice, that fam'ly?"

"Yah, yah. Und dey like it here. George yust need a place dat iss bigger."

Looking around, "Gol-ly, bigger'n this?"

"Dis not big enough for a fifty cows." He petted Edelweiss, and she obviously appreciated it.

"Mebbe when folks like your friends got this much, they don't need to be mean."

Julius looked puzzled for a moment, then he tapped his forehead. "Dat vhat you say iss schmart. Ven people haff too much dollars, zome of dhem be greedy."

"Wouldn't know 'bout too much. I never had money. But people who don't have enough can sure get mean and greedy too."

"Iss your brooder you be speaking about?"

Frieda averted her eyes and went to see the chickens in the corner of the barn.

In his lookout above the farm, Jack practiced viewing the German through the sights of his Krag. Every so often he shifted to Frieda, just to see what kind of a shot a man could get, but then he'd move the little rectangle back to the German and try to keep the nub at the man's heart as he moved around. A couple of times he could have plugged him good without getting Frieda, but the sound of the shot would have echoed up and down the canyon, more than likely within earshot of Sheriff Thompson.

Prob'ly the bastard lawman's down to Brush Creek or Bernard Creek, maybe settin' with old Skeffington or one of the hermits. Jack put his rifle down, dropped to his belly and sucked up another drink of the cold, pure water.

Then he continued waiting for Thompson to ride back past

the German's place on his way out of the canyon. Jack hoped against hope that the sheriff would just keep riding by as he had yesterday on his way in.

⁂

Through a side window, Frieda watched Julius heft the long split rails between the high parallel posts around his garden. He'd told her he was building it higher to keep the deer out and stouter to stop the elk from pushing it down like they'd done on the far side. That way the garden would be ready for his spring planting. *No wonder this farm is so nice. He's a workin' son of a gun.*

An earthquake deep in her core was threatening to break to the surface. She put another stick of wood in the stove and walked around the room like a penned animal. She ran a hand over the pine tabletop, smooth except for the dark knots, then flicked the back of a fingernail across the slats of a chair. She squeezed the lace of the curtains and looked through the bookshelf—most of the books in German, a few in English. There were two volumes of *Oliver Twist*, the one she'd started reading, another in German. Her reading had been so rusty yesterday that she'd got only a little into the book. *If I didn't feel so quivery I'd prob'ly sit down on that nice soft chair and read some more. But I doubt I'd git through a single line of it with this bad feeling inside me.*

Her attention kept coming back to the cradle in the corner. She gently rocked it. In the bottom lay a folded pink blanket knit in a circular pattern that resembled roses.

On a small table next to it stood two pewter-framed photographs. One appeared to be a family standing in front of a farmhouse—an older couple with a young man, not Julius. Shadows in the picture, black as the clothes on the people, made it hard to see the faces clearly. In the other frame a young woman with a wide nest of hair on her head peered boldly out at Frieda. This girl, standing in a fine white gown, had her elbow on a wicker plant stand. The trees and large flowers behind her looked painted.

Could she be Julius' wife? Where is she now? Or is this his sister? These nice pichers sure do give the place a high-toned look. Maybe Jack and I oughta keep 'em … after …

No. Her mind bounded away. *What's wrong with me? I can't keep my mind on anything… . Why'm I'm so jittery? Just ain't used to loafin' 'round while a man's outside workin', even if he ain't gonna be long fer this world.*

The thought sent her back to the window where she observed the quiet strength and endurance of the man lifting the split logs, tipping them in the slot, bracing himself as he straightened the underpinnings when they didn't settle straight. The sun was high over the canyon, and this was heavy work. *A big man like that'd be hungry by now. I'll take 'im out some dinner. Surprise him.*

Filled with sudden purpose, she hurried out the door, around the side of the house, and lifted the heavy double-built hatch of the cellar. She hooked it up to give light while she went down the stone stairs to a dim earthen room smelling of dirt, potatoes, turnips, parsnips, onions, cabbages and apples, the potatoes in a neat pile and the rest in old flour and sugar sacks, open at the mouth. Hanging from the joists were strings of sausages and several smoked hams. She found the pork loin from last night's supper, beside it a small can of juniper berries, a few of which Julius had cooked with the meat, to flavor the schnitzel. In this cellar everything was cool but safe from freezing, and safe from wolves and bears.

Back in the kitchen she diced some apples and put them on the stove with a little water. From a tin-lined bin beneath the counter she added sugar. Like a girl at play, with all the right implements and pans, she chopped potatoes and onions together, poured half-melted lard from the coffee can at the back of the stove into the skittle, and fried the potatoes. The fire was hot from the damper that directed air up through it. The potatoes and onions sizzled and snapped. She stirred in salt and pepper, and then moved the pan to the other side of the stove where it wasn't so hot. On the tin counter top she sliced cold pork loin, then opened the door of a cupboard to retrieve the bread she'd seen Julius put in there the night before. She didn't expect to find several perfect, fresh-smelling loaves on metal screen shelves. *He's a baker! An' this shore is a real good place to store bread.* Cool air came up from the cellar with all the good smells, and rodents would be stopped by the screens.

Pleased that his back was turned when she went out to Julius, Frieda carried a plate of food in each hand. "Figured you'd be hungry."

Julius turned around, and his wide mouth stretched into a big smile. "Ahhh, dat smell goot. Tank you, Frieda. I tink you read my mind. I haff hunger." He took the plate that she offered. "You sit and eat mit? Ve eat togezer, yah?"

Frieda sat on the end of the felled tree from which he would cut more rails. He sat near her, his coat hanging over one of the fence uprights.

He took a bite out of his sandwich and chewed with gusto. Between chews, "I not so goot at reading minds als you."

"Wha'cha talkin' about?"

He swallowed. "Vhat you be tinking? … Vhat be your plans … vhat you do tomorrow … da next day, und so fort?"

What can I tell him? She simply looked down at her boots.

He turned to her, plate on his lap. "Frieda … you be a lofely, sveet woman …" He put his hand up to silence her objection. "Yah, yah, iss true. But vhat iss heppening? Vhy you be here?"

She looked away, upset to hear this again. "I'll leave if I'm gettin' bothersome."

"No, no. You be company for a man who been alone, by himself alla time. Und I like you. But, about you, you say no ting. Maybe *zometing* in dhere," tapping her forehead, "Dat I see not? Zomething dat scare you, yah?"

If I told him he'd probably stab me with his fork. Unable to look him in the eye, "I'll tell you … when I … uh … when I can."

He kept staring at her like he actually was trying to read her mind. At last he spoke, reluctantly. "For now, yah. Ve vait. You tell me later." He moved around on the log and picked up his fork and ate in silence.

She scraped up the last of her tangy, sweet applesauce, savored it, and said, "Hey, you ain't told me much about yourself neither."

"Vhere I came from you already know. Dat be more dan I know about you."

"Born 'n raised in Idaho ain't very interestin'. What's it like, you know, in Germany?"

Taking a forkload of potatoes, he looked at her, then turned his gaze toward the canyon wall across the river. Chewing ever more slowly he said, "Da landt vhere I be born iss very beautiful. In der valley of der Rhein. Der river he run vide und slow. One sees towers und old castles on islands in der river. Quiet iss dat vasser mit big boats floating on it. Quiet und peaceful." He seemed to be looking at that distant scene.

"Quiet 'til ya get to the rapids, then all hell breaks loose, huh?" She grinned.

"No, no, no. Not rapids. Not like your Middle Fork. Der Rhein iss like a … river dat sleep, but down under in der deep he be avake, alife, moving, always moving." Pushing his cooked apples around, he added, "Like you."

"Me? Wha'cha mean?"

Forking up the apples, he took his time with the answer. Quietly, "I tink your soul iss deep, down under where it be difficult to see, but your mind iss alife, moving all der time."

Is that a compliment or an insult? She couldn't imagine a river like that, much less a person.

He wiped his plate with a piece of bread pulled from his sandwich. "I like such rivers. You haff dem in this country—Missouri, Mississippi, other rivers in der east."

"You been back east?"

"Ach yah. I come first to Iova, den later to Idaho."

"So, how come ya left Germany in the first place?"

He blew out a mouthful of air. "Vhat start to happen. My faterland change … Wilhelm, he iss Kaiser becoming. Den tings change. Menner taken avay from der farms. My family, vor many generations dey been farmers, und now dey afraid dey be taken to da military. You understand? Der Kaiser, he been making men go to der army und navy. My fater he not vant to go. He not vant his two zons to be soldiers. My family, my grandfathers, be long time in der church. Christians not make var, not belief Jesus vant fighting und killing other peoples. So my family, ve all come to America. Leafing der Vaterlandt. Ve hope to find a landt vhere menner not fighting. Dat vas in nineteen hunnert, ve kom to America."

"And now men from around here're goin' off to fight Germans." *And everybody thinks you're a fightin' son of a bitch who ain't even human. Jack says he can kill you and nobody'd give a damn. They're afeared you'll kill them first. Like I been sceered …*

"Iss a little bit, how you say, *ironique*? Not so?"

Frieda didn't know that word and wanted to stop thinking about people killing each other, "I kinda thought you was a farmer. I mean …" Gesturing around them, " … what you done here, an' all."

"I learnt vhen I vas a boy to be a goot farmer. But in Chermany farmers vorking in big shipyards, some off dem vorking on undervater boat. Zub … zub zometing."

"There was that ship … the *Lusitania* I think its name was. Mr. Larsen told me about it when we was at the Cove. We didn't buy the newspaper."

Shaking his head, "Yah, yah lotta people dead. Innocent peoples."

"I saw the picture of that ship in the newspaper. Ain't seen a paper in so long I don't know what's goin' on outside."

"Outside?"

"You know, outside this canyon. Guess the whole world's out there, like Germany, places where the sun comes up."

Setting his empty plate on the ground, where Liesl licked it clean, he studied her, puzzled. "Der sun, he come up here too."

"Yeah, I know, but it don' rise here in the mornin', jes' late in the day, when it goes up an' out."

He sat thinking about that. "Der sun he komm down on da canyon vall. Dat vhat you mean?"

"Yup, it's a wonderment," a word Mrs. Taylor had taught her.

"Yah, iss beautiful. *Schön* in my language."

"I'm not religious or nuthin' but I allus see it like God's lowerin' the sun down to us each mornin' like a mother settin' her baby down to sleep." *The way I'd like to put a baby down in that pretty little cradle of yours.*

"Yah, but ven der zun he come down, ve all be avake, not sleeping."

"Jes' the opposite, huh?" She smiled at him, inspired to joke. "Maybe that's why we're mostly kinda backward down here in the canyon. Maybe it's surprisin' we don't walk backwards."

Julius threw his head back and laughed a deep rumble of wonderful sound. He got up and started walking backward with a silly exaggerated awkwardness until he bumped into the fence he was building, causing a precariously leaning rail to drop to the ground. "I guess dat iss vhy ve don't walk backwards, yah?" He laughed even harder.

She couldn't help but laugh with him, and in laughing together and his being silly in front of her, sharing her joke, she felt like she had long, long ago while playing make-believe with her friend Amy in the school recess. Just being alive was fun.

Julius slowed down to a chuckle. "Now I know vhy dey call dis der backcountry, and vhy dey call people in der canyon backward. You be a funny lady. I like dat."

She finished her sandwich. "Is that your family in the picher in your house?"

"Picher? Oh, you mean photograph. Yah, yah. Dat be my family. My mooder send it yust before I come to da canyon."

"That their house they're standing in front of?"

"Ya, in Iova. In dat house I liff fife years too. I been sixteen vhen ve leaf Chermany. Dat be my brooder, Peter, in der photograph. He be younger dan me." He looked at her inquiringly. "Und zo, I haff brooder too, Frieda."

She averted her eyes and pretended not to pick up his meaning. Did'ja like it in Iowa?"

He leaned down, selected a small stone, and threw it far over the garden fence. "Der farm vas goot to us. Landt flat, not so beautiful as Chermany, no hills vit grapevines, but people be welcoming us. Many people from Chermany."

"Friendlier than here, I bet."

"Yah, yah … but you be friendly."

"Wasn't so much at first."

He cocked his head at her and smiled. "I not see dat."

"You said it yourself, I was scared a' you."

"Ah, but scared is scared. Unfriendly is unfriendly … Scared can good reason haff."

"Or *think* there's a good reason. Jes' what is it to be unfrien'ly?"

His little smile struck her as about the friendliest she'd ever seen. "Dat be shutting off da mind und heart to other peoples. A bad vay to liff."

Wish Jack felt that way. "So … you ain't seen Germany for a long time?"

"I been back dere fife years ago, to help my grandparents move here wit da family."

"Did it look diff'ernt? Things changed much back in Germany?"

"Yah, da country be even more closer to war." His big, pitted face took on a sadness. "Und dere be more change … udder ting."

"What?"

Shaking off memories and standing up, "Frieda I moos finish da fence today, before der zun he goes avay."

"Oh, sorry, I've been botherin' you." She stood up with him. *I'll wash the dishes and maybe read more of that book. I think I can read now.*

"Maybe ve eat a chicken dis evening?"

"Yes! I'd love that. I'll cook it —well, after you …" She made a wringing motion.

"Yah, yah, I do dat."

She looked down at the holstered pistol on his belt. "Or do you shoot chickens instead?"

"Oh, no, no." He patted the pistol. "Dis be for little aminals dat eat my garden."

But his garden truck was all in the cellar.

He looked at her and she knew he wasn't telling the truth. Did he suspect something? Was he actually protecting himself? His voice took on a certainty.

"I tell you, Frieda, vhy I haff dis gun mit." He slapped the holster. "I tell you da truth, as I hope you tell me da truth. Animals mit two legs be da most dangerous kind. Not you, Frieda. You be a goot perzon. But maybe some perzon come to hurt you. I see you looking around mit fear in your eyes. I haff my gun here so dat not happen. I protect you. I protect you mit my rifle also …"

Suddenly she couldn't talk any more. Whisking up the plates, she turned to the house before he could see the tears in her eyes. He was protecting her! A man who came to America to find peace! A man she would help to kill.

10

Not until later that day— Frieda inside the cabin and the German still working outside—did Jack see movement. A rider on the far side of the river, the east side. The canyon was in shadow, the distance a little too far to be sure if it was the sheriff. *Couldn't be old Skeffington. He wouldn't be goin' to the Cove fer supplies, would he? A squaw man who eats off the land, snakes and such. 'Sides, his mule died.* Or was he on his way to register for the draft? On a horse he got hold of some way? It didn't seem possible. If it was the sheriff, he must have decided not to visit the German, or he would have used the west trail. Jack believed it was the sheriff, but he needed a closer look.

He grabbed his things and ran up the hill. Having left the saddle on the roan yesterday, he was ready to travel in less than a minute. He galloped the animals up the Sheep Creek trail and turned left on the ridge, once again making up time on the old trail high above the river. The four miles or so passed swiftly, but the animals had to pick their way down the steep and rocky washed-out creek bottom. He tied his animals behind a big rock outcropping a ways before he got to the river trail, and hurried down to a bunch of pines and willows near the water's edge. The river was narrower here, the trail on the opposite side closer to the water. He would get a good look.

It was the sheriff all right! Thompson's long-legged Indian warhorse appeared to be taking his time, but was actually moving like a son of a gun. Jack waited before he fetched his animals, forded the river and followed the sheriff. He was feeling much better now, except for needing a cigarette. The sheriff hadn't talked to the German. Knowing that put him back in the same frame of mind he'd been in before Thompson showed up in the canyon. He told the roan, "Now ol' Jack's gonna get his new place, sure as shootin." Chuckling at his little joke, he rode slowly up the trail, careful not to come up too close behind the sheriff.

But his mind kept turning back to Frieda and the German. He'd seen her climb up in a fruit tree and saw off some limbs at the Hun's direction. That was all right, probably something a farmer was supposed to do to fruit trees and a good thing for her to learn, but earlier in the day he'd seen them eating together. They had laughed, and the memory of that laughter kept stinging his ear like a pesky mosquito. It wouldn't leave him alone. In the cold, still air of the canyon, voices carried half a mile. He'd been only about a quarter mile away, but it sounded like they were laughing right in front of him. Frieda never laughed like that. What was going on?

Were they laughing at him? When he'd been a young boy people used to point at his scar and his callused bare feet and laugh, the bastards. That's one reason Jack liked horses better than people.

Had Frieda been laughing at him? He cuffed the side of his head, knowing he had to pry that out of his mind or he was likely to make a mistake. Besides, maybe they were just laughing over something funny, and that was good. It meant Frieda was softening up the German so he'd lose his wariness. She was simply doing as she was told. Still, Jack thought, getting drunk would help him keep that stinging thought at bay. Maybe get a drink up at the Cove. Then it occurred to him that he would be riding right past Martha Tollifson's place on his way to Meyer's Cove. This just might be a good time to pay her a visit. From what he'd heard, Martha knew how to take a man's mind off his troubles. She wasn't too particular about her men either.

⁂

The cold, still air carried Sheriff "Tommy" Thompson's "Hello there. Anyone home?"

Home, home, home echoed off the canyon walls and died. He didn't dismount. With both horses and the mule gone from the corral, it was obvious that neither Jack Sanders nor his wife was there. But where were they?

Thompson shook off his overactive imagination. *They just went to Meyer's Cove for provisions, like Jack said. He might even check in at the post office for the draft, though I wouldn't lay a bet on it.* He considered the fork of the trail, one going upstream along the Middle Fork, the other heading east along Camas Creek, back toward Meyer's Cove and Salmon City.

I got a capable deputy watching things back in town, and there's a man or two left upstream that might not know of the draft rules. But not enough to warrant spending another day on the trail. Betsy had those apple pies bakin' when I left—a mighty fine repast for a man who's been on the trail. My butt'll be weary enough without taking an extra day out here, much as I like this good autumn weather.

He'd talked to only four men downstream and along the tributary creeks of the Middle Fork. Sanders here at the mouth of Camas Creek made five. None of them had known of the new draft rules, but they'd all been sociable except for Sanders. At the very last minute he'd decided not to talk to the German. There was a possibility of danger. Jack said the man was mean. *Figure I got enough to keep me busy without digging up extra trouble down in this canyon. Talk to a German about fighting his own countrymen? Absurd.*

He reined the appaloosa up the Camas Creek trail heading out of the canyon. He'd be riding through Meyer's Cove. Did he really want to stay in the hotel again? And see the same people he'd already talked to? Or shouldn't he get on up the mountain while there would still be daylight. Maybe lay out his bedroll in the barn of one of the friendly farmers around Panther Creek. That'd cut a chunk of mileage off his trip tomorrow.

⁂

Arriving at the dugout Jack examined the fresh prints where the appaloosa had milled around in front of his door. After satisfying himself that the tracks headed east toward Meyer's Cove, he left the saddle on the roan, threw him some grass from the collapsed barn, and went in the dugout to fill up on mutton and hot coffee. Later he moseyed on toward the Cove, figuring the sheriff would probably spend the night there at the hotel. Jack needed to know what the sheriff did before he could sow his seeds of doubt about Frieda.

The days were very short now, and he'd be lucky to get to Meyer's Cove while there was any kind of light left. The widow Tollifson lived three miles short of the Cove. If he played his cards right, she might let him sleep there and fix him some bacon and eggs in the morning. Widows wouldn't be on Thompson's visiting list, and Jack could use a place to stay while he scouted the lay of the land.

⁂

That evening, having finished the first chapter of *Oliver Twist*, Frieda baked a small chicken with dumplings while Julius again cooked root vegetables. He had a knack for it. They made little joking comments and excuse me's when they got in each other's way. Cooking beside Julius was fun.

With Julius, everything felt like playing. He'd shown her how he pruned the peach trees, and he liked it that she insisted on climbing up the trees, with a boost from him, to cut some branches that he couldn't reach without risk to valuable branches. She'd followed his directions without feeling ordered around. He was gentle and kind about everything, explaining that the trees slept in winter and were not hurt being cut. He explained that they would grow bigger and better peaches next year. Later, they'd had a good time at the river fishing for red-sides trout. She enjoyed teaching him some of her tricks for catching them, and now he was showing her a new way of cooking the trout—steamed in a pot with onion and a sprinkling of sagebrush leaves and herbs from his garden.

"I never knew a man would want to cook," she told him as she took the chicken from the oven.

He smiled. "Did you know most of the great cooks and bakers in der vorld be men?"

That astounded her.

At the table Frieda exclaimed over his delicious trout. Her chicken tasted bland in comparison. She kept trying to eat more slowly, like Julius. She also tried to copy the unusual way he ate—forearms, but not elbows, resting on the table. He didn't hunch over his plate and never used the point of his knife to put food in his mouth. Whenever a bit of food was around his mouth, he wiped it off with a napkin. He chewed with his mouth closed. It seemed to Frieda that this was a nicer way to eat, maybe the way the better people did it.

She noticed the look in his eye, a look that told her he knew she was trying to copy him, but didn't want her to know he'd noticed.

When they were finished, he rolled up his sleeves and started washing the dishes like that was a perfectly natural thing for a man to do, even when a woman was standing there ready and willing to do it. He put the soiled plates, utensils and pans into one of the heated buckets of water, plunged his arms in, rubbed a cake of soap on each dish or pan, and then rinsed it in the bucket of clear water.

With a shy smile he asked, "Maybe you vant to help? Dry and put dem in da cupboard?"

She felt herself ready to weep again. Why, she didn't know. Picking up the towel, she fought to blink away the tears. But as she stood drying dishes beside him, now and then accidentally bumping elbows, she felt herself being pulled toward him like a scrap of iron to a huge magnet. He handed her the rinsed dishes, his hairy arm and big hand dripping, and she felt weak with the effort to keep from leaning on him. He looked at her with those large blue eyes that told her he had been lonely and now he loved her being here with him, and she wanted to grab him around his thick chest and never let him go.

Yet she was here—forced to be here—to help kill him. She needed to warn him. She needed to be as honest with him as she now believed he was with her. But not now, not with the stove radiating domestic warmth and something tantalizing happening inside her. She couldn't break this spell with news like that. He would surely turn on her. Any man would.

After they'd put everything away, Julius settled in the soft chair with a German book. It was understood that she would read on the bed, her place. The kerosene lamp on a table beside him lit his kindly, honest face.

"Why ya got a cradle here?" Frieda asked.

He put the book in his lap. "It belonged to da family dat liffed here. Dey just leaf da cradle here. My friend make it goot, yah. I not vant to feed Mrs. Pigfrau mit dat cradle." He flashed Frieda a little smile. "Maybe Edelweiss like to eat from it."

"Maybe someday you'll need it for a baby."

His brows furrowed. "Dat be difficult to belief, now."

"You never know … maybe someday."

"Ve can only know, ve can only understand da day ve be liffing."

For a while she sat turning that in her mind, and when she thought she understood his meaning, took a deep breath and started. "There's somethin' I gotta …"

But it just wouldn't come out. She looked at the black squares of the window. The wind was kicking up, and in the distance she heard a high-pitched howl of a wolf, desolate, mournful, chilling. Not Jack.

"Yah? Vhat iss?"

She couldn't answer. Continuing to stare at the black night, she knew that if she told him he would wring her neck, or drive her out into the cold. But even now she felt the magnetic pull of him—so peaceful and friendly in his chair. *I never knew men like that was in the world.* She'd been counting the days, and forced herself to concentrate on the fact that it was Tuesday evening and Jack wouldn't arrive till Friday morning. Well, maybe he'd come on Thursday night to be ready for the killing. She would tell Julius tomorrow, Wednesday, in full daylight, which would be better for running and hiding from him, if that became necessary.

She'd have to hide from Jack too, and Jack would kill Stormy. Stifling a moan, she told herself, *I jes' need more time to figger out how to tell Julius. Maybe if I tell him right he'll run away with me. Maybe we could leave the canyon to Jack. But would Julius do that? No, I'm jes' daydreamin' again.*

"Frieda, you start to zay zometing."

Turning back to him, "Not now, I can't. Not right now."

After a long silence, he nodded. "Iss all right. Some udder time. I vait." He raised his book again, his eyes moving over the page.

She went to the bookshelf. "Maybe I'll read some more tonight too." She pulled out *Oliver Twist.*

"I haff two of dem, see?" He was pointing.

"I saw that." The *Oliver Twist* printed in German had gold lettering on a green cover, the English cover was brown. "How come ya got two of 'em?"

"Charles Dickens, he vas my English teacher."

"Your teacher?"

"His writing teaches me, not him in perzon."

"Oh."

"I read dose two books zide to zide."

"Side *by* side."

"Zide by zide, yah. Dat help me learn English."

She took the book to the bed and sat against the pillows. Julius had lit the kerosene lamp on the wooden crate beside the bed.

Oh how I wish I had you here in my arms.

After a few minutes he pushed up out of the chair and slipped his book back on the shelf." I go ins bett now. I sleepy." He went outside for a while, returned and removed his shoes. Then quickly he settled down between his blankets in the corner near the stove.

Frieda couldn't make herself read. This nightmare was getting worse all the time. Worse than her old dreams. She trusted Julius. Her world had turned upside down. She had never felt this pull toward a person before. She felt dizzy, happy, strangely excited just to be in his house.

When she thought he was asleep, she grabbed her coat and trotted through the chill, dark night to the outhouse, hugging the coat around her against the wind. Liesl accompanied her. Back inside the cozy cabin she pulled off her boots and undressed down to her longjohns. She turned down the lamp, snuffing out all the light except the red glow at the seams of the stove. When her eyes adjusted to the dark, she stared at the big friendly lump under the blankets on the floor. Tears rolled silently down her face. She hadn't cried for years, but in the last two days she couldn't seem to stop.

Softly, "*Gute Nacht, Frieda. Schlaf schön.*"

Startled, "Goodnight, Julius. Sleep nice."

I learned me some German words! She crawled under the pretty feather quilt, looked into the darkness and listened to the distant wolves. Eventually his breathing changed. He slept like a baby, as though safe in his own house.

11

On Tuesday evening Jack sipped his beer at the Meyer's Cove Hotel bar. He also sucked deep, soothing draws on his cigarette. He had examined the hotel's pasture where guests grazed their animals overnight. The big appaloosa wasn't there. He blew the smoke out slowly. The sheriff must be camping farther up the trail, maybe anxious to get home. Jack doubted he'd be in the canyon again till at least next summer—unless trouble came to his attention.

Jack had already tossed back a shot of whisky, but was taking his time with the chaser. He wouldn't be able to afford another setup. He hated being out in public about as much as he'd hated talking to a lawman. It upset his stomach to see people all over the place with their mouths spewing stupidity at sixteen ounces to the pound. In fact he'd lost his appetite entirely.

Fer two bits I'd quit this horsin' around. Those dudes gawkin' at me from the bar mirror, fer instance. I'd like to shut those eyes once and for all. But by damn I come this far and I'll finish the job. Folks'll remember what I said about Frieda. 'Sides, that whisky sure went down good; this beer too. Ain't I just a reg'lar fella havin' a drink like those others down to the end of the bar? Shore am. Jes' can't stand people gawkin' at me.

Walter Larsen, proprietor of the town general store, entered with his young helper, Pete Mabry. They looked around and Pete saw Jack at the bar, pointing him out to Larsen.

Larsen walked up to him. "Sanders …"

Jack whirled to see them. Relieved, he forced a smile. "How ya doin', Larsen? Missed you today when I was pickin' up supplies."

"What's this Pete's tellin' me about your wife?"

"Oh, she, uh, goes off by herself ever' now an' then. I jes' asked him if anybody'd seen her in town 's'all."

Larsen's eyes narrowed. "What do you mean goes off by herself?"

"Frieda's kinda taken to … prayin' in the mountains. Gets her closer to the Lord, she claims."

"How long she been doin' this?"

"Oh, jes' lately … two, three weeks."

"Pete says you told him she'd been gone since mornin'."

Jack produced a wistful smile. "Yeah, that's right. Nuthin' new. She run off overnight once. I found her an' she was all right."

Larsen glanced at Pete, then looked again at Jack. "Lot can happen in the canyon at night."

"Frieda takes a handgun 'long with her Bible."

"Still, mebbe we'd oughta organize a search party. Just say the word and me an' Pete can get some men together."

Jack stiffened. "Naw, she can take care a' herself. Know that for sure. She's a crack shot. I taught her. So it ain't no real cause for worry."

Larsen studied him for a long moment. "You'll be headin' back home in the mornin'?"

"Yup. Crack a' dawn."

"If she ain't back by the time you are, Sanders, I wouldn't wait another day to be seriously lookin' for her. You'd need help. I still think a little posse should ride with you in the mornin."

"If she ain't come back, I'll ride back here and gitcha. But, like I said, she'll be alright." He forced himself to go soft-eyed, "Helluva woman, my Frieda."

After they sat down at a table in the corner of the saloon, Larsen asked Pete in a low voice, "Ever hear a wolf talk?"

"Huh?"

"Reckon it'd sound about like Jack Sanders."

"Think he was layin' it on, Mr. Larsen?"

"Thicker'n shit in a stable. The few times I seen him in the store he'd barely gimme a grunt. Snarly sort. None too friendly to his wife neither."

"Well, sir, he sure sounds all lovey 'bout her tonight."

"An' in the same breath paintin' her as bein' wayward. He ain't the smartest rat in the bunkhouse, but I don't take 'im fer a fool neither … Jes' don't figure."

When Jack woke up Wednesday morning, he was in bed with Martha Tollifson. Martha was childless and none too young, widowed a few years earlier when her husband died of consumption. Even Jack had heard she got her private itches taken care of by a couple of men who used this trail.

The bed was unfamiliar, and that's what woke Jack up so early. He looked over at the still-sleeping Martha, thinking she looked her age, all worn out. *Say one thing for her old man, he learned her pretty damn good how to please a man under the covers. Or mebbe it's jes' her nature. I done my best to teach Frieda, but she don't do much more'n lay there like a wounded animal. Martha's more of a woman in that way. If she jes' didn't have that big ol' wart up on her cheekbone.*

When Martha woke up, they had sex again. Afterward, lying in bed together, she ran her fingers across his furry chest.

"You're an intense one, Jack. Say that much for you."

"Kinda like a pent-up stallion, huh?"

She chuckled. "After a few weeks being alone in this four-poster, I can easily welcome a fella like you."

"That's all, a few weeks?"

"If you think you're the only man, Jack …"

He felt his scar stretch in a grin. "Bet I'm the best one, though. Ain't that right?"

"I ain't runnin' no contest."

"Still, if ya compare …"

Martha put her finger to his lips. "If I compare the men around here to my late husband, I'd turn you all out. I jes' need to keep lonely at bay every now and agin, that's all."

They were silent a few minutes, then, "Jack, how'd you like to do something for me?"

He shook his head and grinned. "Gotta give me a few more minutes, Martha. Ain't 'zac'ly a kid no more."

She cackled too long. Continuing to snicker, "Just need ya to shoe my horse. Left front shoe come off, another'n's loose."

She laughin' at me? Naw, doubt that after all her lovin' ways. "Okay. I'll do that right after breakfast."

She got up on an elbow and narrowed an eye at him. "I know your kind, Jack Sanders. Once you're satisfied in your belly an' below your belt, you'll be down the road without so much as a how-dee-do."

With a look of mock hurt, "Naw Martha, I wouldn't do nuthin' like that."

"Yeah, an' cows give cider."

"'Sides, I was thinkin' I'd stay over tonight too. How'd you like that? Huh?"

"Don't know if I could put up with you two nights in a row. Now git on out and shoe my horse while I fix us some breakfast."

"Oh, alright." He sure didn't like her ordering him around, but having missed supper last night, he felt hungry enough to eat a sow and nine pigs and chase the boar a half a mile.

"Goddamn woman," he grumbled as he waited for the little triangular forge to heat up. "'Spects a man to work on a hollow stomach!"

All the time he was squeezing the bellows and sawing off the iron, the internal rumblings came out about as loud as his complaining. And Stormy kept turning her head from the stall she was in and staring at him. Jack took it as the spirit of Frieda giving him reproving glances, or worse, laughing at him. Stormy kept this up while he filed the hooves and heated and pounded out the iron. She kept it up while he nailed on the shoes, with the jughead horse leaning on him. It was a half hour of backbreaking work, bent over like a barrel hoop, and every so often he needed to drop the damned hoof and swear at the lazy animal that was using him for a leaning post. His stomach never stopped grumbling, and he got madder and madder at everything. When he finally pounded in the last nail, he straightened his aching back and strode up to Stormy and grabbed her roughly by the mane.

"Don'chu be givin' me no evil eye, girl." Tugging hard on her mane, "You hear me? Huh?"

Stormy bolted around suddenly, knocking Jack against a stall gatepost. His back hurt.

"WHY YOU GODDAMN MARE! I'M GONNA BEAT YOUR ASS! He looked around for a whip, finding only a coiled length of rope. He tied a knot on one end, let out a few feet, then started for Stormy, swinging the rope …

"Wha'cha think you're doin' there, Jack?" Martha stood at the barn door, fists on her hips.

"Ain't your horse I'm gonna whup, so don'cha fret about it."

"You won't take that knot to any horse in my barn."

Jack's fuse was sizzling to its end. "Martha, that's my own damned mare. Don'chu be tellin' me wha …"

"I mean it. Set that rope down. Now!"

He glared at her but, afraid of not getting any breakfast, let the rope slip from his grasp.

When he joined her in the kitchen, he was so mad he couldn't sit down. Martha was at the stove frying a mound of potatoes and onions in a cast-iron skillet. Looking at him and smiling pleasantly, "Got a sizeable appetite?"

He turned away, a low guttural sound escaping from him.

"Didn't quite make that out."

He just paced back and forth.

Martha glanced at him and rolled her eyes. "How long you gonna keep that up, being mad as an old goat?"

"Shouldn't talk to me like you done, Martha."

"It's about time you gave up chawin' on that."

"Warn't right."

"You know, I'm the one with the right to be riled. Here I give you my bed and body the whole damned night, an' fix you breakfast, and you sulk around like you had your nose rubbed in manure."

"I ain't used to bein' talked to that way."

She spooned out the fried potatoes and onions on his plate, saving her portion for later. "I'd say you ain't used to a woman standin' up to you. Bring your wife by one day, Jack. Me and her, we could have us a good heart-to-heart." She handed him a plate. "Here you go."

He took the plate and looked at it with disdain. "No eggs!"

"Not today. Chickens ain't layin' so regular."

"What about bacon?" He knew for a fact she had pigs and a smokehouse.

She turned to him, folding her arms defiantly. "No bacon today either. Now eat what you got and be thankful for it or you can jes' git out a' here right now."

"You don' mean that after I done all that wor —"

"Try me."

He slammed his plate on the table, sat down and hunched over it, muttering to himself, "Goddamn ugly, wart-faced whore …"

Martha's eyes narrowed and her words came out measured. "What did you say, Jack?"

Digging his fork into his food, "Nothin'."

"Turn around and tell me to my face what you said."

Hunched over his plate, he shoveled a fork-load into his mouth.

She snatched up the skillet and lunged toward him, swinging the pan against the side of his head. Jack dropped out of the chair and sprawled on the floor. When he didn't move after several seconds, Martha knelt down next to him and put her fingertips to her mouth. Blood trickled down through Jack's hair and his breathing was shallow. His eyelids fluttered weakly.

"What'd I do? Heaven help me!"

The door was open and, like the morning before, Julius was out shaving on the porch when Frieda woke up. In the gloom of the canyon before the sun came down, he had lit the lamp on the table. The cabin stood back so far from the river that the sunlight came down a little earlier than at the dugout, but still not much before noon. They had slept late. *For some reason I'm not waking up early like I usually do, maybe 'cuz the bed's so soft. But I sure do look forward to spending the day with Julius.*

When would she tell him?

Not right now. She dressed and went around the house. On the way back she asked Julius if she could milk his cow. She hadn't milked since she'd been a child. Clearly he was pleased at the suggestion.

When the first squirt missed the bucket, she frowned. "I'm sorry. That was dumb."

"No, no, no. You be yust out of practice. Try pulling it straight down."

She did that and streams of milk starting filling the bucket. He smiled encouragement. When the bucket was full, he poured the milk into a can, screwed the big lid tight, and she helped him carry it up the creek where they laid it on its side against a boulder with the water running over it. "Now, it keep plenty cold."

Everything here was easy, like she'd been rescued from under the bucking horse of her nightmares. And the rescuer's face was German.

After they'd fed the chickens and other livestock, and had their own breakfast, Julius turned to Frieda and smiled broadly. "You like to see zometing nice today?"

"Sure." The sun had just poured over the canyon rim and was

starting to come through the window, gleaming off the glass lamp chimney on the table and the pistol next to it.

"It's a few miles avay. Ve ride my horse. Iss goot?"

"Both of us ridin' the horse?"

"Not to vorry. General can easy carry heavy me. You on him he not notice."

As much as she liked the cabin, Frieda was glad to go somewhere else. She wouldn't always be looking around for Jack. And maybe she'd feel freer to confess to Julius why she was in his house.

Julius sliced sausages and bread for the noon dinner, putting it in the saddlebag. She was glad to see him strapping on his pistol. Then he saddled and bridled his horse and lifted Frieda up. He mounted heavily behind her.

When they moved, Liesl followed.

"Oh, all right," Julius said to his dog. *"Komm mit uns.* Ve not go too fast for you."

They rode away from the farm, downstream along the river trail. With his warm strength behind her and his big arms holding the reins on either side, she was content, at peace against the magnet. They rode at a slow, rocking pace.

He turned the horse to ford a shallow place in the river; Liesl swam across. Then Julius guided them down the trail on the east side of the Middle Fork. He took a faint side trail up the mountain. The trail got steeper. To make purchase on the granite scree the horse lurched, and Frieda slid back into Julius, grabbing his arms.

"Should we be gettin' off?"

"No, schtay. Da trail he not zo schteep up ahead."

A little farther up it was as he said. The trail still ascended, but at much less of a slope. Small patches of snow were evident in the shadows, and in the distance they got occasional glimpses of a high mountain. "Middle Fork Peak," Julius called it.

"Lotta snow up there."

"It gives winter in der high elevations."

They turned into a forested area. "You like it here?"

"It's purty, and purty darn cold too." She huddled in her sheepskin coat. He put his arm around her, and she felt safe, the way she'd want a baby to feel in her arms.

"It gives sunshine yust up ahead."

Frieda peered forward to see light shafting through the trees several yards away. She could hear the sound of water. They rode out of the forest into a meadow, at one end of which a tiny waterfall splashed into a creek from about four feet up. It made a small pool.

Julius leaned forward to see Frieda's beaming face. "Zo, you like dis?"

"It's so beautiful here! Why is that water steaming?"

"Iss varm." He dismounted and reached up to help her down. "People can take a bat here. You see?" He squatted beside the pool and put his hand in. She kneeled beside him and felt the warm water, a perfect temperature for a bath.

"I can't hardly believe it! It's a miracle. How'd you ever find it?"

Sitting back in the green grass that grew alongside the warm stream, he clasped his arms around his knees, "I come a long journey across da zea to find dis canyon. From my farm to here iss only a little …"

"Thank you, Julius, for bringin' me here."

"It giffs me pleasure to see you heppy."

The long thick grass of the meadow was mostly brown and bowed from the frost, but along the banks of the stream it grew as green as in summer. Yellow flowers dotted the green. General was munching the dry grass, and Liesl curled up for a nap in the sun, which played peekaboo in the clouds.

"In der zummer all dis grass iss green," Julius was saying,

gesturing over the entire meadow. "And it gives wildflowers of many colors. Maybe you und I should come up here in zummer?"

Frieda inhaled the aromas of pine, sage, and mountain mule ears. "That'd be nice, Julius, but it's nice now. And we're here, and I don't think I've ever seen anything so purty in my whole life!"

She put her hand in the musical waterfall, and joked, "Wanna take a bath?"

He copied her joking manner. "I stink goot, yah?"

"Naw, you don't stink. But I'll bet you've taken a bath here before."

He nodded. "Yah, yah. Like Adam."

"Adam?"

"In der Bible, Adam and Eva."

"Oh sure, the first people on Earth."

"I sit very still in dis pool wit the flowers and green grass all around and da birds zinging, da rock chucks, deer coming out, und I know dat Gott iss here."

This man has such a purty way of saying things! "Well, it sure would be a sight easier'n hauling in all them buckets of water to heat on the stove."

He laughed. "Dat be true. Dat iss true."

"If I lived in your place I'd come here all the time to take a bath." She added, "Come to think, I'd do it now, if you'd like. I mean the two of us." It took her breath away to get that out.

He was sitting beside her, clasping his knees. "You like dat, Frieda?"

Half afraid, "Sure."

Hurriedly they disrobed, each facing away from the other. Frieda heard a big splash. Shivering in the cold and peeking at him with her shirt in front of her, she saw him up to his neck in the far side of the little pool with waves splashing up on the bank. His gun belt lay back from the stream on top of his clothes. Frieda slipped into the wonderfully warm water opposite him, throwing her shirt on the grass. About five feet away from Julius she settled onto the soft bottom and leaned against the cutbank. The warm water just covered her breasts, which floated a little. She felt shy, awkward.

He seemed uneasy too. At last he said, as though fully clothed and sitting in school, "Vhere you be in *Oliver Tvist*? Vhat iss der boy making? I mean vhat iss he doing?"

"Oh, not too good. He jes' met up with a bunch a' thievin' kids an' that fella that's in charge of 'em."

"Fagin?"

"Yeah. He ain't gonna be no good for Oliver."

"Und Bill Sykes, he be vorse yet."

"Guess I'm not there yet. You said it was gonna turn out okay, though, right?"

He nodded. "Yah, yah. At der ending all be heppy."

"I'll keep with it then. I like a story with a happy endin'."

"Tell me, Frieda, how you learn to lofe books. Your parents giff you books? Dey teach you to lofe reading?"

She made a scoffing noise. "Hardly. My ma died when I was five. An' Pa, he had no use fer books. But I had a teacher in school, Mrs. Taylor …" She eased back in the water, her head pillowed on a protruding curl of turf. "She brung her own books to the schoolhouse. She was so patient with me—all of us—showin' us how to say the longer words an' all. Most a' the kids didn't give a hoot 'bout readin'. We was jes' dumb country kids—little clod-brains … But bein' on the farm with Pa an' all, well, I liked readin' about faraway places. Mrs. Taylor helped me picture what was in the books and helped me imagine the colors an' smells, an' all the diff'rent kinds a' people …"

Frieda realized that she'd been gazing at the sky, which was clouding up. She looked at Julius. "Gol—ly, I jes' been runnin' off my mouth like …"

He waved his hand to dismiss it. "You being, how you say, delightful. I like to hear you shpeak like dat."

"Aw, come on. You can't mean that."

"I mean it in my heart." He slapped his chest, which splashed water all the way to her face and made her laugh.

"Please, tell me more about Mrs. Taylor."

Frieda pulled a piece of green grass from its sheath and put it in her mouth, nibbling out the sweetness. "Well, she had a little baby, an' once in a while she had to bring him to school when the lady what was tendin' 'im fell sick or somethin'."

"Had she no hoosband?"

She thought back. "You know, don' recall mention a' that … Maybe she didn't have no husband. Maybe that's why she was so happy an' full a' life." Her smile faded.

Julius was looking at her curiously. "Dat be a funny ting to say. You make yoke." He chuckled.

But she was perfectly serious, and silent—remembering what she must tell him. But she couldn't tell him now. She was naked. She might need to run for her life.

"Vhy you say dat, Frieda? Please." He sat upright with his hairy chest streaming water, staring into her eyes.

She shook her head. "I can't."

He settled back into the water. "Dat be okay. You yust finish your story. I vant to hear it." He looked at her with those honest blue eyes.

She pushed the terrible sadness to the back of her mind. "Well, when Mrs. Taylor brought her baby to school, sometimes he was fussy, an' she would let me hold him. An' sometimes—not always—sometimes that would quiet 'im down. Mrs. Taylor used to say I was so good with 'im it was like I was 'is big sister." She gentled out another blade of grass.

Softly, "Und Mrs. Taylor vass like being your mooder."

She nodded slightly, feeling the tickle of a tear coursing down her cheek. *Why can't I stop bawlin? It's been happening at odd times ever since I got to his place.* Wiping her face with her wet hand, "Before I finished sixth grade Pa moved us farther back in the hills, too far fer me to go to school. He said I had all the schoolin' a girl could want."

"A shame dat be ..."

"Pa only saw school as takin' me away from my chores. After we moved, he worked me to the bone, like he was makin' up for all the lost time I'd spent in school ... No more books ... No more readin' ... I hated my pa. An' got away from him by maryin' Jack. He turned out worser'n Pa."

"Dis Chack vass mean to you, also?"

She glanced at him, then looked at the steaming water as it ebbed past them in the pool. The jittery feeling was coming back. "I don't wanna talk about him. Not now."

After a while, "Frieda, you make me tink of a blue flower—I forgetting der name—a pretty blue flower dat grow near us in Chermany."

"Why's that?"

"It giffs a song about dis flower. People go looking in der voods for it, da *blaue blume*. Dat be how ve say flower—blooma, like you say blooming. Dis blue flower she grows from stone or clay dat be hart as stone, and she giffs good luck to people who find her. People say she be a miracle of *Gott*." He laughed as though sadly remembering. "Ve tink if dis flower can bloom in such a hart place, maybe ve can be heppier in our own lifes."

"I remind you of this flower?"

"Yah, yah. You remind me of dat flower. My mooder, she tell me dat *Gott* lofed da *blaue blume*."

"I never knowed nobody what talked as nice as you, not since Mrs. Taylor.... And your ma, she sounds like she was a real nice lady."

"Yah, yah, she still iss a nice lady, back in Iova. Still liffing."

"An' your pa, wa—is he nice too?"

"I haff a goot strong family. Peter, my younger brooder, und I, ve alvays be goot friends ... I be der best man vhen seven years ago Peter be married."

"Julius … how come you're not married?"

He took a deep breath, and let it out. "Der vass a lady …"

"The one in the picher in your house?"

He nodded.

"Tell me about her."

"Remember vhen I go back to Chermany to help my grandparents move here?"

"Uh-huh."

"Vhen I be dere in der church I meet Gretchen." He closed his eyes for a moment and exhaled a long breath. It rose with the steam into a cold sky, adding to the clouds. "She had seventeen years, younger dan I. Ve be … goot friends first time ve shpeak." He nearly whispered, "Maybe I lofe her already."

Continuing, "I vass only a farm boy. Gretchen vass a lady older dan her years. She vant to be a nurse. I be a … in Iova people say … big galoot. But she … vhen I schtammer, not knowing vhat to zay, she make a yoke about zometing und ve laugh. Yah yah, Gretchen vass a lady, a fine lady."

"She was a nurse?"

"Studying to be a nurse. She vant to help da sick people."

"I could see doin' that, 'specially with animals. Like I done with Stormy."

"Stormy?"

"My horse."

"You take care of Stormy?"

"Yup. She was just a starvin' little baby when I found her. She's my best friend."

"Der horse dat run avay vhen you come to …"

She nodded quickly to erase his thought. "But you was tellin' me 'bout Gretchen. I wanna hear all about her."

He looked almost unreal through the steam now that the sun had gone under the gathering clouds. "She … she … Frieda, dis be a … tragic story." His eyes appeared to be shut. "You like heppy endings."

"I like any story about you."

After a long minute, "I … vanted to marry her right avay und bring her back to America mit me. But Gretchen be tinking she schtay and finish her nurse school. She say dat giff me time to find a farm, mine alone. Not the farm of my family."

"An' that's how you come to be in the canyon?"

"First I be a cowboy in Montana. No goot horse rider. Dat cowboy life iss not for a big galoot. Den I work on construction in south Idaho, building a big dam and canals. When dat be finish I vant to write Gretchen a letter dat she come … but … "

He frowned and pointed at the sky and the snowflakes now drifting down. "Frieda, it giffs bad vetter. Ve go to house now, yah?"

"But we're nice and warm in here, and I wanna hear about Gretchen."

He looked at the horse, now grazing in the meadow where the silent snowflakes seemed to be falling more thickly than over the water. "Ach zo … In a railroad town in south Idaho I meet a Cherman baker. He vant a helper. Dat be Gustof. He teach me baking und ve be friends, goot friends."

"So that's why you're a baker! Oh, I love bakin'! I mean I sure would if I had me a stove like yours."

He smiled. "Ve bake a pie tonight, yah? Apple pie? Or apple cake? I make goot apple cake."

"Gol—ly, let's do it! Cake and pie both! I'll make the pie and you make the cake. But go on, finish yer story."

He didn't speak for a minute. "Gus, he keep telling me," wiggling a dripping finger at Frieda, "'you go fetch Gretchen.' He say, go make farming mit her in Iova."

"Why not bring her to the town where you worked?"

He shook his head. "Not possible for two people to liff on baker's helper money." He blew out air, making ripples on the water. "I vanted my Gretchen to haff a goot life … I hat only a small room, und in dat town it giffs hatred for Chermans."

"It must be real hard to wait when you love somebody. You must love her, a lot."

He nodded, and for a while it seemed he was finished. She waited as the snowflakes continued to fall.

"August two, I go to da telegraphie office and tell der man to zend a vire to my family dat I leaf for New York on da next train and sail to Chermany. I tell dem I bring Gretchen to da farm in Iova." He paused, his voice gravelly. "Dat man, he stop making da telegraph. He say, 'No, it be no use.' He tell me der kaiser had dat day France invaded. War had been started. No more can peoples buy passage to Chermany."

"Gol-ly, whad'ja do?"

The words came out slowly, like each one pained him more. "Vhat can a man do? It be too late … Too far avay … Too late …" He was looking down and she saw that the top of his hair was white with snow.

His quiet voice resumed through the veil of steam and snow that separated them. "Four, fife veeks later. A letter from my parents. Gretchen be dead."

"Oh, no! That's awful. Was there fighting in her town?"

"Nurses been called to duty, also student nurses … Gretchen vass on der front … in France …" His voice broke as he struggled to continue. "She help da vounded men … Gretchen be …" He leaned forward and splashed water on his face, and then sat slumped, staring into the pool.

Frieda hadn't known it was possible for a man to love a woman that much. Yet his love for Gretchen seemed to be breaking Julius. She scooted around the pool and put an arm around his back—the girth and solidity of him—and somehow she knew this man would never break.

He'll go right on livin' and tendin' his farm, an' carin' fer his animals … Oh, dear God in heaven! If he ain't dead the day after tomorrow. I gotta warn him!

But she could hardly do it when he felt so bad.

12

Jack came to slowly and pushed himself up to lean on an elbow. Lumps of potato and onion and shards of pottery lay strewn around him. *Martha hit me with the damned fryin' pan!* Instantly enraged, he tried to spring to his feet, but could only grab the edge of the table. His legs weren't under him, and he slipped in the coffee and grease.

He landed hard, his head throbbing. He lay there a couple of minutes, knowing she had clobbered him hard. *The bitch. Where is she?!* By now his empty stomach was waking up, teased by the smell the food.

Groaning, he rolled over and pulled his knees under him. On all fours he gazed down at a pile of potatoes giving off the tantalizing aroma of the bacon grease they'd been fried in. He grabbed a handful and stuffed it in his mouth. Still warm, it tasted fine except for the grit from the none-too-clean floor. Another good-sized clump lay just ahead so he went to it on his hands and knees and ate that too. He crawled around through the coffee and pieces of the broken plate to glean more of his breakfast, for which he had worked so hard. Finally he managed to pull himself up on his feet at the table.

Touching the side of his head, he grimaced in pain. "Son of a bitch! Wait 'til I git my hands on … Martha … MARTHA!"

Yelling brought agony. "Damn you bitch …"

He looked around the two-room house, but she was gone.

He went out to the barn, but she wasn't there either. He saddled the roan and checked the packsaddle on Old Chief, the effort making his head feel as if it was about to explode. Stormy wasn't giving him the evil eye now, and he hurt too much to strain himself meting out punishment.

As he led the two horses and the mule outside and was about to mount, the crash of a rifle shot stunned him and dirt kicked up near his boots. Hair prickled on the back of his neck, and he was trying to hang onto the frightened, rearing animals when he heard Martha.

Her voice came low and mean from a clump of trees a ways back from the barn. "Now you GIT! Y'hear? I don't ever wanna see your filthy ass at my place again. Got that?" She fired and the dirt jumped again. "Next time I'll shoot straight."

Jack ached to pull the rifle from the saddle-boot and light out after her. That female wouldn't stand a chance against him. But though it about killed him to let her get away with this, he forced himself to remember that it wouldn't do to kill two people on practically the same day. Seething with anger, his head beating a tattoo of hate, he mounted his agitated horse and reined the roan down the fairly steep trail into the wind.

The roan's mane was blowing back at him and he had to tighten the bead on his hat strings to keep it from sailing off. To the northwest the mountains had disappeared behind some ugly clouds. *Shit! Jes' my rotten luck. Ten miles to the dugout and a storm's commencin'.* But his head wouldn't take a gallop or trot.

"Well," he told the roan, "you make tracks an' I'll jes' think on how good it'll feel to send one a' them big soft-nosed bullets through that Kraut. Hope Frieda ain't shot 'im yet. Step along, ol' buddy."

The snow came on like a sudden blizzard. Julius took charge, realizing they needed to get back to the house as fast as possible. Frieda agreed with the urgency. No time to eat the noon dinner he had packed. Struggling into their cold clothes, they ran across the snowy meadow to mount General.

The wind intensified as they rode down the mountain. In the river General slipped on the rocks just as he was coming up on the west bank, spilling them out of the saddle before he righted himself. Drenched to the skin, they mounted again, and by the time they got to the cabin, the snow was blowing sideways. Frieda quaked like the junipers on the hill. She couldn't even talk, her teeth were chattering so hard.

Julius unsaddled General in the barn and insisted Frieda get inside the house immediately. She didn't have an extra layer of flesh like he did. Later, shaking off freezing water, he stomped up the step and opened the door to set the saddlebags on the table, glad to see the lamps lit and the fire rekindled. Frieda's clothes hung over the back of a chair near the stove. Crouched on the floor, shivering and holding a blanket around her with one hand, Frieda was also drying Liesl with an old towel. This touched him.

"Ah, tank you, Frieda… . Liesl, she be a nice lady to you, yah, yah."

"Julius, your lips is blue," Frieda chattered. "Better get out a' them wet clothes or you'll catch your death."

She was a kind, sweet woman, but something she'd said today about her horse didn't make sense. He puzzled over that as he brought in a large supply of cut wood from the porch and piled it near the stove—enough to last the night. *Maybe tonight… she seems to want … But what should I say?* Taking off his soggy shoes and socks, he picked another blanket off his makeshift bed on the floor—Frieda had used one of them—and turned his back, undressing behind it. He felt shy as a schoolboy.

"You vant to put on my extra clothes, till yours be dry?"

"Me? In your clothes? I'd be swimmin' in 'em." She laughed through her chatters.

He laughed with her as he pulled his wet longjohns off his leg, hopping around under the brown blanket he'd draped over his shoulders. "You already been swimming in your clothes." He loved having someone to laugh with, even if she didn't always make sense.

Naked beneath the blanket, he turned and looked at Frieda on the bed. She sat against the pillows, swaddled like an Indian papoose. Her long brown hair hung wet against the yellow blanket. He couldn't help but tell her, "You look pretty, Frieda."

She felt her soaked hair. "Oh, sure. Like a pony that fell in a lake." Her teeth chattered through her smile.

"You need something to warm you inside." *More than coffee.* First he draped his wet clothes over the other kitchen chair and moved it beside the one where Frieda's clothes were drying. They looked so domestic, those two chairs.

Opening his sea chest, he lifted a layer of clothing and removed his bottle of whisky, setting it on the table. He used American whisky like medicine, as some people in the old country used schnapps. *Gott im Himmel,* he also needed to warm his own innards. About to shut the chest lid, he stopped. This would be more than medicine. It would mark a special occasion. Frieda. was helping him get past the death of Gretchen, something he'd begun to doubt he'd ever be able to do. So he unwrapped his two special *becherlein*, small pottery goblets from the homeland, from the folds of his Sunday shirt, which he hadn't worn since coming to the canyon. Pouring a little whisky into each of them, he handed one to Frieda. "This make you warm," he said.

With a smile she took the *becherlein,* and he felt inspired to make a toast. "*Prozit,*" he said. "To our health."

Clearly she didn't understand the gesture, so he showed her how to touch the gray and black cups, then sip the drink.

Pulling his easy chair a little closer to the bed, he tried to explain. "My people in the Rheinland drink vine from cups like these ven ve haff a party. Every harvest of the grapes ve make vine mit our neighbors. My family und all da people around us are proud of der grapes, proud of our vine. All the peoples of Germany drink our vine. Men play the olden songs on their musical instruments. Ve sing and dance and laugh. Und ve drink to our health." He lifted his cup and leaned toward her, touching his *becherlein* to hers as she leaned forward, smiling and clutching the blanket around her neck with her free hand.

In a short time her teeth stopped chattering.

He asked in a pleasant tone, hoping this might lead to why she was here in his house. "Stormy, your horse, is all right in this bad weather? Your brother is taking good care of her?"

Frieda took another sip of the whisky and felt it burn down to her stomach. "Stormy'll be okay."

"You sure of dat."

She's been through storms a whole lot worse'n this."

"Dat be on your farm?"

"No. Well, I was thinking of the storm when I found her in the mountains … I named her Stormy because of it."

"I would like to hear about dat. You tell me. Here, eat your dinner too." He reached to the table and handed her a sandwich from the saddlebag—fortunately its contents hadn't been drenched. He then bit into his own sandwich.

"Well, I've had Stormy the better part a' six years an' don't think in all that time I knowed anybody to tell about her. It feels good to tell you." She smiled at him again. "We was huntin' in late March, me an' Jack. He did the huntin'. I tended to the horses. We was hopin' to find a half-curl ram with some fat on 'im, when we got caught in a spring blizzard. So we sheltered up in a grove a' quakin' aspen. The storm passed in a' hour or so, an' we was jes' gettin' ready to leave the trees when I heard this sad little whinny. An' then I saw her. She was nuthin' but a wobbly little baby with long, shaggy hair. Skin an' bones she was. Purt'near too weak to stand up, an' I think she was callin' out for us to save her. Leastwise, I b'lieve that… . Right beside her lay the scrawny mare that'd died a couple days before. You could see she'd been gnawin' bark an' twigs off the aspens, but that hadn't been enough to keep her alive. Her front teeth was wore clear down to the blood line tryin' to feed her an' her baby."

"*Traurig*. Sad." But was this Jack, her brother? Or Jack, her husband? Julius didn't interrupt the story. He added, "You horse is vite like snow, yah?"

"No. She's a bay, brown. An' she was havin' a hard time

getting' enough a' the good from tree bark herself. She'd even chewed off a lot of hair from her mother's tail."

"Poor little ting."

"Jack was getting' his rifle to put her out a' her sufferin', but I begged him to let me try an' save her. He said, 'She's prob'ly a goner, but she must be a tough little pisser to hold on this long.' So he let me keep her. I wrapped my jacket 'round her head to blindfold her an' protect her head from bangin' on the trees. We tied her front feet together, an' her hind feet, an' loaded her on our mule's packsaddle, tied to the lash hooks. Skinny little thing jes' gave up, didn't even struggle."

"Vhat you feed her?"

"At first, I gave her a mash a' rolled oats an' a little canned milk mixed with warm water. After she growed a bit, I gave her plenty a' good grass, an' before ya could say Jack Spratt she was arunnin' an' abuckin' an' havin' her a time!" In the glow of the memory, Frieda took another bite of the delicious sausage sandwich.

After a time, "You gave her life."

"No. Stormy fought for her own life. I jes' helped her some."

"Ach nay, Frieda, You have made her liff."

Well, I 'spose maybe I did. Frieda loved going over all the details. Between chews, "Ya know, I never really had to break her. She was a mite skittish when I first got on her, but settled down real quick. From the very first we jes' had us an understandin'… There mighta been Jack's roan an' our pack mule in the corral, but I was always Stormy's best friend. An' she sure is my best friend… . Why, one time I was ridin' her to beat the band though some trees, when a branch I didn't see knocked me clean off. I wasn't hurt none, 'count a' the thick cover a' leaves. Jes' shook up some."

Reliving the memory, she laughed. "With one hand I was brushin' myself off, an' with the other I was swipin' away at Stormy's big ol' tongue lickin' me."

Quietly, "Dat be true?"

"Sure is," Frieda said brightly. "Lickin' at my face like a big ol' dog."

"And two days ago your horse trew you und run avay? Dis be not da same horse. Or?"

Stricken, Frieda set the rest of her sandwich on the crate beside the bed.

"Vhat iss?" he said quietly. "You be sick?"

The wind screamed around the corner of the cabin, and Frieda was thinking, *Ain't never a right time to tell a man he's gonna get killed.* "Oh, Julius … I can't pretend anymore."

"Vhat you mean?"

All pretence drained out of her and she wept openly, unable to speak. After what seemed a very long time, she was able to blurt out between sobs, "I been lyin' to you … from the start … I ain't got no brother … an' my husband Jack … he ain't dead."

Julius remained motionless in his chair while, through her tears, Frieda told him the entire story from beginning to end.

Sobbing and sniffing, she finished, "… an' he's comin' to kill you Friday morning. That's the day after tomorrow. I'm s'posed to make sure he gets a clean shot. Guess maybe we'd oughta go to Salmon City … and tell the sheriff."

For a long time he sat as though frozen.

Watching him, knowing she hadn't the energy nor desire to run from him, she saw only his dark silhouette against the gray light from the window. Finally his voice came low.

"It giffs a bad schtorm. Salmon City iss a two-day ride from here, passing by your dugout." He fell silent. Only the ferocious howl of the wind could be heard, and her sniffs.

He rose from the chair, holding the brown blanket around him, and picked up the holstered pistol he'd set on the table.

"Go on an' kill me," Frieda cried, "I don't care."

He stood blocking the light from the window, his face and the gun in darkness.

She choked back her sobs, needing to talk fast. "I never had such a good time in my whole life as these last two days, so I don't mind dying now. I shoulda confessed sooner … I'm glad you took me to the warm spring. I even had fun fallin' in the river, but now it's over. So go on an' shoot me. It's okay. I don't blame you."

"You understand me not." He patted the gun. "I haff protected you mit dis. I protected you yesterday. I protect you today. I be ready for him." Then after a long pause, he added, "I not kill you, Frieda."

She had trouble transferring that from her ears to her mind, which kept telling her: *Any man would kill me for this.* So she remained steeled.

With his bulk enlarged by the blanket and his back to the gray sky and snow in the window, he spoke as though making sure each word was correct. "Frieda, tell me … Haff you vanted to finish dis plan of Jack's? To kill me? To take my farm?"

Steeled, "Ain't no call for you to b'lieve a thing I say."

"Den I be a *dumkopf.* Tell me. Hass it been your vill, your vanting, dat you help him kill me und take my farm?"

She shook her head. "No, I never woulda except to save Stormy. I was buyin' time 'til I figgered a way to … I been meanin' to tell ya all along. Jes' couldn't find the right way to do it."

"I know you been keeping zometing from me."

"I ain't no killer. For this place ner nuthin' else."

"Frieda, I belief dat be true. I belief you be a good person in der heart."

"No I ain't. Ain't at all!" At first she hadn't thought of him as human. She fell to the bed weeping.

Suddenly he was there, pulling her up and embracing her as she wept on his shoulder. He kissed her lightly on the forehead and cheeks. "Frieda, no perzon iss perfect. Gott in heaven knows dat."

This brought more tears. He let her cry, and they held each other as the blankets fell away. Frieda looked up at him. Straightening her back she touched her lips up to his. They began kissing, hesitantly at first, like two people who had not known how, then with ever-increasing passion.

13

Throughout the rest of the day and most of the night they made love, and in between their bouts of ardor they explored each other in body and mind. At first Frieda was almost embarrassed by the woman she was experiencing herself to be. She wasn't sure if it was all right to actually join in the pleasure of having sex with a man, but Julius acted like it was natural, and everything he said and did seemed more than all right to her.

As they lay face to face, Frieda couldn't help but gently squeeze Julius' muscular upper arm, which was encased in surprisingly smooth skin. He slid his hand over her hip and down the deep depression of her waist. She reached around and felt the muscle of his hip, kindling a renewal of passion.

When she came back to the earth for the second time, she murmured, "I wonder if other women feel this good when they're in bed with a man."

In blissful peace, "You be *wunderbar,* Frieda."

"I sure feel sorry for the ones that don't." She snuggled close and breathed in the subtle, interesting scent of his skin, and the air from his nose. She wanted to get inside him.

"Frieda, you be putting my broken parts back together. You make me zo heppy."

Lying there in complete darkness, she forced herself to ask, "Did you do this with Gretchen?"

"No. Ve vait to be married."

"I'm glad we didn't wait. And Julius, I'm sorry you didn't hold Gretchen in your arms like this."

"You not speak off Gretchen now. It giffs in my arms only

Frieda. You understand? Only Frieda. Gretchen iss gone. You be here making me a king in my little house. I never vant anyting different from dis moment. I vant you mit me alvays."

"Me too. I want you for the rest of my life." That moved her thinking to the problem they faced. "Maybe we'd better figger a way to hide from Jack, or … or …" She couldn't say the words, *kill him*, couldn't even imagine it. Such an awful thought didn't belong here now.

Petting her hair, Julius stared across the darkened room. This first storm of winter had come at a bad time, he was thinking. Not a time to ride anywhere, and they had only tomorrow to make an escape, if that was the best thing to do. He wasn't sure—

Frieda asked, "How old are you?"

"Three und thirty."

"Huh?"

"I mean. Thirty-three. I forgot Americans no more zay it dat vay."

"What way?"

He turned over, swung his legs down, struck a match and lit the lamp. With the room coming back into soft focus, he rolled back to her and pulled her into his arms quietly singing:

"Zing a zong of sixpence, a pocket full of rye,

Four und tventy blackbirds baked in a pie … Und now, I hear you zing dat, all da rest of it, please."

"I never heard that before. Four and twenty, uh, twenty-four blackbirds?"

"Yah, yah." He kissed her on the end of her nose. "Dere came an old lady in der bakery of Gustof. She teach me dat. She say all English-speaking children sing dat zong." One big blue eye crinkled up in a friendly smile three inches from Frieda's face.

"Well this girl never sang it. I told ya I was ignernt about a lotta things."

"Ach zo I teach you English now." He chuckled softly, planting little kisses all around her face.

"So you're three and thirty."

"True. And how many years haff you?" He kept smiling, kissing her chin and neck.

"None and thirty."

He chuckled in his throat, "Dat be vhat I tink." He kept kissing her down to her breasts, which he explored with his hands and tongue, and sucked gently on her nipples, causing a dark funnel of sensation to grip her insides.

And for the first time in her life, she felt thrilled a man was responding to her.

"I'd like to have a baby," Frieda said when they reluctantly separated. "Your baby."

"You haff no children, but you be married how many years?"

"Fifteen." She told him how she'd always longed to have a baby. "Maybe it's my fault I never had one. Maybe I'm not right as a woman."

"No, Frieda, you be a perfect voman, a perfect mother. *Gott* knows dat. I vant you to be mother to my zon."

"I want that too. But maybe we'd have a girl. Wouldn'cha like that too?"

Stroking the curve of her hip and waist. "Yah, yah. Dat be goot too. But I vant to teach a son to be a farmer, like my father taught me. I vould love him."

"Me too. I would love him sooo much! I feel so happy I could almost fly, thinkin' about a child that's half from me and half from you … like I been feelin' here in your arms, like we're one whole person with our legs and arms all tangled 'round each other."

"Like heafen …"

"Maybe we'll have a bunch of kids." The sudden joy of it lifted her to an elbow on the pillow. "Then we could go to Iowa and visit your parents. Wouldn't they like to see their grandchildren?"

"Dey vould love dat, und dey vould love you, as I do."

"Oh, Julius. I love you too. Soooo much. "

She slid her hand down his thigh, wanting to feel all of him, the parts with slick, soft hair and the parts without any. Then she piled on top of him, kissing and hugging him.

"Frieda," he groaned …

Later, rehearsing the fact that they had only one more day and one more night before Jack came, they hoped together that fate would intervene and cause Jack to give up on his plan. Maybe his horse would slip and fall on him, breaking his neck. Maybe this snowstorm would blow into something much worse, blocking Jack's way and giving them more time to think. Maybe when he found out Frieda didn't want him any more, Jack would simply forget about her and leave the canyon, maybe return to Challis, where they'd once lived. In the ecstasy of rising love, they felt they could overcome anything if only they could be together. Their love was that powerful.

Later they talked of riding away on General after breakfast and crossing the unknown wilderness heading west, to some town where Jack was less likely to find them; but both of them admitted that even in good weather, a hundred or more uncharted miles in these mountains could kill them as they wandered, seeking passage past dangerous precipices and obstacles. Petting her as he listened to the wind, Julius said, "I tink not, Frieda.

"Maybe we could jes' hide in one of them old dugouts down on Big Creek. Jack'd come after us, but …" The thought of living in constant fear pinched off her words.

Ideas ran out like sand between dry fingers. After a quiet spell Julius said in a low, careful voice. "Dis be my house, my home. My animals dey need me. I can shoot mit my rifle. I vill defend my farm und you, Frieda, or I die trying."

She had told him what an expert hunter Jack was, and she knew she had to trust this wonderful man in her arms. "Yes," she breathed, "Yes." And everything evaporated except the urgency of the here and the now.

At last, exhausted and tender in the wee hours of Thursday morning, Julius and Frieda finally fell to sleep in each other's arms.

They didn't hear the wind stop and didn't know that far less snow had actually fallen than it had seemed the evening before.

⁂

Jack had gone to bed early Wednesday night in the dugout, but had trouble getting to sleep, which was very unusual for him. He missed having Frieda around to keep the fire, fetch water, and cook. His head hurt if he lay on the place where Martha had struck him, but that wasn't what kept him awake. His suspicions had returned. Could it be that she'd been enjoying the German all this time, enticing him, wanting to be touched and fondled by him? Doing things she wouldn't do with him?

The thought was like a packrat running over his bed in the dark. He knew he couldn't catch and kill it. How would Frieda act if she did enjoy a man? Jack had never spent much time wondering how other people felt about anything, so the thought of her with another man … *Goddamn sonofabitchin' German!*

Finally he turned his mind toward the solution, the great pleasure he would take in killing the bastard. He'd be in charge again, not hiding out and following that stupid sheriff up and down the canyon. Not sleeping with that wart-faced bitch and getting clobbered. *By damn, ol' Jack's about to be hisself agin. I'll go on down to that place and find a spot where I can git a good look inside. An' if Frieda's doin' … well, I'll shape 'er up with a lesson she won't be likely to forgit real soon.*

Then he slept.

⁂

Unconsciously, Frieda put her hand across the bed and felt his absence. She woke up facing the window, the dark east wall of the canyon. Only a little of the gray morning light came in the cabin. She heard water splashing in the shaving bowl on the porch and looked over to see the door open just a crack.

She called, "Hey. You up already?"

Julius opened the door a little and leaned into her view, foamy soap on one side of his face. "Zorry, m'lady. I didn't mean to vake you. I be more quiet."

"Your not bein' here's what woke me up. Come on back to bed." He hadn't lit the lamp this morning as he usually did. It seemed like night inside.

"My animals need to eat. Dey not haffing a good time all night. Next time you see me, you not be scratched mit bad vhiskers." He pulled back and shut the door.

She got up, wrapping a blanket around herself, and padded across the cold floor. She opened the door and looked out. He was standing at his little shaving table leaning over it almost to the cabin wall. She smiled at the sight.

"I'll make us breakfast," she told him. "It'll be hot when you come in."

"Ach yah, for zome reason I haff appetite dis morning." He flashed her a grin and continued pulling the razor down his foamy cheek.

"Me too … for some reason." She chuckled. "Ya look kinda funny leanin' into that teeny little mirror. How much a' your face can ya see?"

"Lips und chin."

"I don't think you need a mirror."

"Maybe, I know my face pretty goot. Dis be yust habit." He opened his mouth a little, stretching his upper lip over his teeth while he worked the razor in short strokes under his nose.

She watched him finish shaving around his mouth and chin. Then, still in a dreamy haze from the night before, she said with a little moan, "A kiss'd sure feel good …"

He stepped to the threshold and they kissed long and tenderly, Frieda holding her blanket around them both, his torso cold and wet against her breast. The feel of his gun belt gave her comfort. His rifle was also leaning against the wall by the shaving table. He was being careful. How precious this man was! She soaked up the pure sensation and scent of Julius, loving him so much that it pained her to end the kiss, to become Frieda alone again in the blanket.

He looked deep in her eyes, and she knew he didn't want to separate either. But with one last teasing smack on her lips, he went back to the mirror and started pulling the razor down his other cheek.

She turned inside, smiling back over her shoulder. "Wha'cha feel like eatin' this mor— "

Something moved behind the pigsty. Jack steadying his rifle.

"JULIUS!" she screamed.

Having heard the sound of the rifle's lever action behind him, Julius had already dropped the razor and pulled his pistol. The crash of the rifle mingled with the report of the handgun and the echo of Frieda's scream, all roaring and echoing up the canyon. Inside that cacophony of sound JULIUS, Julius, Julius became ever fainter.

He toppled toward her across the doorway. She caught him, the blanket falling to her feet. For a moment they stood together, but then his rigid body began to relax. He was a big man, his weight more than she could hold, and she bent with him as he slumped to the floor. Some part of her comprehended the great damage that the soft-nosed bullet, which had blown a hole in his side, would have done in his chest. He looked at her, a strange puzzled expression in his eyes.

Blood pooled on the floor. She knelt over him, unaware of the frigid morning air on her bare skin.

Jack stepped up on the porch, nudging Julius with the toe of his boot. "Done my part in the war, ya stinkin' Kraut," he muttered. "This here piece a' shit's deader'n a beaver hat and ol' Jack's back in charge, yesiree-*bob*."

Frieda's expression was blank as she knelt over the German.

Her voice came out soft and quivery. "You wasn't gonna be here till tomorrow."

With seething anger, he bent to her ear, "Well, plans changed. If I'da come tomorra I doubt I'da found anything diff'ernt."

He grabbed her arm, pulled her up, and slapped her hard across the face.

She could hardly feel it.

"I seen how you was with the bastard. Heared ya talkin' all lovey too. You was likin' it with 'im, wasn't ya?" He yanked her close and backhanded her across the face. "WASN'T YA, YA FILTHY WHORE?!" He hit her again and again, now with his fist, but Frieda didn't even try to protect herself. When he finally released her, she fell back on the table.

Jack saw that her face was a mess. *Well that jes' might come in handy.*

Noticing the pistol on the floor, he picked it up, the barrel warm, and stuck it in the waist of his Levi's. "Oh and Frieda, this is for warnin' 'im." Again he yanked her to him with his left hand, and used his right fist on her face a couple of times, good and hard.

Then he stepped out on the porch and picked up his rifle, and the German's. He grabbed one of dead man's wrists. "Help me drag him out a' the house." Jack cradled the two rifles in his other arm.

Like a sleepwalker, Frieda took Julius' other hand, and they dragged his heavy body off the threshold, across the narrow porch, and down the step.

"Now, gitcher britches on and clean up the blood. I told ya I wanted to kill'im outside where he wouldn't bleed all over the house, but a' course ya can't do nuthin' right, standin' in the way like that. Was all I could do to keep from shootin' you too. Come to think, maybe I shoulda."

Troubled, Jack whirled away and strode down to the river trail to where the animals waited, far enough away that they hadn't alerted the horse in the barn. *Sure did git it right 'bout Frieda spillin' the beans to the German.* For the first time since he'd been a boy he felt like bawling, betrayed and hurt. His Frieda! Many years ago, after his mother had scalded him with gravy, he'd thought he'd succeeded in banishing hurt feelings for once and all, but now he was overcome by that same old hurt. *Well by God, Frieda'll never know.*

He led the mule and two horses up to the barn. *Stupid Kraut, lookin' 'round out here with that 22 when he first come out. What a clodhopper. Real stupid turnin' his back like that too. Musta felt safe. Hah! Believed I'd wait till tomorrow like she told 'im."*

As Jack took a rope from the barn and made a loop, he told the roan, "One thing's fer sure, ol' Jack was right on the money about a man goin' silly over a woman. Man's no different from any other animal when it comes to that. They ain't got nothing left over fer survival, 'specially when they been goin' at it fer so long. Jes' never figgered she'd—" He stopped himself. "But now everthing's gonna git right back to the way it was."

He led the roan up to the cabin and slipped the loop over the German's head. Then he mounted his horse, took a dally on the saddlehorn, and dragged the body through the covering of snow to the edge of the small pasture between the cabin and barn. He left it beside a clump of sagebrush just outside the pasture fence. Seeing how the lariat had drawn tight and cut into the stretched neck, a repulsive sight, and not wanting to touch the skin or struggle with releasing the rope, Jack took out his hunting knife and cut the rope, leaving a couple of feet of it attached to the body.

Putting the roan in the barn with Old Chief, Stormy and the other horse, he gave his animals some oats and hay. Then he took a shovel from the barn and one from the packsaddle, and went back to the body.

"FRIEDA!"

She opened the door, clothed but obviously in one of her

stupid spells. She just stood there. Striding to the porch, he pushed a shovel in her hands, nearly knocking her down. "Now git down there and help me dig." With a second look at her, "Goddamn it woman, you're a sight. But it could work in our favor, if I hafta tell somebody how the Kraut beat on ya."

She didn't move.

"Fer the love of Mike, quit'cher starin' off like that an' help me bury the bastard!" He jabbed her in the rear end with his shovel.

14

Julius lay before her half shaved, his neck stretched long, twisted with the rope, which was embedded in the purple flesh. Yet she hardly saw him.

Jack clanged his shovel on hers. "Dig, woman!"

Except for a hard crust on top, the ground was not yet frozen. They worked without speaking. Frieda heard Liesl's whines as the dog sniffed around and her yelps when Jack kicked her, but none of it registered in her mind. All she knew was that she needed this strenuous exertion in the same way she needed air. She could have kept digging all day.

Jack hated digging and soon pronounced the shallow grave "good enough for a lousy Kraut."

The grave would provide only a thin covering of earth, but Jack just wanted the body out of sight. If wolves or bears dug down and ate the corpse, so much the better. Bones were easier to hide. So he didn't put rocks on top.

With the German underground, Jack relaxed and strolled around, taking inventory of his new place.

Frieda cooked Jack's breakfast but forgot to make any for herself, nor did she care. She couldn't make her mind work right, but followed direct orders such as, "Fill my coffee, gimme s'more eggs." She heard little of the running vitriol.

"You bitch! You're no better'n a whore. Traitor too, tellin' him I was comin'. A goddamned traitor! There you was, actin' like a bitch in heat, givin' away our plan, and me out there freezin' my butt off tryin' to keep track of that two-bit sheriff. Oughta give ya the whuppin' you deserve. Why don'cha say nuthin'? How was it with the dumb Kraut? Huh?"

All day long she said nothing. And if he hit her a few more times, she wouldn't remember.

When he reached for her in bed, she didn't resist. She couldn't smell or feel. She was lifeless. He was like a ram or a bull elk, full of envy and desire but no love.

Many days passed as in a bad dream. Frieda worked with Jack, and she rode with him to the dugout several times, moving their possessions. For now they left the heavy sluice where it was, but brought the rest of the tools, the bedding, their clothes trunk, and the sheepskin. Lacking any interest in her appearance, Frieda left the rendered sheep tallow in the dugout.

As they returned to the cabin for the last time, riding the animals past the disturbed earth, the truth slammed into Frieda. It caught her breath. *He's right there, in the dirt. Julius … Julius!* Her breath finally returned, but an ache engulfed every inch of her. She dismounted at the house and removed the roll of blankets from her saddle and carried it inside, all the while hurting. She ached as she helped Jack untie the canvas manta of mining tools from Old Chief and helped him lay it on the stoop. Gradually the hurt concentrated into a pinch on her right side, almost like she'd been running too long.

Jack left the tools on the stoop where he could sort through them later and do some repair. Then he led the animals back to the barn to finish unloading and hang up the tack.

The pinch stayed with her as Frieda went in the house to find places for the things from the dugout. She was carrying the old cast-iron skillet to the stove when she *saw* the bed—the exposed, wrinkled sheets, the chaos of blankets.

Dropping the pan on the floor, she lunged at the bed in a frenzy to cover up the evidence of her sleeping with Jack. She straightened the bedclothes and pulled up the feather quilt, and as she leaned over the quilt, rapidly smoothing it, flinging her arms across it to eliminate every single wrinkle, she caught *his* scent.

Anguish welled up in her. She couldn't stand to think of Jack in Julius' bed. Or eating his food, or sitting on his chair, or using his things. He'd even taken to wearing Julius' shirts. He was like a dog peeing on territory. She buried her nose in the soft quilt, searching for more of *him*—fading, fading Julius. All the unexpected weeping she'd held back during the wonderful days with him now erupted in full force, lasting a long time. Fortunately Jack remained outside because nothing could have stopped her from crying. At first it felt like she'd been broken, like an exhausted horse surrendering to a whip-wielding master. But as the full truth with its successive explosions of sorrow, anger, remorse, and guilt continued to wrack her and she lay on the bed bawling into her hands, a kaleidoscope of colors and shapes blossomed and fractured behind her eyes, and some of the pieces started to come down in a different way.

Julius' death had shut her up in a dark room of her mind with only enough light to move about without really seeing anything. But now light was entering and things began to come clear. *I'm not dead. I can feel. I can remember. Julius said I was like a blue flower growin' in a hard place. He thought I was a good person at heart.*

The convulsions began to subside, and she went to the bucket to wash her face. She wanted to be like that.

Later Jack came in, stomping around the cabin with manure on his boots. He rubbed his dirty hands on the backside of his trousers and sat on the rose-colored upholstery of Julius' chair. "I'm hungry. What's cookin'?" He looked at her with his bight gray eyes while the red scar on his cheek reported the cold outside.

"Ain't had time to cook." Even she heard the edge on that, but couldn't rein it in.

"Well, step lively! I ain't fancyin' the way you been actin'. Slow as a snail on crutches." He grabbed the photograph of the family in Iowa, glanced at it and peevishly tossed it back on the small table where it skidded against the photograph of Gretchen. Both pictures in their metal frames clattered to the floor in a tumult of shattering glass.

Something exploded in Frieda. "Well, I don't like the way YOU'VE been actin'. You're dirtyin' that chair, and now you broke them pichers. Julius loved those people!" She had no trouble holding back her tears; the heat of her anger dried them up before they could show.

He had been slowly rising from the chair, and now, hunched forward with his scraggly chin thrust out, he glared at her. "You … dare … say … that TO ME!" He stomped on the photographs, again and again. "There, that's what I think a' them Krauts." One side of his mouth turned down in a lopsided smirk.

Clear and calm, "You killed a good man, Jack."

"YOU BITCH! YOU GODDAMN BITCH! He snatched Julius' rifle down off its pegs and came at her swinging the butt end. "I've had it with you!" Slashing his weapon at her, "you're nuthin' but that Hun's whore."

Nimble, quick, and very alert, Frieda dodged the rifle as she jumped around the room. Twisting away from a swipe, "First ya tell me to play up to 'im," ducking another, "then ya call me a whore."

Jack kept coming at her. As Frieda jumped out of the way, the rifle butt struck the lamp on the table. A burst of kerosene and glass slivers sprayed through the room. Frieda turned from it, and Jack stepped back to the log wall.

"I was only doin' what you wanted," Frieda yelled, backed against the countertop.

"YOU WAS LIKIN' IT!" he bellowed, lunging at her again with the rifle.

Behind her she felt the butcher knife. She threw it.

He ducked. The tip of the knife stuck in the wall.

He glanced at the quivering knife in the smooth caramel-colored log.

She seized a sturdy piece of stove-wood.

Jack, rushing the pile of wood, brought the rifle butt down an instant too late. Instead of mashing her hand, the blow sent the woodpile cascading across the floor.

Never had Frieda's mind felt so clear, somehow attuned to his moves almost before he made them. With her wood she deflected his blows, and for a while they fought with their weapons, crossing them like swords. The rifle barrel was slim in Jack's grasp and much longer in its reach, but Frieda's wood was lighter and more maneuverable.

The rifle was on a back-swing when she landed a good wallop on the inside of Jack's left shoulder, but in doing so stepped on a piece of firewood. It rolled under her boot. She struggled for footing,

Jack's follow-through landed on her back and pushed her onto more of the loose wood.

She stumbled wildly, trying to remain upright, but fell face forward, dropping the wood and cushioning her face with an arm. She curled into a fetal position with arms wrapped around her head.

The rifle butt crashed into her side, under her arm. Pain stopped her breath. She hadn't yet drawn air when the next blow landed on her forearm. The arm took the blunt force of it, but her head rang and she saw light behind her eyes.

I'll be dead soon, she realized with perfect clarity. Slightly moving an arm so she could see Jack with the raised rifle, she rolled out of the way just before the next blow landed. Her arm didn't respond when she tried to grab another piece of wood. Or was it her hand? She could barely breathe for the pain in her side.

"You've broke somethin' Jack," she managed to say. "Ruined me fer work."

He stood above her with the butt poised to come down, but gradually lowered the gun. Then he started kicking her in the back and rear end, over and over again. She was in a ball facing the floor, but some of the kicks sent her sprawling and she had to keep scrambling back into a ball, trying to turn her less wounded places to him.

"Ya had enough?" he growled.

"Yeah. Dunno what come over me."

For some time they remained as they were, Jack standing there, neither one moving.

Despite the many pains throughout her body, Frieda remained clear of mind and aware of Julius in his shallow grave. She knew she had deceived a good man by not warning him soon enough. Given time he might have saved himself. Now she must deceive a man who knew nothing of goodness, one who based every move on selfishness, a man she knew she could never change.

15

The next morning when she knew Jack would be in the barn a while, Frieda took Julius' whisky to the cellar and hid it deep in the pile of potatoes. Now she felt safer. Lacking enough gold dust, Jack hadn't bought liquor when he'd gone to the Cove, and fortunately he hadn't noticed the clothing-wrapped bottle in the sea chest. She feared that next time he got riled, he'd be drunk and even more violent.

Instead, he was nice to her. He came in from the barn with a barrel stave sawed in two and used it to splint her broken arm, wrapping the oak slats in place with strips of his old shirt. That made it possible for her to do some work. She even forked hay to the horses—clumsily. It hurt to breathe, and at night when she turned over in her sleep, the stabbing pain jerked her awake. Though she rolled back slowly by inches to her good side, the weight of her injury pulled down like the point of a knife into raw flesh, keeping her awake. Yet her mind remained clear. She considered what she could do, and what she couldn't do.

I could sneak out of bed and shoot 'im in the head. That's what I keep comin' back to. But don't see how I could do it in cold blood with him bein' so nice, an' then live here with two dead men. It's almost more'n I can stand to have Julius under the dirt. Sure wouldn't want Jack to be buried anywhere near 'im. And with these ribs and my broken arm, I couldn't dig a grave, and sure couldn't leave him rottin' on the bed. I jes' wanna be the woman Julius thought I am. So that means leavin' Jack, cause I can hardly bear actin' nice to him. He'll kill me if he catches me leavin', but that'd be better'n livin' with him.

She decided to wait for a riding moon and see if her side was healed enough. Again, many days passed.

Meanwhile she kept busy cleaning Julius' house and caring for his animals, though her steps were slowed by the swollen, bruised muscles of her back, hips and thighs. She was able to milk the cow by using her right hand with a little help from her left, and as she milked she leaned her head against the friendly flank, appreciating the warmth of the large body and listening as the flashing white streams sang their way into the bucket. All the animals helped her endure the absence of Julius. Stormy, Old Chief, the roan, and General nickered greetings when she carefully forked them hay. Mrs. Pigfrau and her offspring met her with unfailing pleasure and eagerness. Liesl divided her time between sleeping on Julius' grave and following Frieda around. All the tasks that she had so recently shared with Julius kept his memory vivid and alive while she waited and worked things around in her mind.

So many things had to be right—the weather, the moon, her ribs, and Jack. He couldn't be suspicious or angry. Hanging over everything was the possibility that blizzards and deep snow could trap her in the canyon. One day dark clouds blew in on a cold wind but cleared up again by the next morning. It served as a warning.

Day after day as she watched the waxing moon, Jack was nice to her. She especially appreciated that he left her alone at night. He seemed to understand that even the weight of a hand hurt too much. Besides the injuries and aches, she experienced new and unfamiliar sensations—a sort of lightheadedness and, at odd times, a feeling she might vomit. But she'd been feeling so many new sensations of late; this could be just another, or maybe she was wearing down from the constant pain in her side. Or it could simply be the curse coming on. But though she watched for it every day, her old rags, which she'd brought from the dugout, went unneeded.

A full moon came and went. Each day she thought, *Maybe I should go tonight. But Jack's been sleepin' light, thrashin' around. 'Sides, I prob'ly couldn't stand the jigglin' of a horseback ride. Guess I'll have to wait till next month and hope it don't cloud over.*

Three days after the full moon, above the cold shadows of the canyon, the hue of the pale blue afternoon sky began to deepen. It would be another long twilight and a very cold night with no wind. As Frieda finished skimming the milk and headed for the house, her mind kept running in circles. *There's still a good moon.*

She stepped up to the porch with the skimming pans, and Jack looked at her in a friendly way. "Say, let's us celebrate tonight." He'd been spending the afternoons on the porch whittling or, as he was now, leaning the chair back against the cabin wall thinking about sharpening the shovel and fixing the other tools that were still strewn about.

"Celebrate what?"

"The way things worked out so fine around here." He gestured around the frosty landscape. "I could catch a hen in the barn and you cook 'er up real special. Mebbe you'd oughta bake one of yer tasty pies too. Whaddaya say?" His mangy whiskers twitched in an actual smile.

"I'd like that." Every day Frieda had been gritting her teeth and telling him, one way or the other, that things had worked out fine. She forced herself to smile. "Sure, go git that hen."

Rocking the chair to an upright position, he stood up and stretched his arms out at the sides. "Reckon I knocked some sense into ya." He looked at her in that way of his, eyes glistening with moisture.

"Oh, I dunno. Maybe time smooths things out." She glanced away, but maintained a pleasant expression. *He's wantin' to poke me. I knowed that was comin' sooner or later.*

Inside, she sat at the table and plucked the chicken, dusted it with crushed sagebrush and the same dried herbs Julius had used on the trout. She browned the chicken with onions in

Julius' heavy iron pot, put the lid on, and moved it to simmer on the less hot side of the stove. As she worked, bands seemed to be stretching ever tighter across her forehead. The muscles at the back of her neck and around her shoulders tensed up so hard she could hardly bear it, but she needed to roll out the crust for the pie. When that was done, she felt woozy and had to lie down for a while before cutting the apples.

I really do wanna wait 'til next month. Don't feel like I could ride. Or am I jes' scared he'll catch me? Scared he'll outsmart me. Cuz if that's it, I never will leave … There mightn't be good moon for a long time. And something else was niggling at her. *I wonder what it feels like to be pregnant.*

The only person who had ever mentioned such a thing in Frieda's hearing was Mrs. Taylor, long ago when Frieda was lingering under the schoolhouse steps, unseen by her teacher. The lady was on the steps talking to an eighth-grade girl, almost whispering, "The curse is never visited upon a pregnant woman." And now Frieda was putting that together with what was happening to her.

Maybe I AM going to have a baby!

She sat up on the bed.

A baby jes' like I told Julius I wanted, his baby. Maybe a little boy with blue eyes and light brown hair. A little Julius jes' might be growin' inside a' me!

I gotta git clean away! Save myself for the baby's sake, if there is one. Jack'd believe Julius was the father. I couldn't fool 'im. Oh, how he'd hate the baby! He'd prob'ly kill it. But if Jack raises a hand to 'im, I sure enough would shoot 'im without blinkin' an eye. Or I could go tonight, while I got the chance. In another month Jack might figure out why I ain't on the rags. The moon'll be comin' over the mountain a couple hours after dark—

But Jack wants to poke me. He'll fly into a temper when I won't let 'im. 'An I won't. There's more'n the pain stoppin' me. I jes' can't. That's all. Not ever agin'. Unless I gotta do it t' save the baby. But how can I say no to Jack and get ready? How can I get clean away?

Then she remembered the whisky.

⸙

Jack came in and sat down at the table in a fine fettle. She had baked the chicken and done up parsnips and potatoes the way Julius liked them. Jack wolfed down big portions and topped off his meal with three pieces of apple pie smothered in whipped cream.

"Now I gotta surprise fer ya," Frieda said, putting the dishes in the bucket that was heating on the stove.

He watched as she opened the "cool cupboard," as Julius had called the one with the screens, and brought out the bottle of whisky, which she'd retrieved from the cellar.

Still at the table, Jack grabbed the bottle, pulled out the cork with his teeth, and took a couple of swallows. "Well I declare, whisky!" he said with a big smile. "Real honest-to-goodness store-bought whisky!" He looked like he'd found a glory hole.

She made herself smile too as she retrieved the *becherlein* from the sea chest and poured the brown liquor into the twin gray and black containers.

"I been savin' it for a time when we was celebratin'. Did'ja know high-toned folks drink whisky from these special little cups?" Handing him one, she went right on.

"Now, I'm gonna read to ya fer a little while" She looked at him quizzically, hoping to distract him from what she believed he had in mind. "Bet nobody's read to ya fer a long time."

He had a blank expression as he stood there, perhaps torpid from eating too much, then finally shrugged. "Don't think nobody ever did at all." Jack, himself, had never learned to read.

She turned the upholstered chair toward the bed and sat down, watching him from the corner of her eye, though she was turning pages in the book to find a good place to start.

He unbuckled his belt.

Alarmed, she nonetheless kept her voice calm. "I bet you'll

like listenin' to a story. Did'ja know? The better folks read to each other all the time." Again she made herself smile at him, though she didn't feel good at all in the stomach—too much food nervously ingested in hopes it would spur him to eat plenty—and now she felt nauseous with fear.

But he lay back against the pillows, raising the *becherlein* as he crossed his boots over each other on the bed "We're livin' like folks a' priv'lege. Ain't that right?"

"Sure is." She lifted her cup to him like Julius had taught her. "We'll live real good from now on." She pretended to drink the whisky, but only moistened her lip.

She leaned forward, setting the bottle beside the lamp at his elbow, "Why don'cha take yer boots off an' git comf'terble?" The boots had to be off his feet.

Quickly, for fear he'd grab her, she sat back in the chair.

He put his drink down and started pulling off his boots. It was a dangerous moment, because he was likely to get the wrong idea. Skipping the first pages, which were too difficult, she began reading in her most entertaining manner.

> My mother was sitting by the fire, but poorly in health and very low in spirits, looking at it through her tears, …

Glancing up, Frieda quickly explained that the young woman was afraid she would die giving birth to Oliver, who was telling the story. To her enormous relief Jack looked relaxed on the bed as he drank his whisky.

> … my mother, I say, was sitting by the fire that bright, windy March afternoon, very timid and sad, and very doubtful about ever coming alive out of the trial that was before her…

Strangely, it somewhat eased Frieda's mind to realize that another woman had felt poorly in health and very doubtful about coming out alive from what lay before her.

> … when, lifting her eyes as she dried them, to the window opposite, she saw a strange lady coming up the garden.
>
> My mother had a sure foreboding at the second glance, that it was Miss Betsey. The setting sun was glowing on the strange lady, over the garden fence, and she came walking up to the door.… When she reached the house, she gave another proof of her identity. My father …

"He was dead," Frieda inserted.

> … had often hinted that she seldom conducted herself like an ordinary Christian; and now, instead of ringing the bell, she came and looked in at that identical window, pressing the end of her nose against the glass to the extent that my poor dear mother used to say it became perfectly flat and white in a moment.

Jack poured himself a second *becherlein* of whisky and hunkered down, seemingly quite contented.

> She gave my mother such a turn, that I have always been convinced that I am indebted to Miss Betsey for having been born on a Friday.

"People born on Friday are unlucky," Frieda quickly explained. Skipping ahead, she read about Miss Betsey helping the young woman give birth, and Oliver, the baby, coming to light as his mother died. She read from the next chapter where young Oliver upset Mrs. Peggotry and was sent out of her home to make his own way in the world.

Jack poured himself another *becherlein* of whisky and made himself comfortable in the pillows. Before she came to the end of the chapter, his head drooped and his eyelids slid down half way over his eyes.

Frieda began to stumble more over long words and phrases, and she paused frequently to figure out which lines to skip. Jack's eyes remained shut for longer and longer intervals, and he didn't see that her whisky had lasted the entire time or that it was still full. He groaned and started to curl up on the bed.

"Why don'cha have just one more drink, Jack? We got us a heap to celebrate, and I'm not to the best parts yet."

He blinked as though to clear his head and accepted another drink, which she poured, but that wasn't half gone before he fell sideways, snoring loudly, nearly spilling whisky on the feather quilt.

Stealthily she took the *becherlein* from his lax fingers and set it on the table.

She reached to turn down the lamp at the bed, bringing the predictable stab of pain in her side. But she had learned to live with physical pain. The motion brought to mind another night when she had turned down this lamp. Julius had taken hold of her wrist, looked in her eyes, and said she was beautiful. Carefully she put the quilt and a blanket over him, folding them over from her side of the bed. *Will I have enough time? Can I do this?*

In a controlled panic, she pulled on another layer of socks, another shirt, and put on her fleece-lined coat. She also put on Julius' warm cap with earflaps. Jack had worn it a couple of times, but Julius's scent lingered in it. She opened the "cool cupboard" and sliced off a hunk of ham, wrapping it in a curl of rind. She also took a jar of milk. She rolled up a blanket with an extra jacket and tucked the food inside the roll. Quietly she lifted the stove lid with the special handle and fed the fire as much wood as it would take.

With a last long look around the cabin where she had experienced the most amazing hours of her life, Frieda took the Colt revolver from the old trunk, made sure it was loaded, and slipped it in her deep coat pocket. She turned down the second lamp. Now the only light was the red glow of the stove.

Jack continued his snoring.

Silently she slipped outside, preventing any noise from the latch. Stars of all sizes sparkled above, and half of a lopsided moon perched on the mountaintop. A narrow smear of cloud in the south reflected the moonlight, but otherwise the sky was clear.

Stormy trotted to meet her as she opened the gate. Frieda slipped the bridle on her mare and adjusted the blanket. Biting her lip against the pain, she put on the saddle. In a growing panic to get away, she tied on the blanket roll, forked some hay to the other animals, and mounted.

As she turned up the trail, the roan whinnied after Stormy.

Would it rouse Jack? She flicked the reins and touched her heels to Stormy's belly. The filly swung into her smooth running walk, rapidly putting distance between them and the cabin. Liesl followed, but in a little while turned back to her master's grave.

A powerful mix of terror and purpose pushed Frieda forward. She tried to ignore the pain in her side with each of Stormy's steps.

Stormy, accustomed to spending her nights outside, could see by the light of the moon as well as in daylight. She maintained her fast running walk on the upriver trail. Meanwhile Frieda looked behind her constantly, though the twisting motion pained her terribly. After several miles, however, she knew the roan hadn't awakened Jack, or he'd been too drunk to do anything. Frieda began to hope. She also began to use her time alone to think about Julius.

When they came to the place where the trail crossed the river, the horse didn't hesitate but stepped right into the cold swift water and crossed as easily as she would have in daylight. *After I got to know him, I trusted Julius like I trust Stormy. That must be the first step in lovin' a person.* Frieda hardly noticed lifting her feet from the stirrups to keep from getting the tops of her boots in the icy, chest-deep current.

Stormy continued her fast pace in the quiet softness of the moonlight, and Frieda deliberately immersed herself more deeply in her dreamy state. It helped blunt the pain. She recognized that there was something about moonlight and the shadow patterns that gave her a sense of looking out at the world without the world looking in.

It was like that with Julius, like being in our own private place, not him and me as two people, but us together, like when we was in the warm water with the snowflakes fallin' all around … That must be part of love, feelin' like nobody else can see in. It's a soft, quiet feelin' jes' like moonlight …

A sound interrupted. Reaching in her pocket for the gun, she looked back. But no rider was there. This happened several times, each time causing palpitations in her heart, followed by a melting sensation when she realized it had been only a night owl flapping or a coyote stepping on dry brush.

They came to the dugout and the old corral where Stormy had lived for so long. The little mare paused. With hardly a glance at the place, Frieda touched her heels to her horse and gave a light signal with the reins. Stormy continued up the Camas Creek trail heading out of the canyon. The horse liked the fast running walk and didn't know it brought physical agony to Frieda. She liked the cold, crisp night air. She liked being with Frieda and doing what her friend and companion asked of her, though many times she started to slow when Frieda shifted around in the saddle, more awkwardly each time, and looked over her shoulder.

It was a steady uphill pull, but the fresh and eager little mare climbed at a brisk walk. Many animals of the canyon were out in the moonlight grazing on the hillsides. Deer, mountain sheep, and elk would lift their heads to note her passing, but they showed none of the fear and alarm they would have in the daytime. Fawns and lambs and elk calves grazed near their mothers. A fox moved silently across the road. Far away a coyote called, soon answered by one nearby. Frieda imagined the pups of these hunters snuggled in their dens waiting for their mothers to return with food.

Someday I might have a child waiting for me to come home. Will I live to see it? Maybe a boy. Julius' boy. I sure would love him.

Fear and the protection of a tiny infant that might be inside continued to drive her, despite the intensifying pain in her ribs.

The sky widened as she came up out of the canyon. She began to think about where she was going and worry about the unknown ahead. She couldn't get rid of those troubled thoughts, nor the fear of Jack following. He could be right behind her, coming on faster than she could stand to ride.

Stars large and small blanketed the sky, some twinkling blue or yellow. The moon had sailed toward the west, and she guessed the time to be about midnight.

She took a back trail and skirted around Meyer's Cove. People in the little town might have seen her, and they would have told Jack. Stormy kept up the running walk, and on the other side of town they joined the wagon trail heading to Leesburg. The tension in her shoulders and the constant stabbing pain in her ribs made her yearn to lie on the ground, but she had to keep going all night. If Jack had slept till now, the moon would have gone over the west mountains and he wouldn't be able to see her tracks. But maybe he woke up hours ago and had been tracking her in the moonlight. If she rested, he would catch up.

The wagon road took her past Panther Creek. For hours, pulling uphill, extending her legs on the level, and then pulling uphill again, Stormy devoured the miles. The stretch up to Leesburg was the steepest, but Frieda let her mare pick her own pace, slowing in the toughest places, with an occasional stop to catch her breath. From time to time Frieda stepped down from the saddle and walked beside her horse to ease the burden and reduce the pain in her side.

She finally made a stop at a little meadow several miles from the summit of the Salmon River Mountains. Knowing it was more and more unlikely that Jack would be able to overtake her, and knowing the hardest parts of the ride were behind them and they would soon be on the downhill stretch to Salmon City, Frieda gave Stormy a much-deserved rest. She left the saddle on to keep the horse from cooling too fast, but loosened the wet cinch to ease her breathing. *If only someone could release a cinch and ease my breathing!*

Standing perfectly still with her head down, Stormy showed considerable weariness, and Frieda worried that she had pushed her too hard. Not infrequently loyal horses died overexerting themselves to please their human friends. The moon had slipped over a mountain, leaving them in darkness except for the faint light of thousands of sparkling stars. An icy breeze was kicking up.

Frieda threw Julius' big jacket over her coat, spread the blanket, and lay down on the light covering of snow. The frozen grass yielded unevenly to her weight, and the chill breeze skimmed over her, pelting her with tiny little crumbs of frozen snow. Moaning with relief, she closed her eyes. At last her ribs were almost still. The pain lessened. She held her breath to stop it altogether. But life required air. She breathed shallowly. Very soon her cheeks, lips, and forehead were numb, and a stinging cold penetrated the blanket and came through her trouser legs from the frozen ground underneath. She knew she mustn't lie there any longer. She'd heard of people freezing to death in situations like this. She must get up and move round. Stormy still hadn't stirred. She seemed to be sleeping. Hoping that's all it was, Frieda forced herself not to disturb the good little mare.

Frieda stomped around and waved her arms. Her lips felt cracked and dry. She picked up the jar of milk and unscrewed the lid. Wafers of ice floated in the milk, but it made her feel a little better and somewhat coated her lips. What would become of the cow, *Edelweiss?* But she wouldn't allow herself to lose sight of her purpose now that she'd covered so much territory. Her big worry was Stormy.

The grass beneath the snow crackled under her boots as she walked anxious circles around her motionless horse. For about a half hour Stormy stood with her head hanging low, but eventually she put her nose to the snow and started nudging it away. Enormously relieved, Frieda watched her crop the dry grass and step forward to find more.

While the horse grazed, Frieda kept moving. The cold came through both coats, and her feet were like blocks of wood. Finally deciding the horse was rested, she stepped close to tighten the cinch and felt the warmth of the horse's body. Impulsively she threw her arms around the mare's neck, pressing her face against the icy fur. As she lovingly stroked the frost off the thick winter coat and felt the damp warmth underneath, Stormy responded with vigorous nuzzling.

"Remember when you was jes' a starving little baby and I saved yer life? Well, now I'm a big grown-up woman in a lot of trouble, and tonight you're doing your best to save my life, and maybe the life of a baby in me. I don't know what's up ahead for me, but it can't be as bad as what's behind. So let's get us on up the trail."

For the first half mile climbing toward the summit, Frieda walked as fast as she could beside her horse, warming herself while Stormy kept them in the wagon road. By now Frieda's eyes had adjusted more to the darkness, but clearly Stormy could see by starlight much better than Frieda. Later, when they arrived at the summit, she sat in the saddle looking at the faint light streaking the southeast. Dawn was beginning behind the majestic peaks of the Continental Divide. There would be plenty of light for the ride downhill from Leesburg, and, now that Jack hadn't caught up, plenty of time. But with only a slight nudge, the mare extended her legs in a swift walk. She would be all right!

Today the sun would rise on Frieda, the way it did on most people in the world. Far across the Salmon River Valley the light was slowly growing behind the silhouettes of Freeman Peak, Center Mountain, all that spectacular range defining the Lemhi Valley. It seemed a giant hand was quietly and very slowly turning up an enormous lamp. As she rode, a feeling of hope began to find its way into Frieda's tense and troubled mind. She was riding toward the light with the darkness behind her. Maybe the future held something good for her. It was a warm thought to ponder as Stormy briskly covered the last fifteen miles of their long ride.

By the time they saw Salmon City, the sun was pouring out from behind the mountains. It was about ten in the morning, and the people of the busy little town across the bridge were involved in their daily activities.

The new courthouse, an imposing red brick building, stood right along the road from Leesburg, a short distance from the bridge over the Salmon River. Frieda was glad she wouldn't have to ride through the business section of town, where people would look at her and wonder. Increasingly anxious about what would happen next, she tied Stormy at the hitching rail and gave her a long, long hug—perhaps the last one.

From his office window Sheriff Thompson saw somebody ride up and thought he recognized the horse. Something about the tortured way the rider dismounted caused him to leave his office and step outside. It was a woman in man's clothing, with a darkly bruised and welted face, one he didn't recognize. Her hair was tucked inside the upright collar of her coat.

She looked him in the eye. "I'm lookin' fer the Sheriff — Thompson think his name is."

"That'd be me, ma'am."

"I'm Frieda Sanders, from over at the Middle Fork."

It disturbed Thompson that the bruises were so bad he hadn't been able to recognize her. He made it a point to remember the faces of all the people in his territory, even the ones he'd seen as fleetingly as Frieda Sanders. Normally she was a passing good-looker. "You'd be Jack Sanders wife then."

Frieda nodded.

"Come on in." He opened the door for her, looking over his shoulder at the exhausted horse and wondering where Mrs. Sanders had started her ride. As to who had beaten her up, he wasn't in much doubt. A friend of his who had come up from Meyer's Cove about a week ago said she'd been missing from home.

Noticing the halting way she walked, he ventured, "Looks like you could use a doctor. Want me to send for Doc Johnson?"

"Not now. I got somethin' to tell you first."

He gestured for her to precede him up the narrow stairwell, musing, "I'll bet Betsy's still got the coffee pot on the stove. I'm ready for another cup myself."

Frieda stopped and carefully turned around. "Your wife's named Betsy?"

"Yep." The look in her eyes inspired him to pursue it. "Why do you ask?"

"Last night I was readin' about a woman with that name. She brung a baby to light, but the baby's mother died." She resumed her slow climbing, more like a woman twice her age.

"Well, my Betsy's been called a time or two to help the doc when a lady's time come, but the mothers all lived." Then he stopped to think. "Just where was you reading, last night I mean?

"Down in the canyon."

"You mean you've come all the way from your place? In one night?"

"Yes sir."

"Well, I'll be! That's a two day ride. What time did'ja take off?" By now, they were both on the landing at the door of the apartment.

"I think about nine o'clock. When the moon come up."

"Let's see, that's.... My God! Only thirteen hours! Some kinda record! I'd say that's a real special horse out at the hitchin' rail. And you must be famished. Maybe Betsy's got some hotcake batter left. You could thaw out and fill up at the same time." He was reaching for the doorknob.

"Oh Sheriff, " Frieda said as though to say it before they went inside, "could you put my horse somewheres out a' sight, an' see she gits plenty a' water?"

"Out a' sight? Somebody after you?"

She nodded. "That's what I come to tell ya 'bout."

He assured her he'd have the horse taken care of. "That animal deserves it!"

As he took Frieda inside and introduced her to Betsy, he'd already pretty much decided this was another case of a woman hoping the law could protect her from a husband who let his temper get the better of him now and then. And since the law couldn't, the least he could do was feed her and hide her horse for a while.

The Betsy being introduced to Frieda was a small woman with freckles and reddish hair done up on top of her head. When the sheriff returned after going back downstairs to talk to his deputy about Stormy, Frieda was in the warm kitchen still trying to get her splinted arm loose from two sets of coat sleeves, both with torn linings from the barrel staves. But before long she was savoring buckwheat cakes drenched in Aunt Jemima syrup and drinking rich, creamy coffee.

Between bites she told the sheriff that Jack had shot and killed the German down at Sheep Creek Bar, and he would be coming after her.

Obviously surprised, Thompson leaned forward on his chair. "I was down in the canyon a little over three weeks ago. I saw Jack then. Wondered why you wasn't there."

That helped Frieda go back to the beginning and tell about Jack's plan and how he'd forced her to go make up to Julius, and how afraid she'd been of going there at first.

She told it all, ending with, "I knowed what Jack told me to do was wrong, but he'd a' killed my horse if I didn't do it, prob'ly killed me too. And now I've been part of a murder. I helped with it an' I'm guilty a' that, but Jack done the lion's share."

In this friendly kitchen, bone weary from her long ride and filled with a sudden, vivid memory of Julius, she was overcome by weeping. She wanted to put her head in her arms on the table but bending into that position was too painful, so she had to sit up straight and bawl into her hands with two people watching.

Betsy pulled up a chair and put an arm around her. Until now, Frieda had been so anxious to get her story out that she'd paid little attention to the woman, but here she was, a stranger, touching her like this. Frieda couldn't remember any woman ever doing that, not even her mother. The discomfort of it, with the freckled face up close and twisted with concern, helped Frieda release Julius from her mind.

She stopped crying and looked across the table at the sheriff, who had not spoken for some time, "What am I gonna do? Jack'll come after me. An' now that I done this, he'll kill me fer sure." *An' the baby in me, if there is one.*

Betsy took her arm back.

Thompson didn't say anything. Was she telling the truth? It

sure didn't sound like anything a normal man would do—send his wife to another man. He'd dealt with a number of murder cases and they could be strange, but he'd never had a case where a person confessed to being an accomplice in murder and turned herself in. Her story did fit with the timing of what he had seen at the dugout. And what a ride she had made to come to him!

"Just a coupla questions," he said. "How long has it been since the killing?"

Frieda hated questions like that. She never had been able to keep track of time. "I dunno. I wasn't right in the head for a while, after. It mighta been a month, maybe more. Is this December?"

"January," he said looking down at the table. "Did I hear right? You helped Jack fetch your goods after the killing? Clothes and pots and pans and tools and such? You went to the dugout and you helped haul it all to the German's place? More than one trip, with the mule—over a number of days?"

"Uh-huh," she'd been saying in response to each part of the question.

The sheriff was quiet for a time, then he finally stood up, hitching up his pants. "This is one helluva mess. I'll have to hold you here in jail 'til we investigate. So, if you'll come downstairs with me..."

He was surprised to see a tired little smile on Frieda's face.

"Please let me stay in jail 'til you've got Jack locked up."

"Well, it isn't exactly the best boarding house in town."

"That's okay. And could you please take good care a' my horse."

Thompson was touched by her request. "You can count on that. Whatever happens, I will personally see to it she gets the best of care."

Hearing this, Frieda stood up and at the same time sagged under the weight of her fatigue. Fear and tension no longer propped her up. She had reported what Jack had done and what she had done. It was over. Now she could rest and grieve for Julius in a safe place.

It was all she could do to walk downstairs with the sheriff. He mentioned that her cell was separated from the others, reserved for women prisoners. When she went inside the concrete cubicle with the thick iron bars he was saying something about the folded blanket and the doctor, but she was already on the cot, half asleep.

⁂

Back upstairs, the sheriff told his wife, "No telling what actually happened. I'll have to go back down to the canyon and look around."

"Tommy, I'm scared for you. You saw how busted up she is. He's a real brute. Like to be gunning for you on the trail. You could just as soon wait for him to show up here in town when he comes looking for her."

He patted her hand. "We'll see. Just remember, long as I got you to come home to, I'm not about to let some two-bit outlaw kill me."

16

At the little meadow Jack stopped the roan and crossed his wrists over the horn, examining the disturbance in the frozen snow, still visible even though there had been some wind.

"Yep, ol' buddy, she stopped here all right." Seeing Frieda's boot tracks all over the place made him itchy to catch up with her. He nudged the roan up the road toward Salmon City, reviewing all that had happened.

Yesterday morning when he'd turned over in bed, a ball of pain like molten lead had rocked slowly to a nauseating halt in his skull. Moaning, he waited a long time before he dared crack his eyes open. It was too quiet and cold. Frieda wasn't in the cabin. The damned female had gone out to do the chores before kindling the fire and starting his coffee! He struggled to sit up, and then took another swig of whisky, hoping to take the edge off the pain.

Outside, the sun came at him like a fire blast from the mountaintop. Squinting around, he couldn't see her, then noticed the mare was missing. He checked and found Stormy's tracks leading upriver. *Musta went after somethin' in the old place, an' jes' let me sleep. Mebbe went fer the sheep tallow.*

In the barn he picked up a couple of fresh eggs, not that his stomach would take them. Strangely, the animals weren't eating and they didn't act hungry. Either they'd finished or she'd gone without feeding them. But the hayfork was in a different place. This was too much for his aching head.

Back in the house he finally got some coffee in the pan and lay down again, pulling the quilt over his head to shut out the hard light. Eventually the smell of boiling coffee got his brain working again. Maybe she had tricked him. Maybe she wasn't just headed to the dugout to fetch something; maybe she was leaving him! He staggered to his feet and looked around the cabin. Two coats gone, the Kraut's hat gone, the Colt gone. Then he remembered her reading to him all sweet as taffy. By God, she'd gone last night!

Gave the other horses some grass so they wouldn't make noise. Got me drunk an' played me fer a fool! After I molliecoddled her!

"BITCH!" he screamed at the top of his lungs. "INGRATE BITCH!"

Instant agony forced him back on the bed. But his mind was working. *Maybe she thinks she can hole up somewhere and hide. But she ain't got the brains to pee outside. Needs me doin' the thinkin'. Stupid female! Takin' off like that when she's tangled up in a murder. Why, first thing you know she'll open her damned mouth an' git herself caught.*

That meant big trouble for him too, having her on the loose. *Better go knock some sense into her and haul her back before she runs off at the mouth.*

He needed to stop her, and quick.

He turned the mule, the other horse, and the cow out into the pasture where there was still some grass and water in the creek in case he might be gone a few days. Her tracks were easy to follow.

Near the old dugout he saw she hadn't taken the Loon Creek trail toward Challis. For a while he sat looking at Stormy's tracks. *Maybe headin' to Salmon City. Maybe thinkin' to take the train and leave Idaho. Naw! She wouldn't have the first idea where to go or how to get there, and she sure don't have no money. But if she thinks she's gonna git away from ol' Jack, she's got another think comin.'*

At the Widow Tollifson's place he saw with satisfaction that

Frieda's tracks continued up the trail. *Reg'lar she-devil, that widow. Females is all alike. Can't be trusted.*

Having started riding after noon, he noticed the long cold twilight had already commenced, and he knew it would be too late to continue much beyond Meyer's Cove, so he might as well stay there. He needed to be able to see her tracks. She might have stopped around Panther Creek to hide with one of those clod-busters she was always blabbin' about.

At the livery stable in Meyer's Cove, the man who ran the place let him sleep in the barn. Asked if he'd seen Frieda, the man drawled in a laconic manner, "Ain't seen hide ner hair a' her." He squinted at Jack. "Ol' Larsen over't the store spread it around yer Frieda went missin' fer a while. So I'da heared about her comin' through town. 'Course she coulda took the loop trail." He drew a lazy half circle in the air. His sympathetic expression said a woman missing that long must be in real trouble, or dead.

In the morning just after dawn Jack was awakened by the rattling of harnesses. After a good cup of coffee at the hotel he started up the long pull to Leesburg. He'd finished off his cold sausage. She hadn't gone up the Panther Creek trail. She was headed to Salmon City all right. Now he had left the place where she had rested and was about to the summit of the Salmon River Mountains.

I'll jes' ride real casual-like into Salmon City an' keep my ears and eyes open. That town ain't got no size to it. I'll find her. Teach her a thing or two about trickin' Jack. The ingrate! Oughta wring her neck and bury her right next to her Kraut lover.

The sun didn't warm him much through his jacket, and the trail led him in and out of the trees, from dark shadow to bright light.

About a half mile from town he was planning what he'd say to people when all of a sudden, with the sun in his eyes, he made out some riders coming out of the trees. By the time his eyes adjusted and he recognized Sheriff Thompson on the appaloosa, it was too late to turn and make tracks or hide. So he forced himself to act casual and keep riding to meet them.

"Jack Sanders," said the sheriff in his usual friendly tone, "What brings you up to Salmon?"

"Oh, jes' a little business 's'all."

The two men with the sheriff seemed to be stepping their horses around the roan, and Jack didn't like it. His Winchester Special stuck out of his saddle boot at his right hand, but he wouldn't try anything, yet. He said, "Didn't 'spect t'see ya headed this way, Sheriff, seein' as how you was jes' down in the canyon."

"I heard your wife's missing."

Prob'ly somebody from Meyer's Cove rode up here and told 'im that. Can't believe he's on his way to look for her. With two deputies? Don't figger. "Oh she showed up. She's okay," Jack said, trying to stay calm. Something about the demeanor of the other riders was giving him a case of nerves.

"Guess I'll ask again," the sheriff said. "What brings you to town? Alone."

"Oh, Frieda's feeling poorly. Didn't wanna come in."

"You sayin' she's at your dugout?"

"Yup."

"That where you're livin' now?"

"Sure. Where else'd we be livin'?"

At a signal from the sheriff, a rider who had circled behind Jack came up and snatched the Special out of the boot, backing his horse away as Jack reached for it.

"Dammit Sheriff, ya got no call to take my gun!" That came out louder than intended, but his heart was pounding and he regretted saying that about the dugout. If anyone looked they'd find it empty. And maybe the bastard knew something about Frieda. Maybe somebody told him she was in town. Maybe he'd seen her. But why take his—

"You an' me need to have us a little talk, back at the office," the sheriff was saying.

Jack couldn't hold back. "Well, what the hell! Can't a man ride to town without gettin' a bad time?" He'd half a mind to light out, though the roan would be tired against these fresh horses. "By damn, Sheriff, tell me what's this about?"

The sheriff signaled with his Colt, nodding to the man who wasn't packing Jack's rifle. "We'll keep you covered while Obadiah here puts the cuffs on. Put'cher hands together in front of you real nice-like."

Shit! They got the drop on me! Obadiah had his horse next to Jack and was holding out the open cuffs.

Jack jerked the reins around and spurred the roan. The big horse leaped to the side, intending to turn at a gallop, but Obadiah grabbed the roan's bridle. The roan reared and whinnied. Obadiah's horse stuck with him, Obadiah with a firm grip on the bridle. By now the sheriff was on the other side, jabbing the barrel of his Colt into Jack's temple. "Now just put your hands into those cuffs real nice and slow, or we'll be mopping your brains up off a' Obadiah."

Feeling the cold metal snap in place on his wrists, Jack realized Frieda must have said something.

As the four rode the short distance to Salmon City—Jack next to the sheriff, the other two men behind—Jack reasoned he'd better start telling his story, because the sheriff seemed to have a card up his sleeve.

"Sheriff, I gotta tell ya somethin'. I didn't wanna git into this, fer Frieda's sake, but I found out she was at that German's place, the one I tol'ja 'bout, down at Sheep Crick. Big, mean son of a bitch. He caught her and forced her to go with im. Busted her up real bad. I had to shoot the bastard. Any man woulda done it."

"You sayin' that's how she got busted up?"

Damn, has he seen her? But she wouldn't tell the lawman about the shooting, unless she's a hellava lot dumber than I think she is. "That's right. I shot the Kraut when I seen what he was doin' to her. She was mighty glad to see me too, I'll tell you."

"Well," Thompson drawled, "when we get to my office, you can tell me and a witness the whole story from start to finish."

Jack's mouth was dry. Being in the sheriff's office with his hands cuffed made him feel like a trussed-up pig heading to slaughter. The sheriff just sat there with his Colt on the desk while the deputy stepped out of the room. He wasn't gone long.

The door opened again. "Jack, go ahead and tell us that story about how you rescued Frieda at the German's place."

The deputy had come in with Frieda! Jack's stomach dropped to his boots. She'd been here all along! Her arm was plastered and her face looked terrible. He hadn't realized her nose pointed a little different than it used to, and most of the bruises on her face had changed from purple to green and yellow. Had the stupid bitch told them something? His ticker pounded like a son of a gun.

"Go right ahead," said the sheriff to Jack with a nod.

Jack leveled a stare at Frieda, to tell her she'd better back up his story. Then he launched into a tale of how he tracked her down to Sheep Creek Bar, what he saw when he got there, and how he shot the German.

Thompson turned his gaze to Frieda. "That how it happened?"

"No, Sheriff, it's the way I already tol'ja. Jack wanted the place and shot Julius to get it. He made me go down there to soften 'im up fer the kill."

Jack burst out. "She's not right in the head. Ever since that German—" He was rising from his chair, but the old deputy stepped over and pushed him down with a gnarled hand. Thompson looked like he was out of patience.

"You had your say, Jack; now keep your trap shut."

"She's lyin'," Jack yelled. "An' a wife ain't 'sposed to talk agin' a husband."

"Shut up, Jack," The sheriff said, "This sure as hell ain't no court of law. Now, the one thing both you and your wife agree on is, when I go down to Sheep Crick I'm gonna find a German with a big hole in him. And if I find your clothes in that place and not in the dugout, I'll know who's story to believe."

Damn! Time to pull out the back-up story. Jack forced himself to frown and look down in an embarrassed way.

"Oh, all right. Guess I'll have to tell ya the truth. A real pain in the ass too. Ya see, I been havin' woman trouble fer some time now, and I didn't know Frieda was seein' that Kraut bastard. Once she even run off with him overnight. She didn't show up to home fer a coupla days and I looked fer her all over the canyon. By damn if I didn't find her down there at the Hun's place, and she was liken' 'im!" He allowed his tone to rise. "A goddamned traitor to the U-nited States of 'Merica. Well I seen that ugly Kraut all lovey to my wife. I seen 'em goin' at it, an', well, I plum lost my senses. Couldn't help myself. Plugged 'im good. A man's gotta right to kill a man who's alienatin' the affection a' his wife. 'Specially in wartime, that bein' the enemy an' all."

"So that's when you beat her up?"

"Shore I did! Any red-blooded 'Merican woulda!"

"That the way it really happened, Frieda?" Thompson asked.

Frieda stuck by her story.

The sheriff allowed himself a wry smile. "Well, Jack, we're at war with Germany all right, but I'm sure you know, bein' the law-abiding citizen you claim to be, there ain't no open season on Huns in Idaho. If you wanna shoot 'em, you gotta sign up for the draft and go over there to Europe and do it."

He paused before adding, "And that takes a heck of a lot more guts than bushwhackin' 'em here and beatin' up on a woman."

⁂

Well, ol' Jack ain't about to go under, he said to himself as he surveyed his cramped cell. He had one more story under his hat. He'd tell them Frieda had done the killing in a love spat with the German. She'd found his gun and shot him with it. Jack had told the other stories because he didn't want her to be blamed. He'd been protecting her, but now had been forced to come out with the sorry truth. At the trial he'd give this new story all he had. He figured the judge might feel sorry for a woman who'd been hoodwinked by an enemy of the county. He might let her off, and then Jack would deal with her later.

On the recently installed telephone system Sheriff Thompson rang up the operator and asked for the county coroner, Bill Eastman, a friend of his as well as a vigorous young outdoorsman who owned and operated the town funeral parlor. He told Bill about the arrests. "Looks like we've got a long ride and a nasty job to do."

"The job I'm used to. The ride, well, too bad it ain't for game." He chuckled into the mouthpiece.

"If we find a body, you'll need to hold an inquest. On the way, we can get hold of some fellas that live over that way and have them come in to give you a jury."

"I guess, Tommy, if you coulda found a case any farther from town an' harder to get to, you woulda done it." Bill Eastman chuckled. "I'll make some arrangements an' be ready to ride with you in the morning."

When Tommy and Bill rode up to the cabin, it seemed a peaceful place. A man from Forney and two men from Meyer's Cove had agreed to serve on the coroner's jury and rode in with them. A lonely, friendly dog greeted them. A light snow had covered any sign of the body having been dragged, but as soon as they dismounted, the dog went directly to the shallow grave, sat on it, and whined.

They removed only enough dirt to see a man's body, naked above the waist. They made an inspection of it, noting the bullet hole in the back, the exit wound in the chest, and the short piece of lariat rope around the abnormally long, stretched neck. Then they covered the body with dirt again. If further investigation was needed, it could be done later. The coroner's jury had taken part in the investigation. They agreed that there was no compelling reason to pack the body all the way back to Salmon. The rope, the grave, and bullet wound all squared with Frieda's story. So did the two sizes of male clothing found in the place, and the fact that the dugout was vacant. They would file their report, and that should be adequate to satisfy the law. Those who died in remote areas were generally buried wherever they happened to lie.

The interior of the cabin brought some surprises. Thompson was impressed by the good care and orderliness. The furniture was simple in design, the curtains looked recently washed, and more books—mostly in German, some in English—filled the bookcase than most of the men had ever seen in one house.

They found a German Bible, lists of names, and two letters inside, in German, the return address from a town in Iowa. As they continued their search they found, tucked in a back drawer, a high school diploma from Iowa, a certificate of American citizenship, and a family picture of what looked like Midwestern farmers—they could have been of any nationality, even American. That photo and another of a young woman were still in metal frames from which broken glass protruded.

When they returned to Salmon, Thompson showed Frieda the letters and asked if she knew about the family of Julius Remsburg. She told them about the family.

As the investigating sheriff, Thompson had a responsibility to contact the murdered man's family. He struggled over the wording of the telegram, making it brief because the cost per word would be paid by the county, but wished it didn't have to be so abrupt.

MR. AUGUST REMSBURG>>>
SORRY MUST INFORM YOU JULIUS REMSBURG LIVING ALONE ON MIDDLEFORK RIVER DEAD MAYBE MURDERED STOP PLEASE NOTIFY IF RELATIVE AND IF YOU WANT BODY LEFT WHERE BURIED STOP
SHERIFF TOMMY THOMPSON

The telegraphed reply came the next day:

SHERIFF THOMPSON SIR>>>
DEAD MAN MUST BE SON JULIUS LIVING ALONE BY MIDDLEFORK STOP WE COME TO SALMON BY TRAIN AND RETURN WITH BODY STOP NEED BURY SON AT HOME CHURCHYARD STOP WILL PAY COST STOP
AUGUST REMSBURG

Thompson studied the telegram. They wanted the body shipped back home for a proper burial. It wouldn't be easy telling them that it had been in a makeshift grave, and for a while the temperature hadn't been consistently cold enough to prevent some decomposition. When he'd inspected the body, it was already in pretty bad shape. Bill was making a lead-lined coffin, but such a large and heavy thing couldn't be packed by mule that far. Yet somehow the body must be brought to the railhead. It sure wasn't going to be easy, but at least the family had offered to pay the expenses.

Thompson would offer a capable man the princely sum of $200 to do the job.

SALMON CITY, January 16, 1918 Today Lemhi County Sheriff "Tommy" Thompson handed two prisoners over to Mr. Keeting, sheriff of Valley County. The accused murderers have been charged with killing Julius Remsburg, a naturalized citizen, formerly of Germany, lately of the Middle Fork country. Mr. Keeting traveled around eight hundred miles, via Boise, Pocatello, and Red Rock, Montana, to take the accused into custody. Sheriff Thompson had apprehended the Sanders, neighbors of the deceased, and investigated the scene of the crime, the Middle Fork being much closer to Salmon City than Cascade, the Valley County seat, established less than a year ago. Previously Thompson arranged for the body to be shipped to a small town in Iowa, accompanied by the parents of the deceased, who had come to claim it.

Subscribers will be interested to know that Mrs. Sanders at first refused to ride in the same train with her husband, fearing his wrath after her confession. She was finally placated when Sheriff Keeting agreed to ride with her in the opposite end of the single car of the train, and Mr. Sanders, duly shackled and handcuffed, rode next to Sheriff Thompson, who in any case needed to provide his information to the Valley District Attorney.

17

Idaho State Penitentiary, Boise, June 1918

From the border of the exercise yard where Frieda was bending to weed her flower garden, she glanced up to see the mountains. Morning sunlight brightened the partly barren slopes, very different from the snow-covered peaks in the Salmon River country. Here in the Boise Valley her purple flags stood lush and full with their petals turned down and their fuzzy tongues damp with dew. Inhaling the fragrance of the sweet peas, she noted with pleasure that a fat poppy bud or two might break open today. She couldn't wait to see what colors they would be. Touching her extended belly, the same shape as a poppy bud, she wondered if she would have a boy or a girl.

She hauled a bucket of water from the spigot and watered the plants, enjoying the way they responded to her care. For a moment she paused, remembering the unseasonable yellow flowers in the grass beside the warm mountain stream that she'd visited with Julius. *Guess they got just enough warmth to bloom.* She closed her eyes and could almost hear the musical little creek and smell the pine and sage.

The whistle shrilled. She brushed her wet hands on her striped britches, set the bucket beside the spigot, and went to the door to wait with the gathering women. The prisoners had been walking around the yard before breakfast, *like a flock of black and white birds,* Frieda thought.

Beyond the high fence she could see the men's prison wing, but not their yard. Jack was over there someplace, sentenced to ten to fifteen years for first-degree murder. The trial had been very short. The state attorney told Frieda that Jack would have hanged for sure if Julius hadn't been a German, but the judge thought it wouldn't be right for an American to hang for killing a German in wartime. And the war was still raging in Europe. The prison newspaper reported that even now big guns were blazing, people dying, and towns still burning.

A guard made her way through the crowd at the door. "Frieda," she said, "at ten o'clock I'll come escort you to the hearing. Be ready. Louise Jones could fix your hair. I'll see she gets a pass from the kitchen. Go see her after breakfast." The guard unlocked the door and stepped aside as Frieda and the other women filed past her into the hallway of the large structure, their footsteps echoing.

Frieda's anxious feeling returned. She'd been putting the hearing out of her mind. After only six months in prison, counting the time in the county jail, she was to be interviewed by the Parole Board. Her friends in stripes said that was unusual, because she hadn't filed a petition. They regularly appealed for hearings and felt extremely lucky if their petitions were granted, though almost all hearings resulted in denials. What if the Board decided Frieda should leave? What would happen to her? Where would she go? Where would she have her baby?

She liked the prison—the regular meals, the company of the other women, the library, and having time to read every day. She had a friendly relationship with the guards; they had given her the flower seeds. She slept well and felt safe in her cell. The work was pleasant and not nearly as strenuous as sluicing for gold in the canyon with Jack. And here the variety of work interested her—the cavernous kitchen with its gigantic stove and many gas burners, the laundry wing with the huge vats with electric agitators. She liked hanging the towels, sheets, and black and white uniforms on the long prison lines. Some of the conversations with other prisoners as they pinned up the laundry on parallel lines were quite interesting.

Phyllis had told how she robbed a bank with her husband. Myrtle joked about the troubles of raising two sons on the outside and the funny things the little boys said when they came to visit her in prison. Maud described the pleasure with which she had shot her husband between the eyes when he was sleeping. Frieda told them about Jack and Julius, and how she had gone on her long ride to turn herself in. The others thought that was the most interesting story yet.

It was good having friends, and Frieda felt a kinship with the other women, but she recognized a bitterness in most of them. Their hurt, hate, and anger had created a hardness of spirit. They didn't trust anyone and never would. Frieda realized that her life with Jack had been taking her down the same path; but the beauty of the canyon, her love of Stormy and the wild animals, and most of all, brief as it had been, her knowing and loving a wonderful man had pointed her in a better direction. Even so she was afraid of the outside.

The baby moved just when the guard led Frieda into the interview room. *Maybe a strong boy like his father. Least I gotta little friend with me in this big ol' echoey room.* Behind a long table sat a number of men and two women, all high-toned folks. A large framed document hung on the gray-green wall behind them.

Telling Frieda to sit in the chair before the panel, the guard stood at the wall.

How can I think with all these eyes starin' at me?

They each asked her a question.

"What are you planning to do when you get out of prison?"

Clasping her hands around her big belly, Frieda glanced up briefly at each speaker, but kept her eyes on the swirls in the cement floor. "Don't rightly know, sir."

"Have you learned anything in prison?"

"Yes ma'am, I learned about those big washing machines. You gotta keep your sleeve out a' the wringer."

They tittered.

"Are you sorry you helped kill a man?"

Frieda squinted back tears and swallowed hard. "Yes."

"Do you think you've been punished enough for what you did?"

"No."

After a long silence, "Why is that?"

"I can't never be punished enough. An' it ain't bad 'nough in the pen to be much punishment."

"That's the first time I ever heard a prisoner say that."

The man in the middle, wearing a pin-striped suit, said, "We've discussed your case with the Matron, and we disagree with you. We think you have been punished enough. We also considered your exemplary behavior while in prison." He cleared his throat, turned his eyes to the high ceiling, then lowered his voice to an embarrassed tone, "Of course there's the matter of the impending birth. I understand you're expecting a child in a couple of months?"

Frieda nodded.

The man's voice turned friendly. "You see, we don't have the right facilities in this prison for infants and children, so we think it would better serve you and the people of Idaho to release you on parole. You'll be closely supervised for a year. Then if your record is clean at the end of the year, you'll be pardoned."

They ARE kicking me out. "I'm scared Jack'll git out an' come after me an' the baby. Ain't no door strong enough to hold 'im, 'cept here at the state pen."

The man in the pin-striped suit removed his spectacles, put them down, and looked at her firmly. "Jack Sanders is very unlikely to get a hearing for at least ten years, and from what I hear, his behavior leaves much to be desired. Unless that behavior improves a great deal, he'll serve his entire sentence."

Little Julius will be ten, at the most fifteen.

But the evaluation of the Board held sway.

The day before she was to leave, Frieda said good-bye to the sunny prison yard. Pink and orange poppies had bloomed, and all her flowers were in full color. Outside the high fences, the surrounding trees had fully leafed out above the mowed summer-green grass. On the high slopes above the Middle Fork, the ewes would have their lambs by now. She wondered about the one that had taken such good care of her lamb and about the attentive elk mother and her calf. Were they all still there? Those slopes would be covered with new grass, yellow bitterbrush in bloom, shooting stars, orange paintbrush, and purple lupine. Would she ever go there again? Would she ride into the mountains on Stormy with her baby before her in the saddle?

Frieda held this picture in her mind as she drifted off to sleep that night.

As she was walking out the prison gate the next morning, the baby gave a big kick and Frieda smiled. Surely it would be a husky boy. He would grow into a man with wide shoulders—a strong man who'd be kind and gentle and good-natured. Frieda would be the mother of a good son. To sever the tie with Jack, a prison attorney had already started divorce papers.

The Matron handed her a few dollars and gave her a street-car pass for the City of Boise. "Check with the library about a position," she said. "They told me they could use someone of your quiet disposition, someone who likes books."

On the streetcar riding past many fine two-story houses and the grand Idanha Hotel, Frieda decided that she would someday take the train to Iowa, if Julius' parents could forgive her. Sheriff Thompson in Salmon might remember what station they lived near. Then her child could meet his grandparents, whom Julius loved and respected.

Little Julius, you'll know what a good man your pa was. You'll never have the chance to see him, but you'll know what a good farmer he was, and you'll know why I loved him. I'll make sure a' that. An' if you're Julia, that's jes' fine too. I'm gonna be the best mother that ever growed out of a hard place.

In the Boise City Library where she worked, Frieda took out two or three books each week. She was especially fond of Dickens. Knowing this, the librarian kept a new edition of *Oliver Twist* in a drawer for her. But Frieda just thanked her and said she'd already read some of it, so she wasn't going to check it out.

"You didn't like this book?"

"Oh, I liked it a lot."

"Then why not read the rest of it?"

"Because I already know it ends happy. And the person that told me … well, I'd rather jes' keep that the way we left it."

Late summer had come, and the big war still raged in Europe. In the canyon of the Middle Fork a warm August day was ending and the coming of evening settled softly upon the land. The light lingered for a long and silent time. No person stirred in the cabin, no lamp was lit. No dog guarded the neglected garden.

With confidence and an air of ownership, a young doe led her fawn to this place of delicious browsing—dried raspberries, carrot tops, tasty strawberry leaves, and her favorite, sweet and very large rose hips. These were good things she was not able to find among the wild shrubs in the hills. Before full darkness could shroud the canyon, a riding moon, just one night past full, lifted the shadows with a soft glow of indirect light. The full-bellied doe nuzzled her fawn, and was content.

AUTHOR'S NOTE: Don Ian Smith

We have made a very real historical event the springboard for our work of fiction. Here's how we heard of it:

In 1944 my wife Betty and I moved to Salmon, fresh from graduate school at Northwestern University in Evanston, Illinois, where I had become an ordained Methodist minister. I had asked my bishop to send me to a church in Alaska. I wanted wild country. Instead he sent me to a little church in Salmon City, Idaho, saying "It's just as wild as Alaska and with your wife and little daughter, you'll be better off in the states." The bishop was wise, and here we are, with one significant lapse, still in America's Beauty Spot.*

Our arrival was less than 30 years after "The Murder." Many people in town still remembered and were talking about it. The story had been retold so many times by so many people with different opinions that sometimes it was hard to believe they were talking about the same thing. I was eager to get back to good fishing. Bill Doebler, a fine man, avid fisherman and member of my church, was still the county coroner and operator of the only funeral home in town, as he was at the time of the murder. He set about showing me the best fishing spots in the county. We would camp overnight and often talk around the campfire before going to sleep. His stories of his work as coroner in this semi-civilized county were fascinating, and it was from him that I learned the most about the strange murder.

---

* Ed. note: Don also served 14 years as pastor of Hillview Methodist Church in Boise, retiring in 1983, and returning to Salmon in 2001.

It was Bill who took the short piece of rope from the neck of the victim, put the decomposing body in a lead lined coffin, and gently advised the family members who came to escort the body home, not to try to open the coffin. Bill had a kind and genuine way of dealing with grieving people, and most people would have followed his advice.

I later met George, an older man in Salmon who was a good storyteller. He had been 18 at the time of the murder, had grown up on Panther Creek, and knew the Middle Fork country like the back of his hand.

When the sheriff learned that the family in Iowa wanted the body for Christian burial and would pay whatever it would cost to get it, he at once thought of George. He was in luck. George was in Salmon City buying supplies. The sole supporter of his mother and a number of young siblings, he agreed to bring the body up out of the canyon for $200, more money than he'd ever seen at one time in his life.

George set up camp near the Remsburg cabin, and spent an afternoon digging and painstakingly nudging the partly decomposed body into his spread canvas manta*, using the slope of the hill to aid him. He then sewed the canvas tightly together with his heavy wheat-sack needle and twine, leaving an "ear" at each corner. He also tied the package with rope, for easier handling. Finding a block and tackle used for bleeding hogs, and a sawhorse in the barn, he placed the sawhorse under a sturdy branch of a tree, and used his horse to pull the body to the tree. He then hung the body over the sawhorse where it would freeze overnight. In the morning, with the body rigid in the desired shape, he raised it with the pulley device and stood the mule beneath the tree. The mule showed his good training by accepting the strange load from the sky, ready for the long trek to the wagon road in

---

* Sometimes "mantey," a western word adapted from the Spanish meaning a large leather drape attached to a saddle.

Meyers Cove. An inventive packer, George was certainly the right man for that gruesome job.

Today a body would simply be flown out from a small airstrip located only about two miles from the cabin of the murdered man. River rafters and fishermen who charter flights from Salmon use that strip.

Several news accounts of the murder were published in January 1918 in the *Idaho Recorder* and the *Cascade News*. The article in the text of the novel is a facsimile summarization. The *Payette Lake Star* (McCall, Idaho) published one on March 1. In their excellent book, *The Middle Fork and The Sheepeater War*, Backeddy Books, 1977, Riggins, Idaho, Johnny Carrey and Cort Conley give a short account of the Murder, perhaps as accurate as any. Only three people ever knew the details of what really happened on the Middle Fork. One of the three died at the scene of the murder and the other two gave accounts suited to their objectives. So I have used the event as a basis for a novel, the story of a woman's struggle to find meaning for her life. I have tried to be entirely faithful to the setting and geography.

Don Ian Smith
Salmon, Idaho
October 2004

AUTHOR NOTE: Naida Smith West

I was born in Idaho Falls, Idaho, where I spent my first 13 years of life — except for extended visits with relatives in other parts of Idaho and Montana. My favorite place was the farm of my Smith grandparents in Rupert, Idaho. I loved and admired my Scottish grandmother, as did hundreds of other people. She was the mother of Don Ian Smith, my uncle, who is close in age to my deceased father.

In the late 1940s and early 1950s my father sometimes drove me (and my siblings) from Idaho Falls to Salmon, usually for the purpose of fly-fishing with his brother Don. On one of those trips I recall Uncle Don pointing out the car window as we sped along a paved road beside the Salmon River. He was drawing our attention to the opposite side of the river where a much older, dirt road could be seen carved into the mountainside.

"There's one!" he would call out. "Did you see that?"

Miles apart, the dugouts along the old road looked like mere shadows in the steep, rocky face of the canyon wall. But some of them had been human dwellings, developed from the starts of tunnels where pick-wielding prospectors of a bygone era had searched for gold. My Uncle Don knew about those places. He had a connection with some of the people who still lived in them, some who had been young in that earlier time.

Don was then pastor of the Methodist Church in Salmon, but he also made it his business to visit the residents of far-flung dugouts and mountain cabins. Periodically he would ride horseback on a circuit of about a hundred miles to call on those colorful souls who welcomed him with a cup of coffee and a plate of beans. Sometimes he trailed a pack mule to transport his camping gear and possibly an elk, if in season. A crack shot with a rifle, Don rode the Middle Fork Trail and knew its history.*

Don also established and operated a small cattle ranch outside of Salmon, where his children grew up. His daughter Heather, when she married, acquired the ranch and has actively worked it with her husband ever since—all the while raising children and grandchildren. Heather Smith Thomas has written for decades about her ranch experiences—regular articles and columns for a number of horse and western life magazines, and at least two dozen published books about the western range, the history of horses in America and the West, and the care of cattle and horses.

Don always had an uncanny way with horses. Into his seventies he rode in 100-mile endurance rides. For a couple of months when I was 13, I lived with Don and Betty and their three young children. On Sundays I enjoyed his sermons because he usually began with stories from his life on the farm, ranch or backcountry. Several collections of these sermons, which he calls "Meditations from the High Country," have been published and read widely across the United States. They have recently been reissued.

My father, Arthur Smith, an attorney in Idaho Falls, relished everything about the West, the tall tales, the songs, and the hunting and fishing. The brothers connected over those shared joys. Now let's return to that car, with the two of them in the front seat and me in the back with other kids. I heard Don's enthusiasm

---

* In November of 1957, when I was alone in Germany, homesick for my country and my language, and sadly poking around the cold streets of Karlsrühe on my lunch break, I found myself at a newspaper rack that contained a few American magazines, including a 2-month old, dog-eared copy of *LOOK*. "The Methodists" was mentioned on the front. Turning to that page, I was stunned to see my very own Uncle Don smiling at me from the saddle of a horse in the Salmon Mountains! Beneath the photo: "The Circuit Rider 1957." Surely it was a miracle. I hadn't seen him since 1953 and we had lost touch. That photo and several more of him spoke volumes about my heart's home in the American West.

as he told my dad tales told to him by colorful old hermits. Why, I wondered, would those bearded old men live like that? Without human contact for long periods of time? How did they end up there?

Fast forward more than fifty years.

After three careers in California, one raising children, one academic, one in public policy, I retired to full time writing and later established Bridge House Books, publishing literature of the historical West. In 1999 the mailman brought a manuscript, *Murder on the Middle Fork,* from my uncle Don. We recognized that this was his first book of fiction and would need some rewrite, but I liked the story and wanted to publish it, however at the time was immersed in writing a big historical novel of my own, set on my ranch in California. Additionally I was engaged in many publicity activities for my first novel. So I put *Murder* on the shelf for a while.

A year later Don sent me another manuscript, the life story of his mother, my beloved Grandma Smith. He asked me to edit it and "bring her to life the way you brought the characters to life in your novels." Setting everything aside I plunged into that labor of love. The result is: the award-winning *Symon's Daughter: A Memoir of Elizabeth Symon Smith.* Now, three separate readerships have "met" that remarkable lady: Don's, his daughter Heather's, and my own.

In the summer of 2004, in the middle of writing the third novel in my California series, I realized it would take longer than anticipated and Don might not have the luxury of much more time. So I returned to *Murder.*

Collaborating with my wonderful uncle on these two books has reconnected me with him and my early life in Idaho. Throughout the process he has been patient and jovial, always ready with a wry story when we talk on the phone. He even gave me some good, practical spiritual guidance.

Perhaps this book will remind readers that for all the spectacular beauty of nature, for which my uncle and I share a great love, nature is not enough. People require at least a little civilization and human fellowship, including family if they are lucky enough to have one.

Naida Smith West
Rancho Murieta, California
November 2004

Acknowledgments

We are grateful to our spouses, Betty Smith and Bill Geyer, for their unfailing support and assistance, and to Heather Smith Thomas for moving us forward when we got stuck. We also thank Paul Samuelson, Ruth Younger, and Marguerite Flower for their contributions to structure and editing, and Gayle Anita and Pete Masterson for their separate arts and their professionalism in working under time pressure.

Don Ian Smith and Naida West

Other Books By Don Ian Smith

(see www.highcountrybooks.com)
By the River of No Return
Sagebrush Seed
Wild Rivers and Mountain Trails
The Open Gate
Ranchland Poems
Symon's Daughter: A Memoir of Elizabeth Symon Smith (www.bridgehousebooks.com)

Other Books By Naida West

(see www.bridgehousebooks.com)
Eye of the Bear: A History Novel of Early California
River of Red Gold
Rest for the Wicked (Expected 2006)

If you liked this book and would like to pass a copy on to someone else, or would like one of the other titles from Bridge House Books, please check with your local bookstore, online bookseller, visit our web site at www.bridgehousebooks.com or telephone us at 916-985-7411.